Joseph has finally put the past behind him. Life is everything he has ever envisioned. Justice has been meted out, the ones responsible for the crimes against him and the innocent have been made to pay, and he can finally end his life of violence. Then, in one moment, it is gone. Everything he values has been stolen from him by a criminal looking for a quick payday. So what can Joseph do when, after a life of tragedy, he finally finds happiness, and someone rips it all away from him? How can he go after a man, when he has no clue where the perpetrator is and only a vague idea of what he looks like? How does he find the will to survive when his whole world is gone and the only thing he has left is the need to make the guilty pay?

The chase is on, and Joseph will have to use every resource available if he is to succeed. But what will he do if he actually catches up with the man he has come to hate more than anything?

From the author of *WAITING IN THE SHADOWS*, a crime thriller, and *THE CLOCK*, a young adult mystery/adventure—both with five-star reviews on Amazon.com.

again. But the cops are sniffing around and Joseph fears his secrets might be exposed, until he begins to think that the cops might have a very different reason for sniffing around—one Joseph isn't sure how to handle. Although the book is written in present tense, which I don't really care for, I quickly got over that and lost myself in the story. With a clever and dedicated main character, some unique gadgets, intriguing techniques, and plenty of fast-paced action, *The Chase* is one you'll hate to put down. *Regan Murphy, The Review Team of Taylor Jones & Regan Murphy*

ACKNOWLEDGMENTS

A big thank you to Lana McLeod, for all her help.

And to my friend Ray Cadorette for seeing the things I missed.

The Chase

Waiting in the Shadows ~ Book 2

LEONARDUS G. ROUGOOR

A Black Opal Books Publication

GENRE: CRIME THRILLER/MYSTERY/AMATEUR SLEUTH

THE CHASE ~ Waiting in the Shadows ~ Book 2
Copyright © 2017 by Leonardus G. Rougoor
Cover Design by Jackson Cover Designs
All cover art copyright © 2017
All Rights Reserved
Print ISBN: 978-1-626947-93-1

First Publication: NOVEMBER 2017

Published by Black Opal Books **http://www.blackopalbooks.com**

The Chase

Preface

I wait and wait as the neighborhood slowly quiets down and everyone has long since gone to bed. Finally, he drives into his driveway and parks. His music is booming inside the closed windows for a minute and stops as he opens the door. People here must just love this inconsiderate bastard.

He gets out of the car and, as he closes the door with a slam, I raise the tranquilizer dart gun and sight down the rifle barrel. As he comes around the back of the car and heads toward the front door, I shoot and the dart hits him right in the ass. He screams and jumps as he reaches behind him trying to grab what has just bit him.

The rifle is gas powered so there is no noise to disturb the neighbors. The only noise is Adam as he tries to make it to the front door.

He gets there, but before he can open the door and get into the house, he collapses in a heap unable to move as he loses consciousness.

I wait for a while to see if anyone around looks to see what the commotion is about. Nobody has taken any notice at all. He must always come home and make a racket the way he did before I shot him, so no one cares about it anymore.

When I'm sure there is no one watching, I cross the street and go to the front door, kneeling beside him. I pick up the dart that he managed to pull out and put it away. Dragging him to the back yard, I tie him up nice and tight with his arms strapped to his sides under a large tree.

Throwing a strong rope over a large branch, I tie it around his chest and under his armpits with the knot at the back. Lifting him up and tightening the rope over the branch suspending him in the air, I tie it off. I take two of those dog anchors that screw into the ground and place them in position. I fasten each leg to one of the anchors, thus holding him facing the street. When he awakes, he will be very uncomfortable but not seriously hurt.

At this time, I undo his belt, lower his pants and underwear then use my knife to cut the pants and underwear completely off. Taking off my backpack and opening it, I take out a zip tie and tighten it around his "banana." This done I reach in the pack again and pull out a can of black undercoating spray and give his genitals a good coating. This stuff is like tar and will be fairly difficult to get off.

With him tied up and hanging from the tree, he'll have to call out to the people he has irritated for help. Who knows, maybe someone will call the police for him. With any luck, he's been drinking a lot and will have to relieve himself soon but with the zip tie so tight he won't be able to.

This man is a pimp, and he better learn his lesson this time and get out of the business. If he doesn't, a more drastic measure will be taken—one he won't survive.

Chapter 1

Joseph

And so, after what seems like a lifetime of tragedy and sorrow, after having removed from society, more people than I can, at times, remember, I have dispensed retribution to the perpetrators that caused me and others so much anguish. Now, I am finally able to put the problems of the world behind me.

I have sold my home, quit my job, left what friends I had, and am on my way. I have met and I am going to marry an absolutely wonderful woman named Kathleen. Even her name has an air of refinement about it.

The job I have had for many years has been very fulfilling. I worked in a steel fabrication shop, where I have done quality control, machining, and performed the duties of shop safety representative. This job allowed me to make many of the items that I have used to remove criminals from society.

Too many people that meant a lot to me have been murdered by some of these cretins. This is what has driven me to the point where I found it necessary to find ways to eliminate some of the worst of the undesirables that infest this world. I can hardly believe some of the things I have done.

When Andrew Madison killed my friend Jack during a home invasion, it was an act of brutality. I had to wait quite a while to dispose of him.

Jake Patterson actually gave me a run for my money and almost took me out. The Carlos brothers managed to wing me twice. The Klan was also dealt with in a way that allowed me to kill five members. While I was hidden in the bushes, I had a surprise myself.

Luckily I found a way to eliminate Amy's killer in prison as well as my mother's murderer and a lot of his buddies. The list goes on and on. I am so thankful that Kathleen and my friends have never found out about this side of me. I doubt they would have wanted to associate with me, to put it mildly. I sometimes wonder if it is fair that I am part of their lives. I have a secret life that would revolt them if they knew. Do I even deserve to have them as friends?

Nevertheless, I have found this wonderful woman who has the ability to bring me back to where I can live a normal life. Kathleen owns and operates Rose Cottage Bed and Breakfast, an English style home that reminds her of her heritage. I was very afraid to start another relationship. There is this fear of losing yet another person in my life through violence or of her finding out about the life that I have lived. I have finally looked at my situation from a new perspective.

Rather than looking at my past life the way normal people would look at it, I have looked at it from the perspective of the people that I have saved. I now look at it through the eyes of people who are now alive, but would not have been had I allowed them to be murdered by a hate group or enslaved by sexual predators or people in the drug trade? I am now at peace with my past and eager to move forward in my new life with Kathleen.

We have discussed the possibility of having children and, as I pull into the driveway of Rose Cottage, I see her running toward me. I have not been this happy in a long time. We are to be married in two week's' time and, since she does not have any siblings and her parents have passed away, it will be a simple ceremony and a short honeymoon. I have invited a few close friends like Harry, Brenda, and the kids. A couple of the guys at work are coming for the wedding as well as Kathleen's friends.

I get out of the rental truck which towed my car and we embrace for the longest time.

"I am so glad that you're finally here," she tells me.

"That goes double for me. All I could think of on the drive here was you. I'm glad that it's over and we're together."

The sun is warm on my face. A gentle breeze coming in from the ocean about fifteen miles away blows the fragrance of the roses into my nostrils. Kathleen has someone to watch the front desk, so we go for a short stroll to the back yard and sit. The light breeze tosses her short, wavy, auburn hair from side to side as I look into her green eyes. I tell her how much I love her and how I'm looking forward to building a future together with her.

This woman, I believe, is my soul mate. I don't know if I have ever been this happy, even with Amy. The desire to punish anyone has left me and all I want is to be with her.

Later, I get the truck unloaded, at least for the most part. I will need a little help to unload the heavier things and place them in the house. Kathleen has a girlfriend who is married and her husband is more than willing to help out. We get along just fine. Who knows? Maybe I can start to actually have a few friends.

There is a large empty shed in the back that I can use for my workout room. The back yard has plenty of room for a garden. This pleases Kathleen a lot when I tell her my plans for it.

"I planted all kinds of vegetables at my place in Salem, and I still have plenty in my freezer. We can use some of them for the guests that stay at the B and B. What do you think?" I ask.

"That's a wonderful idea, I'm sure they'll love it. It will

be nice having a garden here too," she tells me.

Preparations are made for the wedding and she is in her element. She is a born organizer and has everything planned well ahead of time. As the days pass by, we start getting used to each other, and I'm on top of the world. I'm happy again and look forward to a normal life with a woman who has her focus on the right things.

When we can, we go for long walks and talk about our plans. The wedding will be on the following Saturday, and Harry and his family have already come to the B and B.

"We are so pleased that Joseph found you," Brenda says as she and Kathleen walk. "We were so worried for the longest time that the things that have happened to him would hold him back from enjoying life again."

"He makes me happier than anyone else ever has too," Kathleen replies.

Brenda and Kathleen hit it off almost as soon as they meet. They are both women who have easy going personalities and make an impression on the people they meet. You would think that we all have known each other for years. The kids who are now in their mid-teens are all excited as Kathleen has asked them to be part of the marriage ceremony. Harry has agreed to give her away. The kids have grown so much since I first met them.

As Harry and I go for a walk one evening, he expresses his pleasure at me getting my life back in order. He and Brenda have been worried about how I would deal with all the tragedy I have had to endure.

"I appreciate your concern and your friendship all these years, Harry," I tell him as I pat him on the back. "It looks like things are finally going my way again. I'm so glad you and the family are here. This will be a wonderful spring wedding."

The wedding is over and Kathleen and I have a few days away from everything. It was a beautiful day and the reception was grand.

One of her friends is taking care of the B and B. All the

guests have gone home and we are in San Diego. The suite we have is luxurious with a balcony overlooking the ocean. We enjoy barefoot walks on the beach as the wet sand cools the bottom of our feet. We go for strolls through the shops in town during the day, partaking of fine dining in the evenings.

"I just love the architecture in this city with its Spanish influence," Kathleen says.

"It is beautiful that's for sure. You know, we can come here for a visit whenever you want. All you have to do is ask."

A long walk along the sea wall has us stopping for supper at the Harbor House for a surf-and-turf dinner overlooking the water, enjoying the sunshine and ocean breezes. We are getting along so great that it almost seems like a dream. The time goes by far too quickly and, before you know it, we are back home. We discuss our finances and what I will do to keep myself busy when I have gotten everything at the B and B ship shape. She looks at my ear, the one that has part of the lobe missing, courtesy of the Carlos brothers.

"Why don't we look into getting that fixed? I have a friend who has a doctor friend. He can easily take care of it," Kathleen says.

After a bit of discussion, I agree to this and we decide to contact her friend next week.

"Money won't be a problem, you know. We'll go to the bank later in the week and pay off the mortgage. I have money saved, and, with what I got from the sale of my house, we'll be quite comfortable," I inform her.

"I had no idea that you were planning this, maybe you should think it over first."

"We're married now and everything I own belongs to you as well. The property will be in both our names, I don't believe in having separate accounts. I want to share with you all that I have. We're a team and my only interest is in keeping you as happy as I can," I say, wrapping my arms around her.

Journal entry: *Life has once again turned around for me. I've had my ear fixed and it looks fairly normal again. All I can do is hope that things stay this way and…*

The time just flies by and life settles into a routine. I sometimes wonder if there is anything lurking around the corner. There has always been something going on most of my life. I try to put it out of my mind and enjoy the happiness I've found. We hit the six-month mark and go out for a celebration. Enjoying a meal at an upscale restaurant, we then go to a show that she has wanted to see.

A garden has been planted in the back yard. It's growing nicely and we are already enjoying the first fruits of our labor. As I am watering the garden one sunny afternoon in the beginning of October, Kathleen calls me.

"Joseph, there's someone on the phone wishing to speak to you."

When I answer, I find out that it is Abe the supervisor from my old job back in Salem Oregon. "How are things going for you, Joseph?"

"To tell you the truth, things couldn't be better."

"We missed you in the shop. Would you be interested in doing a little inspection work for a week or so? There is a particularly difficult project that we are working on and Jim will be away on holidays. There is no one at the shop that can handle the job. We're willing to put up both you and your wife for the time we need you. The company will also pay you a premium for your time at the shop."

I discuss this with Kathleen and she tells me she will try to get someone to run the business while we're gone. If not, she'll stay behind and I can go by myself for the week.

"Okay, Abe, it's a go, I'll be there on Monday."

"Thanks, buddy, we really appreciate this."

Kathleen phones everyone can think of to take over for her and finally finds one that can do the job. We make contact with Harry, and he immediately insists on having us stay with them. On Sunday morning, I have my inspection tools loaded in the trunk, our bags are packed, and off we go. The drive is pleasant and we talk most of the way there.

It's great to see Harry, Brenda, and the kids, who I let wrestle me to the ground. We spend the evening together, getting reacquainted. There is a bit of catching up to do and, by the end of the night, it is as if we were never apart.

The next morning, I'm at work and taking a ribbing from the guys, who are happy to see me again.

"Hey, Joseph, back already, you must have missed us, right?"

"Of course, who wouldn't miss you guys?"

The job is about the same as when I left and any problems are soon sorted out. There are a few new employees, but they seem to be pretty good men and we don't have any problems. The week goes by quickly and before I know it we are heading back home and everybody is happy. I'm asked by the company if I am willing to do this once in a while. After talking it over with Kathleen, I say, "It won't be a problem as long as you can give me a little notice."

Life back home gets into a routine again and all is well. The B and B is doing well and the guests are pleasant to deal with for the most part. At the end of February, I am asked to come back to Salem to take over for Jim again. I'm on my way back, only this time Kathleen can't find a replacement so I have to go by myself. We will miss each other but it is only for a week so it won't be too bad.

"I'm a little late in my monthly cycle, this is not normal for me. I don't want to assume anything, but I feel a little ill in the mornings."

I am so happy that it feels like my feet aren't even touching the floor. I hug her like there's no tomorrow.

"I'll bow out of going to work this coming week in Salem," I tell her.

"No, no you can't do that, I won't hear of it because you know that the company will suffer if you don't show up."

I try to argue the point with her, telling her I would feel better if I was here with her but to no avail. To make me feel better, first thing Saturday morning I head out to a top of the line electronics store and talk to the manager. I tell him what I'm looking for and when we come to an agreement, I ask if it can be installed today.

He says his men are quite busy and are tied up till quitting time today. I offer him a premium and finally get the okay, as long as it can be done in the evening. It takes the man two hours to complete the installation. This is a relief for me and I give the man an extra fifty dollars just to make it worthwhile for him.

"Is it necessary to have a surveillance system?" Kathleen asks. "I've never had any real trouble before."

"You are the most important person in my life and I want you to feel safe in my absence." So with some reluctance, I leave on Sunday morning.

February journal entry: *I am so happy that Kathleen is going to have a baby. I am on top of the world and things could not be better. Who would have thought that…*

I'm staying with Harry and Brenda again and when they hear the news that it's possible I'll be a father, they're almost as happy as I am.

"This is wonderful news. We're so pleased to hear this. Fill us in on the details," Brenda says, which I do.

We have a great time together during the week but I can't wait to get back home. I call Kathleen every evening and, although she misses me, she tells me that everything is okay. It's already spring and I can't believe that we've been married almost a year. *God, I love this woman.*

On Thursday evening, I phone home but there is no answer. This is unusual because she needs to be there for the guests. I phone several times in the next hour, and still no answer. I'm starting to wonder if the pregnancy is going all right or not. I call one of Kathleen's friends. "Have you heard anything from Kathleen?"

"I haven't talked to her in several days, but I'll go over

and see her as soon as I get off the phone."

That feeling of dread is starting to come over me like it did when Amy went missing. I try to phone Kathleen again, but still no answer. I'm beginning to panic a little. I wait for about an hour and, finally, the phone rings. Kathleen's friend Colleen is talking to me. I can tell by her voice that something is terribly wrong.

"What's going on?" I ask.

"Oh, Joseph, there's been a robbery at the Bed and Breakfast. Kathleen has been shot. She's in the hospital in critical condition. You should get home as soon as possible."

Panic is starting to set in as I imagine the worst happening to me again. *Why didn't I follow my instincts and stay home?*

Chapter 2

I'm stunned as I get off the phone and my head is in a whirl. I almost collapse to the floor as Harry grabs me. How could this happen again, why did this happen?

"What's wrong?" Harry asks.

As I tell him, I see the horror in his eyes. He knows how badly I took things when Amy was murdered and now the possibility has become a reality once again.

"I have to get back home, Harry." I get up to pack so I can get on the road.

"Joseph, you're in no shape to drive. I'll take your car home and you catch an airplane back to Kathleen so you'll get there much quicker."

Brenda is already on the phone booking a flight, using her credit card to pay for it. I'm so distraught that I don't even thank her. Harry packs a suitcase for himself and drives me to the airport, getting me on the plane. He sees me off and heads to my car for the long drive to Napa Valley.

I land at the airport in Sonoma and grab a taxi to the hospital. My hands are shaking as I pay the driver and run to the front desk. I tell the attendant who I am and she calls a doctor to come see me. The man introduces himself as Dr. Jim Williams.

"I'm sorry but your wife has suffered a gunshot wound to the abdomen. Her condition is critical and the internal bleeding from damaged organs is complicating efforts to stabilize her. It's also possible that your wife has sustained spinal cord damage, but that is uncertain at this stage. The hospital is doing everything possible, but we're not hopeful at this point."

I am asked to sign papers for medical coverage. The staff allows me a few moments with her, which ends up becoming a lot longer. She is so pale and, for the first time in a long while, I cry. The staff gives me a blanket, and insists I stay in the waiting room.

I stay at the hospital all day and into the night. It is suggested that I go home, which I refuse to do. I want to be close if there are any new developments. It's a long night as anguish takes a hold of me once more.

"Please don't let things end this way for me again," I ask as I look up toward where they say God is, thinking this might just help.

I only sleep now and then and, even when I do fall asleep, it's very fitfully. I'm already awake when the doctor comes to talk to me. There is a grave expression on his face as he approaches. A feeling of dread runs through me, and I start to fall apart as the doctor confirms my worst fears.

"I'm so sorry. Kathleen has passed away during the night, despite all attempts to save her. Upon closer examination, it has been found that she is indeed with child and that even if she had survived, the baby would have been lost."

I collapse to the floor, sobbing. This is the worst thing that has happened in my life. It is even worse than both my mother's death and Amy's because I would have been a father as well as a husband. Two orderlies place me on a bed as a nurse sticks a needle in my arm and I lose consciousness.

How long I am out I don't know. The effects of the drugs have numbed me to the point that I don't realize

where I am for quite some time. It finally dawns on me
when I see Harry walk through the door. Harry is devastat-
ed as he approaches the bed. He stands there with tears in
his eyes.

"I don't know what to say, Joseph, this is awful."

All of a sudden the nightmare comes flooding back to
me, and I realize that life for me has ended yet again. Unable to speak, I cry with the tears flowing in an endless
stream. Under normal circumstances, I would be humiliated
by this display, but it doesn't matter at all anymore. All I
know is that I have lost everything once more and that there
is nothing left for me.

Harry does his best to comfort me but there is nothing he
can do to make anything better. There is no consoling me at
this point, and he soon realizes this. Before he leaves he
informs me, "The police have been here to see you. They'll
be back to ask you some questions when you're able. I'll be
back later when Brenda arrives."

I barely hear anything that he says to me as the nurse in-
jects some drug into my arm again.

When I wake up for the second time, Brenda is sitting
beside the bed holding my hand. For a moment, I see
Kathleen, not Brenda, but that only lasts for a second, then
I'm back to reality.

"Oh, Joseph, I'm so sorry this has happened. Harry and I
will be here for you as long as you need us. I have made the
arrangements for the f—funeral."

The tears start to flow again and she comforts me as best
she can.

Later in the day, a police sergeant walks into the room
and, after offering me his condolences, fills me in on what
has happened.

"The emergency call center received the call originating
from the B and B. Your wife managed to dial nine-one-one
but was unable to speak before collapsing. We saw the surveillance system in the front office and took what was left
of it to headquarters. Our techs have been working on it and

have pieced together what happened. As far as we can determine, a lone gunman entered the premises from an angle so the camera didn't pick him up. It looks like he came up to the camera from the side and struck the unit. This caused the lens to be broken off disabling the video capabilities. What the gunman didn't know, is that the system has an audio system further back on the device and this kept on recording the sounds on the hidden part of the system."

"Your wife was co-operating with the man and gave him the money. He was very abusive with her. Going by your wife's voice, he must have been waving the gun around trying to intimidate her. She is pleading with him to be careful, just before the gun fires and she is shot. The gunman swears and mumbles something, indicating this isn't what he had planned, he then runs out of the office. The car can be heard spinning its tires as it speeds away."

"We believe that he didn't actually plan to shoot her. Until we catch him, we can't be certain of that. When your wife was picked up by the ambulance she was unconscious and unable to give any details what so ever. I am so sorry for your loss," he says.

I'm unable to function after hearing this and any questions he asks receive no answers. The nurse is back and I am soon out of it again and useless to the world.

After another day in the hospital, I am released with Harry and Brenda driving me back to the cottage. The place has been closed until further notice. The next few days are a blur as the funeral takes place.

A pastor from the church that Kathleen and I started to attend gives a beautiful eulogy, telling the attendees about how wonderful a person Kathleen was and that this senseless death has affected everyone who knew her.

He offers his condolences, but they fall on almost deaf ears.

"Do you want us to stay any longer, Joseph?" Harry asks.

"Thank you for all your help but I think that it will be

best if I am on my own for a while," I say while I look at the floor.

When Harry and Brenda leave to go home and I am left by myself. I lose the control that I have so desperately clung to. I remember what the sergeant told me and in a fit of rage, I destroy a room full of furniture. By the time I am done, the room is a shambles and my hands are cut and bleeding badly. I don't care in the slightest anymore as I lose a substantial amount of blood.

One of Kathleen's friends, Marita, finds me lying on the floor and calls an ambulance. Back into the bloody hospital, I go. When I am conscious, the doctor asks me if this was a suicide attempt.

I almost laugh at him. "If that was the case, I would never do it this way. If that was what I wanted, we wouldn't be having this conversation." I finally convince him that all this was a result of a fit of anger.

Sergeant Anderson comes to see me before I am released to inform me that one of the robbery suspects has just been apprehended. A license plate number on the vehicle speeding away from the scene had been taken down by a neighbor and phoned into the police.

"The suspect, Oliver J. Durham, has been identified as the driver. It has also been reported that there was also a second person in the car. The man claims to not know the name of the accomplice in the shooting. He has told the police that he met the man in a bar and the only name he ever heard is Smitty. Durham says they were both low on cash and thought that the B and B would result in a quick payday. He insists that he had nothing to do with the shooting. He was in the car while the robbery was taking place."

"He swears that it was never their intention to hurt anyone. The robber got distracted when he thought someone was pulling into the driveway and discharged the weapon unintentionally. This version is partially fabricated and when we confronted him with details, Durham changed his story to coincide with what we suspect really happened."

Then Sergeant Anderson tells me they have interrogated the man thoroughly. They've only managed to get the nickname and a poor description of the second man involved. The description is vague and can be attached to many average males.

"The only real distinguishing feature is a tattoo on the inside of his right forearm. The tattoo is a pair of dice, each with seven spots on them. When asked about this, the man, who is in his late twenties, said that it means that he makes his own luck. There is an APB put out on the shooter, but we are not hopeful at this point in the investigation. There is no information as to the mode of transportation and little else is known about the suspect."

Chapter 3

After getting a stern talking to by the doctor I have been allowed to go home once again.

April journal entry: *I haven't written much in a long time. I was on top of the world, being married with a child on the way. How am I to go on after my whole life has just gone down the toilet again? If it wasn't for the fact that Kathleen's murderer is out there somewhere, there would be nothing in my life to keep me here. I don't care anymore about anything. The world can go to blazes for all I care. I hate my life…*

I go to the room where I allowed my feelings to get out of hand and survey the damage I did. I straighten things out as best I can. Grabbing a bottle of whiskey, I walk to the backyard. In the privacy of this secluded spot, I proceed to tie one on, really tie one on.

This is something that I have never done before, but at this point, I don't care anymore. I am so drunk that I can hardly stand. I stay this way for two days. The only reason I stop is that I run out of booze and can't see straight enough to get more. The next few weeks are a mess. When I sober up enough, I go buy more whiskey and just lay around in a stupor. It numbs me enough to be able to cope.

I finally have to stop as my insides are feeling the effects of too much alcohol consumption and too little food. It is getting difficult to keep the booze down. The retching is taking its toll and I know it's time to stop.

Without the booze to numb the pain, I sink into a depression deeper than any I have yet to experience. This takes a hold of me unlike any of the ones I suffered in the past. I reach a point on several occasions where I find myself on the verge of ending it.

As far as I'm concerned, there is no reason anymore for life to go on. All I have ever cherished has been ripped away from me. I have totally ignored all of Kathleen's friends and they have now stopped coming around.

The second man has not been apprehended and, although the driver of the getaway car has been sent to prison, it does little to make anything better. The police feel that he knows more than he is saying but they cannot make him break his silence. It is almost as if he is deathly afraid of the man called Smitty. The B and B has been closed now for several months and is starting to show signs of neglect. I just don't feel like doing anything anymore.

Harry called again this morning and told me that he and Brenda are coming out next week. This shakes me up enough to get off my ass and straighten the place up. I have to pull myself together, even if only while they are here. I can't allow myself to be seen like this. I'm ashamed of myself. Kathleen would be shocked if she saw me in this condition. The business was her pride and joy and she would scold me to no end if she saw how I have let the place go.

May journal entry: *I have to get myself together, the place is a mess. I can't let Brenda and Harry see me this way. I have to, I have to…*

The first thing I do is get myself cleaned up. I go to the grocery store and stock up on supplies. When this is all done, I get down to the daunting task of getting the place back in shape. In my run-down condition, this is a big job. I have really let myself go and this is very evident as the task progresses. My physical stamina is so poor, that I am really surprised at how I have gotten into this shape so fast.

By the time the weekend arrives, things are shaping up nicely, at least in my eyes. When Harry pulls into the driveway, the place looks reasonably good. I have desperately tried to make myself look presentable. Going by the expression on Brenda's face, I can tell that I haven't succeeded. She doesn't come out and actually say it but I can see that she is very concerned.

After settling in, Brenda heads to the kitchen and starts the task of making a better meal than I have had since the funeral. After the dinner is finished, she gets Harry to do the dishes and takes me out to the backyard.

"My goodness, Joseph, look at you. Do you actually think that Kathleen would approve of how you're handling this situation? She would be shocked at this. You know as well as I do that she would want you to pick up the pieces and get back on your feet. This can't be allowed to go on."

I hang my head in shame because I know that she is right.

"I am so concerned about you right now. This has to end and it has to end now," she says. "It is common knowledge that men have a much harder time getting back on their feet than women do. This has been proven by the fact that older men don't seem to last long after their spouses die without getting remarried. With women, it is far different, they seem to pick up the pieces and go on. Most times, they really don't need another man, except maybe because of financial reasons," Brenda informs me. "You have gone through so many horrible things in your life but have always come back from them. This time is not going to be any different if I have anything to say about it. Do you hear me, Joseph? If you can't do this by yourself, then I will have to get you some help from a counselor." She takes me by the hand and pleads with me to talk to someone. She won't let me off the hook until I promise to make an appointment. Here is a woman who cares what happens to me and it tugs at my heart.

The appointment is made after a few inquiries. I prefer to talk to a man rather than a woman. This is not because of any reasons other than that I feel more comfortable with a man. My only real conversations as an adult other than Amy and Kathleen were with Jack Peters, a man I met on a vacation. He, despite my best efforts, made his way into my life and became a friend that I could talk to. He, of course, didn't know the side of me that I've had to keep hidden all these years, but a friend, nevertheless.

After Harry and Brenda leave to go back to Salem, Oregon, the day approaches. The day I am not looking forward to, but know I need. How much I disclose will depend on the relationship that develops with the counselor. I cannot tell him the things I have done. The things no one but me knows. If it were to leak out, I would be on the run or in prison for the rest of my life.

June journal entry: *I am not looking forward to spilling my guts out to someone I don't know again. I know this is the only way, but I don't have to like it. Real men don't do this shit…*

So with much apprehension, I walk into the office of James Morton. He is a tall man with a slight build and a long, very slender neck. I wonder how it holds up his rather oversized head. His appearance strikes me as odd, and it must be somewhat evident, because he smiles at my reaction. This must be commonplace for him because he slides right past this, trying to make me feel at home.

"Tell me about yourself, Joseph."

"I've recently had a loss…" I say, and the story begins.

He has a way of putting me at ease as our first encounter progresses. He has a calm almost nonchalant attitude about him. By the time the first session is over, you would think that we have known each other for quite some time.

We have just scratched the surface, only getting to the part where my mother was killed and the way it affected me. I'm actually surprised that I have opened up that much in such a short time. I'll have to be very careful not to let my guard down too far.

"It will do you good to think about starting a journal. It will help you to write down your thoughts. This way you can keep track of your progress," James advises me.

Reluctantly, I agree, not telling him that I already am. As the session ends and another appointment is made, I feel a calming in my spirit taking place. Don't get me wrong, the anger deep inside is there ready to erupt at any moment, but it seems to be slightly more controllable. More like I was when I learned to vent properly, sort of. I feel somewhat embarrassed by all this talk, even though there is some progress made.

Back at home, I look around at the B and B and the property. I see that what I have done lately is better than how it was. It's painfully obvious that it is nowhere near the condition it was when Kathleen was here with me.

This thought starts to derail me, and I almost lose it again. I know that I will never again have what I did with Kathleen or Amy. I must have been a fool to think that my life could ever be normal. Maybe I should change my name to Jonah.

All that has ever meant anything to me has always been torn away. This has always been done by people who were nothing but worthless garbage to be taken out with the rest of the trash. I must have a little of my old self still left in me because when I reach deep inside I manage to regain some control of myself.

Doing a walk around the property, I decide what jobs should be tackled first. I look at the workout room that has been untouched for many months while I was heading in the downward spiral towards oblivion.

"No more, I will not lie down and die, drinking myself to death," I say angrily to myself.

I know I have a long way to go, but I really need the distraction of putting the place back in order. Thank god for friends like Harry and Brenda. I make the decision to start my workouts again. I don't know exactly where I am headed but I know it is no longer downhill.

The following morning, I have a light workout, which is all that I can manage. The job of repairing some of the damage the room sustained in my fit of rage is started. The holes in the walls are filled in. The remnants of the broken furniture are cleaned up. The carpets are shampooed and a week later the house is presentable again.

My second session with James progresses as we get deeper into my life. I talk about how I've learned to handle the tragedies that have plagued me all my life. This is where my guard goes up and my answers are not what James wants to hear.

"I don't think that you are answering me truthfully. Would you like take a little time to compose yourself and start over?" he asks me.

"I can't go into this right now. I'm just not ready," I say.

"That's all right we can touch on the subject later."

Thankfully, he allows this to rest for a while. We discuss my past work and relationships with my coworkers as the session ends. At home, I realize that I will have to give some thought as to how I will bridge this part of the counseling. Having gone through this already in the past, I should have been ready for it.

It finally dawns on me that I haven't used the internet for research in a long time. Not since I left my job at Salem Steel Fabrication. I can't believe that almost a year and a half has elapsed since I left their employ. Unfortunately, I have ignored any calls from them too.

On the net, I find the answers that I am looking for. At the next meeting as we get back into the ways that I handled the deaths in my life, I tell James, "My workouts and my visualizing the perpetrators before me and lashing out at them has helped. I limit myself as to the amount of television news that I watch. In the end, it has been time and throwing myself into my jobs that has gotten me through."

"Have you ever taken any measures to retaliate against these people," he asks me.

I look him straight in the eye. "I thought about it, but couldn't bring myself to actually doing anything. Two wrongs, to me, don't make a right."

He seems genuinely pleased with this answer and the meeting goes on to other areas of my life. *Geez, I've become a good liar.*

There are a couple of times that I almost slip up but manage to stop myself in the nick of time. A few more sessions and things draw to a close.

"Would you like to share what you have written in your journal with me?" James asks.

I am caught off guard and almost panic at the thought.

"I see this makes you uncomfortable. I know these are your private thoughts and you want to keep them to yourself. This is perfectly normal so I won't press the issue. To tell you the truth, Joseph, I have never run across a client that has had as much tragedy in their life as you have. Yet through all the adversity, you have still found the resolve to go on. If you ever find that you need to talk, that things are a little too difficult, please call me," he says to me sympathetically.

"Thanks, Mr. Morton, I'll do that if I need to."

We shake hands and I'm on my way. I wonder if I should destroy the journal. There are things in there that would not be in my best interests to have anyone else read. I'll have to give this some thought. In the meantime, I'll take some precautions to make sure this doesn't happen. If I was back at my old job, I could make something at work to securely safeguard the journal.

After a lot of work, I have the place operating again. With things getting a little busier, I go about the task of hiring a person to help me run things in anticipation. I have several female applicants but opt to hire a male instead. I hire a guy because I don't want any possible relationships happening. He is called Albert Maples. Being of English descent, he appreciates the décor. We get along well, and he learns the business quickly as this is the type of employment he has always had. Soon I find that things are busy, and Rose Cottage is thriving again.

September comes, and I receive another call from my old employer. This isn't the first time they have called me, but it is the first time that I have answered. The times they tried to get in touch with me, I didn't get back to them because my heart just wasn't in it. I pick up the phone and find that Abe my old supervisor is on the other end. He expresses his sorrow over Kathleen and, when he realizes that I am on the mend, asks me a question. "We are wondering if you are interested in coming back to work for a short time. The shop is very busy, and we could use your help."

At first, I'm somewhat reluctant. The more I talk to him, the more I feel that this may be just what is needed to move on. I talk with Albert, who is more than willing to handle the B and B by himself.

"I've talked with my man here and, yes, I think this is a great idea. I can make it in at the beginning of next week," I say as my mood starts to lift once again.

"That's good news, we'll expect you then. If by chance you need anything, just ask."

I call Brenda. She and Harry are thrilled at the turn of events and can't wait for me to arrive on the weekend. I go out and pick up a few presents for the kids, who are now well into their mid-teens.

After packing up my tools and clothes, I am on my way to Salem. My mood starts to darken as I drive away. I find that I am slipping into the spot that will cause me nothing but trouble.

On a long open stretch of road, I pull over and start walking. The walk soon turns into a run. My stamina is not what it was, and I tire fairly quickly, slowing back down to a walk. I make up my mind then and there to get back into the shape I was in before moving to Rose Cottage. On the way to Salem, I stop several more times for a short run. By the time I get to my destination Saturday evening, I'm fairly tired.

The reunion is quite the spectacle, as I am swarmed by the kids who say they have missed me a lot. We settle in and a deep restful sleep welcomes me back. I wake the next morning bright and early, going for a quick run before breakfast. By the time I'm back, everyone is awake, and we chat about what has been taking place in their lives.

We deliberately stay away from my circumstances. As evening rolls around, I go to the car to retrieve the gifts I bought. Harry and Brenda just love the case of wine I brought. It contains most of their favorites which, in turn, pleases me too.

The kids open what I bought them. As Eva opens the box with a fairly expensive digital camera in it, she squeals and jumps into my arms, almost knocking me over. Gordie opens his box, which contains a small television with a DVD player. He is so happy he hugs me too. The kids go to their rooms and play with new-found treasures.

"You've gone way overboard," Harry and Brenda say. "This wasn't necessary."

"If it wasn't for the two of you, I wouldn't be where I am today. Good friends are hard to find," I say in return.

The next morning, I walk back into the shop I spent so much of my life in. The guys are really happy to see me and a few make comments. They mention the fact that I have lost a bit of weight and seem a little the worse for wear. After a few hours, things start to fall back into place. The first week, although hectic, settles into a routine. The evenings are pleasant with Harry and the kids. I ask if I should make arrangements to stay at a hotel for the duration of my stay, but they won't hear of it.

I check back with Albert and find that everything is under control and realize that he is in his element. He asks if I would be interested in selling him the place, which catches me off guard. I tell him I will need to think about it and maybe, if the price is right, we might be able to come to an agreement.

"Harry?" I call out. "The man who is running the B and B just asked if I want to sell the business to him."

"Well, that's a real surprise because your old house has just come on the market too. It's going for a real good price. I hear that the owner has gotten a transfer with his job and needs to sell quickly."

"I think that I'll talk to my bosses and see where this goes," I say.

The next day at work, I talk to Abe my old supervisor and tell him what is going on. He asks me to give him a minute to talk to the management. Half an hour later, I'm called into the office. Management is waiting for me and lets me know that they have been hoping for this. They were a little apprehensive about approaching me with an offer. We work out the particulars with me keeping my old seniority and a deal is struck.

September journal entry: *I can't believe the turn of events taking place in my life. I was in the deepest hole I have ever been in and, all of a sudden, an upside down world shows some promise.*

Wow, is about all I can say. Who would have thought things would fall into place so quickly. I call Albert and we reach a price we are both comfortable with, and another piece falls into place. Harry calls the agent that has the listing for my old home, and we arrange a viewing.

When we get to my old house, I am pleased that the owner has taken good care of the place. I ask to do a walk through by myself. I'm pleased that he hasn't discovered the hidden storage at the end of the basement. We hash out a deal in short order and all the papers are signed. I ask for a bit of time off work to wrap up things at the other end. With minimal effort, I am loaded and ready to move back to Salem.

Before leaving, I visit Kathleen's grave. With tears in my eyes, I say goodbye for what will probably be one of the last times I'll be here. This is way too hard to do very often. As another chapter in my life closes, I find myself driving back into familiar territory.

Chapter 4

Moving back into my old home brings a slew of feelings I didn't think I would have. Thoughts of Amy run through my head. Coupled with the death of Kathleen and my unborn child, things are almost unbearable. It is all I can do at times to function halfway normal. For a minute, I wonder if moving back into this house may not have been a bad mistake.

I manage to put on a pleasant face as I learned to do years ago. I let those that I have to deal with daily know that there will be times when it will be best not to irritate me too much. I apologize ahead of time for things that may happen. The boys say they understand and will try to help me through this time.

Things are unpacked and put in their places. The guys at work give me a hand to unload the heavy stuff and life starts somewhat anew. My old neighbors welcome me back, and work is falling back into the same old routine in no time. The long term rental facility still has all the items that I put away for safe keeping. They are brought home and stored away in the hidden storage area at the end of the basement. The garage has been changed around a bit. With a little effort, I will have my workout area back in a few weeks.

Jim who I trained to do the job of quality control at work is happy to have me to lean on when he runs into trouble. He is a good guy, and I like working with him. He knows when to back off because he has known me for many years. He's learned to deal with my ups and downs. I am glad to be working at machining rather than quality control because there is far less stress on me this way. This allows me to cope with my inner feelings.

I find myself thinking of ways to get the information I need to find the second man in the robbery. I am at a loss as to how to get to him without revealing myself. I want desperately to find my wife's murderer. I have done some horrible things in my life, but these will pale in comparison to what I'll do if I catch up with dice boy. That pair of sevens will change to snake eyes when I get my hands on him.

I went way overboard when I dealt with Jake Patterson, Beth's killer. It won't compare to what I'll do when I catch up with the bastard that ruined my life. *Arrrrhg, I need to get even!* The words just scream in my head. *Please let me find a way of getting the information that I need. I want to hurt him, hurt him bad.*

My workout room is back in order. I get into a rigorous routine as I start to get into better and better shape. It has been eight months since the robbery, and my rages have diminished to the point where I can think things through with a relatively clear head. I still have my moments, but they are now becoming more and more controllable.

On weekends, I do my old mad dash routines in the forested parks. Starting and stopping and jumping over obstacles helps get me in shape fast. I'm getting good with my bow and rifle again too. Starting some of my projects at work again replaces some of the items that were destroyed in my encounter with the Carlos brothers.

I start looking for new things that I can use to bring down the son of a bitch Dice Man when I find him. I know now that it will be when and not if. I practice my martial arts and hone my moves. Debating if I should put on one of my many disguises and go to some bars in the rough area of town occupies me for a short time. If I let some of the bad boys pick a fight with me, I will get back into fighting form faster. It is something to think about.

I run into Bill Henderson, the police detective who caught Amy's killer, in the mall. I am somewhat surprised at how happy I am to see him. We had struck up a friendship when I was living here before. He is the one I called and informed of an impending murder. That was almost a mistake, as he recognized my distinctive voice and hounded me for a while. It took some real ingenuity to get him off my back.

We end up going for lunch together and he asks why I came back to town. He is flabbergasted when he hears the story. "Is there is anything that I can do. I'm astounded at how much tragedy you've had to deal with in your life. I don't know how you've been able to go on."

I want to ask him about getting to Oliver J Durham who is in prison in California. But I'm a little reluctant to involve him, in case I do find a way to dispose of him. As lunch progresses, he tells me that a big drug dealer from Mexico has moved to Salem. Bill has seen a huge increase in crime and is beside himself as to how to handle it. We turn the conversation in another direction just to lighten things up.

We have never had a real close relationship, but there has always been a sort of comrade feeling between us. He asks if I like fishing and, when I say yes, he asks me to go first thing in the morning. I meet him at a spot outside of town and we spend the day together in his little aluminum boat.

Over the next few weeks, we make this a little ritual whenever possible. We go out now and then after work and on weekends and start feeling very comfortable together. He learns more about what I do at work and is astonished when I tell him of the things we build at the shop. He tells me that if he can be of help, all I need to do is ask.

I thank him for his offer to help. As we part company, because we have started to become comfortable with each other, he hesitantly asks me a question. "Would you be able to make a little device for me at work? I didn't know who to approach with this. It's been a stroke of luck running into you. I'd appreciate it if you were to keep it under your hat too."

"I'll be glad to help you out," I say.

Bill gives me a fairly detailed print and heads out before I can ask him what the device is for.

After getting in a grueling workout, I settle in for an evening at home. My training must really be paying off because the guys at work are starting to comment on my appearance. The muscles are building up quickly and my whole demeanor is changing rapidly.

Pulling out Bill's print, I relax on the couch. Studying what Bill wants me to build starts me wondering why he would need this item. It resembles one of the things I built to take out a person's dog that I disposed of. If I am reading this right, it looks like a device that would be planted in an obscure spot and remotely operated to release a stabbing device.

Most of the items can be obtained in various ways, but some need a person with my talents to fabricate. I want to ask him what he intends to do with the gizmo, but decide not to. I want to see where this leads. I'm a little surprised at how he came up with the plans and how well he has drawn them up. Maybe there is a side to Bill that I have, up to now, been unaware of.

On Monday at work, I start to make some of the pieces that are needed to build Bill's device. By the end of the week, I have most of the things done and pick up the last few things at various specialty stores. By Saturday afternoon everything is assembled and functioning the way I think it should.

Bill comes over soon after he is called. Taking him to the toy assembled in the basement, I show him how it functions, using the remote control device. It's obvious that he needs a clear line of sight so the remote will properly activate the tool. This is something that I would have hidden in the bushes with an opening to allow the arm of the unit to swing in an arc.

I ask him what this thing is meant for and he tries to give me a rational explanation, which I don't buy for a second. I smile at him and let it go because I know Bill fairly well and don't want to doubt his motives, but I know something is up. He pays me for the things I had to buy and takes the unit, asking me once more to please keep this to myself.

Having my own things to deal with, I soon lose track of the incident with Bill. The need to have an outlet for my pent up urges keeps resurfacing more and more often. This is the same thing that used to happen to me when I had no way to relieve the frustration of not being able to punish Amy's murderer.

Since coming back to Salem, I've run across a few underground sites that I've been steered to by a contact in the CDC (Citizens Discussing Crime). Even though I tried, I've never managed to find any information about any of these people, which is probably a good thing. This way they can't trace me either. I'm starting to suspect that there are others like me in the business of taking out the garbage. But I doubt I'll ever find out for sure. It takes a while to gain the confidence of the members on the site called V-anonymous, V, I suspect is for vigilante. There are different levels of involvement in some of the sites I use to gather information.

Going online, I quickly find that the information I receive is obtained from people who are in the know. They must either have contact with these people or know others who do. I look for people that don't belong in this world. A few make their presence known to me by the stories that I read.

There is a slumlord that has allowed things in his many rental buildings to deteriorate to the point where several of the young children have gotten so sick that they died. There have been several fires where people have been badly burned, and three perished. This was due to faulty wiring that was not repaired because of the cost involved. Yes, this guy should be dealt with.

There is an accused rapist loose in Santa Monica that has managed to always have alibis provided by friends. When he didn't have one, it has been reported that the victims were terrified into not testifying. A candidate to be considered, he is.

Drug dealers, pimps, and a multitude of prospective targets come on to my radar. My old friends, the boys from the Klan, are often in the news. These misfits seem to pop up all the time. They have this misguided sense of entitlement. The group seems to think they're decent people that need to be able to dominate and terrorize the people they feel so superior to. Yep, I will one day pay them another visit, only this time there will have to be a far higher body count.

There seems to be a lot of mass shootings at schools across the country in the last few years. What the hell is going on to cause so many of these senseless acts among our young people? It can't all be blamed on bullying. My sources must either live or have contacts across the country, because the stories I get are about people that live everywhere.

I'm already getting the itch to make plans, but I haven't been at work long enough to warrant taking time off. I've been asked to go back on the safety committee, which I accept. A major reason for my decision is that I've seen a few things that need attention. The issues are taken care of fairly quickly. Abe calls me into the office, and he tells me how happy that management is to have me back. My old wage is given back to me and I'm asked to continue helping Jim with quality control. *Sweet!*

As I watch the local news about three weeks later, a story piques my interest. The Mexican drug dealer who has created so much trouble in Salem has been found dead on a trail that he runs along on a regular basis. Preliminary reports indicate that he has died from a stab wound to the abdomen with some traces of poison present. There is some bruising in the area of the stab wound that indicates the knife or stabbing weapon was attached to a holder. No solid evidence or weapon has been found at the scene that points to a possible suspect. The dealer's death is expected to have a huge impact on the drug trade in Salem.

Immediately, I think of the unit that I built for Bill and how he had asked me to keep this to myself. I am almost tempted to give Bill a call, but think better of it. I'll let this pass for a bit of time. If it's true that Bill is behind this, I may be able to use this to my advantage. He may feel a little more obligated to return the favor. Becoming fishing buddies has helped form a much closer bond with the man, and I see more clearly than ever what motivates him.

Thinking about Bill and the fact that we now have something more in common, I wonder if it's feasible that we might become team mates of a sort. I've always worked alone and the thought of someone else knowing this about me doesn't excite me overly much. But who knows what the future may bring? I call him up, and we go out to fish for a couple of hours. His wife is at a meeting so this won't interfere with his home life. We get to know each other quite well as we chat in the canoe. I've gotten one with a nice wide bottom. One that is very stable in the water.

A plan of sorts is starting to come together in my mind. The old excitement is making itself known inside me as a slight tingling affects my fingers. For now, this is going to have to stay a lone enterprise but I'm really itching to get back in the game.

In about two weeks, Bill saves me the trouble of bridging the subject with him. He shows up on my doorstep out of the blue. There is a serious look on his face, and I know he is troubled by the knowledge that he has indirectly implicated me in something. It is late in the afternoon, and he has just gone off duty. As he sits in a lazy boy chair, I offer him one of my favorite beers, a Corona, which he gladly accepts. We chat for a while, skirting around the issue that I know he wants to bring up but isn't sure how to. So I give him an opening.

"Why don't you call your wife and the two of us can have a barbecue? I know there's something on your mind. This way we can talk at our leisure."

There's a look of relief that comes over his face, and he makes the call. We have a couple more beers, and I fire up the barbecue while defrosting some T-bone steaks. A couple of potatoes are wrapped in foil on and put on the BBQ as it warms up. Bill is unwinding a bit as the beer takes its effect, and the conversation is guided to where I expect it is going by me. I make sure that we don't actually talk about what I suspect till after dinner is over. I know that Bill is an honorable police detective that has a high moral code. I'll let him tell me what he wants to say, so I can feel him out as to obtaining his help with my problem.

"Hey, Joseph, do you remember the thing I had you build for me?"

"Yes," I say.

"Do you know why I wanted you to make it?" he asks.

"I am pretty sure I do."

"Despite all the efforts of the police department," he tells me, "it has failed to make any difference regarding the drug epidemic that's hit Salem. I've always suspected that you've had a side that no one knew about. I could never prove anything, but then again, never really wanted to. That's why I approached you about the stabbing device. It was used it to get rid of a cancer that has been eating away at the city I love so much."

"To tell you the truth, Bill, I'm behind you one hundred percent. You never need to worry about me. When I offered to do things for you, I meant it."

Another look of relief comes over his face and he relaxes visibly. "How are things going for you? Is there is anything you need?" he asks.

Bingo! This is just the moment I've been waiting for.

"Well, Bill, I've been thinking. Can you do a little checking for me? Oliver J. Durham the driver in the B and B robbery is locked up in prison. He knows more than he's telling," I say. "Is there some way to get the information from him?"

After telling him the whole story he asks me a question. "What will you do if you find out who his partner is?"

I just look at him and he knows not to ask again.

Chuckling, he says, "I'll put some thought into it and see what I can do. I have a lot of contacts in the underworld and in the prison system. I'll do my best to come up with something."

Knowing Bill, I am sure he will be able to help me, especially now that I know what he has done himself—not that I would ever reveal this to anyone. *One favor deserves another, as the old saying goes.*

At work, a situation has come up that requires some intervention. One of the new employees is suspected of trying to bring in a union. The guys in the plant have a good relationship with management. Not wanting this changed, they are more than a little upset about this man pushing his views at them constantly. It looks like he is a union representative sent in to sign up as many employees as possible.

Abe calls me into the office. "How can we get rid of the man? Any ideas?"

I think it over a bit in my mind before answering. "Allan is still in his ninety-day probation period. You should warn him about his spending too much time talking. Also, have his work checked thoroughly by Jim," I suggest. "Maybe we can find some sub-standard work and let him go because of that."

This is done and, unfortunately, his work is good. He doesn't talk too much during work times, so we don't have grounds to let him go. Abe calls me back in the office a week later and seems a little more worried this time.

"The guy's probation is coming to an end and, once it does, the company will have a harder time letting him go. Have you noticed anything?" Abe asks.

"Allan has continued to pester the guys during breaks about bringing in a union. Being constantly told no doesn't slow him down at all. He approaches me quite often too. Abe, I have an idea I need to run past you. I think that we can get away with it and not give Allan any grounds for a lawsuit against the shop," I say and proceed to fill him in on the details.

He agrees to let me try. So I wait until Allan starts trying to talk me in the lunchroom. He tries to convince me about the advantages of a union again. Immediately, I start berating him. Becoming quite insulting and, stepping closer and closer, I tell him, "We're all sick and tired of you trying to force a union on us that we don't want. Unions are a thing of the past, and we don't need one here."

I get closer and closer as he is backed against the wall. Allan is a big guy, well over two hundred pounds and carries himself well. This is probably why the union sent him into our shop in the first place. He is not intimidated. Putting his hands on my shoulders, he pushes me away.

This is now considered assault. I give him a quick shot to the solar plexus and back a step away. He gasps for breath and then comes at me with a swing, which I avoid easily. He realizes his mistake at once. He tries to apologize, but it's too late as I walk into the office.

After talking to Abe, Allan is called into the office. Abe confronts Allan with the situation. Allan tries desperately to justify his actions to no avail. He is told that this is cause for dismissal. Allan goes and picks up his tools.

As he walks past me, he stops. "I could take you if I wanted to,"

I look at him and, with a smile, tell him, "If that's what you want, we can do it after work today. Just wait for me outside the gate."

He stares at me and I can see in his eyes that he wonders if this is a good idea or not.

Allan leaves the building.

Abe is happy with the outcome. The guys in the shop

laugh and slap me on the back, welcoming the old Joseph back. They have fond memories of when I dropped the guy that tried to beat me up a while back in the parking lot. I have to admit that it felt good to get the adrenalin flowing through my veins again. But I do have to be careful not to divulge too much information about my darker side. I'm planning to resurrect the old me—the one that helped so many meet their maker sooner than they expected. At the end of the day, Allan, it appears has decided not to take me up on the offer, he is nowhere to be seen.

It's now Friday, and I've had my workout, knowing that I am approaching peak form once again. It feels good. I keep practicing my martial arts and street fighting moves. I hone my bow work as well as knife throwing. As I practice, it becomes quite evident that I'm getting fairly decent with the nun chucks. I would hate to be hit with one of these suckers.

All of a sudden, my thoughts stray toward Kathleen. My mood darkens, and I feel the hatred fill me. This happens now and then when I least expect it. The old feelings I had when my wife and unborn child were stolen from me come back in a flash. I look in the mirror and see a face that is hardly recognizable. I am almost overwhelmed by the rage that has its hold on me.

It dawns on me that I really need to tone it down and get control of myself. What I need is to start getting some information on Smitty. I'll call Bill in the near future, and see if he has come up with anything. As the evening progresses, I look on the internet to see if anyone, in particular, jumps out at me. Looking at the news shows, I check to see if anybody in the areas around Salem could possibly be a candidate. This way, I may not have to take time off work and still relieve some of the inner stress that's been building up. This stress has created a problem for me ever since the brutal murder of my mother went unavenged for so long.

I have never done any of my extracurricular activities in the vicinity of where I live, but if I am careful, I may be able to make it work. By checking on the internet, I find a dealer in town who sells to high school kids, gets them hooked on meth, and then forces them into prostitution. He has been in jail a few times but is back on the streets. There is a habitual car thief that never learns to stop. This probably isn't severe enough to warrant death, although the owners of the cars may think otherwise.

We seem to have a loan shark in town too. According to my sources, he has gone way overboard collecting debts several times. Nobody has the nerve to testify against him, at least that's what is I hear. One of his latest victims has suffered brain damage and won't recover most of his abilities. I decide this is the guy for me to see first. I get his name and picture online and then find the general area of town he lives in. I'll do a little reconnaissance next weekend, trying to get his routine down.

The following week goes by a lot slower than usual because I'm anxious to get going on my visitation. I have to actually put the brakes on myself, because of what happened the last time I went into a situation not properly prepared. I almost got shot and ended up getting a gash on my forehead when I ran into a low hanging branch on a tree. No, I don't want that kind of thing happening again.

I decide on what I'll take with me when I go looking up Al Domino. He is of good size but not what I would have expected. He is pudgy and soft looking. After an evening of prowling, I find him in a bar in the sleazy part of town. He's laughing it up with his buddies, slaps the occasional girl that passes him on her backside, and thinks it's hilarious.

I have disguised myself enough that even a friend wouldn't recognize me. I'm wearing a leather jacket that hangs just past the beltline. I have on a pair motorcycle style boots with steel toes. Inside my jacket, I have pockets that conceal the nun chucks and my fixed blade, double-edged knife.

In a fair fight, I can take on any but the best of these guys easily. The thing I always try to keep in mind is that these types of fights are seldom fair. Just to make sure that I have all the advantages on my side, I have my semi-automatic pistol tucked away in a handy spot. Tucked in the top of my boot on the inside, I carry an extra magazine. This is probably overkill, but I don't take chances.

I'm near enough to Al to overhear some of his conversations. But I'm out of the way at a table with my back to the wall. This way, nobody can get behind me. I keep a low profile and am pretty much ignored by everybody. I am not the nicest looking face in the crowd with my disguise on so nobody cares to befriend me. I spend several hours listening and watching and get nothing of importance. Getting up to go before I am noticed too much, I head out the door.

Waiting in the shadows of a doorway down the street, I can see if Al leaves by himself. If yes, I can follow him to where he lives. I have to stand there until closing time before he finally leaves with a buddy. Several times while I have been waiting, I've been bothered by drunks and addicts looking for a handout. A harsh word sends them on their way.

It's doubtful that I'll get a chance to deal with Al on my first night out but one can always hope. I follow at a safe distance, always being aware of my surroundings. As they go, Al and his buddy punch out some man as he walks down the street. The guy with Al distracts the man and Al nails him. Then both gang up on the guy who was in the wrong place at the wrong time.

I made the mistake once of taking out one suspect when I should have taken out two. My friend's daughter died a horrible death because of it. These two are both bad, so I plan to do both at the same time. When I get the chance, being on the other side of the street, I make my way past them. Sticking to the shadows as much as I can, I move ahead of them.

I wasn't planning on anything tonight but an opportunity seems to have presented itself. When I am far enough ahead of the pair, I cross the street at an intersection well ahead and walk toward them. I'm sure they must have noticed me as I worked my way ahead of them on the other side of the street. The excitement of the upcoming encounter starts to build in me. I already have the knife in my left hand with the blade pointed upward, lying against my forearm. The nun chucks are in my right hand against my side, out of sight.

As I approach, the pair separates, with Al close to the building and his pal near the edge of the curb. This will force me to go between them. They think this will leave me vulnerable to attack by at least one of them. What they obviously don't realize is that I am already aware of their plan. As the crucial moment comes, I decide to look at Al, giving his buddy the opening he is looking for. When the guy steps toward me, I drop the one end of the nun chucks. As he starts his swing with his left hand, I swing my right hand in an arc that sends the nun chuck swinging into the open side of his head.

The impact is hard and down he goes. As Al steps in, I raise my left knee to block any kick that might come. As he is coming toward me, I swing my arm in a left hook. I deliberately hit him with my fist instead of the knife. He is stunned by the impact and staggers back against the wall. His hand goes to the inside of his coat, but he is too slow. The knife point is pressed against his throat and his hand drops away. With the streets deserted, I am able to take my time and savor the moment.

"So you like to hurt people do you, Al?"

"Do I know you? What do you want from me?"

"No, you don't know me, but I know about you, and what I know I don't like," I say menacingly. Tucking the nun chucks away, I lift his coat away from his body and see a pistol. "Now what were you going to do with that, Mister Domino? You weren't going to be unfriendly, were you? Sorry to inform you of this, but tonight I'll do the debt collecting. The debt you owe the people you've hurt," I say to him.

The blade enters his midsection as a look of bewilderment crosses his face. This is not how things were supposed to go. As he drops to the sidewalk, I finish the job and then do his buddy, making sure they are both dead. I take a quick look around and, seeing no one in the vicinity, take their wallets and head toward my car after cleaning the blade of the knife on Al's coat. When I have the opportunity, I empty the wallets and put the money in the first donation place I find, discarding the rest.

The whole episode has gone almost too easily. But I don't care about that, and the old feeling this gives me is brightening my mood. Despite the fact that I have just taken the lives of two men, I feel good about myself. This has happened far quicker than I was planning on. I usually take way more time to do a job than I did tonight. But when an opportunity presents itself, you have to be ready.

Back in my car, my hands tremble a bit from the injection of adrenalin. The encounter leaves me with a feeling of satisfaction that lasts all the way home. I clean the knife and nun chucks with straight bleach and ammonia then put everything away. The rest of the weekend is far more pleasant than most of the ones I have had in quite some time.

The following week is routine, so I spend a bit of my spare time making some aluminum darts like the ones that I made when I dealt with the Carlos brothers. Back then, I made a battery operated dart gun that used servos for directional adjustments and an electric, high-speed solenoid that launched the darts remotely.

This is one of the things that I love about my job. The things I have made in the past like my double-edged knives and the arrows that have a rubber type material the size of a golf ball on the end, have really come in handy. I used those to knock out a bad boy from a distance before dealing with him.

It seems that I'm getting control of the darkness that envelopes me now and then. Especially since I had the release provided me when Al and his buddy crossed my path. There is a story in the news about their deaths. It is suspected that previous clients, who were unhappy with the treatment they received from Al Domino and associate, exacted their own kind of justice. These two men will not be missed.

I think that I'll wait till a need builds up again before I go after Frank Ashton, the drug dealer who targets high school kids and gets them into prostitution. I am sure he won't be turning over a new leaf any time soon.

Why do they keep hiring guys at work without checking references and doing a detailed interview? Another man is hired, from Romania this time. He claims to have all the experience in the world, but when he is put to the test, he's worse than a rookie. Jim complains about the guy over and over.

Abe walks over to me. "Hey, Joseph, can you tell me anything about Andrei's work? Jim tells me that the guy puts out a lot of scrap."

"To tell you the truth, I haven't had much to do with the man. I have heard some of the men complaining about him, though."

"Can you inspect his work for a while and let me know how it goes?"

"No problem, boss," I tell him.

For the next couple of days, I keep an eye on the guy, first offing his work and catching a lot of errors.

"Hey, why the hell are you checking my work? Who you think you are anyway?" Andrei yells at me.

"I'm the guy who is going to decide how much longer you work here," I say to him.

He speaks to me in Romanian, and I don't think it's anything nice, going by the expression on his face.

Abe comes by later and asks me what I think. I let him know that the company made a mistake hiring the man. Andrei is called to the office and shortly after he gathers his tools and leaves the building. With his free hand waving in the air, he curses everyone he sees. As far as he is concerned, it's everyone else that is wrong, not him.

Chapter 5

Time goes by, and it's fall. The garden I've planted has been harvested. I've made tomato sauce and frozen whatever I could. While it is still nice out, I go to Baskette Slough Wildlife Refuge for the afternoon. It is a warm day and a gentle breeze blows across the water as the ducks keep me company along the bank. I love to come here and be alone with my thoughts.

I haven't heard from Bill for quite a while and wonder if he has made any progress getting a name or some information for me. I'll give him a call soon, maybe we'll go fishing.

I'm starting to feel a need to express myself again and think that I had better do something before I start overreacting to some of the thoughts that sneak up on me now and then. I haven't lost control in a while but I can feel it's on the horizon. Just thinking too much about it is putting me on edge so I get up and go for a jog to lessen the tension.

When I get home, I browse the net to gather as much information as I can on Frank Ashton. I find out where he lives and Google his neighborhood, getting a street view of the area. He lives on the other side of town. I'll have to cross the Willamette River to get to Fillmore Avenue where he lives. There is a school nearby called West Salem High

School but I doubt that he would be dumb enough to deal so close to home. But of course, you never can tell.

I do a drive by his house and find it is a really nice area of town. This couldn't possibly be his home because it's far too nice. It must either be his parents or he is renting here. I have a photo of him from the news so, if I see him, I'll know. I don't think that I want to dispose of him in this neighborhood because it just doesn't seem right. That means I'm going to have to watch him and pick another spot. The problem is that I'm really not crazy about doing some guy from my own town again. Deep down, I feel there is a greater chance of being identified here, in case I'm observed. I have only done it once before and that was Al. I would rather go to another town to relieve my stresses.

Going home, I rethink my plans and look for another target. The more I think things over, the less I like what I was going to do. This issue resolved, I try to find someone in a place that I can go to on a weekend. My scouting and execution can always be spread out over several weeks.

Bingo. I find a story in Eugene, a city about an hour and a quarter south of Salem. The population is almost one hundred and sixty thousand, so I won't have any chance of running into anyone I know. The story goes on to say that the prostitutes in Eugene are controlled by some especially brutal pimps. There is a reporter who claims a few prostitutes have asked for help anonymously as they are afraid to come out publicly.

I will never understand why the police allow scumbags like this to get away with the shit that these pieces of garbage do. The cops have to know about them and what they do. I hate it when guys beat up on girls, I don't care what the reason is. So if the cops won't do something, I will.

After spending time on V-anonymous, I find what I am looking for. Just to make sure, I check with the Citizens Discussing Crime too and they confirm the information.

One of the main culprits is Adam Hutchman. He is going to come a cropper and pay for his deeds soon. After a bit of research, I find out that he lives in an apartment building on Kinsrow Avenue which is near Alton Baker Park. It borders Willamette River, the same river that flows through Salem. I wonder if he likes to take walks in the park. That would make it easy for me to take him out. I have a suspicion that this one will require a little more planning than the last one did. Next week, I'll start watching him.

On Tuesday, Bill calls me and gives me an update on what he has been doing as far as Oliver Durham is concerned. "I've been in touch with one of the guards at the prison. He thinks that he might be able to get Oliver a new cellmate, one that owes the guard a favor. If the guard can pull this off, the guy may be able to have Oliver confide in him and reveal who his partner really was."

I thank Bill and ask how everything is going for him. He tells me that he feels bad about what he has done. But he sees no other way to have handled the situation. I tell him not to feel bad, that sometimes you have to do what you have to do. We make plans to go fishing again soon.

At home, I check the surveillance system that I had installed when I first owned the home. Everything is as it should be after I check the days recorded scenes. Going to one of my favorite trail areas, I do one of my mad-dash runs through the woods. Stopping and starting, then jumping over obstacles gets my agility back to its peak. Wanting to cover as many bases as possible, I need to get into the best shape I can. I'm going to make some of the people, who have made this world such a difficult place, pay.

There is little left in my life that I love, other than payback. Except for Harry and his family and a few guys at work, that is. It would have been wonderful to have lived the rest of my life with Kathleen and a child or two. But that was ripped away from me by a dice tattooed man that I will one day catch up with, or die trying. *So, you make your own luck, do you? Well, we will see about that. Yes indeed, we'll see if that holds true for you.*

At work, there is a new rather large project that we have

started. There is a lot of laser work as well as brake press and machining to be done. This could lead to more work if we do things satisfactorily.

Jim comes over to me. "I'm a little leery of this one because I haven't done much of this particular type of work. I really could use your help with this one."

In reply, I say, "The problem is that I'm far too busy to be of much help."

Abe understands this. "Just be extra careful and do your best," he tells Jim. "If you have any questions, ask the company that made the order."

Things are hectic all week long and I don't see Jim at all. By the time the week end rolls around, Jim drops by. "I think I'm in over my head with this job."

"Is there any particular part that is giving you trouble?" I ask him. He looks at me and I see what looks like fear in his eyes. "Do you want me to come in Saturday morning for a couple of hours and we can go over the blueprints?" I suggest. *I would rather do some scouting but Jim needs my help and who knows? Maybe I'll need him some time.*

We go over the blueprints on Saturday morning. "These blueprints are a mess," I say. "No wonder you're confused. What I think is best is to write down all the deficiencies and leave the rest till Monday morning. I'll call the client myself and see if we can get the blueprints redrawn. Bloody hell, why would anyone call themselves a draftsman and turn out blueprints like this?"

Monday morning Jim and I go to Abe's office and explain the situation to him. Talking things over, I ask permission to phone the customer. Abe tells me to go ahead and see if we can get something better drawn up.

"What the heck is the problem?" their engineer says when I get on the line. "All the other shops have the same blueprints and they aren't having any problems, so why are you?"

Trying to keep my temper in check, I say, "Have you ever considered that maybe they are and just aren't saying?"

"I'll call them and ask them myself," he says coolly in return. "I'm sure they aren't having any trouble, but I'll talk to them."

I wonder if he actually will call the other shops. I guess that I'll never know for sure.

Out in the shop, we keep working on the job till we get a call later in the day. The engineer tells me that the other shops are having trouble too. "They didn't want to say too much for fear of losing the contract. We'll send you new blueprints as soon as possible. Stop work on the project until you receive them. Please accept my apologies."

This is great news, and Abe and Jim are pretty happy with the way it turned out. *I wish all my problems could be fixed this easily.* The rest of the week goes by better than the week before did. This episode gives me the opportunity to work on some of my own projects. It helps when I'm working on the lathe or milling machine. When I'm done with the company's work, I can take a few minutes to throw in my own stuff, allowing me to make some headway.

On Friday evening, I take a ride to Eugene and start doing a little investigating. After a bit of hunting around, I find Adam downtown at a strip place. He walks around like he owns the place. Later, I find out that he is indeed one of the owners.

He's at the bar and asks the bartender for a mirror. He is handed a small plastic framed one that he sets on the bar. As he is looking at something on his face, someone comes up behind him and asks him a question. As he turns around, the mirror is hit and falls to the floor, shattering. He spins around, staring at it with a look of apprehension on his face. He quickly grabs an empty glass and breaks it on the floor too. Then he picks up a salt shaker sprinkling some into his hand and tossing it over his shoulder.

"What the heck is that about?" I ask myself.

Later, when he sees me sitting off by myself, he walks over and sits down. It never occurred to me he'd do this. I thought this was a safe spot in the corner of the room.

"Why aren't you closer to where the women are taking their clothes off?" he asks in a European accent. "Are you gay? If so, why are you here?"

One of his boys stands close by in case there is trouble. "You can have a private show if you'd like that better?"

I decline the offer and this seems to piss him off.

"If you don't like the girls, maybe you're in the wrong place. Get the hell out while you still can sonny," he says, getting in my face.

I'm really going to like our next visit, but I don't tell him that, I just walk out of this hole. I hear him laughing while I leave as he tells his pal, "I think this guy is a coward as well as a gay boy."

At times like these, I'm glad that I am in disguise. He will soon be meeting me under different circumstances. But he won't know it's me till it's too late, if at all. This character has pissed me off, and I'm going to enjoy hurting him. I wait in a rental car that I have under an assumed name. Having paid for it in cash and using fake identification, I'll leave no trail. Parking down the street, I watch the entrance of the club from a safe distance.

Not until after the place closes do he and two others exit the place. They walk to a car with one of the men running ahead to get the vehicle ready. At a safe distance, I follow the group. One of the guys is dropped off and the other drives Adam home to an expensive apartment complex. He goes into the building and deliberately avoids stepping on what appears to be a crack in the sidewalk. After he is inside, I walk over to double check my suspicions. In the spot where he moved away from, as he was heading to the front door, is indeed a crack in the concrete. It appears that the man is very superstitious. *He goes to great lengths to avoid bad luck happening to him, hmmm.*

I've only brought a few items with me because I anticipate that this trip is for surveillance only. I have my knife and pistol in the rental car with me. The Remington bolt action .300 Winchester sniper rifle is hidden in the trunk of the car. Of course, I don't really want to use the rifle. In order to feel actual satisfaction, I need a direct, hand's-on approach when dealing with a target.

As I relax for a short time unwinding before retiring to bed, I turn on the television. The only thing on is a presentation by Billy Graham who is getting quite old. Beside him is his son Franklin who does most of the speaking. I can see why people flock to these men. However, I have someone to find and he needs to pay for what he's done and, to me, this takes precedence. I doubt that I'm eligible for redemption anyway.

The next morning, not too early, I park the rental in a parking lot down the road and watch Adam's building through a pair of binoculars for two hours. At the end of this time, he comes out and gets into his own car heading downtown. It's Saturday and too early for the strip club to be open so I wonder where he's going. He drives to a sleazy area and goes into an apartment complex, again avoiding stepping on cracks in the concrete.

Even this early in the day, there are a few hookers standing around. One of the girls follows him into the building with an apprehensive look on her face. They spend about ten minutes inside. When they come out, she is in his way, so he roughly knocks her into the side of the building. He scolds her about something and shakes a fist at her as she cowers.

He has an envelope in his free hand as he gets into his car. I guess the previous night's earnings weren't enough to satisfy Adam. The guy drives to another area and pretty much the same thing happens here. Only this time he isn't so nice to the girl. It's all that I can do not to go there and lay a beating on the stupid shit. He is about five foot nine and weighs about two twenty. He's soft and has a pot on him. He is not very attractive, to put it nicely.

Adam drives back to his place and stays there the rest of the day. So far there isn't any real pattern that I can make use of. This evening goes about the same as the one before.

The only thing that happens on Sunday is a stroll in the park nearby. This doesn't leave him secluded or very vulnerable at any point. That evening, I drive back to Salem, not much further ahead than I was when I got here. There's nothing of importance on the security system so, after a light workout, I call it a day and head for bed.

The new prints arrive at work and life is somewhat easier for Jim.

"Thanks, Joseph, for your help," he says, coming over to my work station. "I was in big trouble."

"No problem, glad I could help," I say.

When I was working here before I moved to Rose Cottage, I had talked to one of the guys in the shop after I heard him playing the guitar at lunch. I was so impressed by how fast he had learned to play that I asked him about it. He had told me why he improved so quickly. He told me he'd loan me the DVD's that he had used to learn with. Well, nothing came of it at the time. Me being left handed I thought would present a problem.

Peter has dropped off the DVD's and a borrowed left handed guitar from a friend. He's given them to Jim after he asked Peter to look into it. I ask him why he did this.

"You just made my life a lot better and I wanted to thank you," he tells me.

So I guess I am going to have to make time to give this a try. This has actually made my day. I'm quite pleased with this gesture.

During the week, I do a little research online. After a bit of searching, I locate a tranquilizer rifle for sale by the owner. The gun comes with a number of darts and the re-load drugs. It also comes with the antidote to bring the animal out of the sedation quicker. It uses a compressed gas cartridge to fire the dart and is supposed to be very accurate, all things considered. I contact the owner and a deal is struck. I pick it up when I finish work one day after almost an hour drive to his location. Of course, I'm disguised and my plates are muddied for my protection. He gives me a demonstration and explains the things I will need to know about the rifle.

The rest of the week, I make several excursions into the wilderness parks well outside of town. I have an extensive medical kit with me for the project. By the weekend, I have all that I will need. Friday evening, I head out to Eugene and start the surveillance again.

On the front seat of the rental car, I check out a little device. I've been working on it in my spare time on the job. It has taken quite a bit of machining, bending, and a bit of welding to get right.

I also get another project together. It's similar to the things that you see on television once in a while. You grab the tool by the one end and when you press a button and swing, the other end slides out, creating a club of sorts. It's the type of thing military security uses. The extended end is half an inch round solid stainless steel and creates quite an impact when it strikes the intended target. Everything works as it should and, with any luck, I may get a chance to use it on Adam. I also have a couple of other little things that are going to come in handy.

After doing a little research, I found out a few weeks ago that Mr. Hutchman's heritage comes from Romania, as do his associates. This is one of the middle European countries. This could be used to my advantage if I play this right. A person's superstitions can be used against them. An idea I had earlier and have been working on is finalized in my mind. I've done some shopping and bought the necessary items that I will need for the mission at hand.

Watching from a distance, I wait on Friday night noticing the routine is the same as the previous weekend. Tomorrow night, if all goes well, I plan to get things started. Getting a later start to the day, I know it's going to be a long one.

That evening, I pick my spot carefully, making sure that I have several escape routes. I don't want to be cornered. I have a well-hidden location that Adam will be going past and, if things are right, I'll make my move. If the situation isn't perfect, I will, of course, have to wait for a better opportunity.

One of the men usually runs ahead to get the car ready for Adam. At least he did this the other nights that I have been watching. I'm hoping tonight will be no different. As the time for action approaches, I get prepared and dress in the clothes that I got for the occasion. My tools are in order and the supplies are ready. The route has been properly set up with many shields and hiding spots. Hopefully, I won't need too many of them.

There are several alleyways to duck into, and I have familiarized myself with all the avenues of escape. The only thing that I don't like is the fact that there are a few homeless people in the area.

As the time gets closer and closer, I sit and wait anxiously. The patrons have all left and the girls who have made quick dates with clients are gone too. The three men exit the club, and, after locking up, they start walking toward the car and me.

The adrenalin starts to build as the excitement takes over me. As I hoped, the one man runs well ahead of the others and comes close to where I am hiding. Letting out a roar, I jump out and grab the man, dragging him into the alley. With my head close to his neck, I keep on growling. The men start running toward me, and I let out another growl. Seeing me, they hesitate for a moment. I'm sure they can't believe their eyes. I don't finish the man I've got a hold of at this point. He screams as I let him have a glimpse of me in my costume. I howl and run off in time to avoid Adam and the other man.

"What the hell was that thing? There it goes around the corner," Adam shouts as he starts firing.

Just as I round the corner, one of the bullets ricochet's off the wall and narrowly misses me. The shooting, I was expecting.

I hadn't counted on almost getting hit, though. Ducking

away from the corner, I let out a howl that would wake the dead.

"I hit it," Adam shouts.

While keeping out of sight, I empty the contents of a bag I have with me on the ground where they think I have been shot. I hope that the police will be involved and do some tests on it. At this point, I need to get the hell out of here before they come to the end of the alley and take some more shots at me.

Zigzagging my way around the alleys, I make my way back to the car parked several blocks away. Changing out of the costume just before I get back to the rental vehicle, I get in and drive away. When I was running, my path led me past a few homeless people. To add more authenticity to the situation, I gave them a real scare as I growled at them. This ought to give more credibility to the emerging story. I hear sirens as they race to the scene of the crime.

Back at home over the next few days, I check the news as the story emerges. A local club owner in Eugene, Oregon, had one of his employees attacked by what the men swear was a werewolf. The police doubt the tale very much, but a Mr. Adam Hutchman and his men swear up and down that what they saw was, in fact, a werewolf. The person attacked has bite marks on his throat. He is lucky to be alive as his jugular vein has been punctured. The victim is in a state of shock and cannot formulate a coherent sentence.

The police have found blood in the alley where Mr. Hutchman believes he shot the animal. The forensic lab is testing it to obtain a DNA match that they insist will clear up the story.

As the weeks go by the story takes on twists that the police have no way of explaining. The samples of blood in the alley and saliva from the wound sustained by the victim all indeed appear to come from a wolf. Several homeless people confirm the story, saying they too saw a werewolf that night. The police are at a loss as to how to explain this. Mr. Hutchman is visibly shaken by the event and has hired extra security. He is certain that he is being hunted by a were-wolf. In an effort to deal with the trauma of the event, he is planning on taking an extended holiday. Well away from Eugene, Oregon.

When I dragged the man into the alley, I clamped a hinged tool that has the shape of a dog's mouth on his throat. As I was removing the unit from the man's throat, I pulled back, causing wolf-like lacerations. As I ran around the corner during my escape, I was holding in my hand a bag of blood. It's blood that I took from a wolf I tranquilized deep in the park during the previous week. I kept the unit and the blood in a cooler to prevent the saliva and blood from spoiling for use at this time. I guess it is a good thing that I took the wolf's saliva and smeared the portable biter with it. It's sure handy to be working where I do, and that I have the time between jobs to make my toys.

I plan to see Adam again sometime in the future, but for now, I am happy with the way things have gone. Sometimes you can use people's beliefs against them. I am sure he will be looking over his shoulder for a long time.

While I am relaxing in my chair Sunday evening, I go over the events in Eugene. I know that I could have been shot when Adam and his friend unloaded their pistols at me. But I knew that they would be seriously unnerved by the howling. Of course, I hadn't counted on any bullets bouncing off the walls and coming very close to hitting me.

Being from Romania, their beliefs would overshadow common sense, and this has worked in my favor. I almost laugh at the thought of how it must have looked to them. This is the first time I have pulled off anything like this, and it feels great. The reason I didn't kill Adam is because, he hasn't actually killed anyone as far as I know. If I find that he has, I'll revisit him and do away with the man. With society being the way it is, if I take him out now, there will be several others eager to take his place. For now, I will have to be satisfied with him leaving town for a time and continually looking over his shoulder.

Chapter 6

Looking at the guitar, I think that I'll give it a little try. I put the first DVD into the player, and Marty Schwartz takes me through a beginner lesson. He shows me how to tune the guitar and then on to some basic chords. Strumming the chords isn't the easiest thing in the world, but in time it gets better. It doesn't sound too bad, once I get my fingers placed properly, which sounds easier than it is. I get a feeling of satisfaction at actually making the guitar sound okay. After an hour or so, it's time for bed and I think to myself that maybe I've found something to help me pass the time when I need it. My finger tips are a little sore, but it's all good.

Work presents me with a few problems but nothing that I can't handle. Jim seems to be doing all right. Everybody is happy as the management calls a meeting of all the employees.

Abe gives a speech. "All our employees have been doing an excellent job, and we want to show our appreciation by giving each of you something." He gives everyone an envelope, which, to our surprise, contains a bonus.

There is a little item I saw online that I think will come in handy. With part of the bonus, I go to buy it. The flare gun that I want is ordered, having it shipped to a post office box. I've rented it under a fictitious name. The gun may or may not prove useful, I'm sure I'll find out at some future date. All my counterfeit identification and credit cards cost me a fair bit of money but they have kept me safe so I figure it's well worth it.

I've been practicing the guitar during my off time and find it enjoyable. It isn't easy but as I work at it, my playing becomes better all the time. I hear that a lot of musicians get their start in churches. That old time wild man Jerry Lee Lewis is a prime example. I hear that he was finally asked not to play in church because too often he would play the hymns in a boogie-woogie style. That probably would have been interesting as I like that kind of music. A lot of country singers also got their start in churches from what I hear.

Bill gives me a call and lets me know that he has managed to get a new cell mate for Oliver Durham. "When he can cozy up to the guy, he may be able to get Oliver to confide in him. I hope you understand that this is not a quick process, so don't expect results for a while," he explains.

This is good news for me. But I do know that even if I find out the name of Oliver's partner, it doesn't mean that I'll be able to find him in any hurry.

"Thanks, Bill, for your efforts. Why don't you come over for a beer sometime? Or if you want to go fishing again, let me know," I say, which seems to please him.

So now I wonder where all this is going to lead me. I'm curious about how far Bill will go to help me find Smitty. One way or another, I have to get hold of the guy with the dice on his forearm, the bastard that killed Kathleen. Maybe Bill can help me locate the guy. But then if he does that, he'll know that I removed him quite violently from society.

Damn, there's always something in the way to complicate things. If he finds out I killed Dice Man, there is always a chance that he will then investigate my past life a little more in depth. I don't want Bill finding too much out about me.

Although his integrity has been compromised when he

killed the Mexican drug dealer, I wonder if he is capable of going further. The trouble with all this is that it leaves me more vulnerable too.

The weather has started to cool down considerably and has become rainy. This leaves me wanting to go south to a warmer climate. I've grown to love the sunshine and being near the ocean. If I live that long, I may one day move to a coastal town and get myself a boat. The idea of starting a charter service even crosses my mind. This thought actually brings a smile to my face.

I remember seeing a movie called the *Shaw Shank Redemption* with Morgan Freeman and Tim Robbins. Tim escaped from a particularly difficult time in prison. He moved to the Mexican coast, taking most of a corrupt warden's money with him. Once there, he got a boat to work on. Morgan Freeman eventually met up with him there. It seems like a nice kind of life.

I have my doubts that things will turn out this way for me because I always have this need for payback. I had it under control while I was married to Kathleen. That changed in a big hurry when that scumbag stole her from me. He will pay severely for that. He will pay if it is the last thing I do. *I HAVE TO MAKE HIM PAY, ARRRGH!*

As Christmas approaches, Harry and Brenda get in touch with me. "Would you like to spend Christmas day with us? The kids are all excited about it and really want you to come over."

"I think that is a great idea. I don't have any plans and this will make my day, thanks, Harry."

Eva and Gordie are starting to grow up somewhat, and I see a lot of changes in them. I can't believe that they're already well into their mid-teens. Accepting their invitation, I mark it on my calendar.

"You don't need to bring gifts," Harry says, "we're happy just to have you here with us."

Fat chance of that happening. What the heck else, am I supposed to do with my money? I don't spend very much and my bank accounts are quite impressive. I will do a little research and try to get some ideas. Maybe I'll get a laptop for Eva and a new model iPod or something like it for Gordie, who knows?

While watching the news, I'm surprised to hear that some phone company is suggesting that pornography should be accessed on cell phones. They insinuate that there is a growing demand for it, and they just want to keep their customers happy. I, for one, am not a fan of this. Unlike drugs where you can see the effect on a person, pornography rots a person from the inside. Myself, I'm actually embarrassed by this kind of behavior and don't believe much good comes from it. Maybe I'm lagging behind the times but I don't like where this world is heading.

As the news continues, there is a story about an incident which seems to point a finger toward the Klan. This time, a black family has been burned out of a fairly well-to-do white neighborhood in Mobile, Alabama. The big problem is not that just the house was burned. The young couple, who was out for a dinner engagement had a baby sitter taking care of their three children. All three were under the age of eight and the sitter was age fourteen. Attempting to save the children, she also perished in the inferno. The neighbors claim to have seen nothing suspicious and no evidence of wrong doing can be found. There was one strange fact concerning this story. Found in the remnants of the debris, were more empty gasoline cans than the parents had in the garage. The parents also said that they had received hate mail. The letters threatened violence if they did not move soon. Complaints to the police previously had fallen on deaf ears and so no investigation had been started till now. With all the evidence destroyed in the fire, there was little to be done, according to a police spokesman.

This is just another case of discrimination with nothing done to help the African American couple. I've often wondered why they are called black because they appear to be more a brown color to me. But then again, I guess it's none of my business because whites are not really white either…well, most anyway.

There is an earthquake in a third world country and a plea for help is given. I remember a number of years ago when a tsunami hit an area which I believe is called Sri Lanka and money to rebuild was asked for. As I recall there was in excess of five hundred million dollars raised. Several years later most of the money had not been used to rebuild very much for the common people there. I believe the same thing happened in Haiti. I could be wrong but I don't think so. As a result, I am sometimes reluctant to donate very much.

Stories of perverts and drug dealers abound as I watch the television. There are several priests in Catholic churches that are accused of molesting children for the umpteenth time. Nothing has been really proven in court. There are only the testimonies of some of the children reported.

This is supposed to be the largest church in the world and has the worst reputation of all of them. Those who are accused, it seems, are just shifted from one church to another, and nothing is really done about it. What good does this do for religion? I find it very disheartening and finally shut the bloody television off. Should I visit a few of these offending priests? It really is a tempting thought.

I have a desire to visit the Klan again too, as this is not the first time they have been in the news lately. How does this hatred fester so badly in a country that has so much? I find myself wondering why good people sit idly by and let this happen. I guess if you don't think about it and it isn't happening to you, you need not concern yourself with it.

I spend the rest of the weekend tidying up the property, working out, and practicing the guitar. Sticking with it, I'm improving quickly and am thinking of buying my own guitar. Going online, I check for popular brands, read a lot of reviews, and plan to go to a music store soon and have a look at some Fender guitars. This is a brand that I have heard of for years, and they seem to have a good reputation.

I wonder if I will need to order one because of being left handed.

The week at work goes by fairly quickly and, before I know it, the weekend is here. On Saturday morning, I go to a music store in town that has been in business for a long time and chat up one of the older salesmen.

"I'm looking for a decent guitar but don't really know what I should buy," I say.

"Are you looking for an acoustic or electric guitar?" he asks.

"I probably should go with the acoustic so I won't need an amplifier or electricity."

He shows me several in a decent price range and as I am ready to make a decision my eyes fall on a guitar that looks new but has a slightly lower price tag on it.

I ask him about it.

"That one is on consignment," he tells me. "Because it's used and left hand, it's been here for some time. It's a good guitar and the owner is open to offers."

I give him a price that is just over half what a new one is going for and have to wait while he phones the guy. It turns out that the guy wants at least twenty five dollars more than I offered. I quickly agree to the price and, ten minutes later, I walk out with an almost new Fender Kingman acoustic/electric guitar with a built-in tuner. I love a bargain, not that I'm cheap, I just like not having to pay full price.

Too often on the news, I see that a lot of young people are getting themselves into debt, buying things they don't need. They seem to be doing this because the interest rates are so low. We already had some major financial crises and, if the interest rates go up much, we'll have another one. Nobody seems to want to save their money before buying anymore.

Chapter 7

As the winter slowly passes, I find myself getting wound up more and more often. Thoughts of Oliver and Smitty keep going through my head. I haven't had much news from Bill. The only thing that I heard so far is that Oliver's cellmate is making progress, but nothing concrete at this point. So I start looking for stories on the internet of criminals living within a day or so drive from where I live. I prefer places not too close to home as this makes me feel a little more protected. I'm not sure why this is, it just does. There is a person of interest in Sacramento California.

Ivar Ozols is a biker club enforcer who has been linked to multiple homicides in the city. Ivar is an immigrant from Latvia, the news articles say. He was born in the capital city of Riga. This area is known for the extortion practices, the drug trade, and prostitution aspects of organized crime. Maybe this is why he fits into the biker club so well. The club is part of a nationwide gang. It has been in the drug and prostitution trade for years and seems to be pretty much left to its own devices. It would appear that the police aren't particularly eager to tackle these bastards.

Ivar is about thirty years old and looks pretty tough. At about six three and two twenty, he would be quite intimidating to most people. It is a good thing I'm not most people. He has been charged several times but always released due to lack of evidence and witnesses refusing to testify. He has piqued my interest because he is in a biker club. The man that raped and murdered my mother so brutally when I was a teenager, was a biker too. I have no love whatsoever for bikers. Even thinking about it too much brings back some of the anguish I felt as a youngster.

This is going to be my next target. I start to gather all the information that I can on him and his buddies. I don't know right now whether I will take out only Ivar or go for the gusto and make this a group effort. He lives with a couple of other members in a seedy area of the city. They either rent or own a modest-looking house with a large high fenced lot on Del Paso Blvd.

I wonder how the neighbors like the Harleys coming and going. They are beautiful machines, and I have thought about getting one myself several times, but there is always something holding me back. I wonder if many people know about Dick Clark. He was the super clean cut host of American Bandstand, a popular television show years ago. Dick Clark used to ride a Harley along with the Hell's Angels during the off seasons. To me, it just didn't fit, but I guess you never can tell what people are really like.

There is a Doberman chained to a post near the front entrance. With plenty of trees and ground cover, I should be able to hide if the dog is out of commission. Using Google allows me to see exactly where someone lives without ever setting foot in the area.

Back at work, I am asked to do quality control for a week while Jim goes to a family reunion, lucky guy. Most people don't know how good they have it. With family around, you have someone to turn to in times of trouble. That is not so much the case when you are alone. This thought reminds me that I need to touch base with Harry and his family. Christmas is coming and I want to make this time special for all of us.

About midway in the week, I'm called to inspect a job being done by one of the guys in his late twenties. He is married and has a couple of kids and seems a bit out of sorts. I ask Sam if everything is all right. He unloads a pile of grievances about his home life on me. I didn't really want to know all this stuff and almost regret asking.

"My wife and I aren't getting along. She's unhappy with her life," he tells me. "Money is not a problem and she has a part time job that makes her happy enough."

I'm almost afraid to ask for any further information because there are certain subjects I don't want to get into.

"We used to get along great," he continues, "but things have gotten routine and the joy has left our home."

"What do you do in the evenings?" I ask.

"I have a number of projects that need doing around the house. I spend quite a bit of time each day doing these. I help put the kids to bed and watch some television till bedtime," he informs me.

"Is this what you did when you were dating your wife?" I ask.

"Of course, I didn't do that. If I'd done that, she would never have married me," he tells me.

I see a light go on in his head as he gets the point I am trying to make. "Then I suggest you get a babysitter and start taking your wife out once a week, just like you are dating again. Spend more time going on family outings and building a relationship with them. You'll have a happier wife and will, in turn, be happier yourself. All the projects will get done in their own time and shouldn't take priority," I explain.

At lunch, I see him on the phone talking to the little lady. As he passes me he says thanks with a smile on his face. People need to work on relationships because, otherwise, they fall by the wayside. I'm happy for Sam. I wish I had Kathleen back as a tear is in my eye.

Jim finishes his holiday and is back at work. This frees me up to get back to my own job. In my spare time, I work on a little project that I've been developing. The item is something that may come in handy when I go see Ivar. It consists of a thin cable and a quick self-windup mechanism.

I have noticed that there are a number of trees on the property Ivar lives in. There are a lot of leaves and twigs on the ground as well as several patio stones lying around. This gives me a few ideas I might use if the opportunity arises. There are a few other ideas that I want to develop but I need to do a little research first.

The storage place hidden in my basement is getting a little crowded. It looks like I'm going to have to consider some sort of expansion. I can't use up any more of the basement area because it would become too evident if the basement got any smaller.

The Christmas holidays are here and I am looking forward to spending Christmas day with Harry and his family. The gifts for the kids have been picked up and I've decided on what to get Harry and Brenda.

It's the last day of work before the holidays. The plant is shut down at lunch and there is a party. The alcohol is kept to a minimum but the food is just great. There are gifts for everyone and a nice bonus. Management makes a nice speech and everybody is happy. These types of occasions are really pleasant and employees that work in different areas of the shop who normally don't interact much find time to get to know one and other.

When things come to a close, we all wish each other the best and head to our respective homes. "My wife and I are happier now than we've been in a long time," Sam tells me before he leaves. "Thanks for the advice, I really appreciate it."

I am glad that it has turned out for him, he's a good guy. A few days off is going to be nice. It would have been nicer to have a week or so off. Because we're so busy, it isn't feasible at this time.

Doing some more research on Ivar, I find some stories about him and a few of his associates online. It seems that he has been accused of really hurting some of the people he has extorted. Broken fingers, arms, and kneecaps are the least of his offenses. Ivar, it would appear, has some training in keeping people in line. There is not a great deal to be found, but there are hints about some sort of underground military experience. I'd better not tackle him head on, as he will be resourceful and dangerous.

It's time to take my training to the next level. It might be a good idea to start working on developing more power in my attacks. Working on my attack moves as well as my devices helps give me every advantage possible. In the past, I've entered other situations not as prepared as I should have been and almost gotten nailed. If I can, I'll take out several of his buddies at the same time. I missed doing that too. Because of it, someone innocent died. I go off to the park and do my stop-start dashes and try to get my agility to its peak.

When I go after Ivar, I'm going to try not to do the job on their property. A backup plan to do so will have to be made, anyway, just in case I'm not presented with an opportunity to do it elsewhere. The club house may have to be another alternate target. I work on trying to get as much information on it as possible. Familiarizing myself with the surrounding area and escape routes may keep me out of trouble.

While I'm at it, I check the addresses of the police stations and emergency services. This lets me determine how long it will take police to get to each of the scenes because I absolutely have to be gone before they get there.

Surveillance will be on weekends or when I have more than two days off. It takes about eight hours to drive to Sacramento. If I leave early on Friday, I'll have Saturday and a short period on Sunday. This really isn't enough time, so I will see if I can book off a couple of Fridays, and maybe a Monday. The extra time is required in order to have enough time to tail Ivar.

This guy really irritates me. He is like so much of the

cancer that eats away at our society. They make drugs so readily available to our youth who don't seem to have the common sense of a donkey. Once they are hooked or grow dependent on substances, they become slaves to their habits. *What a bunch of fools this generation has spawned.*

I heard that, even if you get clean for a while, the chances are very high that you will end up going back to it eventually. I never want to be a slave to anything. I may, in some way, be somewhat of a slave to my past, but, of course, that is different. Whichever is worse is a matter of opinion, I guess.

Spending a couple of days watching the bone breaker, I start getting some of his routines down. Some useful information is obtained on where he goes during the day as well as what he does during the evening. It appears that he likes to keep in shape and does a little martial arts training too.

I watch from a distance with my binoculars through the window of the local Dojo. Ivar spars with a partner and I see that he uses very unorthodox moves just like I do. This always keeps your opponent guessing what your next move or two will be.

He likes to fight what the uninitiated call dirty. This is a term that has little meaning to anyone who is fighting to win. You never enter into a situation that you know you can't win. So if you are going to fight, you do whatever it takes. If not, you may end up paying for it with your health, or maybe your life.

Ivar has some interesting moves that even I hadn't thought of. He is quick and has a fair bit of power. In a one-on-one encounter, I'm fairly sure I would beat him but these things seldom go as planned. So fighting him head on is not going to happen. I don't take chances and haven't lasted this long for no reason. My ego doesn't need a boost like some people's do. No, I am going to have to think of a fairly safe way to get rid of Ivar the terrible, especially as he is seldom alone.

Tomorrow is Christmas Eve and so I head home in order

to get ready for my time with Harry and the family. I'm actually looking forward to hanging out with them. The kids are a lot of fun and Harry and Brenda are a lovely couple and good friends. On the drive out of town, I see a store that specializes in crystal. Stopping in, I pick up a nice piece for Harry and Brenda. I get the gifts wrapped as neatly as I can. It takes a couple of attempts to get the hang of it. In the end, I manage to do a relatively decent job. To finish it off I pick up a gift certificate to a good restaurant.

On the television, I watch a Christmas program that evening. Just as I am getting into it the phone rings, and I hear Bill's voice on the other end. He says he is just heading out for a church service with his wife. He thought he'd give me a quick call to wish me a merry Christmas and update me on the situation with Oliver Durham.

"There is nothing definite to report yet," he tells me, "but the cellmate is making progress and thinks he may get Oliver to confide in him fairly soon."

"Thanks, Bill, merry Christmas to you and your wife."

The rest of the program I was watching fades into the background as memories of Kathleen take over. I remember the wonderful times I had with her and how abruptly it came to an end. I feel an immense amount of guilt for not being there when the robbery took place. If I had been there, Kathleen would still have been alive. We would now have had our first child. As the tears flow, the rage in me builds to a point where I cannot contain it. I am filled with a pain that consumes me. I feel a loss that I will never be able to satisfy.

I need to lash out and end up going to the garage. In there, I put myself through a grueling workout that has me hitting, kicking, and stabbing my imaginary target. The guy that makes his own luck is going to suffer and suffer badly. It's as if it has just happened. The fury I feel consumes me like nothing has before. By the time I regain control, it is late evening and I am completely worn out. I feel drained. I go into the house and have a shower before going to bed. It would have been better if Bill had not phoned. I haven't lost control like this in a long time and don't want to do it again.

January journal entry: *Despite the amount of time that has passed, I am unable at times to control myself. When will this end…*

Despite the evening I've had, I fall into a deep sleep where all is well and I feel rested the next morning. It's Christmas day and I'll be going over to see Harry and the family in a short time. I get prepared and gather the things I need to put in the car. I am actually in a rather good mood, which surprises me. Maybe working through the tantrum last night has had a beneficial effect on me.

The time is here and I am on my way in a cheery mood. I can't believe how much I've been looking forward to this day. As I walk up to the front door, I am surprised to see the kids run out.

"Merry Christmas, Uncle Joseph," they say as they hug me.

This makes up for some of the short falls in my life. Having them treat me like this gives me that warm feeling inside that is hard for me to explain. Harry and Brenda are in the doorway with huge smiles on their faces. It's almost as if they know how I feel and that this is an important moment for me. I leave the presents in the car and meet my friends. I wonder if everyone has people like this in their life.

We have ourselves a beautiful breakfast of ham and eggs with a side order of bacon. "I know you seldom eat it but like bacon once in a while," Brenda says. "You're quite health conscious, but it won't kill you, so enjoy. There are orange juice and milk and some homemade Christmas cookies that Eva helped me bake."

Because she helped, I make a fuss over them.

Wow, this is the life. As everyone retires to the living room, the kids ask if they can open their presents and are told that they are allowed to start. These kids are well behaved and genuinely appreciate what their parents do for them. Harry reaches under the tree and brings out a gift, handing it to me. The youngsters are right in front of me, watching as I open the box of a beautiful camera with a telephoto lens.

"We thought you would get some use out of it when you go to some of the National Parks like you have in the past," they tell me. "You can take long distance pictures with this and catch shots that you might normally miss. Do you like it, Uncle Joseph? We helped Mom and Dad pick it out," Eva says, smiling at me.

"The camera comes with an SD Card so you can take as many pictures as you want," Harry tells me. "Then you can download them to your computer."

I am a little overwhelmed, at this point, and it must show because the kids get up and hug me. They actually say that they love me and this is more than I can handle. My eyes water up a little. I'm somewhat embarrassed by this display of emotion. I seldom react like this and need a moment to compose myself, heading for the bathroom. It doesn't take too long to get things back in order. With a somber look, I leave the house and go to my car.

"Uncle Joseph, where are you going?" Eva asks.

"I'm not leaving. I'm just getting something from the car," I say.

There is a look of relief on their faces as I walk back, bringing in the gifts for them.

"We didn't mean to embarrass you," Eva says.

"I'm sorry, but I'm not used to this, and it caught me by surprise," I say, a little embarrassed again.

I give them the gifts and, as they open them, a look of surprise is on their faces. They jump up and hug me again.

"My laptop is on its last legs," Eva tells me, "and I need a new one for school. How did you know that this is what I wanted?"

I just shrug and let it go at that. Gordie gets up and opens the big box I left near the front door, revealing a Mountain Bike.

He's beside himself and can't thank me enough. "Wow, this is the best present ever. Gee thanks, Uncle Joseph."

I guess I must have picked the right gifts. This is a better Christmas than I thought it could possibly be. I head out to the car again and get the gifts for Harry and Brenda. Opening the envelope with the gift card brings a huge smile. They open the box containing the crystal figurine and Brenda is the one with the tear in her eye.

"Joseph, this is over the top. You shouldn't have done this. It must have cost you a fortune for all these things. We do love them, though," she says as she hugs me and Harry slaps me on the back.

"You guys are the best friends that I have. I wouldn't be where I am if it wasn't for you, so, yes, it is necessary," I say.

The rest of the day is for the memory books. I use the camera to record the highlights and, as I finally head for home, it feels as if another corner has been turned. Yes, it has been a horrible year, but not everything in my life is bad. There was a point where I wasn't sure if I would make it. The pit I had fallen into almost consumed me. In the end, it was only because of people like Brenda and her family that I was able to claw my way back.

In spite of this, I don't think, even for a second, that I won't be going after the man who almost destroyed me. I'll never stop until I catch up with him. As I strive toward this end, I periodically need a release. I'll soon be looking up Ivar. Only now I'm going to have to make absolutely sure that I survive these encounters. I've got to be around to deal with Dice Man on some future day.

Chapter 8

As the holidays end and work starts anew, I continue my plans for biker boy. Going to the mall, I purchase extra SD cards for the camera. I mark the one that has the photos of Harry and the gang on it. I don't want to accidentally use it when I take photos of my intended target. When I am finished with the hit, I'll probably destroy the card that has Ivar on it so things can't be traced back to me. I mark this one with a capital *I* for Ivar.

As January progresses, I manage to watch the bone breaker, taking some shots of him and his pals. I am surprised on one occasion when I see Ivar with a police officer. They meet in a dark spot and, therefore, are somewhat hidden from view. But not hidden enough to escape the camera lens. I take several photos of them. They are on very friendly terms. This, to me, is unusual as they are supposed to be on opposite sides of the fence.

As they part company, Ivar hands the cop an envelope. Before he puts it away, the cop opens it and takes a brief look at what seems to be money inside. Thank goodness I have this camera. I manage to get perfect pictures of it all using the telephoto lens. I won't do anything about it at this time but look for ways that this information can be used. This cop is certainly on Ivar's or his boss's payroll. He's dirty and helping out the biker club by supplying them with information of some sort. It is so unfortunate that this happens all too often.

How the corrupt police officers get themselves tied into this type of situation is a puzzle. When you swear an oath, you have a responsibility to uphold it. Of course, I can imagine that some people enter the force when they are already a part of organized crime, just for this purpose. Others probably get dragged down because of life's circumstances. *Sometimes it is really hard to know who to trust.*

My plans are starting to come together, and I make the necessary items at work. In my surveillance, I've noticed on several occasions that Ivar and his pals make trips to San Francisco on the weekends. It appears the trip is made for a pickup. They drive in a car and not on their bikes. The drive takes between an hour and a half and two hours each way, depending on traffic.

Following them a couple of times made my arrival back home rather late and left me a little the worse for wear the next morning at work. The ride takes them through some unpopulated areas. They usually have the car gassed up and leave by ten in the morning straight from his house. I'll see if I can get access to the car the night before and rig up my little surprise for them.

Between Fairfield and San Francisco, there are a number of open stretches that are somewhat secluded. If the traffic conditions are right, I can pull off the hit successfully before unwanted attention is drawn to us. It's too bad he doesn't go camping or hiking but it is the way it is.

Purchasing a few items that I need to buy in Sacramento with cash, I get prepared. The rental car is taken back, and I go home to finalize my plans. Watching Ivar on several occasions, I see he has done a number on people who appeared almost defenseless. I would very much like to have stepped in and put an end to it but thought better of it. One or another of his pals has always been around with him so I won't have any hard feelings about taking them out too.

As the weekend approaches, I test all the devices to make sure everything works as it should. Fresh batteries are put in the things that require them. I've come up with two plans to handle this operation. I've got to have a bit of time in the middle of the night to set everything up. Sunday is the day that they go to San Francisco so I book Monday off work. Heading out fairly early Saturday morning, I roll into town in the late afternoon.

I want an inconspicuous vehicle with a good size engine, in case things go sour and I have to make a hasty exit. I've been practicing for years, watching online videos demonstrating how to handle a car in adverse conditions. Now I'm quite the getaway driver.

I transfer all the things I will require to the rental car and rest up at the out of the way motel that I am staying at.

There is someone snooping around the rental car during the evening. Coming up from behind him, I ask, "What the hell do you think you're doing by my car, buddy?"

He tries to run but he has put himself in a spot with no exit. "I'm sorry, I was just looking around."

"Bullshit, you're looking to break in and steal what you find," I say.

He sees the error of his ways when I manhandle him a bit. Because I've been working out so hard, my strength is developed to the maximum. I lift the feather weight off the ground and against the wall with one hand.

"Don't come back, you hear?" I say.

He's gone in a flash. I could have roughed him up easily but I don't beat up on people for the fun of it.

When I go to sleep after setting the alarm for three in the morning, I do so with a feeling of anxiousness. I always feel like this just before I'm about to embark on a maneuver. It takes a while to fall asleep but, when it comes, it comes quickly. Before I know it, the alarm is going off. Getting prepared and, after a power bar and a drink of water, I head off to Del Paso Blvd. Parking down the road from Ivar's place, I survey the scene for a few minutes. With my pistol and the tranquilizer gun, I head toward my destination being careful to stay in the shadows.

The dog is tied up outside and, as he hears me quietly approaching, he gets up and listens for me. When he gets up, I nail him with the dart, waiting for him to go down. There is a slight yelp as the dart hits but not much else as he tries to scratch the affected area. When he goes down, I head back to the car, grabbing a duffle bag with the rest of the stuff I need. I could have taken it with me on the first trip but just in case there was trouble, I didn't want to be loaded down on my escape.

As I enter the property from a secluded spot, I make my way over to the dog and remove the dart. Hiding for a moment, I listen for any signs that I might not be alone. When I'm sure it's safe, I lie on the ground beside the car near the dog. Quickly as I can, I attach two of the devices brought with me, using the industrial grade zip ties. The items are secured. This done, I slide to the back end the car under the gas tank. Puncturing the tank with a tool I made at work, I immediately plug the hole. The soft rubber plug has a screw in the exposed end. Putting a flexible sealant around the plug so there won't be any chance of a premature leak finishes things. Any gas that is spilled is soaked up by the rags I laid on the ground so there will be minimal smell.

The plug is a fairly tight fit and so won't fall out prematurely. I have a short section of thin aircraft cable attached to the screw. The other end is hooked up to a high torque, battery-operated and remote-controlled servo motor. When activated, the motor, which is anchored by zip ties, will pull the plug out and the gasoline will drain from the tank. The drain time, by my calculations, should be less than a quarter hour.

The reason for the plug is to have Ivar and his pals run out of gas if my primary plan fails. I don't want to initiate the primary plan here in the driveway because the car is too close to his neighbor's house.

With everything done the way I want, I slide out from

under the car. Once I know the way is clear, I get my butt the heck out of there. This part of the job is always a little nerve racking and my hands tremble slightly.

In the past, about half the time there is always something that comes up during this part of the job. Luckily, this time, things go according to plan. Before I know it, I am back in the motel and climbing into bed. It takes a bit of unwinding before I fall asleep again. Then it seems like I just dozed off and the alarm wakes me again.

This time, I am a little the worse for wear and it takes longer to get up to speed. I have a quick bite to eat and, after making sure that I have everything that I need including food and water, I'm on my way.

Getting to Ivar's place ahead of schedule, I park down the road the opposite direction that he will be going. He comes out in about half an hour with the guys. Off they go out of town toward San Francisco with me following at a discrete distance. They stay within the speed limits so no unwanted attention comes their way. It wouldn't do to have a cop pull them over and check the trunk, finding the money for the buy.

There are a number of areas that pass through very sparsely populated places on the way to San Francisco. I'm going to have to wait for one of these. It's imperative to wait till there is no traffic anywhere near us before making my move. During the drive, I'm on edge, waiting for the proper moment to arrive. There are no good spots to take action till after we get past Fairfield, about an hour outside of Sacramento. As we get near the best place to do the job, I find that traffic isn't helping me much. There always seems to be some car in the vicinity.

"Come on, give me a break, all I need is a minute to do the job," I say out loud to myself.

This is taking longer than anticipated. I'm starting to wonder if I'll have to wait for the return trip to get this done or just initiate plan two. The distance between us is too much so I close the gap.

I see an opening where there is almost no one around for more than a mile.

I hit the gas and close the distance between us. This seems to take forever but finally, I'm in position. With one final look around, I open the window. I reach out with the two remotes that control the servos that are hooked onto the pins of two grenades that I mounted on the underside of the car.

I point the remotes, press the buttons, and start to back off immediately, not wanting to be too close. I positioned one grenade underneath between the driver and passenger and the other near the rear passenger area.

It seems to take a long time but, finally, there is a double explosion and a fireball erupting from the bottom of the car. It lifts the vehicle slightly off the road, as it crashes into a guardrail, coming to a stop.

Pulling up alongside the car, it's necessary to avoid some of the debris on the road. The only one left alive is Ivar. He slowly turns his bleeding face toward me.

I doubt that he can hear me but I yell out anyway, "Hey asshole, how does it feel to be the one hurting for a change."

As I pick up my revolver and point it at him, he realizes that this is the end and tries to squirm out of his seatbelt. Too late, it is, as I pull the trigger, putting a bullet between his eyes.

This is the last trip for him and there will be no more enforcing in his life. I know someone else will probably take his place but it might slow things down for a bit at least. Stepping on the gas before any of the cars approaching can see enough to identify the one I'm driving, I speed away. Not everyone will see my side of this situation, even if they knew who I had just terminated.

I have seen it too often that some of the bleeding hearts seem to side with the wrong people. They think that the poor unfortunates had a bum start in life, and this excuses them from their behavior. Just because you have a bad upbringing doesn't give you the right to live a bad life.

There are plenty of people with horrible childhoods that turn things around and become wonderful productive adults. It makes me wonder if the bleeding hearts would be quite as sympathetic if they were the ones that the perpetrators had violated. I somehow doubt it. It's the same thing with the lenient judges.

Getting off the main road as soon as possible, I head back to Sacramento on a less-traveled route. I end up heading to Rio Vista and then go north back to Sacramento and to the motel. It's late afternoon and, although I'm tempted to start back to Salem right away, I decide to wait till morning. I've had a big day and need to eat and rest.

Taking a life isn't something that should come too easily. If it did, I would suspect that I had grown excessively callous. If I ever thought that someone might turn things in their life around, I would give them some consideration. Ivar was not one of these. He enjoyed hurting people, and I'm sure he has killed innocents. So ends the last chapter of his life.

On Monday, I'm back home and putting everything back in its place. When this is all done, I check my security system and, after seeing all is in order, I take the SD Card out of the camera and look at the photos on my computer. After making sure there is nothing on it to incriminate me, I wipe it down and put it in an envelope addressed to the commanding officer at the Sacramento Police Department.

The officer who was so chummy with Ivar and took the money will have to do some explaining. That is if the head guy is not on the take too. I guess only time will tell. I'll keep an eye on the news to see how this develops.

Things turned out well this time, but I have to make sure that I don't become complacent. Overconfidence leads to mistakes, which, in turn, will put me in a bad spot or dead, and I can't have that happen before I deal with Kathleen's murderer.

Afterward, it won't matter much, as my primary job will

be done, but between now and then there are people that don't belong in this world.

If polite society and the police can't or won't do anything about it then I guess the problems fall on me. God, I wish it wasn't like this. I don't like living this way because, at times, the burden is just about too much to bear. Despite all going well, I feel down this evening.

Chapter 9

It's funny how the people around you can make life seem better. At work the next day during lunch ,which I usually eat alone while I'm reading, Sam stops by and leaves me a little gift, patting me on the back as he walks away.

"I just want to show you a little appreciation, from the wife and myself," he says.

In the box are nice bottle of expensive whiskey and a note that reads, *"Thanks for the help, if you ever need me, just ask."*

Damn, I have another one of those moments that I don't want anyone to see. He's already left the room, but I will catch up to him later. So with my mood elevated, I head back to my work area after chatting with him for a moment.

Spring seems to be coming early this year and I am anxious to get things going, but know from past experience that it does not always stay as warm as you need it. So I get the gardens ready but don't plant anything.

Coming home from work one day, I find Bill waiting for me. "Hey, Bill, do you want to stay for supper?"

"Thanks but I don't have the time today," he says. "I've come to update you on how things are going with Oliver's cellmate. He tells me that he is close to getting the information and that he should have something solid soon."

"Thanks, Bill, this is great," I tell him. "Is there is anything that you need from me?"

"I'm okay for now but thanks. I may require you to make me something soon. There's an individual in town who seems to be almost impossible to prosecute. I wish that I had something on you, it would make me feel safer, but I know that you won't say anything," he says.

"Bill, at this point I haven't done anything wrong, but, if I do, I'll be sure to let you know."

He laughs. "I know you've got skeletons somewhere in your closet, despite this proclamation of innocence."

I just smile and let him think whatever he wants. We make plans to do some fishing later in the week.

If I were to get a pile of stuff on him, I might consider confiding in him a bit but, at this point, I don't feel secure in doing that. I feel a real kinship with him, despite the fact that we are, for all intents and purposes, on opposite sides of the fence. Of course, I'm on the wrong side of the fence only occasionally, as far as I can see. The rest of the time I walk a fairly straight path with only the occasional detour. *So that makes me okay.*

This has been a good day and so, after a vigorous workout in the garage and supper, I settle in for a relaxing evening. I check online to see if there is much going on as far as Ivar is concerned. There's a story about a rival drug dealer taking out an enforcer that has been on the police department's radar for some time. It seems that the enforcer met with a violent death along with two associates on their way to a drug deal. The police feel this is where they were heading because of the large cache of cash in the trunk of their vehicle.

A police officer who seems to be somehow involved with Mister Ivar Ozols has been put on suspension, pending an inquiry.

It's reported that information has been sent to the department head incriminating the undisclosed officer anonymously. The source of the story remains confidential. Maybe something will come of this.

Harry phones me later Friday evening. "Would you be willing to look after the kids for us?" he asks. "We've got to leave town early Saturday morning and will be back Sunday evening. We don't have anyone else we can call on such short notice. Besides, the kids specifically asked for you."

"Whoa, this is a first for me and I'm not sure that I'm the right person for the job."

Harry laughs. "There's nothing to worry about, Joseph. They have homework to do, and they're not hard to look after. There won't be any diapers to change."

"Well, I don't have anything pressing to do, so I guess I can try. It'll have to be at your house, though." *After all, how hard can it be?*

The next morning, I get there with my overnight case packed. Harry and Brenda leave after giving me a few instructions.

I ask the kids, "Do you have anything that you need to do?"

"Nope, we're free for the whole weekend so we can do all kinds of stuff together," Eva says.

I wasn't really expecting this and am at a bit of a loss as to what to do. "Why don't you think of a few things to do and we can talk about it?" I say.

We discuss a few things and there is one in particular that even piques my interest.

"Uncle Joseph, there's a zip line park in Warrenton, Oregon, that we found online. It looks like it would be fun," Gordie suggests.

After a bit of discussion, we all agree this is the place to go. The first thing I need to do though is to call Brenda and make sure it is okay with them.

"Hi, Brenda, the kids want to go zip lining, but I thought we should ask you first. What do you think? Is it all right with you and Harry?" I ask.

"Zip lining, oh my goodness, do you think it's safe? I

know the kids have been asking us about it but I'm not sure," she informs me.

I hear Harry in the background talking to her.

"Harry says that he thinks it is great and that you're a responsible man. Go ahead, just be careful, all right."

"I'll do everything I can to make sure things go nicely, after all, I am the safety rep at work you know," I assure her. "Okay, guys, we're going zip lining," I tell the kids.

Eva and Gordie are as happy as a couple of pigs in a dung heap. We get a change of clothes and have a quick breakfast then off we go. It's a two and a half hour drive to get to the place, but we are there before eleven 'o'clock. We pay our way in and are setup in harnesses while the guide explains how everything works. A short time later, off we go for two hours of more fun and thrills than any of us have had in a while.

Flying through the air over a lake and through the trees is as good as it gets. The kids have a ball and are grinning from ear to ear. To tell you the truth, I'm enjoying this adventure as much as they are. It's great fun flying through the air high above the ground. We end up going on all the lines several times.

After we're finished, we go for lunch at a Subway and head back home. As we settle in for the evening, the two are still talking about the excitement they felt as they were flying through the air. They thank me over and over. I'm glad that I took on this assignment. I guess this what they call bonding.

The rest of the weekend goes by almost too quickly. I've had a great time with these guys and am a little sad to head back to my place. I sit in my easy chair and reminisce about the weekend. Thinking about it, I might even volunteer to do this again. Who would have thought I could feel like this? One thing bothers me, though. I feel there is something just a bit off with Gordie. I can't put my finger on it but I know deep down that he is starting to change somewhat.

Things are warming up nicely and so I plant my garden, putting in all my favorites. Things, for the most part, are going well at work, and I start to watch the news again as I'm starting to get the itch I usually get when things don't come around fast enough. I want to find Smitty or whatever his name is.

I hear again about the loan sharks or debt collectors in Vegas and how another body has turned up. In the newer online sites I'm in, I hear a story of an individual who let gambling get the better of him and how he got deep into debt. It is suspected that he ran up a tab far in excess of what he could pay. I find out from Seeking Justice and Crime Everywhere that Angelo Carlucci is most likely the man who was sent to make him pay. At least that is the underground story. I don't find too much information in newspapers anymore. I guess they have to be careful of what they print because of a chance of lawsuits.

I've been to Vegas, but only for a day or so when I was on my way somewhere else. To tell you the truth, I wasn't particularly impressed with the place. It is, in my estimation, a place for suckers wanting to throw their money away. But then again I guess it's to each their own. There is a lot of top-notch entertainment there to draw people.

Another story catches my eye. Neo-Nazi members are thought to be responsible for several murders and the continual harassment of minorities. Several of the members are shown in group photos at events. The story fills us in about what their beliefs are. It seems incredible that anyone would follow this kind of ideology. It was brought about by a man who attempted to exterminate an entire race of people. Why would a hate group such as this even be allowed here? This is a country that prides itself on its heritage based on equality? It even says on our money, "In God We Trust."

Maybe it would be a good idea if these people all banded together, bought a large island, and formed their own country. Then they could keep out anyone they didn't like and be happy by themselves. This intolerance is almost archaic and should have been discarded long ago, in my estimation.

I turn off the television because this crap is starting to really piss me off. It seems to me that the only thing there is to see on the news is bad stuff. There are so many stories about terrorists creating havoc around the world. This is another thing that is starting to really disturb me. Things in this world are getting worse and worse.

There are more and more refugees flooding into countries in Europe. Then they try to come to North America. Many of these people are Muslims and, although most are legitimate, many of the terrorists are hiding in among them. This gains them access to the free world. Once they are in a country, it's easy for them to hook up with others of their kind and plot to kill innocents.

I have no idea where all this will lead. I heard some people discussing the fact that Muslims have a plan to defeat their enemy—which, by the way, is us. They want to come over in numbers and take over by out breeding us. By this, they can become the majority in our countries. They do have a lot larger families so where this may end frightens even me.

When I see Mark, one of the owners at work, I say, "Man, am I ever enjoying the book you loaned me."

"If you liked that one, I'll bring you in a few more of Asimov's books."

Up in the office, I have a meeting with two other very pleasant owners. Susan the purchasing agent, Mona the financial head, and I go over some of the records and make a few changes.

At lunch, I see one of the guys outside with a slingshot. He's practicing hitting a target and seems to be pretty accurate. I ask him about it later and he tells me he got the thing at a local sporting goods store for very little money. He mostly uses small round stones but tells me that marbles are amazing ammunition. The one he got is a hunting model and has a lot of power. I think I'll pick one up and see what I can do with it.

After the workday is over, I head to the store and ask the salesperson about the slingshots. He shows me a few types and asks what I would like to use it for. After I give him a suitable answer, he tells me that some of the better ones can bring down animals like geese or a fox and even wild turkeys. I get the best one that he has and an assortment of ammunition plus extra bands. Back at home I practice for a while and get the hang of it fairly quickly.

I want to take a real run at Angelo when I can find him alone. I'll be doing my surveillance first, of course. I'm looking forward to this encounter as I plan to break a few bones before I dispose of this scumbag if I have the opportunity.

I am not sure why I have the need to see him so soon after dealing with Ivar. I wonder if this is related to my wanting to find Dice Man so badly. At this moment, I don't have a clue as to how to go about it. Maybe I didn't have enough of an active physical involvement in removing Ivar. With my workout over, my hands are trembling slightly. I wonder if all the death in my life is taking its toll on my health in ways I don't realize. *No, this can't happen to me I just need to relax the rest of the evening.*

I decide to have a little barbeque and a beer to help me unwind. The steak and baked potato are superb, and I feel a little better. Because of seeing all the horrible things on the television the previous evening, I have a bit of a fitful sleep.

These things are bothering me more than they should. The unfairness of life is irritating the hell out of me. The need to do something about it is building up more and more. I wonder, if my mother was still alive and I hadn't gone through all the deaths of people around me, would I still be like I am? Maybe I should make a habit of reading an Asimov book before bed.

Every now and then, you see people protesting, trying to make changes in government policies and laws. It all seems to be for naught because nothing ever seems to change for the better this way. The rich get richer and the poor get poorer and the downtrodden continue to get walked all over, despite the good intentions of the few. The only thing that the more-determined protesters get is a couple of days in jail and a fine for exercising their rights. Yeah, it's time to get things moving.

I book the following Monday off. I have a three day weekend and head to Vegas to start watching Angelo the collector. I've researched as much as I can ahead of time. After a bit of hunting around, I locate him at one of the casinos that he seems to work out of. I go in suitably disguised with a wig and glasses. I find a spot at one of the one-armed bandits where I can survey the scene and watch him.

I play the machine and don't take any of the offered drinks the girls working the place try to give me. Cheap booze is never cheap in a place like this. They say that Vegas never shuts down, it just goes on and on and on. I must really be out of date or just a totally different breed because the gambling doesn't turn me on at all. The girls in the place are really attractive but I know they only have one purpose. They're here to help the casino make money by distracting players.

I watch the guy as little as possible so I don't give myself away. I see him with what appears to be a boss who signs notes once in a while. I assume it's for credit to some unlucky player. The note carrier heads back to the person and nods to an employee of the casino. This gives the player the finances he's asked for. There are a surprising amount of people who ask for credit during the course of the evening. I would think it'd be quicker if these people just burned their money. They don't appear to be very happy by the end of the night. Oh well, I guess that's their business. We're, for the most part, the authors of our own misfortune, at least that holds true in this place.

Around midnight, Angelo leaves with one of the men and heads to another hotel in the area. He walks into the casino and directly to one of the floor bosses. There is a discussion and the boss hands him a few notes which Angelo reads and then puts in his pocket. What this is about I don't know, at this point, but I aim to find out later. He and the man go into the elevator, ending up on the fifth floor. Racing up the stairway, I see them enter a room after knocking. Getting outside the door as quickly as possible, I listen to whatever is going on inside.

Going by the noise inside, Angelo is here to make a collection. There is a loud discussion inside as Angelo's voice booms out, "You've got twenty four hours to come up with the money. I'm taking your car keys and your license. Try running and we'll visit you at your home and explain a few things to your wife."

"I'll get the money tomorrow, I promise. I'll make a couple of calls as soon as you leave. Please don't hurt me or talk to my wife," the man pleads.

A few more threats are made but no real violence as Angelo and his associate get ready to leave the room.

Before I am spotted, I hide down the hall waiting for them to come out. The two head to the elevator, going to another floor and into a room. At the door, I hear pretty much the same thing happen again. As they walk down the hall, they discuss how much they will get when the gambler pays. So, Angelo gets a percentage of the collections that he makes. This could explain why he is so aggressive when he calls on the debtors.

"We should call the jerk's wife just for the hell of it, once he pays, ha, ha, ha," Angelo says as he walks by the stairwell on his way to the elevator.

Why people get themselves into these predicaments is beyond me. I wonder if they would be so eager if they knew what happens to some of the ones who can't pay. When I think about this, the answer becomes obvious. People will do things, despite any risk. A perfect example is the use of drugs nowadays. People know the dangers of trying cocaine and heroin and still use it for what is called recreational purposes. It is a trend in our society, and I wonder where it will all end. At this rate, I can't imagine what society will be like in another fifty years. It's always possible that things could swing in the other direction and society could straighten out.

The next day, I am back, disguised differently, and at another slot machine, biding my time. I move from machine to machine until he shows up again. The night goes pretty much the same, with Angelo getting a couple of payments for the casino. Other than that, I don't get much chance to pick up any more information about the guy. He seems to be quite competent in his collection practices because all the bosses seem quite friendly with him. He must have a good retrieval record. I see him get a little intimidating with one of the gamblers that appears to have had a bit too much to drink. This is, of course, not done where the public will see them.

The next morning, I get an earlier start and catch him before he heads out of town. This is okay because I have already checked out and had my things in the car. I will be heading back home sometime today, depending on what the collector does. He takes highway fifteen to Barstow and then heads toward Bakersfield.

He ends up driving all the way into Santa Cruz, following the Cabrillo Hwy to Swift Street, and stops at a small but beautiful little home with no garage, just off West Cliff Drive, within sight of the beach. He parks in the driveway, gets out, and heads to the front door. With his keys in his hand, he unlocks the door and walks in. Wow, is all I can say. He must make a fortune as a collection agent.

I wait down the street and survey the property. There is very little maintenance to do on the landscaping so he can leave the place for weeks at a time. The home is small but in this area, it must have cost a lot, especially since it is so close to the beach. I follow him as he heads to another part of town.

He drives to what looks like a care-giving residence and, as I wait in my car, he sits out in a shaded area with a man that bears a slight resemblance to him. The man he is with sits in a wheelchair and to communicate they have to use sign language. I have some signing ability because of knowing a neighbor who can't speak and this is the only way to talk to her.

I guess having a place in town is convenient for Angelo, this way he can visit what is probably a brother. Looking through my binoculars, I try to catch what they are trying to communicate to each other but miss a lot of it. I do catch a question being asked of Angelo by the other man. "Why do you hardly ever come to see me?" Then there is an odd question. "What happened to our parent's money? The will said it was supposed to be split between us."

At this point, Angelo strikes him in the face and shakes his fist at the now-whimpering man. Angelo looks quickly around and, seeing people watching him, he gets up and leaves.

So Angelo is even nasty with an invalid who can't fight back. Has he taken the money, meant for both of them, for himself?

It's getting to the point that I need to start heading home but I now know a lot more about Angelo the loan shark. Maybe loan shark isn't the proper term to describe Angelo because he doesn't actually loan out the money. The casino does this. Angelo is more a loan retriever than anything else.

The trip back takes about ten hours, and I am a bit tired by the time I pull into my driveway. I stop periodically going for a short run to keep the blood flowing.

The next day is slow at work, and I think of ways to handle Angelo. I could rack up a debt that he would need to collect but, after a bit of thought, I soon realize this isn't a good idea.

I could find one of the gamblers who owe a lot of money by hanging around and watching who is losing a lot and meet with him before Angelo can get to him and take his place when payment is expected. He would expect a person that he could intimidate easily and beat up if necessary. I could take him out at that point. This way others who had been hurt severely and those that died at Angelo's hands would get a little justice. Thinking this over too, I realize that the actual person owing the debt could end up being charged with murder if it got traced back to him.

The casinos are not the nice places that most of the patrons think they are. Anyone who can find a way to get an edge, like card counting, is thrown out. The only one that is allowed an edge is the casino. This idea about trading places is put aside while I try to come up with a few decent plans. I wonder if Angelo or his buddy that seems to be around him during collections carry a gun. Until I find out otherwise, I will have to assume that they do.

I head out to the park now and then for some off time relaxation. I like to sit on the shore of the lake in Baskette Slough Wildlife Refuge to watch the ducks and have done this on many occasions. This brings a bit of peace to me as the warm spring breeze blows across the water at me. I miss the time I had with Jack at the Chain of Lakes getaway. We chatted for hours while we fished and had our little lunches. He is probably the closest friend that I have had. Harry and Brenda are close too but it's different than Jack and I had. I wonder how close Bill and I will ever get? Which reminds me that he may soon have some more information for me, I hope.

Chapter 10

Angelo

This is the life is going through Angelo's mind as he sits in his living room with a glass of red wine. A nice stroll on the beach later will top off the day. He bought this place from one of those idiotic people that got in hock over their head at one of the casinos. When Angelo went to collect, the dummy started crying and begging to be given more time to pay. That is not how the game works, you lose, you pay, and quick too. Well, the only thing this guy had was this little house in Santa Cruz. He offered to sell it at fair market price to the casino but that isn't how the casino likes to be paid. Angelo made him an offer he couldn't refuse and bought it with his own money for less than half what it was worth. This way, Angelo paid the casino and the debt was wiped out for the moron. In actuality, Angelo likes this kind of person. He makes a great living collecting the debts from them.

Under normal circumstances, he gets paid thirty-five percent of the delinquent debtor's tab. The casino normally has no way to collect their money when gamblers hightail it out of town, so they figure that partial payment is better than nothing or trying to chase the guy down other ways.

Angelo offered his services to several casinos and came to an agreement, as long as he did his service away from the establishments and out of the public eye. Angelo already knew many of the owners through some of his former employers. It had been difficult, at first, convincing the casinos to use his services. He had to show them that they would not be embarrassed by their involvement with him. Staying in the shadows behind the scenes has been a very important part of his association with them. It would not be good for business if people got hurt on the premises or that things could be linked to the establishment in any way.

The trick in collecting the tabs is to keep an eye on the ones that are going to bolt and follow them when they try to run. A helper comes in handy in trapping the fleeing customers, and that is why he hired Freddy the flunky. Most times the gamblers see the error of their ways and pay up pretty quickly with minimal force required.

Every now and then, he runs into one that either thinks he can get away without paying or just doesn't have the means to get the money owed. It's sometimes hard to tell the difference between these types. Occasionally, he has to ask for the payment harder than the guy can withstand. Then Angelo doesn't get paid at all, and nobody is happy then, but that's part of the business. No use crying over spilled blood.

You can always tell the ones who are going to run by the way their eyes start darting back and forth, looking for the nearest exit. They just leave all their belongings behind and make a dash for the car. Freddy is already by the door when Angelo gives him the signal.

Angelo's bank roll is building up fast, and he always keeps his eyes open for other business opportunities that sometimes come up in his encounters with these fools. He never gambles himself because he knows you can't win in these places. Sure, there are some small payouts that keep the patrons happy but the money is usually lost again when they try to win more.

It's time to go for a pleasant stroll on the beach which is less than a minute walk. Yeah, life is good when you know how to play the game and can spend a couple of days here, now and then.

Chapter 11

Joseph

I'm wondering if I should call Bill to see if there is any progress that has been made with Oliver's cellmate but decide against it. I don't want to pressure him because he already knows how important this is to me, but I am getting anxious.

A big job at work gets my mind on other things as I need to give Jim a hand with some of the checking to see if everything is going right. There are a few items cut on the laser machine that are not made with the proper material. The operator says that he couldn't find the correct steel and thought that it would do. The customer is called and the situation is explained to them. They tell us that the material cannot be substituted and we need to re-cut the parts.

"I think that this is a waste of time," the operator says. "They would never know if we didn't comply. I don't see the problem."

Enough of this shit, it has to be dealt with properly. I call for Abe and explain what is going on. Into the office, the three of us go.

"Do you not understand why a substitution like this won't work? You listen and listen good, Steve. If there is ever a failure in the parts because the wrong material has been used, Salem Steel Fabrication will be held responsible. The company will be sued, big time, and we'll all be in shit up to our eyeballs because we knew about it," Abe says in no uncertain terms. "If it is ever found out that you have done this again, you'll be fired."

Steve is normally a good worker but this cannot be tolerated. "I don't think it was necessary to bring Abe into it," Steve says as we head back to the laser.

"If I hadn't done it, we could all be out of work one day. This is my job, so don't let this happen again. If you can't find the right material, ask the forklift driver or me for help."

Jeez, when will people learn? You spend a life time building a business and, if you aren't careful, you can lose it in a day because someone makes a bad decision.

At home, I sit down with another book that Mark gave me. It is by the same author, Isaac Asimov. He is a science fiction writer that is reputed to be one of the best. I read for about an hour and am totally enthralled by the story. The book is called *Caves of Steel* and is set far in the future. It's as much a mystery as it is science fiction and it's some of the best stuff I have ever read. I even have fantasies about living in the city of Asimov's future.

Mark says that, if I like this one, he has pretty much every book Asimov has ever written. I think I have found another passion to keep me occupied besides the guitar, which I am surprised that I am learning so quickly. It's time for bed. The crap on the television is gone and, in its place, I see myself living in the distant future and loving it.

At work the next day, I make up my mind to visit Angelo Carlucci in the near future. He needs to be dealt with, because I have been hearing about him and his type far too much. It's time to bring some justice his way. The poor slobs that go to Vegas looking for a good time are allowed to get in over their heads. When it comes time to pay the piper, there just aren't the funds and no way to raise them.

At least these are the stories that float around this town, according to my sources. The Citizens Discussing Crime and others have once again supplied me with much of the information I have.

The beatings that are received sometimes border on torture and every now and then one of the poor fools dies in the process. All this is for the love of money. What a despicable world we live in. I think I'll have to find a suitable method of dealing with Angelo, circumstances permitting, of course. Yeah, it's time to meet with Angelo.

As the days pass, thoughts of the book go through my head too. I almost wish that I could live there in that future time. What an adventure that would be. I guess almost everyone, at one point or another, wishes for something like this.

I find a variation of a slingshot I want to try to build. I am already getting excited as I usually do when I start a project that piques my interest and challenges my creativity. I have made a lot of things that I have never found a real use for but they are in my basement anyway. I'm not sure why my mind is always working on something. I wonder if there is something wrong with me, or are others like this too?

I take another extended weekend and head down to Vegas, going through Santa Cruz first on the off chance that Angelo is there. When I get to where he lives, I find that he isn't there, and I start thinking that next time I come down I am going to bring the tracking device I used to keep track of Jake Patterson in Des Moines. I don't know why I didn't think of using it before now. It would have saved me some valuable time.

I head on to Vegas and get there in the middle of the day. I am bushed. Booking into a motel, I go straight to sleep. I wake up about seven o'clock, get myself ready, and head to the casino that he frequents most. He isn't there so I head to another one he hangs around and soon see him on the sidelines nursing a drink. I leave my weapons in the car because I don't want to be found carrying one around in any of the casinos. I don't know if they have metal detectors in these places or not.

I watch Angelo from my vantage point for the next hour while I'm playing the slot machines. Holy crap! I just hit the jackpot. The stupid bell is ringing to beat the band, drawing attention to me that I don't want. It's a good thing I have several other disguises at the motel. I turn my back toward Angelo so he won't get a good look at me at all. If he is too observant, he may remember some detail that I may overlook. He could catch on that to the fact that I'm on his tail, but I doubt that he is concerned about things like that. Of course, you never know. Some people, I'm sure, must have it in for him.

The payout requires that I go to the cage to collect. It seems that I have just won two thousand dollars, which I decide I will cash in. I take it in cash and head out of the casino. No one tries to stop me as they know that I will be back to lose it soon. I stick to the crowds in the streets just to play it safe. I wouldn't be the first guy to have my winnings taken away from me so I keep an eye on people around me.

I go in and out of several places and, when I am sure that I'm not being tailed, I change my disguise in a bathroom, enough to pass for someone else, and head back to the car. Driving around town a bit to make sure no one is following me, I go back to the motel I'm staying at. Of course, in the scheme of things, two grand probably isn't that much in this town. Who would have thought that I'd get lucky at the slots and draw attention to myself?

Later after I rest up a bit, I change completely and go back to the casino. Angelo is long gone so I check out the other casinos that he works for and find that he isn't at any of those either. I may as well call it a night and try again tomorrow.

Angelo is a man who has done extremely well for himself on the backs of the wannabe gamblers that hit the casinos. I never could figure out why someone would take their hard earned money and just throw it away in places like this.

You hear stories of people losing their life savings this way and committing suicide afterward. I have an acquaintance whose husband lost around ninety thousand dollars gambling. They almost split up over it. This not being bad enough, he couldn't kick the habit, went out, and did it again. They lost their home and ended up divorced.

It seems people are always looking for easy money and think this is the way to get it, not realizing that ninety-nine percent of the people here lose their money. Don't they see that it costs a fortune to build and run these places? Where do they think that money comes from? The odds are with the house and they won't allow anyone to take it away from them. No card counters or anyone else who tries to better their odds is tolerated.

The next day, I hear a story through the grapevine about a player who got in over his head and got a beating for it when he couldn't pay quickly enough. Going by what I manage to pick up, it has to be Angelo who is behind this. I almost want to go and visit the man in the hospital to check and make sure that it is Angelo who did this, but I think better of it.

The day is a waste so I head back home to make some plans to deal with the collector. I'm not sure if I should take care of Angelo in Vegas or Santa Cruz. This will require some thought.

Back at home, I check online to see if there is any information about the beating of the man in Vegas. According to the online sites, it seems that Angelo is the one behind the hospitalization of the gambler.

I'll get the tracking device ready to install on his car. I won't be able to tell where he is from home but I won't have to go all the way to Santa Cruz either. I can get close to Yuba City north of Sacramento and I'll be able to see if Angelo is in Santa Cruz. This will save me a lot of time because I am thinking of disposing of him at his home so there won't be many of his friends around to interfere.

Digging the unit out of storage, I check it over. Having removed the batteries before storing it, I get some new long life ones. Once I attach the tracker to his car, I'll be able to keep an eye out as to his whereabouts. I haven't decided exactly how I am going deal with him but I'm sure something suitable will come to mind. Of course, once he is gone, I will have to remove the unit. This is another reason why I want to get rid of him in Santa Cruz and not in Vegas.

If he is alone during his stay at the place near the beach, then I won't have any problem taking the tracker off at night, as long as the police aren't in the area. The last time I tailed him there, he walked to the beach and went for a swim. He isn't a good swimmer but does go out a bit of a distance and floats quite a while. He has a lot of extra weight on him so I am sure he won't be able to hold his breath too long. Maybe the extra weight is why he floats so well. I think that I may just have gotten myself a way to take him out.

I get a membership at the YMCA and get back into swimming. I haven't done too much swimming for a while but I was very good when I did. I'll build up my under water skills and try to develop my lung capacity. After work, for the next couple of weeks, I go and swim for an hour or so. I try to go as far as I can underwater and, as time goes by, the distance increases measurably. I get back in swimming shape pretty quick.

On Sunday, I managed to catch Angelo at the house in Santa Cruz. He doesn't have a garage, so, late at night, I was able to attach the tracker to his car. I don't feel like going back to Vegas any more than I have to. It will also save over two hours driving time not having to go all the way to Santa Cruz if he isn't there. He goes to the beach house every few weeks to spend a couple of days there. He does this mostly on Sunday. That way he is in Vegas part of the weekend when the hobbyist gamblers are there and he can make his visits to the ones that get in over their heads and become delinquent on their repayments.

The weather has been unseasonably warm and this has made it a little more difficult at work. This does make it more pleasant going for the swim time. The heat is taking its toll on some of the guys as their concentration is thrown off a bit and the errors in their work start to pile up. The fans that the company buys help but there are still problems.

One day, the management calls a meeting of all the employees and asks everyone to take a little extra care, or, if they find it necessary, maybe a little vacation time is warranted. A few of the boys who can't handle the heat decide that some time off is a good idea.

I figure that a couple of extra days off in the beginning of the week may be a good idea for me too. It's about time for Angelo to spend some quality time at the beach and this may give me the opportunity to keep an eye on him. On one of my earlier trips down to Santa Cruz, I stopped by a dive shop and picked up two underwater breathing devices. It's a miniature tank apparatus that I can carry out when I swim into deep water and will help me to stay under for a couple of minutes longer than I could normally. If Angelo doesn't show up at the house, I can always go back to work earlier and come back the following weekend and stay the extra couple of days.

So Saturday is here, and I am on my way. I have all the things I need and find a place to stay just down the road on the main drag. The beach he will use is across the road and, when I'm on the beach, I can see his house through the binoculars, which I use sparingly. I don't want to draw any attention to myself.

Chapter 12

Angelo

I sure am looking forward to spending a few days at the beach for a well-deserved rest," Angelo tells himself. "I've made a lot of money from these fools in the casinos lately. The most enjoyable part of the job is when I get to inflict some pain on the slow-to-pay dummies. I actually like it when they have a hard time getting the money. This means I get to spend some one on one time with my customers."

"When I'm finished with them they rarely ever come back to Vegas again. This is okay, though, as there is a never-ending supply of potential clients that come looking to make their fortune."

"Little do they know that it rarely, if ever, happens to the average Joe who comes here. This last guy got more than he bargained for. He didn't have access to any more money. When he couldn't pay all the money owed, he found out how inventive I can be in my techniques at collection. Hope the guy has medical insurance, if not, oh well."

This brings a smile to his face. He is on his way to a peaceful interlude. Today is going to be a day of relaxation and, tomorrow, after a quick shopping trip, he will go out to the beach and float on the water as the stresses of the job just ooze out of him.

Chapter 13

Joseph

Sunday afternoon, I see him pull into the driveway. I knew he was coming ahead of time by keeping an eye on my GPS unit as I drove here, the unit alerting me when he came into range. At least things are going my way for now. I'm in my bathing suit with a towel draped over my shoulders and lots of sunscreen. The sun is hot and blazing in the sky. I feel the effects on my skin.

Luckily, I found a shady spot under a rather large tree. This way, I won't get too fried. I see lots of people lying on the beach with little or no protection. There's even a few that have oiled themselves to get a quicker tan. I guess they must not watch the news much. If they did, they would know about the ozone depletion in the atmosphere and that excessive exposure will lead to skin cancer down the road. I can almost hear their skin sizzling.

Of course, vanity is a large factor in their decision about getting baked. I knew a nurse who was brown all year round. This was not because it was her natural color, but rather that she went to tanning salons in all the off seasons. With all the hype about ultra violet rays being so harmful, you would have thought that her being in that profession, she would have known better. I guess it is as the old saying goes. "You can lead a horse to water, but you can't make the dumb bugger take a drink."

I think it must be a little too hot for Angie boy because he doesn't come out the rest of the afternoon. I decide to go for a swim with my snorkel, goggles, and fins. I want to check out the bottom again and see if there is anything I can use to my advantage.

There are some things on the bottom, like big rocks and a few other things that have been dumped in the past. The depth varies from five feet to twenty feet a little farther out. When I find out all that I want, I head back to shore.

Having the snorkeling stuff will come in handy. I just hope the weather stays calm so swimming is easy for Angelo. I head back to my room and go get a bite to eat. The place I eat at is next door so I am able to keep an eye out for Angelo. Maybe he isn't feeling well, and he may not do any swimming anytime soon. As the sun sets, I head for my room and turn in for the night.

The next day, I am up fairly early and at my post again. The car is already gone and, as I get in my car, I check my GPS, noticing that he is in the downtown area. I am about to make my way there when I see he is on his way back. In about fifteen minutes, he pulls in and parks. Into the house he goes, carrying shopping bags. I guess he has to eat too.

Chapter 14

Angelo

Okay, all the shopping is done and a light lunch has made me feel all right. The sun is shining brightly and there is no wind so the water is nice and calm. This is a perfect day for going out and just floating on the water," Angelo says to himself. "Freddy marveled at my ability to just relax on the water and almost fall asleep. It is almost like I'm filled with air the way I can lay on the water.

"Maybe I shouldn't have slapped Frankie so hard but he keeps accusing me of stealing his inheritance. So what if I did? What the hell can he do with it, anyways? At least he gets to live in a fairly decent place. Piss on it, life goes on. Going to grab my towel and hit the beach."

A quick look around at the edge of the sand, just to make sure an old client isn't waiting to get even. It wouldn't be the first time someone took offense at his collection methods. One guy once came back and tried to shoot him. What the hell, is it his fault that the guy didn't know when to stop gambling? Don't shoot the messenger or something like that.

The only guy he sees that looks a bit out of place is sitting in the shade. He doesn't look like he really belongs here, but then again, who does?

"I should be okay," Angelo' decides as he heads for the shore.

Chapter 15

Joseph

I have to wait an hour after he gets back before Angelo exits the house and heads to the beach in his trunks, carrying a towel. When he gets on the beach, he stops and looks around. It looks as if he is looking for something, his eyes stopping on different people.

They stop on me and stay there for a short time. I'm wearing shades with my towel over my shoulders, and I have a bag beside me. He then continues to the water's edge. I wonder why he was looking at me. Maybe I reminded him of someone or maybe he always does this. I am far enough away so he wouldn't be able to make out any details. I also turned my head away as he started looking in my direction. It's possible that he has made so many enemies that he is always on his guard and looks constantly for possible threats.

He drops his towel on the sand and heads for the water. It is a very calm day and the water is as smooth as glass. As Angelo swims out, there are others in the water but he goes out past them. He doesn't seem to like anyone too close because everyone has the potential to be an enemy.

I make my way to the shore quickly and get my gear on.

I have a small netted bag on my hip to carry the few items that I need. I've got two of the underwater breathing devices that I bought with my winnings at the slot machine. In the bag there's also a light green thirty-foot length of light but strong rope with a loop at the end that will tighten when pulled. It's green so it will be less noticeable in the water. Finally, I have my trusty knife in a bag on my other hip. I get into the water before anyone can see the things I have with me.

Once I'm in, I get the flippers on and check to see where my target is. He has reached a point where the water is about twenty feet deep, and he is far from anyone else. His head is toward the shore so he isn't able to watch what is transpiring behind him.

I head to an area not near him and, even though the bag creates a bit of a drag, it's not enough to cause a problem. When I am about fifty feet from him, I load up on air and put one of the breathing units in my mouth. I hold my breath as I go under the water to conserve the supply of air in the device. At about the ten-foot-depth mark, I take a few breaths and work my way under him.

On the bottom, there are a few large rocks and a big chunk of concrete with a piece of a steel bar sticking out the side of it. I slowly breathe in but not out so there won't be any bubbles going up to warn him. I have the rope with the noose on the end in my hand. As I come up underneath him I reach up and slide the noose around his ankle. I almost miss his foot because of the way the light is refracted by the water but manage to correct the problem before Angelo is aware of it.

I yank on the rope, tightening it as I use the fins to drive myself straight down. Angelo obviously is panicking as he is drawn down into the water. He desperately tries to resurface to get a breath of air. I have the advantage over him because of the flippers, and there is little he can do to slow my descent to the ocean floor. His only thoughts are likely of trying to get to the surface.

Chapter 16

Angelo

*A*rrrrgh! *What the hell just grabbed me? Angelo thinks. How on earth am I going to get back to the surface? What the hell is around my ankle? Is that someone pulling me down? I've got to get this thing off my ankle. Why is he pulling me down to the bottom? How can I get loose? Is he signing at me? What do you mean this is payback for the gamblers and Franky? I can't hold my breath much longer. Please let me go, argh.*

As the air runs out, these are the last thoughts that go through his mind.

Chapter 17

Joseph

I tie the rope to the steel bar in the concrete. The struggling momentarily subsides as I sign to him. I'm sure he gets the meaning of my communication as his eyes bug out, and it dawns on him why this is happening. A final effort is made to free himself as he thrashes around, trying to get the rope off his ankle. But it is now way too late as the last of his air is released from his lungs, and I finish dragging him all the way to the bottom. I quickly retie the rope around the rebar and switch my breathing device for the spare. I make sure the rope is secure around his ankle and, after I pull him as near the bottom as I can manage to secure the rope to the steel bar then back around his waist.

I go up and take a quick peek when I surface to get my bearings and go down again. I don't resurface till I am well away from where I took Angelo down. You never know if someone was watching at the moment he disappeared and raised the alarm.

I am at least a hundred feet away when I have to surface because I am running out of air from the breathing unit. As I get near enough to shore to stand in the water, I look around to make sure no one is watching or distressed. Everything checks out, and I put the things I can into the bag underwater. Back on shore, I gather the towel and bag, walking quickly back to my room and wash everything off to get rid of the salt that will otherwise corrode things.

There should be no cause for alarm for a while unless someone else is snorkeling and finds Angelo. Just in case this does happen, I check out of the room paying in cash, and head for another part of town. It really is handy having false identification and credit cards and any bills that are ever racked up are sent to a post office box, also under a fictitious name.

When it is dark enough, I will retrieve the tracker from his car and be on my way to another town where I can stay overnight and then head home tomorrow. It would have been better if Angelo could have gotten a taste of his own medicine. Unfortunately, there wasn't a chance to do this because he is seldom in a place where I can get away with it.

I don't feel bad for the guy at all. You live by the sword and it is only fitting that you die by the sword. A life of violence reaps a death by violence. This, of course, doesn't apply to me. I'm on a mission.

When a job is finished in a satisfactory way, I like to have a kind of celebration at an upscale restaurant and have something like a surf and turf dinner, accompanied by a Corona. This has almost become a ritual for me and this time is no different. At the restaurant, an attractive young woman asks if I am looking for a date and I almost say yes until I realize that she is a prostitute and so I decline. The only reason I would even have considered it, is for a little company, but I really don't deserve any company. Not from a decent woman at least. I manage to get back home by Tuesday afternoon and finish cleaning the last of the salt water residue from my things before I put them away. The heat wave has broken, and it should be nicer at work tomorrow.

Chapter 18

The guys at work breathe a sigh of relief as things are far more pleasant with the drop in temperature. As the week goes by, it is evident in their work, and management is pleased. That evening, I check online to see if there are any developments as far as Angelo is concerned. I find that nothing so far has been on the news about it but I am sure that it won't be long.

There is a young man who was hired a while back who seems eager to learn the trade. He has an excessive number of tattoos and piercings that pretty much cover most of his exposed skin and a few of the older guys don't like this, so they pretty much avoid him. I don't care one way or another. Although I'm not a fan of it, he can do whatever he wants. He's a pleasant enough guy so I decide to take him under my wing. I like teaching people who want to learn.

I would, however, not make a good teacher in schools because too many of the students don't want to learn. They are just there to pass the time. I have a difficult time dealing with people who can't be bothered to put in the effort it takes to get educated and are just along for the ride or, worse, are troublemakers.

That evening Bill calls. "Hey, Joseph, I phoned in order to meet with you later in the week."

"Friday after work is a good time. Do you want to stay for a bite to eat and a beer?"

"Thanks, but the wife and I are heading out to meet friends of hers at Romeo's restaurant," he says.

I hope that he has some information for me. Man, I hate waiting.

Two days later, Bill leaves a message on my machine canceling our meeting. Something important has come up and he says he'll talk to me later. Crap.

The next day at work, the laser cuts some interesting pieces, so I get the operator to cut a couple of extra parts and hang on to them. The parts are identical to a sickle and are made from high-quality steel. I think that I might be able to use them in the future. Exactly what for, I'm not sure of at this moment but something may come up.

There it is, the story I've been waiting for. A swimmer has discovered the body of a man tied to a steel rod twenty feet below the surface. The body is bloated and takes DNA tests to identify who it is. Once the testing is done a week or so later, the news states that it is Angelo Carlucci a part time resident of Santa Cruz.

The man has connections to the underworld in Las Vegas and this appears to be a targeted death. With the body being in the water so long, there has been no evidence found to link the crime to any suspects. This is good news for me, although I always take great care to make certain no evidence is left behind.

We have an employee by the name of Les and he has a wife named Kate. They relocated several years ago from Ohio and have made this their home. The guy is very good at what he does and gets along with everyone. He helps anyone that needs assistance and can always be counted on. He trains a few of the younger guys and has a good heart. His wife is very attractive and also has a heart of gold.

This sometimes leads to problems for them because, now and then, they are taken advantage of. Kate has a son from a previous marriage who moved in with them about six months ago. They have been trying to help him get on his feet and off the booze, which most guys in the shop don't know about.

Grant Wendal, Kate's son, has gotten a job here a while back because of Les, and a couple of times lately, I have seen Les take him aside and lay down the law. "What is wrong with you? Your mother and I have tried to help you, and all you do is treat her like shit. This drinking and abusive behavior has to stop. We can't take much more of this."

"Yeah, yeah, whatever," Grant replies, walking away, leaving Les shaking his head.

What an asshole. Despite all the help they have given him, Grant refuses to straighten out, plus he has caused a few real conflicts in the shop. I'm sure that this character has mental issues.

It's evident that there is growing animosity between Grant and Les and I know it is going to come to a head. Les is a well-built guy with some boxing and martial arts behind him, and I think Grant may get his ass handed to him soon.

When the opportunity arises, I ask Les, "Is there is anything that I can do?"

"I'm going to tell Grant to find his own place soon," he tells me. "Things at home have been disrupted a lot since Grant moved in and Kate has really been feeling the effects of his abusive behavior. She has had to walk on egg shells whenever Grant is around and, no matter how much he is helped, he shows no appreciation. We can't put up with it any longer."

A couple of the newer guys in the shop who didn't know about his problem have gone for a beer with Grant. They've come back with the opinion that, "Man, this is one guy that should stay away from booze. His whole attitude goes downhill fast as he drinks."

His attitude is bad enough when he is sober and the guys refuse to go drinking with him anymore. It's really too bad because Grant knows his stuff and could be an asset to the shop. This is starting to affect quite a few people in the shop, and the time has come to deal with Grant.

I go talk to Abe about it. He has seen firsthand several times the interactions between Grant and the other employees. He has warned Grant three times about his behavior and has only let it go this far because Grant is the stepson of Les and didn't want to create any hard feelings. I tell him that, if he wants to let Grant go, this would be all right with Les but could he wait till Grant moves out and gets his own place.

"I want to be informed as soon as this happens so I can rectify the problem," Abe says.

I go back to Les and let him know what is going on and to keep it under his hat and let me know as soon as he can when Grant moves out. He is appreciative of my efforts and tells me he will have him out in two weeks. He has already been looking for places for Grant and will tell him tonight that it's time to go.

Two weeks go by and Grant has moved out. Already we see that he is coming in to work hung over and his attitude is worse than ever. It would appear that, no matter how much you try to help some people, there is nothing you can do to change them. They are actually their own worst enemies and end up causing nothing but disruption where ever they go. And it is, of course, always someone else's fault.

Grant got a several-thousand-dollar Christmas bonus, like everyone else, but he even bitched about that, thinking the company had cheaped out. It is so obvious to everyone in the shop that Grant has severe mental issues, and they really feel for Les and his wife.

Abe has finally had enough and calls Grant into the office, giving him the news. As Grant leaves the building, there is a feeling that a dark cloud has been lifted from the premises.

Les's happy disposition returns quickly and he tells me a few weeks later that Grant has moved to another city and that he has stopped all communication with him and his wife, blaming them for this turn of events. Yeah, this is one sick dude.

There seems to be an inordinate amount of mental illness in the world. Why this is, is beyond me. There have been studies done and some researchers think this may be linked to things like flu shots and vaccines for measles and small pox and a host of other diseases.

The diseases have been held at bay but there seem to be long term side effects from what has been injected into the population at large. Autism is thought by many to be increasing dramatically because of this. I wonder if we will ever find out for sure. There are thoughts that civilization as a whole is becoming weaker and weaker.

In the past, centuries ago, the sick and weak died off and only the fittest survived. With modern medicine being what it is, the weak survive and carry their weaknesses on to future generations, thus causing an adverse effect on the survivability of the human race. I guess it makes sense, but who would willingly let their offspring perish to keep the race stronger. I doubt that I would, so why would others?

I have found two more sites over the last year or so that have members with a lot of knowledge about criminals that have so far escaped justice. The site Seeking Justice has shown a potential subject. A relatively new site called Crime Everywhere is proving to be an invaluable source of reliable information. I can't say for certain but it looks very much like there are members of the law enforcement agencies who are frustrated with all the rules preventing them from bringing criminals to justice. It takes quite some time to become a trusted member of these sites, but, once in, there is a wealth of information to be had.

There is an old man who is an occasional speaker at the White Supremacists rallies. With the information available, it is suspected that he is a leftover of Hitler's youth movement. He is in his eighties and was brought into the military at a very young age in Germany near the end of the war. There have been attempts to bring him to justice, but because he was young and there is very little evidence against him, there is nothing to be done.

The ideals of the Nazi party have been ingrained in him and he wears this distinction with pride. He has managed to incite the neo-Nazi groups with his anti-Semitic views. There have been countless incidents of violence, partially because of him. At least this is what the site's members claim.

How in the world does the government allow this? Freedom of speech is one thing but hate mongering is something else entirely. This is an insult to any veteran of the Second World War and anyone with a sense of decency. The Bible tells that the Jews are God's chosen people. Even if you don't think this is right, would you really want to take the chance, just in case you're wrong? I have never been able to understand this type of person. What on earth makes him think that he is so much better than someone else?

Heinrich Schmidt is probably going to be the next person I visit. I have found out through the internet that he was quite a successful business man and has retired to a fairly large tract of land outside Alamosa, Colorado. His property borders the Rio Grande River and is off the beaten track. You need to get there by a gravel road off Route 160 or by water in the river.

This place is going to be a little harder to get to than most I have accessed. There is a lot of open and treed country surrounding his land. I could travel across it to gain access, even though he is near the foothills of the Rio Grande National Forest Park. I'm going to have to give this some thought. Maybe another solution will present itself and I won't have to go to the wilderness at all.

I do some exploration via Google and get an idea of the surrounding area. In some of the news stories, it is reported that he has several Doberman pinschers guarding his property inside fenced grounds. I don't like these dogs as they tend to be vicious animals. Doberman's and German shepherds were used by the Nazi's in prisoner-of-war camps because of their highly intelligent and vicious natures. If you have ever had an encounter with one of these you know what I mean, they can be quite intimidating.

I could use my fence-mounted dog eliminator but there are too many of them. If I go the route of taking him out at his residence, I will have to come up with a solution to this dilemma. I have heard several of his recorded speeches and find the man repulsive at best. The extermination of a race of people horrifies me, but this is what he believes should take place.

Things at work are better since Grant has been given the boot and Les is back to his old self. The atmosphere in the shop has brightened considerably and life is good.

I have been invited to Harry and Brenda's on the weekend and, as it approaches, I start to think that they are always the ones inviting me to their place and it is never the other way around.

I think that in the near future that I'll take the whole family out somewhere. I would bring them to my place but feel that it is a little risky. The kids are curious and could easily discover things I don't want them to.

As the weekend gets closer, I wonder if I should bring something extra or not. I finally decide on some wine and a German torte cake made with real cream and as rich as anything. I've had this cake a few times and found it absolutely delicious. I contact an upscale bakery and order one to be picked up on Saturday.

The kids haven't seen the cake before and swoon over it.

"Oh, wow, what kind of cake is that?" Eva asks.

"It's called a torte cake. It's a German cake made at a specialty bakery in town," I inform her.

"It sure looks good," Gord, as he now likes to be called, pipes in.

They almost drool on the table like that dog in the movie called Hooch. Everyone enjoys the cake tremendously.

"Would you like to take the leftover cake home with you, Joseph?" Brenda asks.

"What do you think kids, should I take the rest of the cake with me?" I ask.

"Ah, well, I don't know," Eva says.

"I don't think it's good for you, Uncle Joseph. Maybe you should leave it here so we can help you with it," Gord says eagerly.

"I think you're right, thank you for thinking of me. Tell you the truth, Brenda, I would prefer a few slices of roast beef for sandwiches if that's okay with you," I say.

"I think I can manage that," she tells me with a smile on her face.

So a deal is struck, much to the delight of the kids. I just love roast beef sandwiches for lunch.

Sunday, I'm back online using Google Earth to get a better idea of the property around Heinrich's house. From what I can make out, he has three dogs and they are kept within the wire-fenced property. The Rio Grande goes past the house about seventy or eighty feet away from the home. The river widens considerably before it gets to his home. It almost looks like a lake at that point and has lots of evergreens near the shore. There are brush and small trees along the bank in front of the house. It should be easy to scale, gaining access to the property.

The fence is along the river too so the dogs can't get to the water's edge without the gate there being open. Of course, the fence along the river appears to not be as high as the rest of property, something that needs to be taken into consideration. I think that I may be able to take care of the dogs using my sling shot. I will have to practice using what I plan to shoot with, so I can get a feel for the load.

The surrounding area is flat and doesn't offer a lot of cover in case I plan to approach the house from that way. I'm going to have to do some real planning on this one. I am sure that despite the fact that the old man is in his eighties he will have a few guns about. This could range from pistols to a rifle and a shotgun. If I was living way out there, that is what I would have, and he seems paranoid enough to have those. Otherwise, he wouldn't have the three Dobie's.

The river flows under a bridge on the main road then through the evergreen trees, widening as it goes past his house and on to its destination. It is a bit shallow in spots, leaving rocks exposed here and there, and isn't very big at this time of year. There are many side roads that allow access to the river and a few spots that allow for a car to be left. I have noticed via Google that a couple of the parking areas are obscured by under growth. There are several places that will allow me to get near Heinrich's house from the more barren areas too. I have a plan developing in my head but I need to fine tune things a bit. I'm going to take a weekend and do a little reconnaissance before I commit myself to any particular plan of action.

June journal entry: *Life is back to normal for me. Well, as normal as it will ever be for someone who always seems to have the rug yanked out from under him. But at least things are bearable and my sanity is fairly stable. Thank goodness for Harry, his family, Bill, and my job…*

Taking an extended weekend, I head out Friday after work to Colorado. Driving through Idaho, Utah, Wyoming, and then through Colorado to my destination. The route is interesting enough and I get there Saturday afternoon. I've booked a room at the Holiday Inn in Alamosa. I go out and have corona with an Italian dinner at the Rialto, pretty good!

The next day, nice and early, I head out toward the Nazi's place. Taking Route 160 out of town and a few gravel roads, I end up a mile or so from his place. Surveying the river, I check the depth and current which flows past his house to where I am. I continue down the gravel road past a gravel driveway which leads to his house beyond the trees, quite a distance in from the road.

Going to a secluded spot well past the driveway, I take out the extra powerful binoculars. In the distance, I see his house and check the surrounding area. There are a number of spots that can be used as a place to watch from, which I may do just to get a better idea of what goes on there and which will help formulate a plan of action.

This place isn't the type that I would pick to live in. The area—away from the river and the wide section, or bay, where the house sits—is dry and there is a very little vegetation, except along the river. You can see the rolling hills in the distance and behind them the mountains. During the day, it gets quite hot and uncomfortable.

The Nazis were well known for their torturing of prisoners during the Second World War. Seeing as how Heinrich is such a fan of the Nazi Regime and their ideology, maybe he would like to experience firsthand what it feels like to undergo the techniques used by them. I'd like to, but don't believe that I will go this route, even though he probably deserves it. I did that with Jake Patterson and it took a while to recover from it.

A simple execution will have to suffice. Under normal circumstances, I would not touch the old man but he has been the cause of many being hurt, and I'm certain people have died because of him. He's agitated groups to the point where they made innocent people suffer. So a time of reckoning is about to descend on Heinrich.

The thing I like the least about the premises is the dogs. They are a vicious breed of animal that has undoubtedly been trained to attack with the intent of maiming or killing an intruder. I would hate to be seen and get caught out in the open with those bastards on my tail.

Yeah, I need a plan that will keep me out of harm's way. I continue my scouting and, later in the day, I find that it gets quite cool out here. Heading back early because it's a long drive home, I review the information I've acquired.

When I was gone, Bill left a message on the answering machine, asking for a meeting and apologizing for canceling before. I call him up and we get together in town at a coffee shop late Monday afternoon.

"Oliver's cellmate has made some progress," he says as we sit at a corner table. "He has discovered that Smitty isn't the accomplice's name at all. The guy is a career criminal by the name of Dennis Jackson. Jackson has committed many robberies in the past and has served time in prison where he had the dice tattoo done. There are, at this time, no warrants for his arrest as it is thought that he has cleaned up his act. I've contacted other jurisdictions and, upon further investigation, it has been found that there are a series of robberies that have been committed in a number of different states. These robberies weren't tied together because of the lack of cooperation between law enforcement agencies across the country. It has taken some time but it looks like the MO in many of the robberies is similar. This has led to a pattern being discovered and it is strongly believed that Jackson is the perpetrator. At least that's what I've heard," he tells me.

"What is the pattern and is there anything else you know about this guy?" I ask.

"Small businesses like B and B's are mainly being targeted in towns that roughly follow the route a driver would go as he travels around the country. The police in several towns have been alerted to the possibility that these types of businesses in their area may be targeted. There are, of course, many different routes that Jackson could possibly take and, hopefully, his luck will run out soon," Bill says, taking a sip from his coffee mug.

Because Bill is on a roll, I don't say anything, not wanting to interrupt his train of thought.

"A few of the victims have been severely hurt and a description of the assailant is similar to Jackson with a few modifications, indicating that he may be disguising himself somewhat. The gun that Oliver Durham described is the same that all the witnesses give a description of. This means that, if he is apprehended with the firearm, a ballistics test will be done. Even if Oliver won't testify against him, he will be found guilty because the bullet that killed Kathleen is in the hands of the police, and forensics will be able to match it to the gun. I think that Jackson is using a vehicle under another name and may have a false identity. There seems to be no record of his whereabouts for quite some time."

My hands are trembling as I hear the news. Can it possibly be true that Kathleen's murderer may be caught and sent to prison? If he is caught, I should be able to find someone in the same prison to dispense justice for me. I would much rather do the job myself, but this would be better than nothing. I know that Bill sees what is going on in my mind as he smiles at me.

"So what's going through your head, Joseph, you thinking of trying to catch him yourself?" Bill asks me.

I have been visualizing this in my mind and zoned right out. As I come back to reality, I catch the smile and flush a little bit.

"I'm sorry. I was daydreaming for a second there."

"I can see that for myself. Just what you're daydreaming about is what concerns me, buddy."

"This is wonderful news; I've waited a long time for this to happen," I say, changing the subject.

I thank him profusely and he tells me that he will keep me posted. I ask if it is possible to get a copy of the route that Dennis has been traveling to see if I can refine the pattern a little more. He says that he doesn't think it is a good idea but changes his mind when I look him straight in the eye saying nothing. Sometimes it is better to keep your mouth shut and let other things do the talking for you.

After making plans to get together to do some more fishing, we part company, shaking hands, and I am on my way home. There is a feeling of elation running through me and I find it difficult to get to sleep this night. To make things worse, I sit in front of the television for a while and catch something on the news about a child that has been severely abused by his mother and stepfather and this makes it even harder for me to sleep.

Fortunately, the parents have been charged and the child is in foster care at the moment. It really irks me to see these things. I feel like finding these people and abusing them for a while. Damn, I hate this stuff. I can't understand the things people do. It's like they have no soul.

I wonder if I should postpone the visit to Heinrich the Nazi for a while and take care of those people that have so badly abused their son. I think they are out on bail at this time, and it might be easy to get to them, but after a bit of thought, I decided to wait and see what happens. There is nothing I can do about Dennis Jackson right now either, so maybe I should just go ahead and take care of the old man.

The itch is getting stronger all the time, ever since Bill told me about Dennis Jackson. I want to get to him quite badly, and it is affecting my work. So I have decided to go see Heinrich soon to alleviate some of this stress. The plans have to be made carefully because I don't want a repeat of what happened to me at George's house.

My approach to Heinrich's house will be by way of the river and the bay. Having figured out a way of dealing with the dogs and, since the house is at least a mile from the nearest gravel road, I plan to rent a canoe with an electric motor on the squared off back end. I found a place in Denver where I can rent one and a jeep to carry it to where I need it. I have been assured that it will suit my needs more than adequately. The propeller is just below the rear end of the canoe and has a guard to prevent any damage to the prop in case a rock is hit.

I will be coming upstream rather than down because this will make it easier to get back to the vehicle in case there is a problem. I'll be somewhat limited to the amount of stuff I can bring with me, so I need to choose carefully. I select my semi-automatic pistol that I loaded the magazine with a pair of latex gloves on, this way there won't be any fingerprints on the shell casings that might be left behind.

I pack two extra magazines and my semi-automatic twelve-gauge shotgun that has been altered to accept a couple of extra shells. My trusty knife is coming along for the ride.

Finally, I pack my slingshot, which I have a real purpose for. My slightly padded leather bomber jacket also gets added to the pile.

It gets quite cool at night so I will need to have something warm and durable to wear.

I book off two weeks. One of the guys asks what I plan on doing. I tell him I'm heading for the mountains to rent a cabin. Unfortunately, there are no real mountains on my way to Colorado. I will just use some of the photos that I took at Yellowstone the last time I was there if I feel the need to show any photos.

The day arrives, and I am on my way. I could stop at Salt Lake but decide to continue on to Rock Springs instead. Having been to Salt Lake before, I want something different and stay at the Comfort Inn just off Lincoln Highway.

The next day sees me in Denver where I pick up the Jeep and canoe. The person helping me load things up shows me how to hook up the electric motor to the canoe and how to recharge the batteries if I deplete them. The canoe is strapped to the racks on top of the jeep. Then loading my stuff in the back, off I go, removing my disguise when I get out of town. My car is left in a long term protected parking lot. Driving through Colorado Springs and turning right at Walsenburg, I head for Alamosa, booking into the Super Eight. So I am not a familiar face, I'll probably change hotels again at least once during my time here.

I've been training real hard and can run a long distance in case I have to bee line across the desert back to the jeep. All my supplies are packed, along with food and extra water. I'm starting to get the jitters like I always do before any mission. Even trying to plan as carefully as possible, there are always things that you can't foresee. My biggest concern is those bloody dogs. I have a plan to deal with them and hope it works out the way I anticipate.

Sometimes I wonder if Heinrich would feel the same

way he does if he were born Jewish and had been thrown into a concentration camp during the war. It really is a shame that people like him can't experience what they so much want others to feel.

The next day, I make a trip to the area near his property to make my final preparations. Going to a supermarket, I get the things I need and head back to my room, trying to rest for the following day. I need to sleep in because it's probably going to be a long day.

In the late afternoon, I head out, traveling down the back roads, and make my way to the river downstream from his house. There is a bridge over the river and this is where I unload the canoe, taking it down to the water when the way is clear. Tying it up under the bridge out of sight, I get the batteries, paddle, and motor.

When everything is hooked up and my supplies loaded into the canoe, I take the jeep to a spot nearby. It's out of sight from anyone that may travel the back roads. I have a couple of flashlights, one big and one small. When I'm approaching the property, there can't be any light spotted by the dogs or Heinrich, so they will have to be out. At this time, I'll use my night vision goggles.

The water level in the river is a little lower than I'd like. When I came out last time, it was noisy enough to mask the sound of the electric boat motor which runs very quietly. Despite the fact that the dogs have excellent hearing, I think I'll be okay. The water does look like it's deep enough, so I probably shouldn't have to worry about scraping the rocks that are here and there in the river.

I picked this particular time because there will be a full moon tonight and this will help light my way if I have to remove the goggles for any reason. I jog back toward the bridge and wait for it to get dark. Staying away from the road, I use my binoculars to keep an eye on the house through the trees, waiting for all the lights to go out. The occasional vehicle goes by but, by the time I am ready to get moving, all is quiet.

At about nine thirty, they go out and, after waiting another hour, I get the canoe going. I don't push it very hard, not wanting to run the batteries down, but manage to make good headway toward the property guided by the moonlight. Here and there are little narrow spots in the river that causes the water to make more noise. This works in my favor, but I have to go a little slower here because of the likelihood of impacting a rock.

This makes me wonder if anyone else has ever tried to get rid of the man way out here. As I get close to the place, the river widens and the trees become more abundant. I start to ease off on the power, going as silently as I can. Luckily, the water makes enough noise to mask my approach. There is a small island, like strip of land, in the middle of the wide section of the bay.

When I am close enough, I tie up to a tree at the edge of the island, on the far side of it, away from the house. I should be out of sight of the dogs here. I tie it up near the front of the canoe, otherwise the gentle current will swing the front of it in the direction of the water flow and may cause me a problem.

I get hold of my slingshot and, opening the bag I have with me, I pull out several pieces of steak that I have laced with a powerful tasteless sedative. I could have used a strong poison, but I couldn't locate any that was fast acting enough and also tasteless. Loading a piece into the pouch of the slingshot, I pull back and fire it over the small trees in front of me, to where the dogs will probably be. I do this until all the meat has been sent over the fence then wash off the slingshot. The sedative was tested on a stray dog in Salem to make sure it worked properly.

After waiting half an hour, I untie the rope, making my way across the water to the shore at the edge of the property. After quietly tying up the canoe, facing the way I want to go when I return, I check my knife and the pistol in my holster, undoing the safety strap but leaving it there until I get to the fence at the top of the bank. This way, I'll be able to pull it out quickly in case of trouble.

Taking care not to slip and fall, I ease my way to the top as quietly as I can. Looking through the fence, I try to see if I can spot the dogs. There is one lying on the ground near the fence and another closer to the house. I don't see the third one but am fairly confident that it is out of commission somewhere on the property too.

I go to the gate as quickly as I can with the big flashlight in my hand but not on. Just as I open the gate and start reaching for the pistol, there is a growl and I'm hit by the third dog. I only manage to get my arm up at the last instant as it clamps down on my left forearm, and we both tumble down the bank to the edge of the water.

My face is slapped by the brush as we roll down the embankment. Holy crap, the pain is excruciating and disorients me for a moment. The dog is fairly big and has a grip like a vise.

I have had unpleasant experiences with these types of dogs before so my thinking isn't at all clear. Luckily, we are right at the edge of the water with the dog trying to pull me off balance as I'm on my knees attempting to shake it loose.

It takes all that I have to keep my wits about me. With my free hand, I grab the dog by the collar and drag it into the water as it is latched onto my forearm. I turn it on to its back in the water that is chest deep and, taking a deep breath, push the dog down underneath me.

I would have thought that it would have let go at this point but it doesn't. It is struggling for what seems an eternity and, finally, it lets go of my arm. I hold the bugger down with my good hand and wait as long as I can. When I am out of air myself, I stand up and gasp air back into my lungs, still holding the dog down.

My heart is thumping like a jackhammer. My hands are trembling from the adrenalin as I try to regain my composure. I am really lucky that my arm was flat in the dog's mouth so that the bite was on the top and bottom of my forearm. If it had been sideways, I'm certain that it would have broken the bones in my arm and incapacitated me.

It's also fortunate that I had the heavy leather jacket on, as it protected the arm to some degree. Another stroke of luck is that we fell down the bank so close to the water, giving me the opportunity to drown the dog too. Otherwise, I might have been in a real pickle with the dog shaking me so violently. Slowly, I make my way up the grassy bank, resting at the top, nursing my arm for a bit.

I check out the house, relieved to see that no lights have come on. I remove the jacket and inspect the arm at the spot the dog clamped down on it. There are some abrasions but no punctures. It is quite sore but still functional, so I gently massage it to ease the pain.

My heart is still racing, and I take the time to get control of myself again. Why the third dog was not out like a light is bothering me, and this could have turned out much worse than it did. I couldn't use the knife because it's on my left-hand side in a position that was hard to reach with my free hand. The pistol fell out of the holster when we tumbled down the bank, which I've retrieved, so I couldn't use it either.

If you have ever been attacked by a dog like this, you will understand why I was shaken up. I locate the flashlight, leaving it off and holding it with the left hand, leaving the pistol in my good one.

I approach the house as quietly as I can, taking the time to use the knife on the other two dogs, not taking the chance of either of them waking up prematurely and wanting to play too.

As I come near the main window from the side, I see some movement inside. Damn, I hope there aren't any more dogs around this place. A closer look inside the house and I see Heinrich walking toward the window with a pistol in his hand. He must have heard something during the ruckus with the dog. His thin form is slightly illuminated by the dim light from a room at the other end of the house.

This must have just come on when I finished the dogs.

Otherwise, I would have noticed it. Ducking behind a bush, I try to see what he is going to do. Slowly, he makes his way over to a sliding glass door, opening it, and takes a few steps outside away from the house, turning on a flashlight panning it around the property.

"Come here, my boys," he calls out to the dogs.

He waits for a sound that doesn't come. Stepping away from the house a few paces, he stops when he spots the dog dead on the ground and turns quickly to re-enter the house.

As he turns, I am there, having come out from behind the bushes. I knock the gun out of his hand, turning on my flashlight and shining it into his eyes.

"You dirty rotten pig, why have you killed my pets?" he yells at me.

He continues to shout some obscenities at me and starts backing up as I get closer.

"Stop right there, shut your mouth, and get in the house, now," I say to him.

In the living room, he sits on a sofa. "Who the hell are you and what do you want? Do you really think there is anything worth stealing here, you fool?" he shouts with a heavy German accent.

"I'm not here for anything like that, old man," I say. "You have been spreading hatred all your life and caused many people pain. People you think of as inferior, but in actuality, you are the one who is inferior."

"They are nothing better than animals, these people I speak against."

"Whoever taught you that?" I ask the demented old man.

"Who else but our Fuhrer? He was a man of vision. He made Germany a force to be reckoned with. If those stupid Japanese hadn't brought the Americans into the war prematurely and if that traitor Einstein had not turned his back on the motherland, it would have all turned out different. Germany would now be in control of the world and the rest of the swine would no longer exist," he screams as spittle flies from his lips.

I explain to him that the debate is over and what I am here for. He's told that he's one of the things that are wrong with the world. His ideals should have died along with that scumbag Hitler. The lives of the people he and his kind have persecuted for so long will be better off, knowing he is no longer among the living.

I tie him up with the rope I find in a closet and fasten it to the couch. I finally have to gag the man as he just screams at me on and on. I do a little search of the house and find many Nazi mementos and a lot of propaganda. I start a fire in the fireplace and one by one I throw it all into the fireplace. All the while he is cursing me and the Jews that he has hated all his life.

I could sit down and debate this with him, but it would be a waste of time and just delay the inevitable. People like this have an unreasonable hatred in them that can never be explained. I doubt very much that they even know the real reason they feel this way themselves.

An idea was, at some point in their lives, put into their heads and, for them, it became a reality. So, no, I won't bother trying to convince him he is wrong. Burning his mementos has infuriated him so much that his eyes bug out as he attempts to hurl obscenities at me, but the gag stops that.

I sit down in front of him and take a DVD out of my jacket pocket. Luckily, he has a player and, after drying it off, I place it into the DVD player.

I force him to watch the entire movie by smashing his foot whenever he closes his eyes or tries to look away. The movie is about all the Nazi war criminals that have been caught and executed. By the time it is over, he is almost frothing at the mouth.

I look at the man and see the product of a bygone era. Much of what is wrong with the world is sitting right in front of me. It makes me wonder if some of the Middle East leaders are just replacements for the man that Heinrich idolizes. So much hatred is in this world, and for what? Many examples of this can be seen on the internet. A perfect example is Revenge dot com. How this is allowed is beyond me. Free speech is one thing, but this crap goes way overboard.

With the DVD finished, I take his pistol in a gloved hand and, when I am certain he knows what is about to happen, I put a bullet right between his eyes. I thought about burning his house down too but I might not have time to make my get away if I do that. I am sure someone would see the flames from a distance and call the fire department.

As I am about to leave, another idea comes to mind when I see his supply of firewood. The property around his house is cleared away of trees for close to a hundred feet in all directions. I stack some wood about twenty feet behind his house. Then, I make a small narrow row of very dry firewood, leading to the house, placing it so the fire won't go out along the way. When I have everything ready in the canoe, I walk back to the small pile of wood and ignite it.

If all goes well the fire will take about half an hour or so to travel from the pile along the pieces laid out with crumpled newspapers, inserted here and there to make certain the fire doesn't go out. As it burns it should go through the sliding doors and into the house to the couch and chairs then continue till the whole house is on fire.

This has all taken quite a while because of my sore arm, but is well worth it. I quickly get back to the canoe and, with the big flashlight pointed ahead of me, it doesn't take long for me to get back to the bridge. Running to the Jeep, I drive back to the spot where the canoe is. After loading everything up, I see the house is starting to really catch fire. By the time an alert is received at a fire station back in Alamosa, I am almost back to the room. After washing up and seeing to my arm, I am exhausted. Lying down, despite what I have been through this night, I am out like a light.

The next morning, I have a breakfast and check out, wanting to leave the area before anyone has the chance to put two and two together. As I drive back to Denver, I keep the radio tuned to the news, waiting for any word on the death of the Nazi. So far nothing, but I'm sure it will come out sooner or later. I take the canoe back to where it was rented, then drop off the jeep, taking my time going back home.

I get home well ahead of the end of my time off and decide to let soreness in my arm diminish before I go back. It is a good thing that, when I was rehired back into my old job, one of the conditions the company agreed to was that I would retain the seniority I had when I left. This gives me the amount of vacation time that I had before I quit. If not, I would have had to work my way up to this point again.

Thinking back, I wonder why the third dog was still on its feet. The only thing I can think of is that the other two must have beaten it to the meat every time. The one that attacked me was the smallest of the three. Either that, or it was on the other side of the house when I fired the meat into the back yard. This all could have turned out a lot worse. The animal could have caught me by the throat, which is where it would have bitten me if I hadn't managed to get my arm up in time. When I think of this, a shiver runs through me. It goes to show, yet again, that you can't plan for every contingency. This is a man who should have been removed many years ago, but I guess it's better late than never. It's four in the afternoon, so I decided to sit down and have an ice cold Corona. Some might not, but I think I deserve it.

Chapter 19

When I say the guys at work, I don't mean everybody, just the few I have a bit of a relationship with. These guys are nice and, once in a while, we go for a beer after work. I, of course, don't hang around with anybody too much because sooner or later something might slip out and suspicions will then be raised. I can't afford to have this happen, so I know that I can't have a normal life like the regular people of this world.

This is okay, though, because things don't work out for most of the people I have known and I wouldn't want anything happening to any more of them. Anyone that I have gotten too close to has been hurt. I am really glad this hasn't happened to Harry and Brenda because I could not bear to be indirectly responsible for some calamity striking their lives. Maybe I should keep my distance from them too for their wellbeing. I don't like this idea much because they are one of the facets in my life that help me feel at least somewhat normal. In this respect, I am a lucky man, despite all that has happened to me.

The garden in my backyard is doing well and, now and then, I see a deer in the greenbelt that runs behind the house. This is why I have the garden fenced off so they can't eat up the vegetables.

I do enjoy watching them when they come around, as they are one of the beautiful animals in the wild. Other animals I really like are horses. They are so majestic and run like the wind. Thinking about them, I make up my mind, then and there, to try my hand at horseback riding and look up some stables online. It's not cheap but then again there must be quite an investment in one of these animals. On Saturday morning, I call to arrange a riding lesson. When I get there, I find out how big they really are. Having never been up close to a horse before, it takes a few minutes to get used to it.

"What experience do you have?" Ben, the instructor, asks me. When he finds out that I have none, he blinks. "Why do you want to learn to ride?"

I tell him, "I think these animals are beautiful, and I've always wanted to learn but never gotten around to it."

"Okay, the first thing you need to do is to make friends with the horse." He smiles. "You also have let the horse know who is in charge. It works best for both of you if it isn't the horse."

Once the rules are established with the horse, we saddle her and start the lesson. Ben walks the horse around with me in the saddle for a few minutes and then hands me the reigns. He tells me how to make the horse do what I want inside the corral. It doesn't take long at all and I relax, guiding the horse where I want her to go.

"I've given you a mare because they're not as rambunctious as geldings or stallions. Every now and then the horse will give a little buck and if you're not ready for it, you could end up falling off. It's a long way to the ground," he warns me. "If this happens, you might have a hard time getting back on. The horse will run if you chase after it."

We go out on the trail and I even manage to miss most of the branches that come my way. We are out for about an hour, and I'm having a blast. We go at a slow trot and it takes a bit of getting used to because, at first, I am bouncing up and down so much I can hardly see. Ben tells me what I am doing wrong and shows me the proper way to absorb the shocks with my legs and time the ups and downs, which make it a whole lot easier.

"We'll leave the galloping for when you have a little more experience. It is a lot easier to fall off the horse at a gallop if it decides to turn when you're not expecting it," Ben tells me.

This makes sense, and we head back to the stables.

"Thanks, I really enjoyed this. I think that this is something I'm going to continue. I'd like to learn to saddle and unsaddle the horse too if that's all right?" I ask.

He seems pleased to hear this and tells me that most people can't be bothered learning this aspect of riding. They just want to get on and go.

Back home, I have a real feeling of accomplishment as I shower and get supper ready. Ben told me that I will probably be quite sore tomorrow morning from the riding. He said that most beginners are not in very good shape and find it difficult to get used to the first few times.

In the morning, I wake up expecting a bit of soreness but there is very little discomfort. Being in the shape I'm in has helped a lot. This reminds me that I wanted to go to the park and have a serious workout today. I have a light breakfast, pack a lunch, and head to a park with long trails, several ponds, and a few streams. I start things off with a nice jog, and I end up on the bank of a beautiful little lake well into the woods.

I listen to the sounds in the air. There are a few ducks in the water and birds in the trees. I'm just relaxing when a big splash scares the ducks and I hear a couple guys laughing. I look over. About a hundred feet away, there are three boys in their late teens throwing more rocks at some of the other ducks in the water.

"Hey, guys, is it necessary to try hurting the wildlife?" I ask the boys.

"Why don't you just screw off?" one yells back at me after he sees that I'm by myself.

They walk away and I am left by the water by myself. I take off the backpack and have a drink of water, enjoying the warm sun. There is a noise behind me and, when I turn, I see the three lads standing there, no real surprise.

"You should learn to mind your own business. We can do what we want, asshole," the leader of the group says to me.

He takes a step forward as he is talking, and I know exactly what he is going to do because of the way he is moving. His right hand comes at me straight out from his shoulder and, as it approaches, I step to the left.

As he is coming forward, I grab his arm and pull, forcing him past me. Because we are on a downward slope, he can do nothing to stop himself and, just to make things worse, I stick my foot out and trip him, sending him face first into the water.

I turn slightly sideways so I can keep an eye on him and his buddies at the same time. I look at the two standing there with their mouths hanging open. "Well, what now?" I say to them.

They look at me and shrug. I pick up my stuff and walk back to the trail toward my car. I guess the two were a little smarter than the one in the water. I pick up the pace and figure that I might as well get the rest of my workout done.

This has been an interesting week, including the distraction in the park. The horseback riding has been an experience that I want to partake of again. It's better than I thought it would be. I really like those animals, they are such graceful creatures.

I check online and see there is a story about the Nazi zealot and his demise. *The fire department and the police were called to the blazing home of the Heinrich Schmidt and found a deliberately set fire. The fire department arrived at the scene of the blaze before any of the surrounding forest caught fire. It has been determined that this has been an execution because the autopsy reveals Mister Schmidt has suffered a fatal gunshot wound to the head before the fire was started. It has also been determined that the fire was set in such a way as to allow the perpetrator of the crime time to make his getaway. The owner's dogs were also victims of the assassin's work and one was found floating in the water, well downstream of the property. No clues have been left behind by the murderer, and it is suspected that there will be no arrests in the near future. Further details will be released as they come to light.*

Aside from the abrasions I received from the dog, this has gone well and another evil person is dispensed with.

July Journal entry: *Despite the way things have worked out, I wonder sometimes if I am actually any better than the people I kill. I know the ones I deal with are guilty of horrible things and, with them gone, many other innocents are spared much pain and anguish. But I still wonder sometimes about this…*

Chapter 20

During the next week at work, we receive a new contract from a recreational vehicle manufacturer. There are several different parts that we will be making, and this keeps the shop humming. The general attitude around the shop is happy and, to celebrate things, the management has a barbeque for lunch midway in the week.

We normally have half an hour for lunch but today we get an hour. This is always a bonus and makes everybody even happier. There are sausages and burgers with potato salad, as well as salads and pop to drink. This keeps morale up for quite some time and shows the men that management appreciates their hard work. There is even dessert afterward before the guys go back to work. The rest of the week goes by that much better because of this kind gesture.

Thursday, Bill calls me and says that he has some of the information that I requested. He asks if I will be home Saturday morning, saying he will drop it off when I tell him that I'll be there.

In the morning, Bill comes by, and I offer him a coffee, which he turns down because he has a meeting that he has to attend at police headquarters. He opens a large manila envelope and takes out some papers and a large map of the United States. On the map are a series of Xs drawn at different points on a red line which has little arrows placed on it.

"The red line is a path that the investigating officers from several jurisdictions believe that Dennis Jackson has been following performing the robberies. The line starts a considerable distance before Rose Cottage in Napa Valley and continues well across the country. The sheets of paper give the time and location of suspected robberies Jackson has committed."

There are a few Xs that have been erased and I ask about them.

"These are spots that have been taken off the list for one reason or another. There have been several towns where the authorities had been notified as to the possibility of Jackson's possible future presence but, up to now, none of these have amounted to an apprehension," Bill says.

The path seems to be erratic, which appears to mean he picks new locations at random as the mood strikes him. I would like to strike him myself. Bill, of course, sees this in my facial expression.

"You need to keep this to yourself, all right? This can cause me a lot of problems because these actions are definitely against police policy," he lets me know.

"You don't have to be concerned with this. I know how to keep a secret," I tell Bill.

As soon as I say this, I realize that I have divulged something I maybe shouldn't have. Since we know some things about each other already, I try not to sweat it. I thank him after he tells me he will get me the information on any new developments as they occur and he leaves to go to his meeting.

Studying the map, I try to piece together the events pertaining to Jackson, looking for a pattern. I'm sure the police have already done this but I have a more personal interest in catching up with Dice Man than they do, so I might spot something they haven't. Hopefully, I may also be able to think a little more like Jackson than the police can and come up with a clue. After spending a few hours processing the information, I remember that I have to get to the horse stables for my next lesson.

I manage to get to the stable on time, dressed in jeans and a shirt, but no cowboy boots. They may be good around horses but I would feel silly wearing them anywhere else.

As promised, Ben takes the time to show me how to saddle and bridle the beast. This will take a little practice to do properly so the horse feels comfortable with me doing it. The saddle straps that go under the horse needs to be tight enough that the saddle and rider don't slip and end up under the horse. This is an exaggeration, of course, but you get the idea.

Once this is done, we go out on the trails, and Ben teaches me more about handling horses and what to expect in different situations.

"You should know that occasionally the horse will see something you don't and may turn unexpectedly. It may see a rock or a hole in the ground and the horse will suddenly change direction without any warning, so be ready for it," Ben tells me. "When this happens, if the rider is not paying attention, he may lose control or fall off the horse. This can actually spook the horse more and it may bolt, making it difficult to catch it and remount."

But today is not one of those days and the riding lesson is a pleasant one. We follow trails up slopes and through creeks, around bends, and through grassy fields with the sun shining down. A gentle breeze bends the longer grasses back and forth. I watch as some of these grasses are swayed when the gusts make their way across the meadow. You can follow where the wind is going by which areas are affected, interesting!

There is a hawk circling above, looking for a mouse or whatever it likes to eat. A murder of crows becomes noisy as we pass by under the trees they are congregating in. It is a relaxing afternoon and almost makes me wish I lived out on a ranch and could do this all the time. This, of course, is just a pipe dream and, like most things that you get too much of, it would be fun for a while but becomes common place and the novelty wear off soon enough. This is something that you would have to grow up doing to become a way of life.

As the afternoon ride comes to an end, we head back to the stable and Ben shows me the proper way to remove the saddle and bridle from the horse. He grabs a brush and gives the horse a rub down that helps the animal to relax and dries any sweat build up under the saddle. The horse seems to enjoy it enough and, afterward, I pay for the lesson.

"Is there a charge for the extras, like saddling and unsaddling the horse?" I ask.

"No, I'm happy that you are taking an interest in this aspect of riding. When you saddle and unsaddle the horse in the future then give it a rubdown, it will make things easier on me," Ben tells me. "Were you sore after the last ride?"

"I was actually only a tiny bit uncomfortable the next day and that went away quickly enough."

"Most people, because they're not in very good shape, are so stiff the next day that they can hardly move, so you must be in pretty good shape," he says.

I thank him for his help and am on my way back home, feeling pretty good.

Harry calls later that evening and says that he was just wondering how I am doing.

"Can we can talk Sunday afternoon," he asks me.

"Of course, how about you come over sometime around two o'clock?" I suggest after a second.

"All right, that's great, thanks, Joseph."

The rest of the evening I spend going over the map and reports. I look at where the robberies took place. What type of businesses they are, as well as what time of day it is. What the sizes of the towns are and the areas where the crimes take place. How much money is taken. What the time interval is between robberies. Is he alone or is there a second man involved? What kind of vehicle is driven by the suspect? How many people are hurt and how they are hurt? I write down and categorize everything that I can, looking for any pattern that I might be able to find.

The red line doesn't appear to be following any obvious pre-planned route but does stick to smaller towns that could be thought of as weekend getaway spots. I imagine this may be because the police forces in these places are considerably smaller than they are in the larger cities. This way, a real organized effort can't be made quickly, allowing Dice Man time to leave the area unhindered.

I need to get updated reports as they are available, in order to anticipate Jackson's next move. There will always be several possibilities and so I may have to wait for a time when the targets are limited to as few as possible. I try to figure out how long the money lasts him so I might be able to ascertain when he will strike again.

I have a prison photo of him but it is suspected that he has attempted to alter his appearance as much as he can. I know I would if I was him. So I study the picture and I get some copies made and start making changes that seem most obvious to me so, if I ever get on his tail, I will have a chance of recognizing him. I compare these with a couple of police sketches as described by victims.

Harry comes over the next day and we go to the backyard and have a beer together. After the chit chat is done, I ask him what is on his mind.

"I hate to mention this but I just don't know what to do. Eva met some guy at the mall who is about five years older than she is. He has been phoning over and over, trying to talk her into meeting him at various places. She has refused and asked him to leave her alone, but he continues to call, almost harassing her," Harry tells me.

Eva is growing up to be an attractive young lady. She understands that the young man's behavior is not as it should be. You can't force someone to go places with you if they do not wish to and, no, does mean no. It doesn't mean keep bugging the person until they agree.

"I don't know how to handle this situation," Harry continues. "The boy hangs up whenever I get on the phone. I've called the police and they've told me that there is nothing that they can do about it until an offense has been committed."

"Do you have a name and picture of the kid?" I ask.

He pulls out an envelope from his pocket. He has come prepared.

"I'll see what I can do about it. Do me a favor and don't ask any questions about how this is handled, all right?" I tell him.

A look of relief comes over his face and I see that this has really had an adverse effect on him. I am not a parent but I really like this family and won't tolerate anyone causing them problems.

"Just out of curiosity, why did you pick me?

"There has always been an air about you that indicated you aren't someone to be trifled with. Besides, you're the only person I could turn to, so here I am," he informs me.

I guess I can live with that. We say our goodbyes and I look at the photo and check out the address Harry has written down. Where he got the picture from I don't know and really don't care. All that matters is that I have it. Where the kid lives is in an area of town that is known to be a rather unsavory place that has a reputation for drug deals. I suspect that Joey Mandol has a plan for Eva that is not conducive to her happiness.

I take a disguise with me, as well as the nun chucks and my knife, which is tucked away but handy. I go to the address and do a drive by. I don't see him around so I suspect he may be in a spot where drugs might be sold. It takes a while driving around different streets but I finally spot him in a group of people that look like trouble. Before I left home, I had a little work out just to limber up, in case I ran into him, and it now seems that it might have been a good idea.

There are four guys there, all around twenty years old, give or take a year or two, and they seem to be having a good time. Everyone who passes them gives them a wide berth, trying not to draw their attention. The odd person does make direct contact with Joey. A quick exchange is made and they are gone. I decide to get this over with as soon as possible so I put the binoculars down and park the car a few streets away. With my toys in position, I walk back in their direction. I stop at a place across the street and wait to watch the group. There is an alley near me and I plan to use this to my advantage.

I stand there, just watching the group, making it obvious that I am there to see what they are doing. It doesn't take long before they notice me, and they start discussing the funny looking character across the street.

Joey, who seems to be the leader, yells at me asking what the hell I think I am looking at. I give him the finger and walk toward the alley. This is not something these guys want to tolerate, and they start crossing the road, swearing at a driver who has the audacity to honk at them. I walk to the back of the alley, knowing in advance that there is no way out and I'm sure that they know this too.

It doesn't take long and the four of them enter the alley and position themselves in a way that allows me no exit. Joey has a real smirk on his face. He's about six feet tall with a rugged build. His friends are, for the most part, a little less impressive, but look like they'd be trouble for the average guy.

"You just made the biggest mistake of your life, asshole," he says.

"Oh, really? You going to teach me a lesson by yourself or do you need the whole group to keep you safe?" I ask.

A few curse words and he starts forward and, as he comes toward me, I see him gesture for the rest to join in. They come at me quickly, as one group, with Joey in the lead.

As they get near, I bring out the nun chucks and lay out

Joey with a quick flick of the wrist. It happens so fast that it catches the bunch completely off guard.

They only hesitate for a moment and pull knives as I jump back and forth giving them little to lash out at. One by one, they go down, being struck by a kick, a fist, or the swinging piece of hardwood. The last one standing turns to make a run for it but, alas, too late. Crack and down he goes. These boys are obviously not used to anyone who knows how to defend himself.

As the last one falls, I grab them one by one and dump them in a pile at the end of the alley. I make sure to stack them in very embarrassing positions and go back to Joey. I take the knife out of his pocket and open it. It's not as sharp as I would have expected it to be so I put it aside. I put away the nun chucks and bring out my own knife. I have him propped against the wall and give him a few good slaps across the face. I made sure not to hit him too hard so he wouldn't be out for long.

As he comes around, he realizes what has happened and a look of concern crosses his face. I give him a demonstration of what a really sharp knife can do by shredding his clothes. I look him in the eye with the coldest most threatening look I can give him.

"I have a message for you. Do not ever call or contact Eva in any other way, ever again. If you do, you will be seeing me again and you won't like what happens." I say this to him very slowly, looking him in the eye.

Just to reinforce that thought, I pick up his knife with a rag in my hand and slowly bury it to the hilt in his thigh, holding my hand over his mouth to stifle the scream.

I place the point of my knife against his chest where his heart is. When he has enough composure to hear what I'm saying, I tell him, "If I have to come back, I'll push my knife into your heart, understand?"

He nods quickly.

I believe that I have made my point. I am sure his intent was to get Eva hooked on drugs and then pimp her out.

This, of course, will not be tolerated, hence the drastic actions on my part. I let him know that any of the other girls he is trying this with have to be left alone too. I'm sure there would be several others.

I call Harry when I get back home and tell him things have been dealt with. "I don't think there will be any further calls, but if there are, let me know immediately."

He thanks me profusely and I know he wants to ask what happened but he doesn't. So, with a feeling of satisfaction, I call it a weekend and go to bed. It is surprising how this kind of activity can lighten your mood. I really am cut out for community work.

At work the next day, there is a problem with a department that produces clutch rods. These are steel rods made from three-eighths inch round bar cut to a specific length, depending on the application. They have a three-eighths fine thread put on each end of the rods. One end has a left-hand thread and the other has a right-hand thread. This allows adjustments to be made on the linkage without removing any connections. The length of the rod and thread applied depends on which vehicle it is used on.

The problem is that the size of the thread is critical as the rods, when completed, are zinc coated which increases the size of the thread. If the threads are slightly oversize when they are machined on in a lathe with a threading head attached, it causes a problem. Even though you can get the nut on easily it is too big when the coating is applied and then the nut goes on too tightly and has to be forced. I am sent over to the threading department and asked to see if I can fix the problem. The man named Frank that is usually there is quite competent at this job. Unfortunately, a relief worker has had to take over while Frank is helping in maintenance. I have worked with Frank in the past and always enjoyed his company.

When I get there, I see Luke is standing by the lathe, waiting for me. Luke is an okay guy but not terribly good at this type of work. Some people you can teach easily and

others have a harder time learning to do slightly complicat-
ed jobs correctly. I take a look at Luke's last few rods and
notice that the threads are very rough. This means that the
threading inserts in the head have a chip on the leading edge
that cuts the threads. The first thing that needs to be done is
to replace these with fresh ones.

I show him how to do this the right way and then how to
reset the sizing aspect of the job. The depth stop now has to
be reset also so that the thread is the proper length. When
this is done and a few slight adjustments are made, I show
Luke how to measure the finished product in order to get a
good part. I get him to make a few parts and then have him
call quality control to get the work approved.

This done, I am free to go do my own work. I don't mind
teaching someone how to do these jobs but this guy is more
difficult to teach than most. I doubt that he will be here
much longer, but then again who knows?

I prefer machining some of the jobs for the pipe handling
units for the oil rigs more than many of the jobs that come
my way. Some of the guys don't always like doing this
work because they have to deal with the supervisor of that
department. I actually don't mind Kevin, as we have set the
boundaries in our relationship long ago. We know where we
stand with each other and don't cross these lines. We actually have some nice conversations when he is in a good
mood, which sometimes is not the case. Of course, with
some of the men under him, he can become somewhat offensive and so they don't always care for the man. I even
like to set up and run the presses now and then. It is a job
that sometimes allows you to go on autopilot. You need to
be aware of what is going on but not intensely so.

The week goes by and it is Friday late afternoon and I
finish my grocery shopping, heading to my car. A homeless
man is sitting on the grass at the exit of the parking lot. He
has a little handmade sign asking for spare change. I have a
few bucks but don't give it to him. Instead, I ask if he wants
a bun to eat. He asks if I have butter or something to put on

it. I am slightly taken aback by this question. I would have thought that if a person is hungry it wouldn't matter, but I guess I have run into a fussy homeless man. I just drive away and leave him there. I, myself, don't mind a bun by itself, but this guy seems like he is just asking for help because it is the easy way to get money. I really don't have any use for people like him. I actually do like helping people who need and want help, but not this type.

Because it is Friday and I am going to horse around tomorrow—literally!—I decide to go out to the park and have a good run and workout. I tidy things up, grab a bottle of water, and head for Baskette Slough Refuge. This is one of my favorite places. It reminds me of the times I had with Jack Peters the old man who befriended me. I still think about him now and then, getting angry at his untimely violent death. I try to put this out of my mind and start at a brisk pace on the run.

It's funny how a place as beautiful as this can stir up such feelings of anger. As usual, I stop at the small lake and stand on the shore, feeling the gentle breeze blow my troubles away. The sun is warm and the ducks are having a good time, like they always do. I think about Ellen Prescotte, the young blonde grade school teacher who taught at Garfield Elementary. She almost met with a horrible death at the hands of Jake Patterson, Beth Peters's murderer. She was a very pretty girl and, under other circumstances, I might have been attracted to her. She, of course, couldn't hold a candle to Kathleen, but then again, I have never seen a woman who could.

This line of thought is starting to depress me so I get myself moving and really push myself in order to get my mind back on track. Finishing up the run, I cool down for a few minutes and head home. It's such a nice day that I figure I'll defrost a steak that I got from a private farm that is allowed to butcher their own grass-fed cattle.

The big thing nowadays is the hype about grain fed cattle and how great the meat is supposed to be. What most people don't know or realize is that cattle are not grain-eating animals. They are grass eaters. Grain is not their natural food and is given to them to fatten them up far quicker than they would normally. This makes the meat far less healthy for a person than from grass fed cattle. Plus, all the antibiotics and hormones given to them really have an adverse effect on the consumer's health. Just take a look around at the size of people today and the point becomes obvious. I blame the problem more on our government and the greedy unconcerned corporations than the consumer. But you do need to educate yourself or you get taken advantage of.

Again, I need to get back on track and deal with things that I can change and not the things that I can't. The steak and potato are cooked and the salad without too much dressing is eaten. The steak is not quite as tender as some of the expensive store bought ones but tastes like a steak should. This being done and having a small piece of cherry pie, I wash the dishes and once again nothing is broken. I am getting fairly good at this. There was a time when I would break or crack something every time I washed things up. I spent a fair bit of money replacing dishes and glasses in my career. It also pays to buy better quality items, as they are more durable.

As I am getting down to studying the map and crime reports, the phone rings. Call display tells me that it is Harry. I answer and he asks me to come over for dinner tomorrow evening. I tell him his thanks are enough but he says he and Brenda want me to come by for a meal with their family in appreciation. I accept the invitation and then get back to my work.

I find a few more items of interest with respect to Jackson during the course of the evening. I think that I just might be on the right track and possibly one step closer to finding a pattern. There is nothing definite yet but I feel that I'm getting somewhere. Saturday, I'm at the ranch again, enjoying the lesson and building a bond with Ben and the horses that I ride. After tidying up, I get ready to go to Harry and Brenda's.

As I walk up to the house, Eva comes running out and gives me the biggest hug she can and kisses me on the cheek. "There have been no more calls and I'm so relieved. I was really afraid of this guy and didn't know what to do," she tells me.

"No problem, I'm just glad that I was able to help you out," I say in return.

With this, we head to the house and Brenda repeats Eva's performance.

"How did you convince the kid to stop calling?" she asks me.

I just shrug and decline to answer. Harry tells her not to ask anymore and whispers, sorry. I don't think they would have much sympathy for Joey but I don't want them to know this side of me.

We sit in the living room and Harry brings me a Corona, nice and cold, just the way I like it. The kids are asked to go get something and Harry and Brenda tell me how much they appreciate my help. I tell them that I would never allow anyone to hurt them if there was anything I could do about it, and I leave it at that.

The kids come in carrying a gift-wrapped box and put it on the floor in front of me. They look up and smile, grinning from ear to ear.

"This isn't necessary," I tell them

"Yes, it is, why don't you open the gift, Joseph?" Brenda says with a smile on her face.

I do this and see an ultimate barbecue kit with all the extras. Inside the box is a gift certificate for the butcher where I get my meat from.

"This is great," I say

I am delighted by this thoughtful gift and get a tear in my eye. Crap, am I beginning to be a bit of a softie? These people have come to mean so much to me and this is again embarrassing because real men don't cry. Shit! I wish this didn't happen. The only one who is just a little off is Gord. He smiles enough but there seems to be more of a change in him. Maybe he's just getting older and this is causing changes in his behavior.

Brenda goes to the kitchen to check on dinner and, a few minutes later, we are seated at the table, enjoying a wonderful lasagna dinner. Brenda knows this is another one of my favorites and cooks it to perfection.

Lord help anyone that hurts these people, I vow mentally. I know what will happen if anyone does, and I quickly get rid of these thoughts because I am too easy to read when I have this stuff going through my head. The evening is as pleasant as any I have had and, as I am ready to leave, I thank them all for being my friends and get out the door before I embarrass myself again.

This night, I sleep very soundly with no nightmares or unpleasant things interrupting the night, which is nice since all-too-often I have disturbing dreams. The next day, I go online to see if Joey and his buddies are in the news but find nothing. I didn't think that they would go to the police because even they aren't dumb enough to want to draw attention to themselves. There are no new developments as far as Heinrich Schmidt is concerned either, which is good news for me. His dog was found many miles downstream but this offers the police no clues because there are no wounds or marks of any kind found on the canine. So once again it looks as if I am in the clear.

As time passes, Bill periodically drops off new information, which helps me form more and more of a pattern. I feel I am getting closer and closer to predicting where he will strike next. I have been able to predict within three to four small towns where he will strike next. When I can get this down to two, I will be going on the hunt to see if I can draw a bead on him.

His description is getting better all the time and, although there aren't any clear pictures of him, the police sketch artists are drawing him pretty much the way I have envisioned him. The anger at this point threatens to boil over again and I need to get a distraction real quick. Despite all the time that has passed, I still flare up over this man. I go to the garage and have a workout so hard that I am drained by the time I am finished. It surprises me how close I still get to losing control periodically. The thought of someone having this kind of effect on me is disturbing. I have gone through so much in my life, you would think that I'd be able to control myself better by now. Isn't that what counseling was for?

I know that it will be my downfall if I let this happen when I am closing in on Jackson. He hasn't been out of reach of the law this long for no reason. He must be smart and resourceful and probably unpredictable, like Jake Patterson was. Maybe he has that animal instinct in him too that allows him to sense when he is in danger. Jake almost clobbered me with a club because of this instinct, and I can't allow anything like this to happen again. I have to, no matter what, find and take out Kathleen's murderer. This is what has given me a purpose for living. Although lately, there have been other things that have kept me going. I think that I am going to have to find an outlet again soon. The satisfaction Joey and the boys brought me is starting to wear off. Time to go online again.

Chapter 21

I've found several potential targets online. A couple of them, unfortunately, are a little close to home. I don't like dealing with people that live in or near Salem. I feel somewhat vulnerable doing things here, so the choice I make will have to be elsewhere.

There are the big cross-border drug dealers who bring in large shipments from Mexico that I would love to dispose of, but I think this operation may be beyond me. They are too well organized and have huge firepower, and I hear they like to hire ex-mercenaries to do their dirty work. These guys are professionals and are maybe a bit too much for me.

I have been bothered by the constant offenses of a slum-lord in San Francisco. He has been charged several times with offenses that have caused death and severe injuries to many of the tenants in neglected buildings that he owns. He never seems to be imprisoned. He is only fined and left free to continue his life.

There is also a pimp in Seattle who has been charged with the beatings of several girls that tried to start new lives and get out of the trade. He got off, due to technicalities and insufficient evidence. Also worth a look is a coach who has been charged with the sexual molesting of young hockey players in his charge.

It's a good thing I'm not one of the parents.

There is a story that pops up in the news about priests that continually molest the young boys who are entrusted to them. This is something that irritates the shit out of me. These men are supposed to be above this kind of thing and preach about salvation, and yet they are allowed to continually abuse these boys.

The Catholic Church is the largest in the world and the governing body, in my opinion, has done little to correct this obscene practice. How can it be allowed to have so many young lives ruined and have no one really be held accountable? It is a crime that is supposed to be punishable by imprisonment for anyone else, but this doesn't happen to the priests at all.

This affair has been swept under the carpet for so long and angers me to the point that I want to do something about it. The general public seldom hears who the offending priests are. The only thing that stops me from doing something is the fact that there are certain things that go against the grain of everything a person learns as they are growing up. Killing a priest is one of them. So, for now, I will have to refrain from that. Maybe I could remove the offending organ on the priest instead. *Hmm, something to think about.*

I think maybe the pimp should be my next visit. I hate it when someone beats on defenseless people. I start doing some surveillance on Adam Broadman after I learn as much as I can online. Seattle isn't too far away and I can drive it in about three and a half hours.

I've learned that he drives a fancy car that he likes to show off now and then. He periodically enters it in car shows. It's a 1938 Chevrolet Street Rod and must be quite a sight when he checks on his girls, driving this thing. His girls, like he owns them, yeah right! The car is a beautiful red with off yellow stripes running down the side. I think it is worth about thirty-five thousand. It's not a rare car but still pretty impressive, except for the fact that this sleaze ball owns it. He must think he is someone who should be noticed, even though he is nothing but a stinking pimp.

I've found out where he lives and see through Google that the garage he keeps the car in has a remote control operated multi-sectioned door that goes up on tracks over the car. I am thinking of having a bit of fun with this guy before I actually deal with him. I need to do something to lighten things up for me. I seem to have taken everything so seriously for a long time with these types. I am going to see if this guy will change if I take another approach to dealing with him.

I don't see any cameras on the outside of his house when I do a little surveillance. I am sure he will have a security system installed inside the house, though. He lives in a house with a small wall around the perimeter and a two car garage that has two doors. The top of the doors have several small windows in them so I will be able to look inside. The only time I saw either of the doors open it was the one closest to the front door. This is where he parked his everyday car and, being where I was, I could glimpse the street rod on the other side.

After a couple of weekends of keeping an eye on Adam the pimp, I decide on how to make his life a bit less enjoyable. How this guy would be tolerated in this fairly pleasant neighborhood is a bit of a surprise. The people living near him can't possibly approve of his lifestyle. But then again, when I have seen anyone around as he comes home, they seem to turn their back on him and go inside.

I imagine that if something were to happen to Adam, they would not be overly sympathetic toward him. So I get together the items that I will require for my little escapade, as well as a couple of my toys, and head out on Friday after work.

I made a little device at work this week that will come in handy. Adam is, so far as I have seen in the past, always out till late, keeping an eye on the girls working for him. I was planning to do the job while he was home but have decided to take care of it while he is out so that he won't be able to do anything to stop what I have planned to do. I wait till everyone in the neighborhood is long asleep at about one in the morning. Adam doesn't get back on the times I have watched him, till about three, so this should give me plenty of time.

The houses on either side of his are a fair distance away, so my plan shouldn't endanger them much. I sit in my rental car down the street and wait. When all has been quiet for a long time, I grab hold of the things I need, as well as my knife and pistol. Disguised in old clothes and a ball cap, I carry the stuff with me, sticking to the shadows and keeping a wary eye out.

The dog spray is handy, in case I need it for a dog or some other pest. There is a fair bit of cover all the way to the driveway and along the edge of the driveway toward the house. Taking hold of my flashlight and, after looking around to make sure it is safe, I shine the light in through the little window at the top of the garage door. The Street Rod is there and out goes the light.

The tool I made at work slides under the door. It is made from a piece of quarter-inch-thick steel plate with a thirty-degree bend in it, about two and a half inches from the end. The rest is about a foot long and gives it a lot of leverage so the door is raised about an inch easily when I step on the long end. This is all I need to do what I have come here for.

There is just enough flex in the door mechanism to allow this movement. I tried this on a door before I came here so I knew there wouldn't be a problem doing this. I brought with me a large flexible plastic container, the type you get in boxes of wine, only bigger and a lot stronger. I attached a five-foot length of garden hose screwed on to the spout, securing it with construction adhesive and hose clamps so it wouldn't leak. I did this after I filled the container with a mixture of oil and gasoline.

Sliding the hose under the door as far as possible, I then step on the container which is lying on its side. The mixture is forced out through the hose flooding the garage floor under the car. When the container is pretty well empty, I grab another smaller container and do the same thing, only this one has straight gasoline in it. The reason for the second container is that I want it to ignite easily, as the oil and gasoline mixture sometimes is a little harder to set on fire.

When all is ready, I move the empty containers away from the door and check to make sure I am not standing in any of the gas. The concrete around the tool is saturated so I pull it out and move it over. Because the bottom of the door is against the concrete I cannot ignite the gasoline from outside so I brought a long nose barbecue lighter with me which I slide under the door and, after a quick look around, pull the trigger. The gas lights up and the flames spread inside the garage under the car.

I grab most of my things and run like hell, sticking to the shadows as much as I can. I have left the trunk undone but down and toss everything in on a plastic sheet and close it. Jumping in the car, I drive away, being careful not to draw attention to myself by driving too fast.

I go to a phone booth I spotted earlier and call the fire department after I see the blaze is well underway. The only thing I really want destroyed is the car. I left one empty container so it would be obvious that the car was targeted. I hear the sirens in the distance and head back to the room I rented. I'm sure that Adam the pimp won't be happy about what has happened to his car. I wonder if he has insurance on it, I kind of hope he doesn't so this will then piss him off even more.

The next morning, I take the rental car back and head home. I was thinking of taking care of Adam the next weekend but I am sure he will be somewhat on his guard so I'll wait a while. I just hope he doesn't take it out on the girls. I don't think this will be the case because I left a little note which I tied to a rock and threw through his window at the other end of the house as I was leaving. No fingerprints were on anything that I left behind because I wore latex gloves at all times when I worked on the items.

The note only had six words on it. *I'm coming back for YOU soon.* I'm sure he'll know exactly what the note means after what happened to his prize automobile. Having nothing happen for a couple of weeks should fray his nerves a bit. I have a feeling of satisfaction as I drive home. On the way back, I have an idea come into my head about what I can do next time to Adam.

At home, I go over the information I have on Dice Man and his activities. Online, I see if there have been any more robberies in any of the towns I suspect might be hit by him. There is nothing new so I am going to have to wait for his next move, in order to make plans to intercept him sometime in the future. Spending a little time on the guitar helps me relax and have a bit of enjoyment.

The weather is cooling down at night and the growing season is almost over. I go to the garden and make plans for what I'll do with the things I have left. I've really enjoyed having a garden and, when I'm working out here, time just slides by and the problems of the world don't seem as bad.

Later, I settle down with another book by Isaac Asimov. This one is the next book after *Caves of Steel* and is titled *The Naked Sun.* I also have the following one, *The Robots of Dawn.* I have only just started it and already I wish I could be there. What I wouldn't do to forsake this existence here for a life in the far off future. Maybe it is the sign of an absolutely fantastic writer when he can have this effect on his readers.

I knew it was going to happen sooner or later. The kid named Luke who works on the clutch rods has sent out a bunch of work that does not conform to the prints. A lot of rods have been sent back to the shop and the management has received a call, informing them that this can no longer be tolerated. If it happens again, the contract will be given to another supplier.

The company has no option but to terminate Luke's employment and train a new employee. Frank has been asked to take over the operation in that department for the time being. It is too bad for Luke but he was warned several times and now has to look for another job.

Frank isn't happy about this and Don Winters head of maintenance will be short-handed for a while. Don, though, is a very capable man and will be all right. Besides, he can always call on Gerry who is the head of Tool and Die to give him a hand. Gerry has more experience in these areas than anyone I have ever seen. I sometimes think that there is very little that he can't do. I periodically need Gerry's help and he invariably has an answer to my problem, not always but almost. Don is pretty much the same way. I like the guys I work with at this shop and get along with most everyone.

About a month has gone by and I am sure that Adam Broadman must be starting to feel safe again. I hear online that he is still no better with the girls, though. I head out on a Friday after work, getting to Seattle in good time, and check into a room at a motel not too far from where pimper boy lives. Renting a car that blends in, I take a couple of toys with me. I'm thinking it'll be a good idea to harass him once more, just to make his life miserable.

I wait until late and drive to a spot down the road from where he lives. If all goes well, he should get home at his usual time, which is around three in the morning. I'll be waiting in the bushes near his house across the street with a clear view of him as he parks in the garage and gets out of his car to go into the house.

He has up to this point never closed the garage door from inside his car. He has needed to walk around the back of his car and outside his garage because there is not enough room between his car and the closed door. When the time approaches for me I position myself, I'm back in the shadows, when the way is clear, and station myself so I can take advantage of the opportunity if presented.

As I approach the house, I realize that he won't be parking in the garage. The doorway openings are still boarded up from the damage caused by the fire. I would have thought this would already have been repaired. Maybe the insurance company has delayed the payout because of arson. It's possible they suspect him of lighting the place up himself and are investigating him thoroughly. Oh well, too bad for him. This makes it easier for me, as he will be an easier target for what I have in mind.

I wait and wait as the neighborhood slowly quiets down and everyone has long since gone to bed. Finally, he drives into his driveway and parks. His music is booming inside the closed windows for a minute and stops as he opens the door. People here must just love this inconsiderate bastard.

He gets out of the car and, as he closes the door with a slam, I raise the tranquilizer dart gun and sight down the rifle barrel. As he comes around the back of the car and heads toward the front door, I shoot and the dart hits him right in the ass. He screams and jumps as he reaches behind him, trying to grab what has just bit him.

The rifle is gas powered so there is no noise to disturb the neighbors. The only noise is Adam as he tries to make it to the front door. He gets there but, before he can open the door and get into the house, he collapses in a heap, unable to move as he loses consciousness.

I wait for a while to see if anyone around looks to see what the commotion is about. Nobody has taken any notice at all. He must always come home and make a racket the way he did before I shot him, so no one cares about it anymore.

When I'm sure there is no one watching, I cross the street and go to the front door, kneeling beside him. I pick up the dart that he managed to pull out and put it away. I drag him to the back yard and tie him up nice and tight with his arms strapped to his sides under a large tree.

Throwing a strong rope over a large branch, I tie it around his chest and under his armpits with the knot at the back. Lifting him up and tightening the rope over the branch suspending him in the air, I tie it off. I take two of those dog anchors that screw into the ground and place them in position. I fasten each leg to one of the anchors, thus holding him facing the street. When he awakes, he will be very uncomfortable but not seriously hurt.

At this time, I undo his belt, lower his pants and underwear then use my knife to cut the pants and underwear completely off. Taking off my backpack and opening it, I take out a zip tie and tighten it around his "banana." This done, I reach into the pack again, pull out a can of black undercoating spray, and give his genitals a good coating. This stuff is like tar and will be fairly difficult to get off.

With him tied up and hanging from the tree, he'll have to call out to the people he has irritated for help. Who knows? Maybe someone will call the police for him. With any luck, he's been drinking a lot and will have to relieve himself soon but with the zip tie so tight, he won't be able to.

I leave him exposed and facing the street as I gather my things. I could have killed him but thought this humiliation would be enough for now. As far as I know he hasn't killed anyone, so this may make him rethink things.

If he is in the news again, a more permanent solution will be presented to him. I reach into the backpack and pull out a note explaining this and the fact that he should get out of the business. With the latex gloves still on, I put the note in his wallet, so there won't be any chance of him losing it, and hightail it out of there.

The next morning finds me on my way back home. Sunday, I go and tend my garden with a smile on my face. I have watched the news and seen a story about a suspected pimp hanging in a tree. It seems one of his neighbors took a video of the incident, with Adam carrying on and struggling before the authorities got there, and put it online for the entire world to see. It has since gone viral. Now everyone knows his face and what happened to him. A reporter was sent to his home after he was released from the hospital to find out what happened to Adam Broadman. Unfortunately, Mr. Broadman refused to open the door and asked to be left alone. Gosh, what a shame.

Chapter 22

Almost every Saturday morning, I have been going for a horseback riding lesson, and I am now good enough to go out on my own. As much as I like having Ben along, it is really pleasant riding where I want to and going at my own pace.

It's so warm and sunny out that I stay out longer than normal. I listen to a stream as the water tumbles over rocks and the birds sing in the trees along the bank. The horse and I get along well and, if I was in a better position, I would consider buying a horse of my own and keeping it at the stables. Unfortunately, I never know where my path in life will lead me.

Sitting on the bank of the stream, basking in the sunlight, I lean my back against an old maple tree. Sitting there for a few minutes, I think of nothing at all. My mind goes blank as I enjoy this time. The horse snorts and brings me back and, at moments like this, I feel at peace. I wish that the rest of my life was like this, but alas it is not to be.

This evening, after Bill has given me more updates on Jackson, I go over the new information and add it to the file. He has hit two more small businesses. One is a small owner-operated motel with four units and the other is a B and B on the edge of a small town.

After the horse riding, I go to the mall and buy one of those large maps of the continental United States. It is six feet wide and four feet high. I have a left over sheet of plywood downstairs and have a frame made to hold it up so I can pin the map to it. I'm going to write on little Post-it notes, and stick them to the route marked in red that Jackson has taken during his trek around the country.

This map shows a lot of the small towns and will give me a way to get a better idea of how to track him. I've bought a box of those colored pins used in offices and use different colors to indicate the patterns that are developing. I mark these on the map and try to plan what his next move will be and when he will strike approximately. The latest B and B that he hit is in one of the towns I thought might be on his route and I try to guess what places to add to the list of the next group of towns.

Standing back, I take a look at the map and notice that there a couple of spots that take an erratic turn. He seems to go in a direction at times that doesn't make sense. You would almost think that he makes some decisions on a roll of the dice or he does this to play it safe. I can't see anyone doing something like this unless it is for that purpose. It's all a waiting game, but I feel that I am getting a little closer all the time. I want very badly to get hold of him but know that I will have to keep my head clear in order to catch up with this guy.

I watched the news last night and saw a story about the arrest of a middle aged man who had been accused of molesting his eleven-year-old daughter. He claims he is innocent but the evidence is telling another story. An older daughter who had moved out several years ago backed up the accusations being made by the young girl. When asked by the police why the older daughter left the younger one without reporting the father, she said that she had talked to the police but nothing was ever done about it.

I cannot, for the life of me, understand how a man can do this to his own child. I have an even harder time understanding how a man can be drawn to such a young girl. If he gets out of this mess, I will be seeing him. I may not kill him but he will never be able to sexually abuse anyone again when I am finished with him. I have a difficult time sleeping this night, as I keep having visions of this despicable human being in my head. What a horrible world we live in. How can a girl who has something like this happen to her, live a normal life? Yes, I will be seeing this guy if he gets off.

After a couple of weeks, the story resurfaces, and I hear on the news that the man who molested his kids is actually going to prison. Finally, something is done the way it should be. This guy is going to have a horrible time being incarcerated, as many inmates take a dim view of this type of crime. They themselves are fathers too and will undoubtedly exact payment on behalf of the kids. This at least makes me feel a lot better.

One of the brake press operators named Mike has himself a ponytail and is now and then made fun of about it but he is a real nice guy. The press is used to bend the material to specific angles consistently. He comes over to my department now and then, and we chat about all kinds of stuff. He plays guitar. He is way better than I am and offers me advice about guitars when I need it. He's a real fan of Schechter guitars, and I like Fenders, but he doesn't hold this against me.

This day, he asks if I have the time to make him a set of alignment guides for his machine. I ask him to draw out what he requires. He does this and, because I am not real busy, I go outside, grab the material, and cut off what I need. I do all the machining in short order and bring him the finished pieces. He can't thank me enough and lets me know that he owes me one. I like helping the guys out because I quite often require their services to complete my little projects too.

I have, on occasion been, caught by one of the supervisors doing a personal job and been asked what I am working on. When I say to them "Ask me no questions, and I'll tell you no lies" they understand and don't bother me.

I work hard on all the jobs given me and my scrap rate is extremely low, so they just consider this a perk for me. I, of course, try not to abuse it and, besides, I do some personal work for them periodically too. I can honestly say that, aside from the horrible things that have happened in my personal life, I really enjoy the type of jobs I do. I get a wide variety of work all over the shop and most of the guys are great to be around.

The Klan is in the news again and is suspected in the death of an entire family when their home was burned down. They moved down from New York City and made the mistake of buying a home in a white neighborhood. In New York, the racism is not like it is in the Southern states and so the folks had no idea what they were getting themselves into. Either that, or maybe they thought that they might be treated as they were up north. How this way of thinking ever got like this is a mystery to me. You would think that this insanity would have been left back in the eighteen hundreds. I believe that my next visitation is going to be down in Dixie.

It's no longer the oppressively hot and humid time in Alabama, so I am going to start making plans. It looks like my destination is just outside Mobile on the north side of the city. Through a fair bit of painstaking research, I find out that there is a good size event planned for next month. A man by the name of Benjamin Norwood a longstanding member of the Klan whose father and Grandfather were part of the ruling class of the Klan, is hosting the meeting.

From what I can ascertain by way of Citizens Discussing Crime, Seeking Justice, V-anonymous, and Crime Everywhere, this is to be a full dressed meeting where everyone is to be in their garb. There is to be special entertainment provided on the last evening when the full dress code is to be applied.

The only thing is that the site of the last evening is to be revealed only on the second-to-last night. I am certain that the person who has relayed this information must be a Klan member. The information is not readily obtained by everyone who goes online, and the only reason I manage to get it is that I have had to reveal things about myself and things I have done to a number of core members. I don't like having to do this but it is the only way I can access some of the more secretive information.

This gives me an idea which could gain me access to the meeting itself on the last night if I can find out where that location is. I'm not sure why the last evening would require wearing their hoods and gowns, so I plan to attend fully prepared.

I Google an aerial view of the property where all but the last meeting are to take place, and I plan to fly out there on a weekend to do some reconnaissance, so I know the layout, from firsthand experience. I have dealt with the Klan once before and heard the speeches made by their leaders. I found the members to be a particularly vile group of people. I cannot see how anyone who professes to be a Christian can follow the Klan's teachings. It goes against everything that Christianity is supposed to stand for.

Benjamin lives in a beautiful home at the end of Bayou Road near an area called Creola. The property is off by itself and has the Tensaw River running behind it along the back edge of the acreage. There is an expanse of lawn and a lot of trees in groups as well as large individual trees. This place should be fairly accessible once it starts to get dark.

Benjamin, it appears, owns a rather large construction company. He has a lot of connections in politics and a fair bit of influence in what goes on in the district he resides in. There is even a photograph of Benjamin with the Governor of Alabama. I doubt, of course, that the governor would be part of a group like this. The photo could be one that many a politician would pose for with a great many people he would hardly know, at least I hope so.

As I make my plans, I start dropping hints at work about

taking a holiday soon. I book a flight to Mobile for the coming Friday after work. I finish up little projects whenever possible as the week goes by. In preparation, I pick up little items that I may require for my upcoming time at the meeting. Then I gather some flexible plastic tubing and two soft flat rubber bottles that hold about a cup of fluid each. Finally I check online for materials that I can use and go about obtaining some. I think I'll go about this venture a little differently than the way I did last time I had an encounter with the Klan.

Catching my flight, I land at an airport outside Mobile, Alabama. Having reserved a rental car ahead of time with my credit card and driver's license that have been purchased long ago for this purpose so as to keep my true identity hidden, I pick it up, driving less than twenty miles to town. Getting a room at the La Quinta Inn, I settle in.

It is evening, so I'll wait until tomorrow to scout around a bit near Benny's place. Instead, a little sightseeing around Mobile is in order. It is one of those cities that you hear about but seldom get the chance to actually see.

Going to the historic downtown area, I see some gorgeous architecture. These buildings are unlike anything I see back home in Salem, Oregon. The building at the botanical gardens is fabulous, as are many of the others in the area.

When I ask someone on the street where a good place to eat is, I'm directed to The Brick Pit. With my GPS, I manage to find the unassuming place and have their specialty, barbecue ribs. Wow, is the best way to describe this meal. These are the best ribs I have ever eaten, and it almost makes me want to live here so I can get these all the time. I think I will come back here before I leave and fill up on them.

Back at the Inn, I relax for a bit before hitting the hay. After a light breakfast, I have a short drive to go check out the area where Benjamin lives and see if I can get a plan together. I get to Vaughn Drive and cruise the area. It looks like the best way at this time is to come to the property by way of the river. There are a couple of boats tied up to a dock at the back of the property, which I'll have to disable if I end up using this as my entry/exit point.

The roads in and out of the area are far too restricted for an easy exit. The problem will be getting a boat that I can use and then dump after I get to my rental car when I finish the job. If by chance I am pursued, I may have a problem getting away if the people chasing me know the area and manage to cut me off from my escape. They may be driving on the roads along the river and keep me in sight before I can get to my car. It's always possible that they may have access to boats other than the ones I disable.

I'm going to have to really think this through and come up with a plan that I can refine more to my liking. After I do a considerable amount of driving around, I find a rental cottage not too far from Benjamin's place. It is downstream on the Tensaw and the other side of the river. At this point, I'm not sure if this is good or bad. Benny's area doesn't have enough streets on it near his house, so escape would be more difficult from there. Where the cottage is may buy me the time I require.

Contacting the owner, I find out that it is a short term rental and that it can be rented by the week. Asking if there is a small boat that I can use, he tells me that one comes with the rental. He asks me a few questions and I let him know that I am a writer and will need the cottage for a week in about a month to finish my novel. Giving him a fictitious name, which is written down so I won't forget it, I let him know that I'll contact him in the near future. I'm not sure if I'll use the place or not but maybe I can work a plan around it.

August Journal entry: *I want to make Benjamin and his cronies pay for what happened to the people that burned to death in the fire. I know by the CDC and the other sites that he is one of the ones responsible for this travesty, even though no real evidence has been found linking them to the crime. This is another reason I think one or more of my sources is a Klan member. My biggest worry, though, is punishing someone who is at one of these meetings but not really a hardened Klan member. These types may still have a chance to redeem themselves and…*

I continue to check the area, familiarizing myself with escape routes and other possible locations for a base of operations. At the end of the day, I head back to the room and, after getting cleaned up, I head for The Brick Pit. The ribs are just as good the second time and, after eating my fill, I tour the city, taking in the sights.

In the morning, taking a last scout around, and after checking out of the room, I go back to the airport. The rental is taken back and I board the plane, heading back home.

Getting home by late afternoon, I relax for the evening. A plan starts to come together and I mentally prepare myself for what is about to come. I've already obtained a few of the materials I will need for the encounter with the Klan. I've come up with an idea that will help me to identify the members that are going to be eliminated and the ones that are not. My main objective is to take out the ones who have made a career of causing nothing but pain for those who have done nothing except be born into the wrong race.

I don't believe in guilt by association. Just because you are in the crowd doesn't always mean that you are really part of it or think the way they do. Sometimes, people are in situations because of peer pressure or because it is expected of them by elders.

I have seen, firsthand, youngsters getting into a gang or being at a party and doing things they feel they have no choice but to do, even though they know it is wrong. Everyone there is cheering them on and to back out is to lose face and expulsion from what they think, at the time, is a group they really want to be part of. It seems all too often that appearance to others means more to people than being who they really are. This must, in the end, cause people a lot of unhappiness.

On the weekend, I get my things together and do a lot of online research, looking for a couple of items I want to use when I go to Mobile. Finding one, I put in the order for it, including two neon white fluorescent markers sending everything to a rented post office box. I also find the other item I need and order four of them. They are battery operated, remote controlled, and only four inches long. Best of all, I find that I can activate all four at once from a distance.

The order is put in and I get everything in just over a week. Just to make sure, I get extra stuff and decide to try it out on a large dog that I catch on the poorer end of town. Most of my plan is falling into place but, as usual, there are always contingencies that can't be prepared for. In the past, I have had many close calls and I know that this could be the case again. I will be entering the group this time and mingling with them so I'll need to be ready for confrontations constantly. If I get caught, I am sure that they will take exception to what I have in mind.

All my things are together and I let management know that I'll be gone for at least three weeks. I'm asked where I will be going for so long. I tell them about the Thompson Chain of Lakes in Montana. It is the place I met Jack Peters, the old man whose friendship started a series of events that cost at least five people their lives. A couple of the guys ask me to take some photos to show when I get back. Luckily, I already have these from my last trip.

The owner of the rental cottage is called and a week's stay is booked with the option of extending it by a week. He asks me about my novel and I tell him that I have hit a roadblock and that is why I need the time alone. He asks me what it is about and I tell that I really shouldn't say, other than it is about a vigilante. That taken care of, I finalize the plans and, check to make sure I have everything that I will need.

With me, I'll have two pistols, two knives, and a sawed

off semi-automatic shotgun. I have a long line attached to a grappling hook and, of course, my specialty walking sticking with the spearing mechanism. I made up a holding apron to keep the things in place when I enter their midst. I check all the batteries, find that they are mostly the cheap types, spend the extra money, and get good ones. I wouldn't want anything to fail at an inconvenient time.

The quick-dry white neon markers are in place and I have loosened the tops so they come off easily. I check to make sure nothing leaks and pack it all away. I contemplate taking my bow but decide against it. It will be too cumbersome and noticeable. I have a tube of slightly flexible glue that dries soft and isn't uncomfortable. Hopefully, this will help me to leave less evidence behind and increase my chances of getting away with what I am going to do.

As the day to leave approaches, I contact the lad that takes care of my house when I am gone and am informed that he will be away at camp. Crap, I should have thought of this before. It's too late to change my plans, and I ask if he knows anyone who can do the job for me. Unfortunately, he can't think of anyone, as his buddies are going with him.

I finally have to resort to looking online for a lawn maintenance outfit that can do the job for me. I locate one and ask to have the person that will do the job come over so I can show him what to do. A young lad named Arthur arrives, and I show him around the property and ask that my vegetable garden is included. He hems and haws and tells me that this is not included in the services he is hired for. I ask how much it will cost me to have it included and, when I hand him two twenties, he says that should do it. Oh well, such is life.

Chapter 23

Saturday morning sees me on my way and, after a long sunny day on the road, I make it to Cheyenne, Wyoming. The end of the second long muggy day gets me to Little Rock, Arkansas, giving the air conditioner a bit of a workout. I stay at the Wyndham Riverfront and go for a swim in their pool to get the kinks out and help relax me. After this, I go to the steakhouse and, because it is fairly late in the day, I get the seniors size and spend an hour relaxing before I hit the hay.

Getting up a little later the next morning since it will be a much shorter drive, I get to the cottage around supper time. Thankfully, the mugginess has dissipated somewhat, making it far more pleasant to be outside. Too bad the mosquitoes are alive and well here. Oh well, I guess that's why we have repellent.

I go to a small restaurant and, after a nice meal, I relax in the cottage, which is close to the Tensaw River not far from Gunnison Creek on whose shore I am staying. I check the boat that is moored at a small dock and find that it is topped up with fuel and running nicely. It also has oars in case of trouble.

Just so I can get used to it, I take it for a trial run and locate Benjamin Norwood's property. It's a good thing I have my GPS unit with me. Otherwise, I would have a much harder time finding it.

Stopping the boat a little ways past the property, I row my way back, which is downstream making it easier. This way, I can have a good look at the shoreline and landscape, taking some pictures to study in order to plan my route. There is a dock with two nice-sized expensive boats moored in the water.

There are several large trees just past the dock, as well as brush and shrubs on the river bank. This will give me a place to tie up the night of the full-dress meeting. I still don't know why they will require everyone to be in their full-face hoods and robes. Is it possible that the entertainment that evening will be such that they don't want to know who does what?

The lawns and gardens adjoining the riverbank will provide lots of cover, to keep me hidden until I'm ready to join the affair. Being well away from neighboring properties is probably why the meetings are being held here.

I have paid for my time here in cash and shouldn't be disturbed by the owner or anyone else. I told him the reason I came here was to be alone so I could concentrate on my book. Funny, I should have chosen this as an excuse for being here because I have a hard time putting more than a few sentences together properly.

My laptop is with me and kept locked up in the rental car. I find a place in the cottage to hide my stuff when I'm out in the boat. There is a loose panel in the main closet and, with a little coaxing and some screws, I get things to work the way I need them. It pays to have a toolbox with you at all times.

The big event for the meeting is four days away on Saturday. I found out from the online sites that there will be things leading up to the finale the evening before and throughout the day of the planned event.

I'll try to get a feel for the mood of the get-together on Friday evening and keep away Saturday during the day so as not to alert anyone to my presence. Driving around the neighborhoods during the day gives me a feel for the area. Traveling up and down the river and waterways on all sides, I familiarize myself with all the possible traps and escape routes that I may need.

The water is murky with all kinds of silt in it. If you were to accidentally drop something in this, you would never be able to find it again.

As Friday evening approaches, I get the night vision goggles out and ready. When darkness comes, I am upstream from Benny the host's place. I slowly make my way near the bank and tie up to a small tree, using a knot that only requires a tug on the loose end of the rope to release the boat.

Climbing the bank through the brush, I get to the top quite muddy as it has recently rained. I'll need to make sure this doesn't happen on Saturday evening. It will be a give-away that I'm an intruder. With the night vision goggles, I watch what's going on. This event is a little smaller than the one in Hattiesburg that I attended on my previous encounter with the Klan. Because this group is smaller, it is held indoors, at least tonight it is. There could possibly be more people gathering tomorrow night but I will have to wait and see.

The total seems to be about twenty at this point. The faces I see are mostly the ones that I have researched and are leaders of various sects of the Klan. This may make my job easier because, so far, none of these men are deserving of mercy. The stories I have read on these people include the burning of houses with occupants inside. For being in the wrong place and of the wrong color, people have received beatings and even been shot. These are all suppositions at this point, as nothing concrete has been proven, but my sources are almost always correct.

Innocent people have suffered much at the hands of these men and others like them. I can hardly believe it when I see a pastor of a church in attendance. The only way I know he is a pastor is because of an article I found online. This man is an even bigger disgrace to humanity than the rest are. Talk about a wolf in sheep's clothing. I would normally never do anything to a man of God, but this person cannot possibly be one of God's workers.

It surprises me how people like this can make out so well financially. You would think that people dealing with these men would have an aversion to being around them. Is society still in the dark ages when it comes to issues like this?

For now, though, I have to concentrate on the job at hand because I will have my hands full just getting in and out alive of the situation I will be entering shortly.

Keeping to the shadows again, I watch what is going on. Luckily, there are no dogs or guards around and with everyone inside the building, I make my way next to a slightly open window. Listening to the speakers here tonight, I hear plans being made against a group of civil rights members.

"We need to think about possible solutions to the handling of this thorn in the side of us righteous people," the speaker says.

Righteous people? What the hell are you talking about? You stupid morons, you're not righteous people, I almost yell out.

Crap, I came close to blurting it out loud! I need to keep myself detached from the situation, or my chances of success will go down dramatically. I have to be in a frame of mind tomorrow night similar to what they have or I could give myself away.

I keep listening at the window to a separate discussion as one of the members says to the head man that he has the quickest solution to the civil rights problem. A bomb is laughingly suggested by the member. After this, as the leader addresses the group, security is discussed, and everyone is warned not to say anything outside this room about where the next night's meeting is going to be. If anyone were to let it slip, the entire group will be held accountable and arrested. This point is driven home several times just before he tells the group the location of what will be one of the biggest events this group has seen in years. The spot is a secluded area not too far from here and has all the amenities but no dwellings anywhere nearby. I'll take a ride tomorrow morning to look the place over.

"Everyone has to keep their mouths shut about this thing tomorrow night, I hope you understand this," the leader says one last time.

The rest of the lecture goes on with points of view expressed, and I realize that, except for the bomb part, this is basically the same as when I was in the stand of trees at the meeting of the Klan in Hattiesburg. The only other difference is that there is very little yelling and there are actual plans being made here. I hear a reference made to the events of tomorrow evening and that this will be a time to remember.

The meeting becomes informal and I overhear a member telling the Grand Dragon (stupid name), "I've got all the components for a bomb ready to be assembled, if need be."

The leader gives his approval. "Get it ready but don't tell any of the others about it yet. This has to be done right."

The two are right in front of the window with their backs turned to me.

I decide this is an appropriate time for me to leave because I have what I need and, as I hide in the bushes on the bank, the members start leaving the building. Getting down to the boat, I untie it and push it away from the shore, letting the slow current take me downstream. As I start floating away, I notice a place to climb up the bank that will allow me to stay clean if I need to come back here, which I doubt.

Back in the cottage, I go over what I have learned this evening. This batch is far worse than the ones in Hattiesburg and, if I don't find any on-the-fence members tomorrow night I may well take out as many as I can. I brought two types of liquid with me. I will have to decide which to use when I go to the meeting.

I have a very tough time getting to sleep this night.

The problem weighs heavily on my mind, and I am at a loss as to which way to go. I fear that this is another one of those forks in the road and, once a decision is made, it will not be able to be undone. This could very well put me in a position of being more of a monster myself, worse than anything I have ever done. These men are the worst of the worst and deserve what they get, but there may be a few coming that still have time to change. What to do, what to do?

After many hours of tossing and turning, debating back and forth, a decision is made and will be followed through, no matter what. I fall asleep and dream—dreams of horror and violence. Waking at two in the morning, I lie in bed for a while and finally fall back into a better, deeper sleep, waking far more rested, even though it is still before sunrise. After having a long hot shower and breakfast, I feel still better and make the preparations that I now feel will be best in the end.

Early in the morning, I take the boat and head farther upstream to where tonight's meeting and the so-called festivities are to be held. It isn't difficult to find because it's the only building in the area, despite it being so secluded. The grounds and shoreline are very similar to Benjamin's place, where all the meetings so far have taken place. There is a dock with boats here too. The grounds are not as well maintained but nice, considering how far out it is. Maybe this has been taken care of specifically for this event. There must be a road for the members to drive here but I don't want to take the chance of being seen so I head back to the rental.

The day goes by as I do a little more scouting and finally head into Mobile and see a few sights around the city. I make a trip to The Brick Pit and have a wonderful meal of ribs again. I don't fill myself too full and take the extra back to the cottage and put them in the fridge.

Evening comes slowly, and it will soon start to darken. I

pack all my belongings and put them in the car, in case a hasty exit is required. Taking what I will need, loading it into the boat, I turn the car around so it is pointing toward the road.

In the boat, I have the converted apron and my things under a small tarp, just in case I am intercepted on my way to the meeting. I stay on the opposite side of the river, go past the first property, and continue past the one where the meeting is tonight, using the oars to get close so as to not draw any attention.

When the way is clear, I cross to the side Benny the bomber's property is on. Using the oars to maintain direction, I let the boat float back to the spot I noticed earlier. The meeting is starting to gather momentum, and I am not observed at all as I disable the two boats moored at the dock.

I wait around till there are only a few still outside. The word soon spreads that the entertainment will commence in half an hour. The ones who are still outside are in full dress with hoods and robes concealing their identities. Picking my target when the time is right, I make my move. Up behind him I sneak, and, with a quick smack of a club, he is out like a light.

Quickly dragging him to the bushes, I make sure that I am not seen and strip off his outfit. Once this is removed, I slide the blade of my knife under the rib cage, stop his beating heart, and slip down the bank to the boat to gather my things. Once I have everything I need placed where I want it, I put on the robe and hood. I take a moment to mentally prepare myself and head for the building where everyone else is.

This is actually quite unnerving as I walk slowly in amongst the enemy. There seem to be about a dozen more people than there was last night. I try to keep myself apart from the members that I want to exterminate. I am forced to talk to some of them when I am asked direct questions, but I manage to keep the answers as non-committal and short as I can. I familiarize myself with the layout and pick the best spots to place my devices. This is actually the easy part, as few pay any attention to me. There is a real buzz of excitement in the air as everyone looks forward to whatever is planned.

The hood is stuffy and uncomfortable as I smell the previous owners scent still lingering in it. Why would anyone want to wear these things? I hear conversations and pick out the people I may spare going by some of the hesitant replies. The people I pick don't sound like they are hardline members. In order to know who is who, I use the white neon marker to draw a line on the backs of those I want to remember. Since the robes are all white, except for the ones in the highest positions, the marks are not visible to anyone.

This being done, I wait to see what transpires before I make my move. I have everything I need in place and wait for the announcement. Finally, the top man, Mister Dragon, wearing a red outfit, stands on a small podium and calls the meeting to order. After a short speech, a signal is given and curtains at the end of the room are drawn apart. I am shocked at what I see. I cannot believe that this is taking place.

Standing on a row of chairs with a noose hanging beside each of their heads is a group of African Americans. They have their hands and feet tied and are gagged. They are of various ages, and the group is made up of both males and females.

Standing behind them are Klan members to keep the group from falling off the chairs. "These kind folks were asked to participate in the entertainment this evening," the speaker announces.

The crowd laughs, some laugh hysterically, as the drugged people on the chairs are still aware enough to be frightened by the proceedings. Their eyes are bugged out and several of the girls are weeping.

"These people have been taken from various areas around the state and come from the slums," he announces.

"They will never be missed and will end up in the swamps, food for the alligators, after tonight's festivities." This brings another cheer and the speaker takes a bow.

I have made sure that I am near the bathroom door and I duck in quickly. I'm almost sick with what is happening here. I don't believe anyone would think this possible in our fair country. I see why a remote place was picked for this evening's event. My heart is racing as I enter the bathroom. I'm alone and head to a stall and, as I close the door, I reach inside the robe and from my belt I remove a gas mask. I take off the hood and put on the compact mask and then replace the hood.

Just then someone comes in and bangs on the door of the stall I am in. A hooded face looks over the top of the door.

"You better hurry up, things are about to get fun. You don't want to miss the excitement," he says enthusiastically.

I turn around to flush the toilet and pull the mask away from my mouth.

"All right, thanks, I'm on my way," I reply in a gravelly voice, flushing the toilet.

He turns to leave as I open the door, heading out. He suddenly turns around and comes back towards me.

"What do you have under the hood?" he asks me.

I hit him as hard as I can in the face, knocking him to the ground just as he is about to yell out. Down he goes banging into the trash container. As quickly as I can, I drag him into the stall farthest away from the door. Propping him up on the toilet, I use my knife to finish him.

Damn, why did that have to happen? It's a good thing the group is whooping it up and the crash is only heard by the one closest to the door. He looks in my direction as I come out.

"Tripped on the garbage can in there," I mumble as I walk by with my least visible hand holding the mask away from my mouth under the hood while I talk.

He nods his head and turns back to rejoin the so-called festivities.

I walk into the room and press a button on the remote in my pocket inside the robe. The battery operated fogging devices that I placed around the room are activated. Coming to Alabama, I brought two types of liquid with me. One is a tranquilizer, which will just knock people out for a while, and the other is a little more permanent. At first, I wasn't quite sure which to use. It's a good thing I chose the tranquilizer instead of the poison.

In the frenzy of the situation, nobody notices that there is a slight fog starting to drift across the room from the four corners.

The speaker continues his speech. "This is the proper thing to do and that this is the right of the Klan. We, the members of the Klan, should be allowed to dispense justice to those who are not members of the chosen race."

The people on the chairs are to be hung for the entertainment of the group as the ultimate event of the Klan's gathering. He has stretched out this part of the speech, wanting to have everyone savor this moment as long as possible.

I make my way over to the area where the people are on the chairs. As they and people around the room are starting to collapse, I catch most of the people on the chairs before they hit the ground. The members behind them are already out of commission. A few of the group try to remove their hoods and make for the door. They are too late and are on the floor long before they can make it outside. I leave the foggers running for a little longer just to make sure everyone is unconscious.

The first thing I do is carry the captives outside and cut their bonds. Next, I dim the lights and pull out a battery operated black light and check to see who has the marks on their backs. The black light makes white appear bright in the dark. With the neon white marker, the mark appears even brighter and I can quickly see who I have marked.

The ones who have the mark, I yank the hood off of and proceed to dispense justice to everyone else in the building.

A single shot to the brain makes for a quick clean kill. I do this with my pistols that have silencers attached. These silencers I made at work from a metal tube filled with baffles to absorb much of the sound. The pistols have an extended barrel to attach the silencer to. This way, the sliding mechanism that reloads the pistol is not interfered with. Being this remote, no one is likely to hear any gunshots but I'm too far away from the rental to take any chances with this.

My bullets, of course, are always loaded into the magazines with latex gloves on my hands. With spent casings left behind, there would be prints and DNA left if I got careless. I take care of the targets quickly and once this is done I collect the foggers and bag them so things are ready to be taken with me.

The enormity of the situation is starting to affect me. My hands are beginning to shake a bit and my breathing is becoming difficult. I collect my things and get outside, removing the hood and gas mask after making sure there isn't anyone around that is awake. I stay out of sight of the former captives, as a few of the first ones I took outside are starting to slowly regain consciousness.

Before leaving the building, I grabbed a couple of cell phones from the dead members and laid them on the ground. The number for the FBI and this location are written on a note stuck to the phone on the ground by the now-free prisoners. When they get their wits about them, they can call the authorities for help. This done, I head to the boat, grabbing a few good sized rocks from the shore.

Once I am on my way, I remove the robe and tie the hood inside the sleeve. I then place the rock on top of the spread out robe and tie it around the rock nice and tight. This done, it's dropped into the dirty water and sinks to the bottom. I can't have any DNA around to tie me to this evening.

The bag in which I have the foggers, remote, black light, and everything else to be disposed of, is made of cloth. When I have the extra rocks in the bag, I tie it up and lower it into the water too. The trip back seems to take forever as the little motor chugs away. I keep expecting to run into a police boat or member of the Klan all the way back. The return trip is dark but not dark enough to impede my progress much. The moon is full enough to light the way, so I don't use my flashlight and, despite my apprehension, I don't encounter anyone on the way to the rental.

After getting back to the cottage, I get cleaned up. Then grabbing a bag, I quickly toss out the stuff in the fridge, except for the ribs. I'll dump everything else here that can possibly incriminate me in a garbage bin on my way out of town, along with the disposable phone I used to make the reservation for the cottage on. Locking the place up, I leave the key inside, dropping it through slot put there for this purpose.

The rental car is taken back when I finish transferring everything back to my car. In no time, I'm on the road, driving on Jefferson Davis Highway heading toward the city of Jackson, where I will stay overnight. By the time I get a room, I am exhausted. I have a quick shower and lay down on the bed but sleep doesn't come.

I warm up the ribs in the microwave and go through the events of the night. There is, of course, a real up side to the way things turned out. The abductees would have been hung if I hadn't intervened. I was originally going to use a poison gas to deal with the Klan boys but, since they had prisoners there, I have a real feeling of relief that the plan was scrapped.

The evening went far better than I would ever have thought it would. There are a total of about twenty-two dead Klansmen at the scene and nine that were left alive. I am not sure if these will change their ways or not, but they now have a good reason to re-evaluate their lives.

I spared them only because of the way they were reacting to the conversations going on around them. The best thing is that the seven people that were kidnapped have been saved and their families spared years of pain and sorrow. So I'm now not just a justice-seeking vigilante, I am also a justice-driven mass murderer. I'm not sure if I should be happy or extremely sad that I have, in my opinion, been driven to this point by a lifetime of tragedy. I've come a long way down this road and, despite the hardness that has dulled my sensitivity, I still feel like crying.

Lost in my thoughts, I forgot to turn on the news and I now find a station that plays the day's events twenty-four hours a day. The biggest story to hit the news in a while is the mass shooting death of twenty-two members of the Klan, including two who were stabbed.

The FBI is involved and, although there is a general description of the events, it appears as if the abduction and planned hanging of seven African Americans that has been thwarted isn't mentioned. The spokesman only gives a limited amount of information of the crime committed by the unknown assailants. The story comes out only a bit at a time and takes quite some time to come to light.

No one at the gathering has any idea of what transpired. The FBI has arrested the surviving members of the group. The arrested individuals claim to know nothing of what was to happen at the meeting and denounce the FBI for its allegations.

The authorities are skeptical of the version of the story told by surviving members, even though they don't actually say what was supposed to transpire.

A spokesman for the Klan from Hattiesburg denounced the entire story as nothing but propaganda, saying that there is a conspiracy by the government to take away the rights of law-abiding Americans. The announcer relays this with a rather sarcastic look on her face. More information will be announced as the investigation continues.

This turn of events sets my mind at ease, and I fall asleep not waking till ten in the morning. After a long hot shower, I gather my possessions and go for breakfast. As I hit the road again to put as much distance as I can between me and the scene, I think of what I want to do for the next few days.

I finally have the thought that I may spend some time where Jack and I met. This will allow me time to reflect on the things we discussed as we wiled away the hours fishing.

I pull out my phone and find the business card for the Thompson Chain of Lakes Resort. I book a cabin and head out for the long drive.

Chapter 24

It takes two days for me to get there. I buy my supplies in Kalispell Montana before I get to the resort. Pulling in late in the day, I pay for my first two nights in advance so there won't be any worries on the part of the owner. He vaguely remembers me from when I was here with Jack Peters.

I get a nice little cabin and unpack my stuff. I've already rented the small boat and fishing gear as well as the bait. By the time I'm settled in, I'm too beat to go for a run so I open a Corona and sit on the porch in a rocking chair. The sun is setting off to my right and has a calming effect as I look over the scene in front of me.

My thoughts go back to the episode in Mobile. I am in a mild state of disbelief. It's almost as if the whole thing is a dream and not the reality that I know it is. The enormity of the situation is really starting to impact me. I know, without a doubt, that these men were about to hang seven innocent people and that they were making plans to murder civil rights workers in a bombing. The one individual had all the items required and had just received the go ahead, and he would have assembled the explosive device.

So why do I still have these doubts about my course of action? It doesn't make sense. I shouldn't have any doubts at all. Is this being caused by this thing called a conscience? I also realize that I came close to being caught when I was changing in the bathroom stall. It seems that I have caught another break. I wonder how long my luck will hold out. It was quite unnerving being in the midst of all the Klan members. I'm sure, if they caught me, it would have been my neck in a noose.

I decide to take my beer and go for a walk along the shore. Absent mindedly, I pick up a small flat stone and skip it on the surface of the water. It jumps on and on and finally sinks. The memories of Jack come flooding back. He was beaten to death and then his daughter Beth was brutally murdered. She was murdered because I failed to deal with a second individual that was with Jack's killer. If I had dealt with him too, she would still be alive. The guilt I feel leaves me wishing that I had not come here.

Despite the long drive and being tired, I realize that I need something to get my mind off this train of thought. I put the beer away and go for a run. I make this a hard run. Maybe this is my way of punishing myself for letting Beth down. By the time I am finished, I am so exhausted that I just go to bed, falling into a fitful sleep.

Dreaming of being chased by unknown villains that are continually close to catching me, I wake up in the middle of the night with a scream, covered in sweat. My hands are trembling and my head is in a whirl. This is not the first time I have had dreams of this sort and, each time, I barely escape those chasing me. I make up my mind that I will leave this place in the morning.

After a long night, I wake to the sun shining and the birds chirping. I go for a last walk along the shore before heading out. As I'm slowly walking, I make sure my thoughts stay away from Jack and Beth.

The last thing I want now is to chat with someone but that is exactly what happens. Actually, this isn't a chat but a monologue.

As I have my face turned toward the water, someone

comes beside me and, before I can get away, an old woman starts talking to me.

"Do you know how lucky we are to be able to enjoy this spot? Through the efforts of many, the pollution and outside world have been kept away from here," she tells me.

I am taken aback by this line of conversation.

"We need to be thankful to those people who go out of their way to make a difference in the lives of others that are unknown to them. A place like this is a haven for anyone needing a respite from the rigors of life, don't you think?" she says.

The older lady just keeps going on, despite the fact that I don't want to hear it. What finally gets my attention is when she tells me, "I just heard on the news about what happened outside Mobile, Alabama. My goodness, this group has been a blight on our society for far too long. Those horrible people deserved exactly what they got."

At this point, she turns and walks away when she is called by a man sitting on the porch of a cabin nearby.

I am left standing there, not knowing what to do. This one-sided conversation has caught me off guard, not that she actually said all that much. The statement about the Klan being a blight on society has had an effect on me. I'm not so sure if I should follow through with my plans to leave.

Chapter 25

Linda

The little old lady mumbles quietly to herself so that her husband can't hear. "For the life of me I don't know why I went up and talked to that young man. Well, it wasn't much of a conversation, as I did all the talking. He seemed as if he had the weight of the world on his shoulders. I was just going to ask him if everything was all right when George called me. It seems like George needs me to do everything for him these days. "Hey, Linda, can you get me this, can you make me that, and so on." Maybe I should have told him to get his own coffee. After all, he does know how, for goodness sake. I think that I will try to catch up to the young man later. I think he needs my help and, since our son died in that dreadful car accident, I have been so lonely. I do hope he stays for a while."

Chapter 26

Joseph

With this happening, my attitude has lightened. The old lady didn't say all that much, maybe it was just the way she said it. I'll stay one more day.

My thoughts just need to be kept moving in the right direction, and maybe a little fishing will help in that department. After a little breakfast, I'll see how I feel.

What the heck, I came here to fish, and fish I will. Gathering my stuff and making sure that I have a snack and water with me, I launch the boat. With any luck, I can catch enough for a decent meal. Maybe I shouldn't have eaten those ribs. They were the best I ever had, and I could have kept them in the cooler. Oh well, too late now.

Out on the water in the sun, I'm glad I brought the sunscreen and a hat. I go to some of the spots Jack took me to and—wouldn't you know it?—I've had a few nice hits. The perch are kept in the pail of water and I keep right on going.

Parking the boat under a tree near the shore on the opposite side of the lake and relaxing, I cast the line into a spot I think might be good. Bingo, another strike, and this one fights like the dickens.

When I get him in, I see a fine specimen and realize that

I have much more than I need and wonder what I should do with the extra.

It is already late afternoon and I don't have a clue where the time went. This is just what the doctor ordered. I clean up the rod and head back toward the cabin, taking my time and not disturbing things any more than I need to.

I park the boat on the sand and take the fish to the cleaning area. The woman that filled my ear earlier is on the porch with an old man who seems to be taking a nap. She gets up and, after tucking him in, heads my way.

Crap, I'm not in the market to get acquainted with any old people. Not that I don't like them, it's just that I don't have a lot in common with them.

"I'm sorry for prattling on this morning, I don't know what came over me," she says.

"That's okay I really didn't mind." A little white lie can't hurt, I guess.

"How was the fishing? You were gone a long time," she says.

I show the old lady the pail. Her eyes light up, and I know that she would just love it if I would offer her a couple. "I have too many so why don't you take a couple of them," I say.

"That is so generous of you. You know, I have the best recipe for perch. I've won cooking contests using it. Why don't you clean them, and I'll cook them for all of us. You won't be disappointed, I promise," she says, almost pleading.

I was hoping to be alone but I don't have the heart to turn her down. I finish cleaning them and let her take the whole batch with her.

"George will be so very pleased," she says. "He hasn't had this dish for quite some time."

As I watch her walk away, carrying the fish in a plastic bag, I actually feel good about the whole thing. Heading into the cabin, I get washed up then sit on the porch with a Corona. The old man has roused and comes over, asking if he can sit and join me. I get him a chair and we have a beer together. He doesn't talk much but what he says always means something. In other words, he doesn't bother with useless small talk.

"We've been coming here for thirty years," he tells me. "In that time, little has changed at the resort and, for this, we are thankful. I sometimes feel I've started to become a burden for Linda, but she doesn't complain. We lost our son in an automobile accident four years ago. He was around your age. We were so happy having him later in life because, for a while, we didn't think it would ever happen. This is probably why Linda came over and intruded on your time this morning."

I realize that her talking to me is what turned my thinking around and made me stay. Going by what she said about the blight, I wonder if there is something that tuned her into the fact that I might have had something to do with the Klan thing a couple of days before. Naw, how could she even have a clue? She would have to be psychic. She probably came over because she was lonely and missing her son and noticed that I had something on my mind too. I think women have this kind of instinct.

Chapter 27

Linda

T hank goodness that young man decided to stay a little longer," Linda says as she sets herself to the task at hand. "I was almost sure he was about to pack up and go, especially when I kept on talking. I'm sure he wanted me to be quiet and leave him alone. Surely, he must think that I'm a wicked thing when I said that those dreadful Klan people deserved what they got. I'm not even sure why I said that." She realizes that she is talking out loud and giggles to herself.

"I wonder if I should have been so forward about the fish. I do hope he enjoys the way I cook them. Oh, I am sure he will. Everyone always says how good my recipe is. He somehow reminds me of Gary. I wish he hadn't died. He was such a wonderful boy. I see George has gone over and is chatting with the young man. Is that a beer in his hand?"

Linda finishes all the preparations for the meal and decides to have the young man eat in their cabin. That way, he can leave when he wants to, rather than when she and George decide to go home. After setting the table, she goes to the porch and calls George and the young man to dinner.

Chapter 28

Joseph

The old man finishes his beer just as his wife comes out and calls us to dinner. I quickly wash my hands and head over. I'm sure the old woman means well and has tried her best, but how bad can she ruin the fish. I can always catch more tomorrow if necessary. The old man is actually not a bad guy. He's interesting enough and has been around so has quite a few stories. I go to their cottage and Linda, as she insists that I call her, asks me to take a seat.

The table is all setup with a red and white, checkered tablecloth, and it is all quite homey. Sitting down gives me a nice feeling of family, much like I have when I go over to Harry and Brenda's.

Linda brings out the dinner and a cold glass of milk. She spoons out a good portion of a fish and rice dish with a few vegetables on the side.

After saying grace, we dig in and, wow, she wasn't kidding. "I must say, this fish dinner is about the best I have ever had."

A big smile is on her face, and I am sure I just made her day just like she has made mine.

When I am finished, Linda asks if I have room for a little more and proceeds to load up my plate. I'm quite full as she puts a slice of cherry pie in front of me. I ask her how she knew this was my favorite and she just smiles again. The rest of the evening goes by very pleasantly and, as I head for the door, I tell both of them that I appreciate this very much.

As I head back to my cabin, I am reminded of how, now and then, you can be surprised by people. I was ready to leave this morning and now I don't want to. I'll go out tomorrow and see if I can't catch a few more fish.

Chapter 29

Linda

What a nice young man, Linda thinks, making sure that it isn't coming out of her mouth. *I wonder why he isn't married. He did seem to enjoy dinner with us tonight and George was very happy to have him here. It was almost like having Gary back again. Joseph seemed to like us too which is nice.*

I wonder if he would still like me if he knew that I have been very naughty at certain times in my life. I don't think he is the type that would approve of the way I dealt with those awful people who hurt their children. Not even George knows what I have done. The poison I gave those bad parents was quick and somewhat painless, but it had to be done.

Some people don't belong in this world and should be removed, just like the neighbor that used to beat his wife. Well, he doesn't do that anymore, he doesn't do anything anymore. There were a few others, I'm not sure how many. It's so hard to keep track of these things. Maybe I should have kept a diary and then I could have reminisced once in a while.

A smile crosses her face as she thinks back on her life.

No, I'm sure Joseph would not approve of this kind of thing at all. I wonder if he might visit us once in a while, which would be nice. Of course, I can never let him know that I am sometimes a naughty lady, despite the fact that they were awful people. How many were there, eleven or twelve? It's so hard to remember all these things.

Chapter 30

Joseph

I manage to catch another bunch of fish and, after cleaning them, Linda asks if I would let her cook them for us again. How can I turn her down? She is as nice a person as you can find. She cooks them, using another wonderful recipe, and I go back to my cabin stuffed again.

Sometimes, I think that these kinds of people are brought into your life in order to keep things in balance. So, after another pleasant couple of days, it's time for me to head back home. I've had a nice time chatting with them when I wasn't fishing or on a run. I even took them on the boat for a ride around the lake, showing them the sights. They seemed to really enjoy that.

Linda gave me their address and phone number and asked me to look them up when I could. I hope nothing happens to these folks like it has to most people that come into my life. Despite these concerns, I think that I might try to keep in touch with them periodically.

When we say our goodbyes, George and Linda give me a hug and say they will miss me. I think I will actually miss them too. They are such kind and gentle old folks. Their son was lucky to have them.

I wonder if Linda would have been as nice to me if she knew what was in the trunk of my car and what I've used the things for. No, these things don't sit well with ordinary people.

I stop for lunch in Boise Idaho and, as I leave the restaurant, I hear a couple of young kids in their late teens harassing an elderly couple. They are quite abusive and frighten the old folks considerably—big mistake, especially after my meeting Linda and George.

As I walk by, I grab the biggest boy by the hair and keep right on walking with him in tow cursing and swearing. I go around the corner of a building and run him face first into the brick wall.

This takes the fight right out of him, and I proceed to explain to him how his lack of respect won't be tolerated. When I am sure he knows what I mean, I give him a few hard shots to the solar plexus and one to his bleeding face, just to reinforce the lesson. The other kid, seeing what was happening, runs for it, leaving his buddy to face the music alone. I leave before the couple has a chance to get a good look at me.

On the road again, I start to wonder what has happened to the youth of today. There seems to be a real lack of respect happening. It can't all be attributed to youth, there has to be more to it. Is it that their parents aren't teaching them properly?

I sometimes wonder if the movies they watch and that god awful rap music are somewhat responsible. I have listened to some of this garbage and found that it is all cursing and disrespecting others. Why this stuff has lasted this long boggles my mind. I don't see the drawing card with this crap. Oh, well, I'm sure I'm not the first person to ask this question.

I get back home late in the day and decide to unpack the car tomorrow morning. After settling in, I'm out like a light as I think about Linda and George. The morning brings a warm feeling of being home again and still having a couple of days off before I have to go back to work. After a light breakfast, the car is unloaded and my stuff is put away in the storage area in the basement. After going for a nice long run, I check the property to see how things have been taken care of. Everything looks okay but not as nice as when the young lad I normally have takes care of it.

Monday, I'm back at work and getting in the groove. Jim has had no real problems with quality control and the young guys that I have been helping are coming along fine.

After work, Bill calls and drops by, giving me an update on the investigation involving Jackson.

"He has been quiet for a while but pulled a robbery two days ago. Here are the particulars that I have been sent. Is everything all right?"

"Everything is, except for this, but I'll be okay, Bill. I hope you know how much I appreciate this."

"I know, Joseph, just be careful and don't do anything drastic."

"No worries, buddy."

After he leaves, I check online on all the sites I frequent to see if there is anything to be found on Dennis Jackson. I figure I may as well use all the resources I can to try tracking this man. Finding little, I take the information I have down to the basement and plot the data on the map. It sure has helped that I have always kept in touch with Bill all these years. We have become quite good friends and spend a fair bit of time together, going fishing and doing other things. I have on several occasions made things for him and this has created quite a bond between us. This can, of course, not take too much of his time as he is married and sometimes works long hours.

Looking at the information, I realize that Dice Man went in a totally different direction than I would have anticipated. It's almost as if he doubled back in order to throw anyone that might be looking for him off the trail. I guess I won't be going after him anytime soon.

I haven't heard much about the incident outside Mobile

so I check online to catch any new developments. There is a story that insists there had to be at least two people involved in the murder of the Klan's members. The prisoners have been intensely interrogated but no new information has been found. The abductees, as it comes out, haven't been able to shed any light on the situation either as they were drugged and quite out of it.

The empty shell casings provide no clues at all. A spokesman for the Klan insists that there were no illegal plans taking place that evening and that the people involved are either mistaken or outright lying.

"The Klan is a reputable organization that is only looking out for their fellow Americans welfare," he goes on to say.

"Yeah, sure you are," I mutter to myself. "Why didn't I record the leader's speech? It would have been damning and proved to the world what you people really are."

I have the idea of converting a walking stick into one that fires a bullet. When I think about it, I'm not sure if I want it to fire when a trigger is activated or if I want it to fire when I push it against a target, much like an underwater shark gun operates. Either way, I am going to have to be able to activate and deactivate it, so it doesn't fire accidentally, that would draw everyone's attention pretty quickly. I play the scene in my mind and have the walking stick fire accidentally as I use it to brace myself. It would almost be comical. I think I'll just forget about it. Too many things could go wrong with it.

Meanwhile, I see an ad online for rubber bullets, the same kind that riot police use. These items have a velocity of about two hundred feet per second because of a smaller charge, which is about the same speed as a slingshot. They are only accurate for approximately one hundred feet, thus limiting their use.

This could come in handy, so I order some and have them delivered to my post office box. I do this from a public phone and am told that payment will have to be received first because of the mailing instructions. I send the cash and hope that I receive the goods. Again, I don't want anyone to be able to track me down, so I do things the safest way possible. I still have a supply of grenades that I got through a contact and wonder if there is any way to launch them remotely, another idea for future consideration.

One of the new employees at work in his early twenties seems to be a little spaced out quite often. He is really nice but there is, at times, the aroma of weed on him. I don't care what he does after work but, because I am on the safety committee, I can't overlook this. I tell him he can't do this on the job and, if it happens again, I'll have no choice but to report him. He thanks me for giving him a chance and says that he won't do it on or before coming on the job anymore.

As the week wears on, I update the map in the basement and try to anticipate where Dennis Jackson will strike next. Of course, even if I get the town right, I may not get the establishment that he decides to rob correct. Maybe I can try to get a better idea as to what type of place he likes to rob, and this will help me figure out where to wait for him. Of course, if I am waiting for him, I will need to be unobserved myself, or I could end up being a suspect. I gather the information and get a better and better idea as to how he thinks. If I can try to be him, it may serve me well.

Chapter 31

The weeks go by and then turn into months, and my plan for the Dice Man starts to take shape. Bill tells me things that are happening in town now and then. He knows that I never repeat anything he says to me and uses me periodically as a sounding board. I feel that there has been a change in the detective.

There is a group in town that is tied to organized crime and, with the use of high priced lawyers, has managed to thwart the law at every turn. Bill's frustration is growing out of control and so I ask if there is anything I can do to help him.

He says he has an idea and asks if I can make an item he has drawn up for him.

I have the feeling that he might know more about me than he has let on, otherwise, I doubt that he would be asking me to do these things. He doesn't tell me what it is for but I can figure it out.

Looking the plans over, I see that what he wants is not that far from things I have built before. I'll ask if he can acquire a couple of the main items so I don't use my own alerting Bill to the fact that I have this kind of thing. I give Bill a call and let him know that I can build this but that he will have to supply two parts.

I take care not to mention the actual thing on the phone because you never know who is listening.

"I can get them to you in the next couple of days," he says.

The next day, I drop by a major hardware store and pick up all the things I need and, when I get home, proceed to put everything together so I am ready for Bill.

When he comes over and drops off the stuff, I tell him that all I have to do is tighten a few screws and everything will be done. We go down to the basement and I finish the job. I ask Bill how he will be able to handle this if, by chance, he becomes a suspect in this incident.

"Do you have an accomplice to help you in case of trouble?" I ask with a slight smile.

"I'm reluctant to involve anyone else. I know what you're asking but I don't want anything happening to you. Besides, I don't anticipate a problem with this," he tells me with a look of concern on his face.

"You wouldn't be the first person to make that mistake. I think that you need some backup."

He laughs. "I can't involve any of my fellow police officers in this because I don't know how far I can trust them."

Bill looks at me. It seems to dawn on him that I am actually serious and a smile crosses his face. I look at him without saying anything and wait. I can see the wheels turning in his head.

"Just what do you think that you would be willing to do?" he says, finally.

"You could keep watch with a rifle while I plant the devices. I'm not familiar with firearms so this would be your job." I don't want to let Bill know too much about me and, this way, I can still help him out. This, of course, will build an even closer bond between us and may be of use in the future. I would never use this to blackmail him, but he would feel more obligated to reciprocate.

"Let me think about it." He gets up to leave and I throw

in one more tidbit of information that he may not have thought of.

"I'm in way better shape than you are and I can probably defend myself better than you, too."

Again the wheels are turning and a blank look crosses his face as he is probably thinking back to the time he came around the corner of my house surprising me and I almost took him out.

"I will let you know this weekend, okay?"

"No problem," I say.

October journal entry: *So what now? Indeed, what now? All these things have been nothing but a distraction, even the Klan in Mobile. They were, of course, the biggest distraction of all, but a distraction nevertheless. What keeps me going, that for which I live, is killing the swine that murdered my wife and my child. I feel I am getting closer to intercepting this man, but am also very leery of this encounter. This guy cannot possibly have been able to outwit the police for so long without being really good at what he does. This means he is going to be dangerous and I had better be careful.*

This thing with Bill might just help our future relationship along, but even this…

The rest of the week has no surprises and, before I know it, Friday afternoon is here. I go for a good run and workout and then have a shower.

As I am getting dried off the phone rings, and I notice by call display that it is Bill.

"Hey, man, what's up?" I ask.

Bill asks if he can come over and tells me he can be at my place in twenty minutes. I ask if he wants to eat here and he likes this idea. When he gets to my place he tells me what is going on.

"My wife is out of town for the weekend visiting her elderly parents. Dinner being made for me is just what the doctor ordered, thanks. Like a lot of guys, I can't cook worth shit."

"Then you're in luck because I can, as you already know," I say, at which he smiles.

I already have the steaks defrosted and the potatoes are warming up on the barbie. Out of the fridge come the Coronas, and the topic of the visit is put aside till after we eat. I check the potatoes and on go the steaks. We start our salads and, by the time that's done, the steaks are ready.

"I can't get over how well you can put a dinner together," Bill says expressing his appreciation after we're finished.

"It's either learning to cook or starve and I don't like going hungry," I reply.

The plates are put away and we get down to business.

"To tell you the truth, Joseph, I've fretted about putting you in harm's way. I haven't been able to come up with anything better and realize that you are probably in a far better position to pull off the planting of the devices than I am."

He stops talking and I know that this is bothering him.

"I can't believe that I have gone down this road and feel somewhat guilty about it," he continues. "This goes against what I have always stood for and now involving you further than I did the other times I asked you to build me something."

"Don't worry too much about it. I wouldn't have volunteered if I didn't want to do it." I say.

I really want to let him in on part of my alternate life, but habits formed long ago tell me this isn't a good idea. Once the cat is out of the bag, it's really hard to put it back in.

We spend the rest of the evening making plans on how to carry out the operation. I insist we go to the place where he wants to carry out his plan of action. I get myself prepared, and we head out.

The place we end up at is a secluded residence with plenty of cover. I have my binoculars with me and scout the area. There are no dogs. The surveillance cameras are fairly obvious and will be easy enough to avoid. There are no armed guards, making things even easier.

I ask Bill exactly where he plans to put the devices. "I was going to put them in a spot where the patio meets the house," he tells me. "When the group is outside, I'll hit the remotes and take out the main people."

I kind of shake my head and let him know that I think there is a better way to do this.

"I thought this way would work pretty well," he says.

"How long are you planning on hanging around to wait for the right people to take position? Plus, they might hear the winding mechanisms."

This quiets him quickly. "Do you have a better idea?" he asks then.

"Which of the cars outside are the ones that will be occupied by the top people?"

"The two that are the most likely out of the three vehicles sitting there are the two on the left," he says.

"Will everyone there fit into two cars?"

"Yeah they'll all fit easily," he says.

"We'll do it tonight at about four in the morning. Go home and meet me here, a few blocks from where the home is located at three-thirty in the morning. All right, Bill?"

"See you then."

Back home, I go downstairs, get some zip ties, and go to the computer to find out what the undercarriage of the cars is like. Once I have what I want, I get ready and go to bed, setting the alarm. When it goes off, I get moving and, with my knife, pistol, and a bag loaded with the devices, I head out.

Parking a safe distance away, I make my way to the edge of the property dressed in black. Using my night goggles, I look things over. Everything is dark and the cars are in an easily accessible place. It's a good thing they aren't parked in a garage, or I would have to rethink things. I decided to do this without Bill being here so I won't have to explain why I'm so good at this kind of stuff.

I stay in the darkest places as I move toward the automobiles. When I am as close as I can get using the cover available, I take a last look around. When I feel safe, I get to the side of the first car and slide under far enough to attach two of the units to the appropriate spots. This done, another quick look and just when I am about to lie down and go under the car a light comes on in the house, shit!

The light is not in a room on my side of the house but comes through a doorway leading to another room. I stop in my tracks and, with my heart beating a little faster, get ready to run. After a minute, the light goes out and, after seeing that nothing is happening, I slide under the car, fastening the devices. Now, the second car is rigged too.

At the third car on the side away from the house, I place a short roofing nail at the bottom of the tire, pointing up and against the driveway. I take my knife and reach around to the inner side of the tire near the rim and stick the knife in just enough to let out the air. I consider doing this to the rear tire too but think better of it. With the nail being where it is, it will look like the puncture happened on the road. If two tires are done they will know it was sabotage immediately.

As the tire deflates, the nail is pushed into it as the car lowers. All I want from this action is to force everyone into the two rigged cars, thereby completing the job more thoroughly. A quick look around from my vantage point behind the vehicle, and I'm off.

I make my way back to my car and wait for Bill to show up. Fifteen minutes later, he drives up and comes over to my window.

"Well, are you ready?" he asks.

"Sorry, but it's already done."

"What do you mean?" Bill says, surprised at this.

"I couldn't sleep and got here early. I did a quick scouting job and rigged the two cars and flattened the tire on the third car, forcing them to all go in the two vehicles," I say, a little sheepishly.

"You could have been caught," Bill says.

"I took special care to make sure everything was all right. I'm sorry but the opportunity presented itself, and I grabbed it while I had the chance. And, besides, I might have lost my nerve if I waited any longer," I tell him.

I hand him the remotes and say the devices are placed where they should be.

"I fastened them with industrial zip ties, so there won't be any chance of them falling off."

Bill looks at me and I smile in return.

I think that Bill has learned something about me that I wasn't keen on him finding out. This relationship is fast becoming a partnership rather than a friendship. Where this will end up going to, is still up in the air.

Back home, I have a bit of a time going to sleep. Things are going through my head and I wonder if this is the start of something that may get out of hand. I haven't minded this so far, but I have always been a solo act and this has suited me just fine. I've always been able to make all my own decisions, without having to worry about what's going on in someone else's head.

The decision on what targets to hit needs to be my own, because different things motivate me than they do Bill. It is possible that I am again over thinking things, and this may just be an occasional event. But, somehow, I don't think this is going to develop that way. I'll have to play this by ear and, if necessary, feign fear of getting myself in too deep. I can always say that my somewhat sensitive nature is holding me back and that this episode has left me unsettled for a long period of time.

I'm not sure if he will believe me or not, but this is already bothering me. Not for the reasons I will give Bill, but for my own preservation. Can Bill actually live with this type of life? After all, he has a wife and needs to take her into consideration. Bloody hell, here I am still over thinking this again.

Two days later, the story hits the news. "There has been

an obvious hit on a group of men living on the edge of town. These men, it has been suspected, have underworld ties and have contributed to the increase in crime in the city of Salem, Oregon. The evidence points to the fact that explosive devices had been attached to two of the vehicles the group used. A third vehicle was disabled, forcing the men to use the two sabotaged cars. Lead detective Bill Henderson, on the scene, described the crime as disturbing and obviously an attempt by a rival group to oust other members of organized crime out of Salem. It is the detective's hope that this does not become a turf war where innocent people might be hurt. Further information will be made available to the media as the case develops."

Well, Bill seems to have thought this through fairly thoroughly. He looks to be in full control of himself. Being in the force all these years has taught him to handle himself in all situations. This is, of course, good for both of us.

Speak of the devil, the phone rings and there he is. It's the middle of the week, but he would like to come over on his way home. I'm a little apprehensive about it but agree to see him. A short time later, he pulls up and knocks on the door. He is a little sheepish at first. He tells me that he knows he has involved me in something that he probably shouldn't have but saw no way out. He goes on to say that he was a little surprised that I went ahead and placed the devices before he even got there and did it so competently.

"I decided to look online as to where to place the explosives and that's why I was able to do it easily," I tell him.

"Most people are very nervous about handling explosives the first few times and I am surprised that it didn't seem to bother you at all. Have you had experience with this stuff before, Joseph?"

"No I haven't, but these things have to be pretty safe or they wouldn't be used so much in the military. All you have to remember is not to pull the pin, and you should be okay," I tell Bill, "I was a little jittery when I got home, though. Not because of the grenades but more when I was under the cars, and I thought I might get caught. By this time, it was a little too late to back out, so I finished the job and got the heck out of there."

He smiles and takes this at face value because he can't do anything else. He tells me he is sorry that he had to get me involved.

At this point, I say, "Despite my nervousness at the time, it really was a little exhilarating. I felt good about being able to help the community in some way."

Bill laughs and slaps me on the back as he walks out the door.

So, in spite of my reservations, I actually feel all right about the whole thing. It's a good thing that I have learned to think on the run. This, of course, comes from having to do this to protect myself all these years.

I take out my guitar and start strumming a bit. I have learned a fair bit about playing and know what chords go together and which don't. Of course, if you play a wrong chord, it's pretty obvious as it sounds bad. I run through the chords in the key of A and before I know it I've come up with a little tune that kind of sums up my life. It's called "In the Shadows" and tells of a person lurking in the shadows of darkness, waiting for a particular person to come along. I catch myself and wonder if I should even write the lyrics down. This could really get me into trouble if anyone ever found the song and knew anything about me. I put the guitar away and, as I lay in bed, the tune continues going through my head. I hope I haven't started something here. *Leonard Cohen's voice could make this song really come alive. Stop it!*

At work the next day, the men are told that we will be having a barbecue on Friday at lunch. This is to show appreciation to the employees for all the hard work that they have done. When Friday gets here and we are sitting down, management brings out a number of wrapped gifts that will be handed out when names are drawn from a bowl. I volunteer to do the drawing as long as I have ample time to write my name on several pieces of paper. My offer is turned down.

The meal is great and there is a variety of meats and potato salads as well as greens. I decide to stay away from the smokies. They taste great but when I read the label on a package of them in the store, I saw that one smokie has the equivalent of about seventy to eighty percent of a person's daily intake of saturated fat. When I saw this, I was almost floored.

The lunch is done and the names are drawn. Management knows what is in each gift so they hand out packages that are suitable to the individual. My name isn't called but that's okay. I can buy anything I need or want, but some of the guys have families and aren't in that position so I don't begrudge them at all.

Some of the gifts are really quite exceptional and the boys are really happy to get them. One of the young men that just had a child won an entire set of good quality pots and pans, and he is almost dumbstruck. Another man received a gift certificate to an upscale restaurant and is very thankful to management for this. When all is over, the employees applaud management to show their appreciation. Because it is not too far from quitting time, the shop is closed up for the weekend so everyone feels that they have gotten something extra. As we all go home, the mood is jubilant and the weekend is off to a great start.

Bill pops by for a visit and drops off a report on the latest escapades of Dennis Jackson. Heading to the basement after supper, I go through the materials in depth. It appears that the randomness of his targets is becoming a little more predictable and the last two towns he has hit are ones that I guessed at. If I can keep doing this fairly consistently, I may take a stab at intercepting him at what I think will be one of his targets.

His path over the past year has led him in a roughly oval circle around the country, and he has been heading across the lower states, making his way closer to the western part of the country again. The last place he hit was in Arizona and I anticipate that he will start heading north soon. I figure that the next one or two robberies will put him in California. If he gets somewhat closer, I'll be able to get to the probable targets before him and wait for him. If I happen to miss the mark, I will only lose a day or so here and there and try to intercept him at his next robbery.

I'm going to have to figure out how to tail him and make my plans to take care of him. It will be difficult to follow him without tipping him off if I do manage to spot him. A number of scenarios run through my head.

I could involve Bill, but I would prefer to leave him out of it if possible because of what I plan to do to the man that murdered my wife and unborn child. I don't want him or anyone else to ever know about it. If I run into trouble, I can always bring Bill into the picture as a last resort. It will be essential to check, ahead of time, the areas around each of the places that I anticipate Dice Man to target.

A spot to carry out my plans for him has to be located. I need to find a place that is out of the way and very private. Maybe a deserted cabin in the woods somewhere would work. If I can find a couple of them at various points, each one farther north than the last one, I can always pick the one that is closest to the place where the scumbag is apprehended.

There is a feeling of apprehension building up in me. Maybe, just maybe, I'll be able to get to this guy in the next few months. As I think about this, my hands start to tremble a bit. If I am right about my feelings, then I'm going to have to make sure I stay in peak condition so I will have the best chance I can of succeeding in capturing this bastard. It would be easy to kill him from a distance with my rifle, but that isn't how this freak's life is going to end. I'll make sure to take a good shovel with me. I feel it in my bones that the day we meet is coming closer.

After spending a few hours online checking various out of the way places, I'm able to find a few spots where there may be a deserted cabin. I write down the locations of all the potentials. I continue with this on Saturday and plan on going to scout the areas next weekend.

Trying to cover all my bases, I may take the tranquillizer gun with me so I can use it to immobilize Jackson. After that, I can take him where I want to. I like this idea the best so far. I like this because, if I wound him too severely with a firearm, there is always a chance he could go into shock and die on me prematurely. I can't have that happening.

Sleep this night is an elusive thing because the adrenaline is already flowing in me. This is not a good thing. I don't want things to get to a head prematurely, because that will just wear me down. So I decide to try something new. I visualize all my thoughts as being right in front of me. Then I reach out with my hand to take hold of them. When I am able to do this, I place them in a drawer and close it, with the plan to bring them all out again tomorrow when I wake up. It takes a little while but it works. I heard about this technique on an interview with a hypnotherapist on television. Who would have thought that a simple thing like this would do the trick? I sleep the rest of the night and wake up well rested.

Sunday is spent relaxing around the yard keeping things in order. Later in the afternoon, I go to Baskette Slough Refuge and go for a run. Once I get to my favorite spot by the large pond, I sit on the bank. At this point, I let my mind go blank and try not to think of anything at all. I watch as the ducks go about their activities. The birds are chirping in the background and a warm breeze makes itself known. The wind sways the branches of the willow trees nearby. The water ripples slightly as it glides across the surface ever so softly and gently caresses my face, which is tilted up toward the sun. Being here alone seems to recharge me somewhat as the sights and sounds around me calm my spirit.

There are a few large white billowing clouds drifting across the sky and, for a few moments, I am at peace with the world. These moments are few and far between, so when I have them, they become a precious thing to me. I manage to stay this way for about half an hour.

A thought enters my mind, and I recall Linda and George and wonder how they are. They were such a nice couple, and I think of how nice it would be to have these folks for neighbors. George is showing his age but Linda looks very spry. What a pleasant gentle woman she is. I sure hope nothing ever happens to her, as she seems to be so fragile. I still wonder what made her ask about the Klan incident. I would almost have thought she knew something about me being involved. Of course, this is silly. How could such a kind-hearted old lady know anything about the ills of the world?

As I sit and ponder the way my life has gone, I wonder, as I have on occasion, just where I would be and what I would be doing if by chance my mother had not been murdered. I wonder if I would still have met Amy or Kathleen. Would I have gotten into the same trade that I am in or would I have gone in another direction?

I am sure that I would never have done the things I have done. I'd never have killed all the people I have. But, then again, so many more would have suffered at the hands of those that met their end because of me. These thoughts run through my head and get me nowhere. It's useless to ask these questions because there are no answers. You can't change what has already happened, so I head back home.

I have heard social service workers on occasion defending the actions of the underprivileged when they have turned to lives of crime. Tonight, I see an article about a person who had a very difficult time while growing up. He was beaten by his father and then by his older brother and bullied at school. Jesse ended up in a job no one wanted. He was a chicken plucker, removing feathers in a factory processing chickens. Jesse became a sickly paranoid person, going nowhere.

One day, he bought a ventriloquists dummy and went to work practicing. When he got good, he joined the military becoming part of the entertainment corps, making people laugh hysterically. He went on to become a very well-known person after landing a part on the Andy Griffith Show. His name turned out to be Jesse Don Knotts, the famous sidekick in the Andy of Mayberry show. This proves you can make something of yourself if you try. You don't have to let circumstances defeat you.

The rubber bullets have arrived, and I pick them up later in the week. The guys are still talking about the barbecue and the gifts. This has left a lasting impression on the men and the company will reap the benefits of the gesture for some time to come. Jim has been doing a good job on quality control and lets me know that things are really going well in that department. I do my job and don't have any problems, except when one of the guys catches me doing a personal item and asks me what it is for. He has caught me off guard and I don't have a ready answer for him. The bright idea hits me out of the blue.

"If I told you what this is for, I would have to kill you."

He laughs and walks away, much to my relief.

I have sometimes found that when everything is going well, there is something down the pipe that screws things up and causes a big shemozzle. I hope, for once, that this isn't the case. The rest of the week goes okay and, just for the heck of it, I go pay a visit to Adam Broadman, the pimp in Seattle. I haven't heard anything in the news about him so he may not have done anything serious lately. This could also mean that he is more careful about being caught too.

When I get into town, I do a drive by and notice that his house is for sale. The repair work has all been done and the sign is in the front of the house. Good, maybe he has learned something from our last encounter. I drive downtown to where the girls working for him always hung around and see different girls here. There is a guy hanging around who looks like he would be their pimp. I doubt any pimps share their locations with other scummies, so maybe Adam took my advice to get out of the business. I pull over by one of the girls and ask for Adam. She tells me he isn't around anymore.

"Say, honey, would you like a date? You won't be disappointed," she says as she smiles at me.

"Thanks, but I'm not here for that," I say as I'm driving away. "Well, well, I'm actually glad that Adam seems to have gotten away from this trade. I was going to finish him off but decided to give him a reason to be afraid and maybe learn something. Maybe he will do a turnaround and become a decent citizen."

Just to make sure, I go back to his neighborhood and park a little distance away. I walk to the house next door and, when a young man comes to the door, I ask him what happened to his next door neighbor.

"Ha, ha,haaaa, Adam was hung up in a tree with his pants pulled down and his junk was all tarred. After the incident, he was a changed man. He didn't make any more trouble around here and always walked with his head down. The house went up for sale shortly after the repairs were done, and Adam ended up moving before it sold."

That's all the young kid knows of it and goes on to say that everyone around the area is happy that he is gone.

I decide to stay the night in town and go to the Needle Restaurant located on top of a high tower. Expensive is a good word to describe this place. It's not for the average person, but the view is incredible. You see the snow covered Cascade Mountains, the ocean, and city in the revolving restaurant. This must be why the prices are so high. It couldn't have been cheap to build this place. The food, nevertheless, is very good and I come away feeling pretty satisfied.

The next day at home, I check some of the things I may end up taking with me when I go after Dice Man. I want to make sure everything is in perfect working order. I clean all my guns, the pistols, and rifles, as well as the semi-automatic twelve gauge shotgun.

I look at the watch that I modified. On the underside of

the watch, I drilled tiny holes and threaded them into each of the four arms that the strap attaches to. I made a flat plate that has a small blade attached to it. The super sharp blade swings out against a stop from between the watch and plate. I have never had the opportunity to use it but if I were ever captured and tied up I might be able to use it to cut the ropes. It is not particularly comfortable but could, one day, save my life.

Having picked up the rubber bullets, I go out to try a couple on a few different targets. Despite the fact that they are rubber, they do a fair bit of damage. The accuracy drops off rather quickly after the initial one hundred feet. So I will have to be careful about their use. I start to make a list of what I will bring with me and head up out of the basement for supper.

While I am getting the barbecue fired up, the phone rings and, seeing it is Bill, I answer it.

"I'm just checking in to see how you're doing," he says.

I use this chance to further mislead him. "I got the shakes once I got home and it ended up bothering me more than I first thought it would."

"I'm sorry that I got you involved, and I don't want to get into the habit of handling things this way. I think that this could lead me further down a road that I don't want to go. I've been giving this all a lot of thought, and I want to try to make this the last time I deal with difficult situations the way I did. I joined the police force, wanting to make a difference but not to do it the way the criminals handle things. I'm actually ashamed that I got you caught up in it all and would like it to never happen again. Can you try to forget that the incident ever happened? Please accept my apologies," he asks.

I let him know that my lips are sealed and that he doesn't need to worry about me. He goes on to say that he will continue to keep me informed about the activities of Dennis Jackson and that he won't ask me what I will be doing with the information.

So, it's a good thing that I kept my mouth shut. None of this pouring your heart out and, regretting it later for me. This is just another lesson to be learned from and reinforces the fact that I am on my own, no matter how things look at a sentimental moment. A feeling of relief comes over me. This has been weighing on me more than I thought. I guess I haven't lost anything as I am still on my own like I have been most of my life.

Monday, an incident comes to light as one of the guys, who has never really integrated into the shop very well, tries to sell what has to be stolen property to a fellow employee. The goods aren't from our shop but must be stolen nevertheless. He has gotten hold of a number of televisions and laptops and is selling them at low prices. Andrew, one of the young guys, lets me know about it, and I go see Abe about the incident.

The police are called and a meeting is set up. A pair of plain clothes detectives come into the office and Andrew, the lad who was offered the stolen electronics, is asked to make arrangements to see the merchandise. He is not keen on this plan because he fears retribution, so I volunteer to be the buyer. I go and talk to Bud, looking around before I say anything.

"Hey, Bud, I'm looking for a laptop and a cheap television and heard that you might be able to help me out.

"Sure, I can do that. I've got a few that I can show you. I'll have to be paid in cash though," he says with a grin on his face.

"No problem."

Bud is so eager to make a sale that he doesn't even question my willingness to buy from him or how I got the information. We agree to meet after work today at a place where he has the goods stored. Instead of walking into the office, possibly alerting Bud, I call Abe on my cell phone. He lets the detectives know where and when the meet is. We then come up with a method to let them know when to move in.

The rest of the day goes by quickly, and I follow Bud to the location of the stolen property. He has hidden everything in his garage and, when he opens the door and walks in, I look inside and see there are a lot of items. With my hand still on the outside door handle, I make a motion, signaling the detectives to move in.

"I can give you a real good deal on some of this stuff," Bud says as he goes inside. "What exactly are you looking for?"

Bud starts to show me some televisions and I am just telling him what I want as the door flies open. As the detective comes through the door, Bud runs to the back of the garage and kicks another door open. Just as he starts going through it, he finds himself confronted by a second detective who is waiting for him.

We are both placed under arrest and handcuffed. Bud is put in the back of a police cruiser and taken away. When he is gone, the handcuffs are taken off me and the detective thanks me for my help in the recovery of a substantial amount of stolen property. I was arrested along with Bud just to make sure he didn't know that I was involved in him getting apprehended.

So, another bad apple is no longer working at Salem Steel Fabrication. I make a call to Abe. "I just thought that I would let you know that everything has gone according to plan, and Bud has been arrested."

"Thank you so much, Joseph, the company really appreciates what you have done. Is there any chance that he'll try to get even with you?" Abe asks, concerned for my welfare.

"No, he thinks that I was arrested along with him so he doesn't have a clue that I was involved at all. Can you go out and talk to Andrew to make sure he keeps this to himself?"

"Sure thing, Joseph."

At home, I settle in with a Corona and fire up the barbecue. It's too bad that Bud had to get caught up in the business he did. If he had applied himself at work, he would have made decent money soon enough and could have had a good life. Now I doubt that he will ever get a good job again. I could be wrong, of course. I was wrong once before, I think.

Harry calls me up after supper and informs me that Brenda's birthday is coming up in a few weeks and he is going to throw her a surprise party at the house. I'm told that presents are not required, and they will be happy just to have me attend. All right! I'm looking forward to this.

The next day I have a chat with Andrew to reinforce Abe's talk with him. Letting him know what transpired and not to let Bud know that any of us were involved in his getting caught. I also ask him to keep it to himself that I helped to trap Bud and that I wasn't actually arrested. He is more than willing to go along with this as Bud would be upset at him too if he found out.

Bill drops off more information for me, and I can see he is uncomfortable. I come straight out with it and tell him to stop feeling any regrets. "You did what you thought was the right thing to do. Having constant second thoughts is self-defeating and only causes undue anxiety. There was no other way to handle the situation, and I don't think less of you for it. I actually respect you more now than ever. We won't discuss it unless something comes up where we need to, okay, buddy?" I say to him, slapping him lightly on the back.

This seems to take the strain away from him and he leaves with a much lighter mood.

I take the information downstairs and go through it. Jackson is heading exactly where I suspected. He has hit two more B and Bs in the towns I thought he might go to. The first place he went to was Wickenburg, Arizona, and the second is Blythe, just inside the California border near Arizona.

Both are small towns and each only has two or three places that he would be likely to target. The robberies are three weeks apart and the descriptions of him are close to what I anticipated. There are police drawings that keep me informed as to how he disguises himself.

The vehicle seems to be different each time, which makes me suspect that he either borrows the car from someone or steals it. He must bring it back because there are seldom reports of this type of vehicle being stolen in the areas, as far as I can find out. This is what I would do in his position. With the car being stolen and then brought back, the owner most of the time might not even know it was gone if it is done right. If a plate number was given to the police and they tracked down the car, the owner would be a suspect and attention would be diverted.

This robber, on occasion, has hurt people who have been too slow in giving him what he demands. Several people have been hospitalized and a few have permanent disabilities because of Jackson. It will be a real pleasure dealing with this bastard.

One of the next towns I think he might go to is Salton City on the edge of Salton Lake either that or Brawley, but I think this town might be a little big for him. Besides, there are too many potential targets here for me to cover, so I would never be able to guess the right one.

I make the decision to keep tracking him until there are only one or two towns available and the likely targets are slim. If I go to places with too much potential, I'll be running around in circles. So despite that fact that I am chomping at the bit, I'm going to have to wait a little longer. Payback is, at this point, the driving force in my life, so I have no choice but to wait and see if my guesses are right.

On the news, it's reported that a suspected prostitution and pornography ring is operating in Los Angeles. The police have been trying to curtail their activities with no real impact. The men reportedly are from Colombia and, if the information is correct, they attract young girls with stories of stardom or a new life, get them hooked on drugs, and force them into porn movies and prostitution on the streets.

These men have been charged and their faces are shown

on camera, actually smiling at the reporters. They have yet to serve jail time as they have the best attorneys money can buy and some loophole is always found. Either that, or someone else takes the fall. How this happens baffles me.

I record the story so I can get their names for future consideration. These men are in our country and force our citizens and immigrants into horrible lives, just so they can make money. How this country has allowed this to happen is beyond me. What possesses people to want to watch this kind of shit? It seems that society has really fallen morally and too many think that anything goes. Well, it goes until it happens to them.

Maybe the land of the free should be re-evaluated. There needs to be a price for this kind of freedom. I believe that I have just found my next targets. I'm not sure that I will be able to make a big dent in this business, but at least there will be a few less participants.

I get the proper spelling of the names and start my research. I try to find addresses but, so far, I must be looking in the wrong areas. This type of person I find despicable. They don't belong in our country—or anywhere else, for that matter. I wonder how many lives these men have ruined. What the hell is wrong with the world today that such scum is allowed to flourish? Where are the people that say they care? Is everyone just turning a blind eye to these problems or are they afraid of offending the wrong people?

I'm starting to think that many of our politicians are almost as bad as the lowlifes that infest our land. The other end of the problem is the fact that, for this type of…for lack of a better word…entertainment to flourish, there has to be a market for it. I need to put this down for the night because it's really starting to irritate me, bloody hell!

Being Saturday when I wake up the next morning, I go horseback riding. I have been busy the last two weeks and have missed the opportunity to get away from it all for a couple of hours.

I go off by myself and enjoy the solitude of the streams

and trails through the woods. I get off the horse beside the stream and let it have a drink.

The birds are making a pleasant background noise as the water tumbles over rocks in the stream. I could get used to this if I didn't have other plans already made for me by my circumstances in life. The air is cool as it gently blows through the trees. I even take the time to smell a few of the wild flowers. The next hour, following trails in and out of the woods, brings me a respite from my concerns.

Before heading back to the stables, I take the horse across a meadow where the wind causes the grasses to sway back and forth. Running along the ground, stopping periodically to sniff the air, is a weasel. It finds a hole in the side of a small mound and, after sticking its head in, disappears into it.

The horse suddenly changes direction, avoiding a small ditch, and I almost lose my balance in the saddle. It's a good thing we were going at a slow pace, otherwise I would have been on the ground. I pat the horse on the neck as we head back.

After dismounting and removing the saddle, I give the horse a nice rubdown. As I am working near the front end of the animal, it turns its head and touches me on the arm in a gesture of what I take as friendship. It seems that the horse and I are becoming buddies. I go and pay Ben and, after a little chat, head home.

Doing what needs to be done around the house, I do a little tour just to see that nothing is getting away from me as far as maintenance is concerned. Everything seems all right, so I go online to get some information on the Colombian porn producers. I finally find a story where their entire names are given. Luis Rodriguez seems to be the leader and the others, Miguel Dias, Carlos Rojas, and Manuel Garcia are his crew. I make a few inquiries with the CDC and the other sites and get a lot of the information that I want.

They all seem to live at the same place. The home is a huge modern-looking house that is the last residence on the high side of Ceanothus Drive in the Laguna Beach area. Laguna Beach is an absolutely gorgeous spot, a little too heavily populated for me but beautiful, nevertheless. This place is perfect as it backs onto the foothills and is easily accessible from the rear. I don't have a plan at this point but at least I know where they live and that's a start.

I don't know why the whole group resides in one place, but the residence is large enough to give everyone some privacy. I wonder if any of the girls are kept there. I rather doubt that this would be the case, but you never know.

I'll have to find a few spots to put my car while I do some surveillance. I should be able to gather some information while watching from a distance during the day and up close at night.

Chapter 32

Dennis

So where to next?" Dennis Jackson asks himself.

He knows he has been lucky and needs to make sure he is careful. He makes his choices, usually, by looking at maps and staying away from large towns. The cops in the bigger places have more resources and can set up roadblocks much quicker than the smaller ones. Besides, the cities that are too big have access to helicopters, and they could present a real problem.

He chuckles to himself. "I don't know why I worry about this shit. If I was some rank amateur, I would have been caught long ago. I'm not going to be caught and go back to prison. Been there and don't like it."

He knows that he has honed his skills to perfection. He tried having a partner a couple of times but, hell, why should he split the money and leave himself open to a double-cross. You can't leave yourself vulnerable to these assholes. That was why he went to prison in the first place. In order to get a lighter sentence, a two-bit rookie turned him in. It took a long time to get even with him. Dennis had to do a lot of favors in order to exact his revenge. Some of these favors are things he doesn't like to remember any more than he has to.

"The only good thing that happened to me in prison is when I got the idea for this wild tattoo." People ask him about it all the time, and his answer is always the same. "I make my own luck and don't leave things to chance."

"So where to next?" he repeats. This money should last me for a week or two but I don't want to run too short because then I have to pull a job before I'm actually ready."

Dennis knows that he could probably get a regular job because he is a fairly personable type and can sway people fairly easily, but why would he want to? Free money is so much more fun and rewarding than the lousy wages that the average dope makes. He is not a dope and nobody better ever call him that. One guy said something like that to him once and almost didn't live to regret it. He had to eat through a straw for a long time.

This brings a smile to Dennis's face. "I never did like that jerk, anyway. He always thought he was better than me. He might have had a better education, but I do in life what I want, and that idiot is a slave to his job and that fat wife and ugly kids of his."

This always makes Dennis feel good. *Yeah, this is the life.* "Okay, Salton City, here I come. It's where I'm going to go because it looks like the best place to pick up some more money. The amount of money better be a lot more than the last one."

The small paydays piss him off.

Dennis enjoys talking to himself. He has some of his best conversations this way. He does occasionally get some odd looks, but who cares?

Chapter 33

Why the hell are these women so stupid? Why can't they just do as they are told? I get them the best drugs money can buy and give them a job at the same time. They don't want the job, at first, but that doesn't last too long. Take away the drugs and a little slap here and there, and they soon come around," Luis Rodrigues says to no one in particular. He also likes to talk to himself now and then.

He has been in this business for a long time. Luis started working for Rafael back in Colombia when he was a kid and moved up the ranks quickly. He had a real penchant for this life. When he had the chance, he grabbed the reins of power when Rafael least expected it and became the head of the group. Later when he got the chance, he moved to California, and he loved it as soon as he got here. He has to fly back and forth to maintain control in Columbia but is thinking that he'll take the offer made to him by his top man down there. It would relieve a lot of pressure and the chance of a coup. He makes the call and a deal is struck with the finances being transferred to his offshore accounts.

"Yeah, this really is the land of opportunity. Where else

can you get so much for so little? You don't even have to
pay all that much to stay in business here. God bless America, oh, yes."

Luis likes to live in the same big house that his friends
and employees do. The girls live in the other place, the one
that is not as nice as this home. The movies themselves are
filmed and produced in an area of town that has some light
industry going on, and the girls are brought in the night before so no one is the wiser.

There are men living with the girls in the second house
and they get to have some fun with them, as long as they
don't mark up the girls. This would be bad for business because the bruises are picked up by the cameras and those
fools who buy the movies don't like the girls hurt...well, at
least not most of them.

What a country this is. You get rich from these people
who get their kicks by watching others doing what they
wish they could. Luis never did like watching this shit much
but has no problem making money from it.

You would be surprised at how fast the young men learn
not to hurt the girls. Luis made a real example of one of the
men who did what he was told not to do. Now this, Luis did
like doing. It was fun beating the boy half to death while the
others watched. Maybe he should look for a reason to do it
again.

Of course, there is one young man that Luis has other
uses for, but this is only done when Miguel, Carlos, and
Manuel are not around. Luis likes women but, now and
then, he needs a different kind of entertainment. Philippe
knows not to ever let on about their relationship. He knows
that he would be the next one beaten if he were to say the
wrong thing, ever.

Money buys anything in this country, it doesn't matter
how you get it. Some of the movies that he has made are
even considered art. Of course, Luis has other people make
the movies. After all, that is what he pays them for. So what
if he takes all the credit and most of the money? So far, he

has managed to avoid any kind of prosecution. Money placed in the right hands and a recording of the transaction has paid big dividends.

Miguel and the other two are in charge of producing the movies. This way, he doesn't have to see what the girls are made to do. Who knows? One day he might even put this life behind him. If only he didn't have so many enemies. There are still men in Columbia who would like to get him alone.

Chapter 34

Joseph

Now that I finished making the arrows that have the modified end on them, I need to try them out. I debated a while as to what caliber to use and finally went with a twenty two long rifle shell. The end of the arrow unscrews and the shell is inserted. When it is screwed back together the shell sits in front of a firing pin. The pin is the end of a hardened, thin, slightly pointed steel dowel that is inserted into a tight hole drilled into the end of the arrow. There is a small light spring inside to hold the shell away from the pin until impact. When the arrow hits a target the momentum slams the firing pin into the end of the shell and it fires.

Heading out to a remote area, I try out a couple of the arrows. Everything works like a charm. All you need to do is make sure that the target is hit fairly straight on. A glancing shot doesn't always work, because the shell doesn't hit the pin hard enough or at all.

There is no damage to the arrows that hit the mark straight on, and I only lose one arrow that is bent because of hitting a tree wrong. I used a thread with a high helix angle so it only takes two turns to unload and put a new shell in.

The noise is not particularly loud, which I like. The end of the arrow is larger than normal so it doesn't penetrate the target. If possible, I want to retrieve the arrows before I leave the vicinity, and not having it stuck in somebody will help expedite my escape. Now that this has been tested, I will make enough to be certain that I won't run out.

With these things, I should be able to take out someone from a distance fairly quietly. There isn't much noise made when I hit a target that is similar to a person. I could just use a regular arrow but this will cause a lot more damage, even if it isn't a killing shot. Plus, these arrows can be put to other uses, making them invaluable.

At the end of the week, I have twenty arrows made and a box and a half of shells. That should be plenty. My arsenal is building up fast and so I go on to my next task. I made some explosive arrows a while back, and I look these over to see if there are any improvements that can be made. These items work much like the arrows I just made and do a lot of damage when used. I haven't had to use them during any of my dealings so far but they would have come in real handy when I went after the Carlos brothers. I might not have gotten shot twice during that encounter if I'd had them then.

I wonder what will happen if I have a twelve gauge shotgun shell attached to the end of an arrow where only the metal casing is secured. Will the shell explode, sending pellets in all directions? Maybe this can be an experiment for the future when I have nothing to do.

In my mind, I see the face of Dennis Jackson, and it is all I can do to control myself. I desperately want to find him and show him my displeasure. I will get him, oh yes, I will get him for sure. This will be the settling of a debt too long in the collecting. You would think that after all this time my feelings would have subsided more than they have.

November journal entry: *I have been without Kathleen for what seems an eternity and yet when I am not careful I can easily fly into a rage over my loss. So far, I have been lucky that I haven't been seen when I do lose control. Thank god, for my friends who help me to cope. What would I do if I didn't have them to…*

It has been three weeks since Bill last dropped off any new information for me and I'm glad when he phones. When he comes over, it is late Saturday afternoon and it's Corona time. We sit and talk for a while, and it's nice to see that we have managed to put the last incident behind us. He seems to be doing quite well, and I ask how he and his wife are getting along. There have been a few times when the job has gotten between them and she was more than a little unhappy with him. He tells me that he is learning to prioritize the things in his life better and it shows.

I tell him I'm glad as he asks if there is anyone in my life. I say there isn't anyone who can compare to Kathleen, and that I have no interest in looking. There is a girl at work who was interested in me for a while but she finally got the message. We finish our beer and he hands me an envelope. He tells me that the police have made little real head way into the case and hopes that I get what I want from the information. We say our goodbyes, and I go downstairs with the package.

There is another robbery and it is north of the Salton Sea. It's not an actual Bed and Breakfast but a motel in Mecca. It seems that this is the closest thing to one in the town. The Salton Sea was once a thriving tourist spot. As time went on in the nineteen seventies, it started accumulating deposits of salt and other minerals, being a lake with no exit. It became so unhealthy that the entire tourist industry collapsed. This influenced my decision to choose Mecca as one of Jackson's next targets.

I look the map over and try to locate what I anticipate will be the next target. I have a feeling he'll swing south again before heading north as the weather starts to warm up again. Yucca Valley seems like a good choice and Desert

Hot Springs is my second pick. If I were to go to either of these towns, I should have a monitor so I can listen in on police calls. I might then be able to get a description of the car and somehow abduct him, ditching him in the trunk till I can get him to the desired location. How to abduct him is the question of the day, though.

I decided to look online for rubber bullets that will work in one of my pistols and find some for my caliber, ordering a box. The only reason for these is because I don't want to kill the bastard, this comes later. I don't think that there is a need to procure a set of handcuffs if I have him in my trunk as the zip ties should be adequate.

I find a Uniden Bearcat scanner that should do the job nicely. It seems easy to use and only costs me about two hundred bucks, when all is said and done. I manage to locate one in Seattle and pay cash for it. The salesman will never recognize me if he is asked to describe the customer who bought the unit. After trying it out for a bit, I get the hang of using it pretty quick. At least with the scanner, I can listen in on any reports on a robbery that is or has happened and get news quickly if I'm in the area. I'm not sure why I never thought about getting one of these before. It would have kept me informed when I was carrying out one of my…for lack of a better term…escapades.

I sure hope that I am in the vicinity when Jackson pulls off a robbery and just after it is reported so I can nab him. I really need to think of a way to apprehend him without having a shootout or something stupid like that. If I can locate him and find out where he is holed up, maybe the tracker can be attached to his car like was done with Jake Patterson and Angelo. That way tabs can be kept on him at a distance. It sure made my job a lot easier with Jake, as there was no way I could have kept track of where he was without it. He was way too street smart to follow without being noticed. I doubt very much that I'll get the opportunity to make this happen with Jackson.

I plan to wait with Jackson till he makes his way closer

and I am fairly sure of the place he will hit. Maybe I'll be able to tail him a bit after he leaves the scene of the crime if I can figure out which direction he will most likely go.

I keep my martial arts up and go online now and then to sites demonstrating what is considered to be dirty fighting. It's good to learn as many of the tricks as possible. It doesn't matter how I win any encounters because I know without a doubt that the types I go against will do anything to win. That is why I train so hard and, if at all possible, strike first and strike hard. You may not get a second chance. Fight from a distance if you can because, no matter how good you are, anyone can get in a lucky shot or have a friend behind you with a gun.

As soon as I can, I'm going to go through all the information I have on the robberies. I want to see how much money he gets each time and calculate how long it lasts him. I have an idea forming in my head, and I need the research to verify my suspicions.

The weekend comes, and I take an extra day off and head down to see Luis and his buddies. I need to occupy myself while I'm waiting for the bastard that I really want.

After getting into LA, I find a place to stay. With only a minimum number of my tools of the trade with me, I don't plan to do anything more than watch and pickup information on these stinking lowlifes. These men offend my sense of values to no end. I find people like this and their customers to be vile. If there wasn't a market for this crap, these idiots wouldn't be making this shit. I may try to find out where they produce this stuff and see what can be done about it. The only way I can get this information, though, is to either follow them or extract it from one of the boys, which means having a heart to heart with him. In this respect, I have become quite callous over the years, but only when dealing with this type of person and not done to excess.

Finding a motel that meets my needs and getting a rental car, I do a little scouting around Luis's area. I notice that the modern-looking home he and his three friends have adjoins a rolling hills area that is above the rear of the property. There is a lot of ground cover that will provide adequate places to observe from, plus there are rises and low spots to hide in. Because I was unsure of how close I would be able to get, I picked up a more powerful set of binoculars. These are twenty-power glasses and considerably heavier but they give me the ability to watch from a greater distance before putting myself in a precarious position.

The hills are quite high above the home and allow me a superior vantage point. It is fairly easy to find a spot to hide as the sun is shining brightly and no one seems to want to venture out into the hot dry hills. I wear a rather large hat that blends in with the scenery. The back of the house has a series of large windows that overlook a pool.

With the sun behind me, I can look inside the house on the different levels and get a good idea of what is going on. The windows are tinted against the sun but still allow me a view. I spot two people in the house and Miguel in the pool. Luis is not visible at the moment and could be anywhere. I start looking for weak points that I can use to my advantage. To my surprise, there is a cross mounted on the wall. Why they would have this here is beyond me. Maybe they think if they pray once in a while, that their sins will be forgiven. I'm pretty sure they better think that one over again.

There is a low wall around the back of the concrete pad that surrounds the pool. It's about three feet high and there for decoration only. There is a path that leads into the hills that comes up from the side of the garage. It looks as if there are faint tire tracks on it from a quad.

Soon, I'll have to get a better vantage point, one that will allow me to get to the car more quickly, in case I need to follow one of the boys when he or they go somewhere. I find a spot down the road from their house and park under a tree. Pulling out a map, I familiarize myself with the area. Having the map out will also dissuade anyone from looking at me too closely, thinking that I am a tourist, which I guess

I am. The rest of the day is a waste of time as I don't learn anything. I come back in the later evening and again learn nothing.

The next day, I catch Miguel and Carlos driving away and have to run to my car in order to follow them to a residence off by itself in a rather run-down section of the city. The windows are all covered from the inside which doesn't allow me to find out anything about what is happening inside. I am pretty sure this must be the place where either the videos are made or the girls are kept. A few people come and go throughout the morning and, using the binoculars, I get a peek inside when the door is open. What I see confirms my suspicions, and I'll see what can be done about this place down the road. There is no security that I can see, and I doubt anyone would break into the dwelling because of who is here. When I take care of the scumbags, I'll put this place out of business one way or another.

Now all I need to do is figure out how to take out these guys. I decide to go back to the hills behind their house and see what I can come up with. It would be nice to just blow the place up but there is always the chance a somewhat innocent person is in there. I wonder if there is a way to get the floor plan to the house. I'd like to get in there and do a super-fast mop up and then burn the place down once I've killed Luis and his boys and cleared out anyone who doesn't deserve to die. I have my doubts that I will catch all of them in there at the same time, though, unless it's done in the middle of the night. What to do? My time here is about done and, though I have learned a few things, I still don't have a concrete plan.

Chapter 35

Luis

Okay, Miguel and the other two are at the movie house and tell me they have the latest batch ready to distribute," Luis says to Philippe. "They will be out of the house for the rest of the day, and we won't be disturbed."

Off they go to a more private part of the house.

Later, when Luis is relaxing by the pool he thinks that he is almost ready to call it quits. Another year or two, and he will have all he needs to disappear and start a new life on some remote island. He is not sure if Philippe will be coming with him. Luis is starting to tire of the boy. He actually likes male company less and less and is thinking of becoming celibate. He has done in life all he has ever wanted to do and would like to just continue with his artwork. He has become quite a good artist in his own right and would like to pursue this avenue in his retirement years.

Chapter 36

Joseph

On my way home, I get stuck behind an RV that has a motorcycle on a trailer behind it. The long winding hill we are on doesn't allow me to pass safely so I am trapped here for about ten miles. When I finally get an opening, I floor it and fly by the unit. The rest of the drive is uneventful and I get home in the early evening on Monday.

After I get everything unpacked and put away, I look at the answering machine and listen to the one message earlier today from Harry. He asks that I call him immediately when I hear the message. When I get him on the phone, he tells me that Gord is nowhere to be found and that he hasn't been to any of his friend's homes.

"He's been gone for about eight hours and Brenda is frantic."

"What can I do to help?" I ask.

He tells me that it would be nice if I could check the mall Gord frequents, and I am on my way, after I grab one of my photos of him. This is something that he has never done before and is somewhat out of character. When I get to the mall, I do a quick walk about and see no sign of him. I then head to areas that he might go to and show his picture, with no results there either. I see a group of kids his age and decide to ask them. Everyone says no, except for one, and, when he looks away, I know something is up. I fix my eyes on him and wait for him to look at me.

"What?" he asks.

I don't say anything and he starts to mumble.

"Where is he?" I finally ask.

He looks down and says that he is with one of the older kids from school. He tells me the location after a bit of prodding.

"Don't make the mistake of phoning the kid, or I'll be back to visit you, understand?"

The kid just nods with his eyes all bugged out.

The place I go to is an area that I would have thought Gord would know better than to go to. I knock on the door and a kid about eighteen opens it. I tell him why I am here, and he tries to slam the door but my foot kicks it open. I tell him to get Gord or I call the cops. He starts to give me some lip as I advance and decides that may not be a good idea.

"Get him, or I get you. Take your pick."

To reinforce this, I throw a kick right over his head, and he almost runs to the other room. There is a bunch of yelling and finally, Gord is dragged out of a room and stands in front of me, completely intoxicated. I don't say a word. I just throw him over my shoulder and leave.

I then phone Harry and let him know that I found him and that I will bring him home shortly. Gord babbles some nonsense, to which I don't bother replying. I'm sure he will have enough time to talk when he gets home. Harry and Brenda, as well as Eva, meet me when I pull up. Brenda is crying when we get Gord out of the car and into the house. I decide to let them deal with this problem alone and slip out to the car. I sure hope he doesn't get caught up in the booze thing, I've seen it happen too many times already.

Chapter 37

On the weekend before I leave to check on the porno boys, I go online and check with the CDC site that has given me so much information in the past and then the other sites I use. I have learned to do my searches on all the sites and through several different computers, using a browser that hides my IP address, so that it appears that my questions are being asked by many separate people.

I don't get anything useful, so I head out and, after I get there, I spend a fair bit of time in the hills. As evening approaches, people start arriving. Tables have been set up inside and a wide variety of food is brought in and placed on them. There is a portable bar near the pool with a bartender mixing drinks for the guests. There appear to be several influential people here that I can't place, but they seem to command a great deal of respect from others. There are no working girls that I can see, so this may be an appreciation party for favors done. I assume these are politicians and people who have been paid to look the other way when needed.

Maybe Luis is trying to achieve an air of respectability in the social circles. There is a band playing music that is more of a refined type that seems to appeal to the women present. They are obviously wives and girlfriends. Just for future consideration, I video the scene. Who knows what use, if any, this will have? Nothing of any interest happens for a while so I head back to my room.

So Luis travels in circles that I would not have expected or so, at least, it would appear. This, of course, could just be an infrequent episode and maybe I am reading more into it than I should. It could be that he managed to get everyone together for a purpose that is totally outside his pornography business. I sure hope so, for the sake of the people attending.

I take a trip to the site outside of town where the movies are made. This is the place that I learned about when I followed the three amigos in order to get a better layout of the area. I familiarize myself with quick ways out. After doing a bit of ground surveillance, I find a back entrance that I use to gain entry into the building. It is difficult to get in but, once in, I manage to get a fair idea of the interior configuration of the rooms. It appears that the work has been suspended because of the party. This is a stroke of luck for me. A plan immediately forms in my head. There is a lot of equipment and supplies in the building, as well as a few stashes of which when opened reveal themselves to be drug storage containers. If I play this right, I can do some major damage to the Columbians' business. I only need to come up with a decent plan for the boys themselves, and I'll be good to go.

Chapter 38

Luis

The party has been a success and we may be one step closer to breaking into a nationwide distribution network for our products," Luis tells Miguel.

"Yes, then we can make some real money."

"The business has come a long way in the time we have been in America," Luis admits.

"The councilman has the contacts we need and his cut will be minimal. A lot less than we thought he would demand," Miguel says.

"We are on our way to the big times!" Luis replies.

Off to their separate quarters the men go with a feeling of satisfaction. As Luis drifts off to sleep, he is thinking that his retirement may have to be postponed for a while. Why would he want to give up such a lucrative venture prematurely?

Chapter 38

Dennis

As Dennis makes plans for his next withdrawal from the B and B that he has chosen to visit, he sees that his RV is starting to show signs of wear. There will be problems if he doesn't take care of those things soon. This means he will either need to repair it or purchase a newer one. Either way, it is going to cost money, more money than he has. This means that he will have to take a greater risk and pull several jobs quickly or have a much larger payday than he has had in quite some time.

He doubts very much that he can get a better unit for very little extra cash. When he was younger, he would have intimidated some clown into making a swap for a better RV. Those days are gone now, since he is more or less on the run. At least no one has any idea what he really looks like or what mode of transportation he uses.

Too bad he had to shoot that good-looking woman in the Napa Valley about a year ago. He hadn't meant to do this but things turned sour, and he had fired the gun accidentally in all the excitement. It wasn't a pistol he was used to and the trigger required far less pressure to shoot than normal.

That idiot he had partnered with had gotten himself

caught and sent to prison. The guy didn't know much about Dennis but any little thing can hurt. Dennis just can't remember if he mentioned anything about living in an RV and moving around the country this way. Dennis likes traveling in decent weather. That is why he is down south in the winters and up north in the summers. Just like those snow animals or ducks, or was it birds? Whatever!

He has to figure out a way to get more money quick with minimal risk.

Chapter 39

Joseph

I finish off a few rush jobs at work and make my final plans of how to handle Luis and the boys. I believe that this will need to be a two-stage job. It looks like I'll have to make my preparations on site over the course of two weekends. I would rather do it in one because of the risk of having my preparations discovered and alerting the men.

Most of the materials and supplies are already on hand. I received my last items during the week and am, for the most part, ready to start the first stage. The production center of the operation is in a very light industrial area. This means that people frequent the area mostly during the day and it is relatively deserted at night.

On the weekend, I go back to the Laguna Beach area and hide in the hills behind the home on Ceanothus Drive. Waiting long enough to make sure that all four men are there and, when it is dark, I head back to my room. After setting the alarm for three in the morning, I try to fall asleep. As usual, this is not easy as plans keep rolling around in my head as I look for flaws and areas of improvement.

Finally, I drift off and, before I know it, the alarm goes off. I've left my car directly in front of the room and, because there is a light directly over it and the fact that I have a steering lock visible, I am not overly concerned about possible break-ins. After getting ready, I drive out to Laguna Canyon Road and to the street slightly away from the building.

This area is quite out of the way and appears to be deserted. I'm dressed in black and, as I carry the dark duffle bag, I blend into the night. Getting to the back door, I put my ear to the metal wall, listening for any sounds. All seems quiet and I manage to open the door again with minimal prying and effort. I try not to do any damage or leave marks. The lock system is very inferior, which surprised me the first time I broke in. Just to make sure, I check that I am not monitored by any cameras that may have been recently installed.

All is clear and I cautiously plant the devices I brought with me in spots they will not be noticed. There are quite a number of things I need to place. This is going to be a two-stage project, and I will have to start things remotely when the time is right. I would like to have done the entire job in one night but too many details have to line up for that to work flawlessly.

It takes half an hour to get everything set and me out the door. It takes an extra minute to get the bloody door secured properly again. I think I may have done a little damage to the lock, hopefully not. Without a key, I can't be sure about that.

Back in the hills behind the Columbians' house, I watch for a short time, but nothing is to be seen, as all the lights are out. I can't make a move as I can't be sure everyone is in the house and that there are no guests sleeping over. This is why I couldn't take action tonight.

This being Saturday, I can't wait until tomorrow night because it is a long drive home and I need to be back to work on Monday. I'm going to book an extended weekend when I get to work. Maybe I should take a week off just to be sure. But, then again, if I do that, I may not be able to take enough time off to deal with Dice Man. I'll have to keep this job down to a three-day weekend.

Monday comes and finds me having to rework a pile of work where the customer has made extensive drawing changes and much of the job has to be started over. This puts us behind schedule and means I may have to work Saturday. I tell Abe that I will work overtime during the week for straight time pay to see if I can get things caught up before this weekend. That way I'll still be able to have the three days off.

I have myself geared up to do the Columbians this weekend and don't want to take the chance of having my things discovered. I end up working four hours a day extra and, by Thursday, I have things caught up. I am asked why the hurry by a couple of the boys and I let them know that I have camping plans for the weekend, prompting one guy to ask if I want company.

"Thanks but this is the time I use to regenerate and I need to be alone."

I think he is a little disappointed but this can't be helped. I am known by most to be a loner and maybe even a bit antisocial but I do try to go out with the boys now and then. I have to keep this to a minimum because it always leads to too many questions.

After work, I go for a run and then pack up the last of my tools ready to load in the car after work tomorrow. Friday is an easier day but seems to drag a bit. Checking the weather for California I find that it is going to be warm and sunny for the next several days. This is good for me, as I am not fond of waiting in the rain for the right moment to present itself. After work, I load up everything that I want to bring with me and store it in the hidden compartment in the trunk.

It's a nine-hundred-and-seventy-mile drive so I have asked for a couple of extra days off. After driving just over fifteen hours, I get to my destination and go to sleep for the day. This serves my purpose well, as I want to hit Luis and the boys in the evening tonight to make sure they are all there. I will have to watch for quite a while after supper to make certain.

Hopefully, there won't be a party again, as this will force me to postpone things.

I wake up groggy and have a long shower then go for a good meal. I rent a car near the motel so I can walk to the rental place. When the coast is clear, I move the things I need into the second car.

After finding a good safe place to park the car, I hide in the hills behind the Columbians' house and wait, to keep an eye on things. I haven't brought anything out of the ordinary with me, just in case someone goes for a walk and spots me, which has happened once. I managed to look like a bird watcher, at the time, and the person just waved and went on.

I continue to keep an eye out for potential interruptions as well as watching the house, because the last thing I need is a bystander to be present when I want to make my move. The tension starts to build as the evening progresses.

I see movement in the house from time to time and see Luis, Miguel, and Carlos but not Manuel. In the driveway one of the cars is missing so I am going to have to wait. It is nine o'clock and too early for what I want to do, anyway. I feel like leaving for a bit and coming back later but this may not be a good idea. I then won't know for sure that every-one is in the house, plus extra guests could arrive by taxi or with Manuel. I relieve myself a short distance away, which also allows me to scout the area at the same time.

Half an hour later, Manuel comes driving in. Damn, he isn't alone. There is a man in a suit with him, who looks like a businessman. He could be anybody. Maybe he is as bad as them and maybe not, so I am reluctant to take him out with the rest.

I haven't seen any weapons around at any time up to now, but that doesn't mean there aren't any. I doubt very much that these men would be unarmed in this house. There is nothing to do but wait. It's a good thing I brought a little food and water with me. I find I need to dig a little hole and really relieve myself. This I do a little distance away, covering it with sand and put a rock over it so I won't accidentally step in it.

Time drags by, and I start to wonder if the visitor may spend the night, but at eleven-thirty a taxi rolls up and the man leaves. Finally, I manage to catch a break. I'll have to wait till about two in the morning before I make a move one way or the other. I settle in and make myself comfortable. It starts to get chilly, and I put on a dark jacket. The moon illuminates things just enough for me to be able to keep a wary eye out.

All of a sudden, there is a rustle in the brush about a hundred feet away from me. I snatch up the night vision goggles and scan the area, looking in the general area that the noise came from. It takes about thirty seconds before I spot the intruder. A coyote is looking for a meal and, as I make a rustle of my own, he spots me and, because I am much larger than he is, he leaves. I run possible scenarios through my head to pass the time. It goes by very slowly, and I almost fall asleep a few times. I pour some cold water into my hands and wash my face now and then to keep me alert.

When two o'clock arrives, I reach for the duffle bag, remove what I want from it, and lay the rest of the stuff inside the opening, ready to grab if I need it. The light from the moon is just bright enough to see my things so I can grab the items that I want.

I have my semi-automatic pistol in the holster on my hip and the knife in its sheath on the other side. The Remington 300 magnum rifle with a scope is propped up beside me. The bow is ready and the arrows, in the order I plan to use them, are in front of me.

The moment has come and after a few deep breaths, I pick up a large stone. Moving closer to the back of the property I throw it in a long arc through the air and into the pool. There is a large splash. Well before Luis and Carlos come out to see what is going on, I am back with the bow in my hand and an arrow in place. Just as I thought it would be, they are standing there, gesturing with pistols in their hands.

I let loose with the first arrow at Luis. As it strikes him in the chest, I have another arrow ready to shoot it at Carlos. Just as I am about to let it go, he fires the pistol at the hills and turns to run into the house. I let her go and catch him as he is entering the door. If I had not already known where he was going to go, it would have been a much harder shot. I decided to use regular arrows first as my accuracy is better with them.

So with two down, the lights come on inside the house as Manuel and Miguel run down the stairs. As they reach the bottom, they see Carlos on the floor with an arrow in his back and both duck behind a bar in the living area.

I fire three arrows with the twenty two shells in them three feet apart near the top of the window in front of the bar, providing weak spots in the glass. The next arrow has the explosive charge and it impacts about six feet lower. The glass now weakened higher up shatters and leaves a huge opening. With the rifle, I shoot several rounds into the bar, and both duck out of sight through a doorway leading to where I think the garage is before I can nail them. This has to end quickly now because I am sure someone in the area must have phoned the police by now.

The light from the garage door opening hits the driveway and out comes a quad with both men on it. Instead of running away, they turn up the hillside heading in my direction. Crap, I no longer have the option of hightailing it out of here.

Miguel is on the back and is firing an automatic weapon in any direction he thinks may be the hiding place of the intruder. Manuel turns this way and that, trying to illuminate a target, making it difficult for me to line up a shot. I have no choice but to give them a target so I jump and, when I know I have been spotted, I duck just in time as a hail of bullets come my way, several hitting the sand and narrowly missing me.

I am in a low spot so quickly run to the right, going up-hill but still hidden. They are so busy driving and shooting where I was that they don't see me thirty feet away to the side and just high enough to line up a shot which takes out Manuel. The quad hits a dip and flips over.

Miguel is in the dirt, scrambling to retrieve his weapon, and manages to find it as I come running at him. I have the pistol in my hand and, as he raises the gun, I fire several shots, one hitting him in the shoulder. He drops the weapon, screaming in pain and, with the other hand, gropes for the pistol in his waistband. By this time, I am close enough to fire a fatal shot which I do as I shout, "Visa expired, ass-hole."

I run back toward my things and shoot Manuel on the way just to make sure he is dead. Picking up the rifle, I put one in Luis and Carlos just to make certain they are dead too. I gather my things, heading for the car at full tilt. This whole incident took longer than I was hoping it would and may have left me more vulnerable than I planned for. I have to get out of here as fast as I can because, in the distance, I hear sirens wailing.

I'm out of breath and my heart is pounding as I make my way to the car. I hope I have enough time to make good my escape. I figured out ahead of time that the police will be coming from the more heavily populated part of the city where the main roads are. I throw my stuff in the trunk and get behind the wheel as the sirens are screaming toward the house from the other side of the property, one street over.

I head toward the suburbs at what seems like a snail's pace. I want desperately to floor it, but I want to attract as little attention as possible. Luckily, I found a place to park that was very close to the hiding spot I had, which allowed me a fairly quick and safe exit. Well, as safe as one could hope for.

I drive toward Laguna Canyon Road with the adrenalin still coursing through my veins and, luckily, have no problems on the way. When I get there, I park in a dark spot and grab hold of the things I need. I sneak near the rear area of the building and, while I am safely hidden in the shadows, I take the first of two remotes and press the button on it.

Nothing happens for a while but this doesn't surprise me. I wait for about ten minutes and finally see some smoke coming out of gaps in the doors and high frosted wire mesh windows. The fire inside the building must be going nicely, having been ignited by the incendiary devices I placed throughout the place on my last trip here.

With no one exiting the building, it is safe to assume that there is no one inside. I'm sure anyone in there would have vacated the place by now. Being a metal building, there are not enough combustible things inside to burn it to the ground.

When the next remote is activated, I get back to the car and, as I am driving away, the explosives go off, destroying everything inside the building. This is why I have placed a number of grenades attached to remote controlled devices in several places near the products stored here. The units are much like the ones I used to get the attention of the Carlos brothers.

By the time the fire department gets here, I plan to be back at the motel and will run the rental car back to the agency. I walk back in less than five minutes and, having packed up my things in my car already, I park down the road in the early morning hours after I phone the authorities alerting them to the goings on at the house where the girls are kept. I am pleased to see that the place is raided and, from a distance watch, as the inhabitants are loaded into police vehicles.

A bright sunny morning finds me in Bakersfield, where I get a room so I can sleep. I am bushed beyond belief. This has been a long ordeal, and I need to rest. Despite the fact that I am exhausted, I have a difficult time getting to sleep.

The events of the previous night keep running through my head.

The incident took much longer than I had expected, and I was almost hit again by the rain of bullets from Miguel. If the police had been nearer the area, I might have been in a real predicament. I realize that my plans should have been refined further.

If I go after Jackson this ill prepared, I won't be going home again. I can't count on luck to get me through too often. Jackson, I think, is far more dangerous than these men were.

They could easily have turned the tables on me if they had been a little better prepared. They must have grown somewhat complacent after living in the Laguna area for the last number of years, a fatal mistake. I start wondering why on earth I jumped up to get their attention. It was one of the dumbest things I've ever done. Ten more seconds, and they would have been close enough for me to shoot, anyways.

I find that, every now and then, I need a wakeup call to put things in perspective. This isn't the first time I have almost been killed. My hands tremble a bit as I think back on other times I found myself in big trouble. It's really a wonder that I'm still alive.

Chapter 40

Back at home, I keep an eye on the news to see what I can learn about the Laguna incident. The police announce that they at first thought that this was an underworld hit. It seems that the authorities had been keeping the boys under loose surveillance. The recovery of undisclosed items found at the scene is now leading the investigation in a direction that makes it look like this may have been an individual's or a couple of people's effort at retaliation.

The police are looking into the possibility that a parent of one of the girls forced into prostitution and pornography has taken the law into his own hands. Specialty made items found at the scene are an indication of the abilities and possibly the background of the assailant and will be investigated further.

Oh, oh! Should I be concerned at this point? Have I left a trail that could one day connect me to this crime? It seems unlikely, but if too many dots can be connected, I may have a problem on my hands. I wonder if they have any DNA samples. I try my best to leave no traces behind but things got out of hand on me there, so who knows? I hope no one stumbles into the stuff I buried under that stone.

The story continues with the discovery of a home where

girls are held against their will and forced into the pornography and prostitution industry. It also comes to light that a video has been obtained, involving certain politicians and influential business men. These people, it is now suspected, may be involved with the Columbians and this part of the investigation will continue. *Good, maybe these people might be held accountable. It's a good thing that I sent the video into the right people.*

Another story is brought to light. There is a mass exodus of refugees, migrating to Europe. The numbers are absolutely staggering. A great number of these are coming out of Syria. As I recall, there was a cry for help from these people a few years ago when a civil war started taking place. They begged the world for help against a vicious dictator. The world governments turned a deaf ear to their plight. Now the cost of the refugee situation is a burden on everyone. I often think it would have been better to help them defeat the dictator then. This crisis may well have been avoided if we would have jumped in. We do it everywhere else.

I go back to work Tuesday in a bit of a somber mood. I am still upset at the stupid thing I did and am kicking myself in the butt for it. The guys ask what is wrong, but I don't really comment. The work week goes by slowly and unpleasantly for me, so on Friday after work, I go for a hard run in the park. This still doesn't really help, so on Saturday morning, I go riding for most of the day. Being alone with the horse seems to do the trick.

As I ride the trails and spend time beside the meadows and streams in the sunshine, I feel a gradual release from my inner turmoil. The horse doesn't ask anything of me and seems happy just to be here. I find that having some alone time with this animal comforts me. I have a nice lunch with me and give the horse my apple, which it seems to enjoy. By the end of the afternoon, I am starting to get back to myself and feel a burden has been lifted. A few decisions have been made and, in the end, I chock things up as another learning lesson. After giving the horse a nice rubdown, I pay Ben and head for home with a different attitude.

Having finished a hearty supper, I decided to look at the "Jackson room," for lack of a better term. I go over the map and the notes that I have pinned all over it. Because of the way things could have turned out last weekend, I decided that I will look at the entire route again. I want to see if there is anything that I might learn, that I may have missed before. Looking it over, I try to figure out what may have contributed to his decisions to hit one town versus another and possibly use it to my advantage.

As the evening progresses, the phone rings and the voice on the other end brings me back to reality. Harry informs me that the final preparations for Brenda's birthday have been made and tells me what he is planning to do. He tried to keep it a surprise but she knows him far too well for him to pull it off successfully.

"It would really please Brenda and the kids for you to be there," Harry says.

"Of course, I'll be there."

It is three weeks hence so I'll have plenty of time to get her something special. I ask if he has any ideas for gifts that she would like, and he informs me that this is a no-gifts party.

Fat chance, I think.

I hope he isn't planning on introducing me to any young ladies. I have already had a mother and two wives murdered on me, and I am not in the market for another. Some things in life are just not meant to be. Harry, Brenda, and the kids have become the closest thing I have to a family, and I am looking forward to this event. I ask Harry how Eva and Gord's little problems have resolved.

"No problem as far as Eva is concerned. I am a little worried about Gord, though. He's changed quite a bit in the last while since the drinking episode. Brenda and I really don't know what to do about it. We've talked to him, and we just can't get through to him like we used to."

"I'm sorry to hear that. Hopefully, he gets himself back

on track. If there is anything that I can do to help, just ask me," I say, wondering if I actually can help.

I go around the house taking care of things, and, as the time slips by, an idea comes to mind. I think that doing something else has given my subconscious mind enough time work in the background and put two and two together. When I was coming back home from the surveillance of Luis and the boys, I got stuck behind an RV with a motorcycle strapped to a trailer towed behind it.

It dawns on me that this is how Jackson gets around the country without being spotted. Who would think that a vacationer is pulling off robberies all over the United States? This would make living quite inexpensive and he can park where he wants. Maybe even park in a farmer's yard and work off any fees, if he is handy. This way, he can wait for things to blow over before he moves on after he pulls one of his heists.

This throws a whole new twist in finding Dice Man. The excitement is already starting to build in me. I believe that I have made a major jump ahead in catching this bastard. The game, I think, is really afoot now. I feel a little like Sherlock Holmes at the moment, as the frustration level in me lowers perceptibly. A smile crosses my face as I visualize this episode coming to a conclusion, one way or another, in the not too distant future.

Sunday morning, I start to prepare the garden for spring planting and, when I am finished, I have this desire to go to Baskette Slough. After a workout, I'll spend a little time relaxing on the shores of my favorite pond. As usual, I do my mad dash and run routine, working up a real sweat.

As I wind down, I make my way to the water's edge. A light breeze ripples the water surface and I see the occasional fish jump.

I spot a sunfish in the grasses near the shore and idly watch it as it hunts for breakfast. I am not sure why, but I really like this particular breed of fish. Maybe it's the coloring or the fact that when you catch one, they really put up a fight. You don't keep these, as there is no meat on them to speak of.

My mind drifts here and there as I contemplate any possible courses of action. The first thing I am going to do is double check on future possible targets for Jackson. As time goes on, I anticipate that he will start heading north. When the robberies happen in towns that are within half a day's driving distance, I will start checking all the spots I think he may hole up. My chance of spotting him is probably slim, but slim is better than none.

Back home, I'm in the basement in front of the board. I have gone over his travels around the country many times. Some things seem to follow a pattern, and some things don't. I have begun to be able to anticipate his moves better, but not accurately. I look at possible places that he may hit and base them on the availability of RV campsites in the area.

This narrows things down considerably. I test this theory out by going over the map and checking for the RV sites where the robberies took place. After about three hours, my eyes are getting really tired, but it looks like I've hit the nail on the head.

Checking online, I discover that there is always an RV campsite within about ten miles of the robberies. I feel very certain at this moment that I will, in the near future, be catching up with my target. All I can do right now is wait for him to head north in my direction. I hope he doesn't make a directional change leading him away from me. Maybe Bill will have some more information for me soon.

At work, I'm a little distracted the following week and end up screwing up a small job. To cover myself, I quickly cut some replacement pieces and redo the work before anyone is the wiser.

I start thinking of looking online for a place that I can take Jackson to when I finally get him, concentrating on remote places in the mountains where someone may have a cabin.

It will need to be one that is away from civilization and not frequented too often.

I also think of what I will need to take with me when I finally have a chance to apprehend him. This weekend I'll do some scouting for potential places.

Chapter 41

After considerable thought, Dennis thinks that he may have figured out how to make the payday bigger so he can make the repairs to his RV.

"I think I will have to find a B and B that caters to a little more affluent clientele. If I can hit the place at the right time, say at breakfast when most of the patrons are eating, I can rob them all at once."

He would normally not do something this daring but he needs the money.

"I'll have to check out where the best place is and hit it pretty soon," he says to himself. "Better look at the map and see if I can find some place and then check on the internet to see if it is popular enough."

If he can't find one to suit his needs, he will just have to hit several in succession. He has done this a couple of times before but doesn't like to push his luck too often. After a bit of searching, he decides on a rather large B and B in Desert Hot Springs. It's pricey, so the people staying there should have quite a bit of money.

"Now I need to plan how to hit this place and, if someone gets hurt, tough. It won't be the first time, and certainly won't be the last. Money, I need money. Why should those stinking old people have it all?"

Chapter 42

Joseph

Looking for a suitable gift, I end up going to the mall and drop in on a store that specializes in feminine products. After talking to a salesperson, I make my purchase and head home to wrap it. I hope Brenda likes what I bought her.

The day of the birthday party comes and goes with everyone enjoying themselves. Brenda likes the gift. The kids and I play a few games and make plans to go to the Zipline Park when the chance comes. I think this may be a good idea because even I notice a bigger change in Gord. Later, I manage to get the boy alone and have a chat with him.

"Hey, buddy, what's up? You don't seem yourself lately. Is there something wrong?"

"Nothing's wrong. Why are you asking me that?" he says defensively.

"I've noticed a pretty big difference in you, and I'm a little concerned. Are you hiding something that's bothering you? Your mom and dad are worried too."

"I'm not hiding anything, so leave me alone. Besides, you're a fine one to talk about secrets. How did you handle Eva's problem?"

He walks away, at this point, leaving me stunned. This lad that I have known for so many years has changed dramatically. He has the look of someone who is either drinking or doing drugs. Short of watching him to see where he goes at night, I'm at a loss as to what I can do. Unfortunately, I am too preoccupied with finding Kathleen's killer to follow up on this. I feel sorry for my friends as I'm sure that this will get worse for them.

The next day, I head out into the mountains in northern California, near Modoc National forest, not far from Klamath Falls in south central Oregon. I take some of the more obscure roads and find two pretty much-deserted cabins off by themselves. They are about twenty miles apart, so this gives me options at least.

The next weekend, I go a little farther south in the mountains and find another good place that, although out of the way, is easy enough to get to. I GPS all three places in favorites and head back home.

Bill drops by with the next batch of reports. We make plans to go out fishing at a new spot soon. When I'm alone, I go through it all and find that I am on the right track as far as where Jackson will probably hit. If he hits either one of the places I think that he will, I will then try to anticipate his next move and see if I can be in the vicinity. With a little luck and a lot of planning, I may have him in my sights in the next while.

Going through town on my way to one of the guys at work's home, I pass a bar and, in the alley next to the establishment, I see some activity. It is late afternoon and seems a bit early for a couple of drunks to be having it out. I pull up and park down the street, unsure if I should get involved.

Because it is still cold outside, I can get away with having my face covered by a balaclava. I throw on an old worn-out coat from the trunk and head back toward the alley. As I am approaching, I hear someone begging for mercy. From what I hear of the conversation, the one being beaten up has been fooling with a married woman. He is being taught a lesson. I hang around the corner out of sight, just to make sure it doesn't go too far.

Shortly after, the two men beating up the guy give the man a warning and start to leave. This is my cue to get away too. I don't have a lot of sympathy for the guy because, if it was my wife he was fooling around with, I would probably do the same thing.

For the next week, I keep an eye on the news online. I am waiting for the story of a robbery at one of the places I hope Jackson hits.

Chapter 43

Dennis

O kay, I'm camped at this run down RV place and my piece of shit fits right in," Dennis mutters. "Geez, what a bunch of losers live here. I really need to do something about that hunk of junk. I barely made it here when the radiator hose went on me."

He wonders what will go next. He goes to an outlet on the motorcycle, and gets a new hose. His reserves are dwindling, and he needs a couple of good scores to get back on his feet. He has made up his mind to hit two well-known businesses. He'll hit the one in Yucca Valley first and then the one in Hot Springs Desert immediately after.

He makes his plans as to how he will do these places, in order to maximize the profits. When he is done at both places, he'll get rid of the stolen car and tie the duffle bag to his motorcycle taking the back roads to the RV site. If he has to, he can cut across fields to make his escape. Good thing the bike is good for off-road traveling.

In the RV, he gets the trusty pistol ready and straps on the long bladed knife. *It's surprising how fast people want to cooperate when the knife is used on some old loudmouth. You don't even have to kill the guy, just slice him up a bit.*

After a little scouting around, he finds an older car he can use. These are easier to steal than the newer models. It's parked on the side of a house where no windows are and, being a stick shift, will make it easy enough to roll out to the street, start, and drive away. If he has a bit of luck, he may get the car back without the owner even knowing it's gone.

"Okay, this Saturday morning, is it. That gives me two days to case the places and find the best routes for the escape."

Chapter 44

Joseph

This waiting is getting harder because I know that the time Dice Man and I will meet is approaching. Arranging the things I plan to take, I start immersing myself in my workouts. The stress level is building, and I almost flare up at one of the guys on the job. I catch myself in time to avoid a scene. Stepping back from the task is imperative, in order to keep things looking normal. Luckily, nothing much is happening at work, so I manage to finish a project I have been working on. The weekend comes, and there it is.

Chapter 45

Dennis

Friday night comes, and Dennis makes the last of the preparations. Setting the alarm, he goes to sleep after tossing and turning for a while. The excitement is building in him. Most people would be nervous at this point, but not him. He was born for this kind of work. He actually hopes someone needs to be persuaded to hand over his possessions. Pleasant thoughts go through his head as he falls asleep.

The alarm goes off, with soft music waking him up. It is five-thirty in the morning and still dark enough to push the bike out of the park before starting it up. No use waking the old farts, having one of them ask about the noise later in the day.

He makes it to the neighborhood where the car is and stashes the bike out of sight for retrieval later. Getting the car is easy enough, as the doors are open and it has a manual shift transmission. He preps the ignition before pushing the car out onto the street. Quietly starting the engine, off he goes with no one the wiser.

Thoughts of some of his earlier jobs go through his mind as he drives. There was the middle aged man in North Dakota last year who put up a fight when he was being relieved of his money. Dennis had to show him the error of his ways and, in doing so, pistol whipped him harder than he had intended. He heard on the news later that the man had suffered brain damage and would never be normal again. Why would someone put up such a fight over money which is so replaceable?

Then there was the woman who kept nattering at him when he had the gun right in her face. How stupid can you be? A good hard smack in the forehead shut her up fast enough. There was only one incident that he regretted and that was the shooting of that beauty in Napa Valley. Not because he cared about her dying, but because she would have been so nice to have for a while if he had made the time for it. How was he supposed to know she was pregnant?

"I wonder what the stupid husband is doing now. Oh, well, his problem doesn't concern me, on with the job at hand."

With his disguise on, he heads toward the place in Yucca. He arrives at a quarter to eight and parks near the entrance. A quick look around and he heads into the front door. The desk man smiles and asks how he can help. Great, finally someone who wants to be of assistance. Dennis pulls out the gun and asks politely for the cash in the drawer.

The smile is gone and a short-lived look of defiance crosses the clerk's face. It's funny how quickly that changes as you cock the revolver. The drawer opens and the cash is handed over.

"Okay, get your ass out here and come with me to the breakfast room. Do I need to explain?" Dennis asks.

"No, no, please don't hurt me," the young man pleads.

They walk into the room together and Dennis makes an announcement that he is here to relieve them of their money and valuables. An older man starts to protest and he receives a fist to the side of the head. Dennis hands the desk man a bag and orders him to collect everything.

At this point, he pulls out his knife and lets all those present know what will happen if there is any trouble. A woman starts to scream but it is very short-lived as the point of the knife is placed against her cheek. A trickle of blood runs down to her chin and she trembles so hard that he has to slap her to get her attention back to the issue.

He is actually enjoying his time here so far. The rest of the guests can't get their things into the bag fast enough. He sees a woman with a rather large diamond on her finger and tells her to remove it as well as her expensive watch. Very little more persuading is necessary and the job is done. Just to finish it, he takes everyone's cell phone, too. As he is about to leave he also grabs a bite to eat from the table near the room entrance. There is a warning given to stay put for ten minutes as he quickly leaves and drives away.

Dennis heads in the opposite direction that he actually intends to go. He does a double back, using a few side roads. It takes longer than he would like to get to Hot Springs Desert and the next target. He grabs the next bag and, after looking to make sure that the way is clear, heads into the place, going toward the front desk. He makes a quick detour away as a couple heads out the front door.

When they are gone, he goes to the front desk and has to say something to get the girl to look up so he can make his wishes known. The pistol frightens her enough to gain the cooperation he desires. As they head to the breakfast area, an old well-dressed couple is just heading out but are convinced to go back in when he brings out the knife as a further incentive.

The routine is explained to everyone as the girl is told to gather all the valuables and cash. Some stupid old man, who seems to think he is above this kind of treatment, vehemently objects and refuses to do as he is told. Dennis walks up and uses the knife to inflict enough pain to convince everyone that it is in their best interests to do what they are told. The man's money and valuables are taken by the girl, and Dennis is on his way with a similar warning given to these guests too. As he is leaving the building, a man runs to the front counter to grab the phone. Dennis rushes back, in time to use the gun to beat the man unconscious. Those watching the scene run back into the room and he makes his way to the car.

He drives into town and back to where the car was taken from. No one is about. He puts all his loot in the duffle bag then drives the car into the spot where it belongs. Just to slow things down for the owner, he locks all the doors and quickly walks to the bike. Strapping the duffle bag to the back of the motorcycle, he takes all the back roads he can. There are sirens in the distance as he drives slowly back to the RV.

The old folks in the camp are just getting up, and he is in his unit without having to talk to anyone.

"Let's see what we got this time," he says to himself as he sets the bag down on the floor. "This went great and I even had some fun for a change, ha, ha, ha."

Chapter 46

Joseph

The story hits the news. A double robbery has taken place, one right after the other. One happens in Yucca and the other in Hot Springs Desert. The MO is the same and I have no doubts that it's Dennis. The amount of cash and valuables taken is quite substantial, and several people were badly injured. The worst was a man who attempted to call the police and was beaten severely. He is now in intensive care. These places are both in the towns that I thought would be targeted.

With the close succession and size of the proceeds, this means he was in need of money to fix or replace his RV. That can be the only reason for this desperate behavior. Otherwise, why take that kind of chance? Is he still in the area of the robberies or has he moved on? If I thought that there might be a chance that he was still there, I might head down and see if I could get a line on him. I have my doubts that he would stick around that long, so I may as well wait. He may or may not need to pull another job for a while. It will depend on his financial situation. All I can do is anticipate his next target and move on from there.

December journal entry: *Will I ever catch up with this guy? This task has kept me occupied for so long. What happens when I finally do catch up with him? Will I have peace or does this go on forever and…*

Christmas comes and goes. Where has the time gone? It seems that it's going by faster and faster as I get older. I'm sure this is only in my mind and others look at things like this differently.

There have been no further robberies that Jackson has committed for some time. Bill dropped off the last reports a while ago, and I feel that something will break in the next few weeks. I have nothing to base this on but gut instinct.

There are two directions that he can head. One is toward Bishop, California, which is on the east side of the mountain range that contains the Sierra National Forest and the other is on the west side in the general area of Visalia, which is located between Bakersfield and Fresno. There are several small towns around there that will suit his needs when he decides to strike again.

The need to find a release is building up in me more and more. The frustration of not being able to get at the bastard is weighing on me. Maybe I need a distraction other than him. I check in with the online sites to see if anything relevant can be found. I am certain that there are several law enforcement members using these sites. Some of the information could only be obtained by them.

There is a long standing discussion about a drug dealer in Sacramento that continually escapes justice, no matter what he does or how hard the authorities pursue him. I decide to do some investigating on my own to make sure of the facts before I do anything I may regret. I find as much info on Murray Gerard as I can and, indeed, he is who the group says he is.

I locate his address and decide to do a little scouting. He lives on Storia Way in the Elk Grove district in the southern section of Sacramento. The homes on this street are really nice, and it seems like a peaceful area. This means I will have to deal with him in a more suitable section of town. No need to disturb this community unduly. I book a few days off and head out Friday after work to see what I can find out.

It takes just over eight and a half hours to get there, so I book a room at a motel and crash for the night, making sure I set the alarm on the car and park it in a bright area. The desk man assures me it is safe. I'm out like a light and, before I know it, it is morning and time to move. After a shower and breakfast at a nice family restaurant, I head out.

I wonder what the fascination is nowadays with the drug scene. It seems that a large percentage of the population uses recreational drugs. How in the world did things get this way? Alcohol and pot are okay but some of the stuff out there is scary. Who would really want to live life in a daze rather than experiencing all that life has to offer? I once heard that a fairly large percentage of people living in the largest cities of America seldom or never actually leave the city entirely to go on a trip or vacation. I thought this was a little far-fetched but have heard this more than once. I also wonder how some people on drugs can afford to live like this.

I see what would appear to be my target's car in the driveway and park just around the corner under a tree to wait. I go through two bottles of water and a couple of protein bars before he comes out in the late afternoon. I follow him to an area of Sacramento that is known for its undesirable elements. Murray drives an expensive model BMW and parks it outside what looks like a popular club. He leaves his car on the street locked up and walks inside. Because it is early, there are not a lot of patrons so I stay outside for a while.

There is a restaurant on the other side of the street so I kill some time there. I manage to get a window seat in a booth and order the healthiest thing on the menu. I pay for the dinner before I eat, in case I have to leave quickly. After a couple of hours, things start to get busy at the club, so I go in. I get a beer from the bar and head to the most obscure spot I can find that has a view of the entire interior. I see Murray at a table with another man and two girls.

He is about one ninety and looks to be in reasonable shape. The guy with him is bigger and I would guess that this is his bodyguard of sorts. He looks mean and his eyes keep moving around the club, looking for signs of trouble. I make sure I'm not caught staring at them. Nursing my beer as long as I can, watching things, I have to order another to avoid making the waitress suspicious.

A woman sitting with a couple of guys tries to make eye contact with me but I stay away from this. I'm sure it is a ploy to get me into a fight with the guys. Finally, some girl sits down across from me and asks if I want to buy her a drink. I ask if she is with anyone here and says she isn't. In the interest of appearing normal to those around me, I buy her a drink.

She has to do most of the talking because I mostly just look at her and keep quiet. It takes a while but she finally gets the hint and, after getting another drink out of me, leaves. Various people come and go from the table Murray sits at. They are probably buying drugs and, later in the evening, two men stand at the table and say a few words then all of them leave the club.

I get outside in time to see Murray and his friend get in the beamer following the other men. I almost lose them a few times but manage to keep them in sight. They drive to a warehouse district, and I have to follow at a greater distance to avoid being spotted. They all get out and go into a building, which looks like a storage place of sorts. A light goes on in a room on the second floor and stays on for about half an hour, after which everyone comes out and leaves, going their own ways.

I decide to stay here and check out the facility. After waiting for an hour, I make a move, doing a thorough scan of the area, just in case anyone returns. I grab a few tools from the hidden compartment in the trunk and head to the building. There is no foot or vehicular traffic in the area at this time of night to hamper me as I check the front entrance, looking for security systems.

I've gone online on occasions to learn as much as possible about disarming these systems. With no alarm system to disarm, I don't find anything else that I can't handle but go around the building to see if there are any other options. There is a door on the side which allows me a safer entry and, after a minute, I am in. There are boxes and crates stacked in various places on the floor. A stairway leads up to a small second floor and, using my flashlight, I head up.

There are a couple of offices with a desk in each. I doubt very much that I will find much in these but look anyway. A rudimentary search finds nothing of importance. I look around the rooms and still don't find much until I look under the desk of what appears to be the main office. Under the mat that looks like it has been moved recently because of the dirt trail, I find a rather large safe in the floor. Unfortunately, my safecracking skills aren't what they should be so I may have to leave empty-handed. It is secured to the floor so taking it is out of the question.

I did notice in the second room a number of stains on the floor and believe that they are from spilled blood. Interrogations must have taken place here. A steel chair over the stains is anchored to the floor and probably had someone tied to it. After a thorough search, I don't find a lot, but there are so many spots on the main floor where stuff could be hidden that it would be a daunting task at best. I have the information that I need at least. Murray is guilty of some bad things and so are the men that came here with him.

I'm just making my way to the back door, when I hear a noise at the front door. A key is being inserted and turned. I'm close to the back door and can sneak out if I want to but decide to stay for a bit. The side of the building has two other escape routes, so I should be okay. With my light out, I hide near the door behind some crates. Three men enter the building, turning on lights that illuminate a walkway to the stairs, which they follow.

There is no talk as they head toward the stairs. I have my pistol and knife with me and so feel safe enough for the time being. If they are unarmed, I won't even need these. They end up in the main office, turning the lights on. As I listen to the conversation, I realize that Murray is the man who owns the building, not the guy he met in the club. There is laughter upstairs and, from my vantage point, it is difficult to see what is going on. I am tempted to move to another spot but fear to make any noise.

There is a tinkle of glasses and a toast is made. Great, hopefully, they will drink themselves into a stupor and make my job easier. There is plenty of talk, but I only pick up parts of the conversations. From what I do hear, business is good and there are several deals in the works. They spread over a couple of months but I, of course, don't have this kind of time so I need to make a decision.

I was not going to do anything, at this point, or even this weekend, but an opportunity has presented itself, and I do have the means to take them all out now. I'll need to move closer to the stairway and stay underneath it, waiting for the men to come down. The stairs are the metal type that has no back, giving me an idea. I very slowly maneuver myself into position, taking great care not to make any noise, and wait. It takes an hour for them to finish what they are doing, and it is almost two in the morning at this point. I have to do a few stretches now and then to keep from getting stiff.

As I am waiting, the lights go out upstairs, and the men start down the steps. One by one, they pass me and, as the last one steps in front of me on the stairs, I reach out and grab his ankles and pull. He trips and falls down the stairs, landing on the guy in front of him. The two go down on the floor as I come around with the knife, which I bury in the standing man's abdomen before he has a chance to do anything.

The guy lying on the floor with Murray reaches into his

coat as I kneel on his chest, pinning his arm, and stab him under the chin and up, killing him instantly as the long double edged blade enters the brain. By this time Murray is getting to his feet with his hand inside his jacket. He is already pulling a revolver from a holster, but I have the pistol pointing at him. His hands go up, immediately releasing the firearm, which clatters to the floor.

"W—What do you want from m—me," he asks in a stuttering voice.

"I want you to go up the stairs, with no sudden moves."

"Do you know who I am?" he asks with a fearful look.

"Of course, I do that's why I'm here. Now move."

When we reach the office, I tell him to open the safe. He starts to protest but thinks better of it as I aim at his crotch. He goes to it and spins the dial, missing the intended number and has to start again.

This time he gets it right and pulls the handle, opening the door. I tell him, "Remove the contents and, if there is a gun in there, you won't have time to use it."

He does this as I have the pistol barrel pushed against the back of his head. With everything on the desk, I see a lot of cash in bundles and quite a stash of drugs. The thing that interests me most is a book which probably contains the names of people I suspect are contacts and clients of Murray.

"What's in the book?" I ask.

A look of real fear crosses his face. "If you value your life, you'll leave that book alone."

"Why is that?" I ask.

"Those people are influential and can't be touched. They'll have you killed. There are even cops on the list. Take the money if you have to, but leave the book or you're a dead man," he tells me as he sits down in the chair.

Having everything I need, I grab hold of a cushion on a second chair. Holding it against the barrel of the gun, I shoot. Down he goes, falling out of the chair. With gloved hands, taking all the drugs, I carefully open the packages by the toilet. One by one the contents are flushed. It takes a while to dispose of all the crap with my rubber gloves on but, finally, it's finished.

Locating a bag, I load it up with the cash. There must be a small fortune here, but I don't bother counting it as I won't be keeping it. The book I tuck away and then make a fairly hasty exit.

This evening did not go as I planned. It was only going to be a surveillance trip but turned out to be far more. I'm not sure what to do with the large amount of cash at the moment, so I think that I will sit on it for the time being.

The book is another story. I think that I'll put it to the online sites and see what they have to say. There are some influential people in the book, and I'll have to be careful with it. Everything will, of course, be done anonymously for obvious reasons. Back at the motel, I get to bed after a quick shower and drift off. Late Monday finds me back home with one more day off, which suits me just fine. I'm still tired from the late nights I've had.

Chapter 47

Dennis

Wow, who would have thought that the score would have been this big? Those old farts had a ton of cash with them and the jewelry is worth a fortune. I'll have to find a fence to unload the stuff, but it's still money in my pocket," Dennis says, talking to himself, again.

After counting all the money, the total tally is well over thirteen thousand dollars. When the other stuff is unloaded, there should be seventeen or eighteen thousand. He knows he'll only get paid a small fraction of what the jewelry is actually worth, but this is the way it is. He'll have to lay low for a while, but when the way is clear and he has sold all the stuff, he should be able to get a lot better RV and have worry free travels for some time.

"Have to make sure there's no incriminating evidence left behind when I trade this piece of shit in," he says to himself. "Yeah, this has been a really good haul."

He wonders if this is the way he should do things from now on. A few people got hurt but that was their fault, not his. *Sometimes you have to listen and do what you're told.*

"I'm sure some of those stupid old people have learned a lesson from me."

A smile crosses his face. He feels good about himself.

Chapter 48

Joseph

After giving it some thought, I go to donation centers like food banks and shelters for the homeless and drop off large cash donations. I go to different cities and towns to do this and make sure that I am well disguised. Women's shelters receive several very large donations and kid's centers get the rest of the money. These are worthy organizations and deserve the help. At least this way, some good comes from all the heartache the drugs have caused.

I put the problem of the book to the CDC and other safe sites. What I finally do is relay the story of how the book was obtained and send it to the DEA. With too many influential people involved, I don't want to take the chance of it falling into the wrong hands. Nothing is certain, but this is the best way to do something about it that I can think of. Hopefully, the proper people get hold of the information in the book and these people are dealt with.

At work, things have slowed down and there are a few layoffs. It is never a pleasant thing when this happens, and I feel sorry for those who are let go, even temporarily. All too often people have spent too much on Christmas and have some major bills to pay this time of year.

A month has now gone by since the robberies Jackson has committed. I think that he will strike again soon. I'm certain he pulled his multiple jobs because of a financial problem and that was probably RV trouble. If this is the case, then I am sure he either fixed it or bought a newer one and so will need some more money soon. With this in mind, I keep an eye online on the two areas around both Bishop and Visalia, California, to see if his type of robbery has taken place in these areas.

Another week goes by, and there it is. An armed robbery takes place in the town of Bishop that matches Jackson's MO. I would have thought that he would not have done it here because of the lack of escape routes from the area. Visalia would have been a far better choice in my estimation because there are so many places to take refuge.

He is either very confident or he is getting careless. Either way, this may be a major stroke in my favor. The excitement builds as I start getting myself ready for when I think he may next resurface.

After studying the map thoroughly, I decide that he will either head into Nevada and a little place called Hawthorne or toward Lake Tahoe. If he picks Lake Tahoe, my bet will have him heading back toward California, somewhere around Yuba City. There are far more places to hide in that area. Only time will tell which direction all this will take me.

It's still pretty cold and snowy, but I check with Ben and see if it is advisable to go horseback riding. He tells me that it would not be a problem if he could go with me, so Saturday morning off we go. My heavy clothes keep me warm, for the most part, but my hands are quite chilled from holding them up on the reins for long periods.

We dismount and get the blood circulating by walking the horses for a while. Afterward, we give the horses a rubdown and Ben invites me inside for a hot lunch. I spend another two hours with him as he tells me about how he got to be the owner of the ranch. He asks me about myself and I give him the lowdown on my life…well, what I want him to know at least. I like the man, as he is a no-nonsense type and a straight shooter.

Chapter 49

Dennis

So now Dennis has a newer RV and doesn't have to worry about the damn thing breaking down too often. He decides to go to a bar and see what's going on. Maybe he can get some info on possible ways to make some money. He has tried his hand at cards but isn't good enough to make much from it. There is a guy at the bar with quite a wad of cash that he makes the mistake of pulling out of his pocket. He must think it impresses people who might be watching when he pays for drinks. Dennis isn't sure if he is the only one who notices it. This is Lake Tahoe and you can expect some people to have a lot of money on them. Maybe he'll keep an eye out for more of these types and who knows? Maybe he'll get lucky.

His cash is getting to the point where he will need to replenish it in the next few weeks.

"Maybe I should have bought the cheaper RV. I'd have more money left, and it wouldn't be a concern yet," he mutters.

The evening wears on and it's getting near closing time, or at least it should be. There are no other potentials in the bar. The guy who is, by now, half in the bag, gets up, goes

to the bathroom, then heads for the door. Dennis noncha-
lantly gets up to go too. The guy walks unsteadily down the
street toward a hotel as Dennis waits for an opening. He has
his knife in his hand inside his pocket.

Picking up the pace, he closes the gap between him and
the idiot. He is now about ten feet behind money man and is
about to make his move as he takes a quick look around. He
sees nothing but, as he turns toward the man again, a pair of
headlights comes around the corner ahead of them.

Bloody hell! A cop car makes its way down the street in
his direction. Dennis walks into the alley where he was going to force his meal ticket to go. He waits for the cops to
drive past and comes out of the alley just in time to see his
intended victim walk into the hotel. Shit! He could have
used that money. That stupid idiot, he is sure, will just lose
it in the casinos or drink it away, anyways. Of all the luck,
now he will have to make other plans, geez.

It's too cold in this place, so as soon as he pulls his next
job he is going to head west and back into California. At
least it is nice and warm there.

Chapter 50

Joseph

So it looks like it might be an early spring and I can start going back to my favorite parks. Bill dropped by with the reports on Jackson's activities in Hot Desert Springs and Yucca. I don't tell him that I already know of these as I have been keeping an eye online. We have a pleasant visit.

"How are things going for you, Bill?"

"There are things happening in town and I think that some high up officials may be dirty."

"How do you plan on handling the situation," I ask.

"I'd like to take care of this by the book, if possible."

I know what he means when he says this and don't push it.

"If you need my help just ask," I say.

"Thanks, but I would like to handle it my way if I can."

We call it a day and he goes home to his wife. I wonder who those officials are. Corrupt people in politics are nothing new, of course. I wonder if they go into politics with this course of action in mind. Or do most go into it with good intentions and just get sidetracked along the way? There have been stories about presidents that lost their way many times. Nixon, Clinton, and even Kennedy had things reported about them on many occasions that weren't kosher. Maybe this is one of the pitfalls of power.

There seems to be an inordinate amount of rain this season, and I start to wonder why. Maybe when I don't have a lot to do I'll go online and see if there are any answers.

At work, the thing nobody wants to happen does happen. A man running the press fails to follow the safety procedures and has his hand in the press when it is cycled. Because it is in manual mode, as soon as he removes his foot from the foot pedal, the press stops the cycle.

There is a scream that's loud enough wake up the dead. I run over to see what has happened. The man is screaming as I check the situation but I manage to tune him out and focus on what needs to be done.

I notice that the ram is in its lower-most position, meaning that if I continue the cycle freeing the man, no more damage will be done. I do this and the man falls to the ground continuing the screaming. He has lost most of his hand in the press and, no matter what, there is nothing that can be done to reverse this. This is the type of accident nobody ever wants to see happen.

When first aid comes to take the man to the infirmary, an ambulance is called. About half the men go home for the rest of the day after this incident. The screaming continues in my head for the rest of this day and several more.

This is not the first time something has happened to this man because of being in a hurry. You would think that he would have learned. I feel so sorry for the man and, as is the case in situations like this, you wonder if you could have done something more to have prevented the horrible accident. No matter what, there is always a feeling of guilt that stays with you. The accident was his own fault, but the feeling is still there.

Gerry the tool and die supervisor pulls the die out of the press, takes it outside, and pressure washes it clean. He is not the squeamish type as he has been all over the world and seen things like this more often than he would like. I really admire this man. There is very little of the man's hand left in the die because of the high tonnage the press exerts.

It is a long, long day. I could have gone home too, but the screaming would still have been in my head, so I might as well be at work. The foot switch is removed from the press by Don in maintenance so that the press can only be operated by a dead man's switch which requires both hands on switches outside the press to activate it. This probably should have been done long ago, but sometimes it takes an accident to bring an issue to the forefront.

A couple of weeks go by. The incident at work has taken my mind off Jackson for a while.

Chapter 51

Dennis

Have to get some money soon. I'm starting to run low, so what place around here can I nail?" Dennis says, talking to himself again. He is doing this more and more often.

He drives around the outskirts of town and locates a suitable establishment. There are actually several on Stateline Avenue, and he is tempted to hit two in a row again. After mulling it over, he decides that they are too close together and the risk of getting caught is too great.

He walks around the area to see which will be the best place to visit. Finally, he decides on the one that has the most cars in the parking lot. Hopefully, there will be enough income to tide him over for a month or so. He doubts that the score will be anywhere near the size of the last one, but one can always hope.

Too bad the cops had to turn the corner when the drunk was ready for picking. Dennis hasn't seen any other dummies that are as easy as him since.

"Okay, I'm going to wait for Saturday morning then hit the place. Better see if I can locate a car to grab and dump, so I can walk back to the RV Park. Maybe after I lose the car, I'll just go to a restaurant nearby for breakfast. This will be the last thing those cops will be expecting. Yeah, stupid cops!"

Saturday rolls around and the car has been taken from Carson City, just down the road, with Dennis getting there by bus. He may take it back and maybe not. It will depend on the circumstances.

Okay, a drive by and the show will be on the road," Dennis thinks.

He drives around slowly and then into the lot, surveying the scene. Nothing seems out of the ordinary so in he goes. Up to the front desk and out comes the pistol. A look of horror is on the girl's face, and she seems incapable of following his directions. He uses the butt of the gun to give her a little thump on the forehead. This wakes her up nicely and the money comes out of the drawer. Off they go to the breakfast room, and everybody in there gets the idea quickly. The money and valuables are dropped into the bag held by the desk girl. Only one old bag isn't doing what she is told and this irritates Dennis to no end.

"That's it, you effing old hag. You were told what to do, so what the hell is the problem?"

He swings the pistol as hard as he can, impacting the side of her head. There is a loud smack as she hits the floor. There is blood coming out of the cut in her scalp. She doesn't move at all. There are screams in the room that are quickly stifled when he points the gun at the offenders. He grabs her purse and throws it at the girl.

"Put it in the bag, stupid," he yells at her.

The idiotic old woman has just ruined his morning. How is he supposed to put up with this crap? Why can't people just do what they are told, and make his life a little easier? He takes the bag from the girl, still fuming.

"Everybody stays here and no cops, or I'll come back and kill everyone here, got that?" he screams at the frightened patrons.

Making for the door, he gets into the car and leaves. His

head is spinning and he almost runs a red light. He knows he needs to regain control, or there will be an altercation with the police. He knows how that will turn out and drives back to Carson City a little more carefully.

After dumping the car back at the owner's house, where he is almost caught in the act, he catches a bus back to Lake Tahoe. The bus drops him off near enough to the large B and B that he just robbed.

He can see the flashing lights of the cop cars. He resists the temptation to walk by the place. It would be a laugh, but only if he isn't spotted. Some of his clothes are the ones he wore during the robbery. He walks back to the RV, sits at the table, and wonders what went wrong. "Why do those people make me do these things?"

The week goes by slowly. Dennis wants to leave and head toward California where it is warmer but doesn't want to take the chance until there are no more roadblocks. It has turned way too cold for him to take the bike for a ride to check things out. The police have been checking every vehicle leaving the area, in hopes of getting a break in the case.

It has been reported that a senior citizen struck by the gunman later died in the hospital. The reporter said that the lady is married to an influential politician up from Texas. As a result, an all-out search is being conducted, which so far has yielded nothing concrete as to the identity of the perpetrator. The police even asked a few people in the RV site some questions but, luckily, Dennis wasn't one of them. He should be able to convince them of his innocence, unless, of course, they search the RV.

By the end of the week, the roadblocks are removed and the way is now clear. Dennis plans to leave tomorrow morning and gets everything ready.

"Shit, why did the old hag have to die? She caused trouble for me during the robbery and afterward too, stupid woman. On the road again."

Dennis thinks he should write a song about it.

Chapter 52

Joseph

There it is on the internet, the story I've been waiting for, only this time he has killed someone again. It appears that he is becoming more and more violent as time goes on. Dice Man needs to be caught and put down soon. Unfortunately, he can easily head in one of two directions. One will take him to Reno and across Nevada toward Utah or Idaho. The other direction is across the mountains to California, probably hitting Yuba City or Chico.

My money is on California because it is much warmer, and I believe that has been one of the driving forces in his tour of the United States. One more time, and I will take time off and try to intercept him. That is, if he goes where I want him too.

I also hear a story on the news that personal debt is at an all-time high. I think that the ultra-low interest rates are not helping things. If the rates go up much, there will be a lot of people in trouble. This is a scary thought because everything else will be affected too, including my job. Not that I need to worry about it, but there are too many guys at work who would be in trouble financially.

One thing that kind of pisses me off is the fact that, despite the interest rates being so low, the credit card rates are still way up there. It is like we are being fleeced and the government sits by and does nothing. Well, the people with outstanding balances are screwed over, not me because I don't owe anything. But it pisses me off, anyway.

Bill drops by and hands me the latest report on Kathleen's killer. This seems to be bothering Bill too.

"I don't know why this guy hasn't been caught yet. Things are getting more and more out of control with this bastard. What is he going to do next?" Bill asks.

"How come the different police departments around the country don't cooperate more with each other?"

"Everyone wants to be the one to catch the guy, and it is also a matter of sharing resources. Future budgets play a part in it too," he says with a stern look on his face.

We have a coffee together and I ask how his local problem is going. He tells me that things have not improved, but there is an investigation now looking into the situation. Hopefully, something will be done.

"There is a new element in town that has taken control of much of the drug trade in the area and, so far, there has been no progress made in curtailing the situation."

"If you need my help in any way, just ask me. I won't require any answers about what anything is for."

He thanks me, says he hopes he won't have to resort to that kind of action, and off he goes. I like Bill. He's an upstanding guy.

Just to make sure I'm ready for Jackson, I raise the level of endurance I set for myself. I start training harder and practicing more with a wide variety of my toys. My knife throwing is actually getting good, and I toy with the idea of finding some sparring partners, in order to get some extra conditioning in.

I go online and look in the Seattle area which will keep me out of the line of fire with any of the locals here. I find a gym that specializes in mixed martial arts—the type used in cage fighting. They are looking for people to help keep their upcoming talent in shape and warn that it will get rough. This is not a job for the out of shape or faint of heart.

I give them a call. "Will I be allowed to attempt inflicting pain on your boys?"

The man on the other end laughs a bit. "You will be going up against some pretty tough guys and you should make sure your medical is paid up."

"Is this Saturday morning a good time?" I ask him. "Do you supply the gear I'll require?"

"Your enthusiasm is commendable but don't expect too much."

We make the arrangements and I get ready to leave Friday after work.

Saturday morning, I enter the gym after a light workout. This way I won't enter the ring cold. I meet the manager and he gives me some head gear and light gloves. My workout clothes are fine and hide what is underneath quite well. I am introduced to a young man who seems nice enough. He tells me he will start slow and allow me time to ready myself before going all out on me.

We enter the ring barefoot and start sparring lightly. As things progress, he starts becoming more and more aggressive. So far, he hasn't made any hard contact with me and is a little surprised that I have actually gotten in several fairly hard hits myself. He has come to realize that I may not be the easy target he thought I was.

As things escalate, he manages to connect with a good shot to the ribs with his foot that I didn't see coming. It knocks a bit of the wind out of me, and he goes for a takedown. I barely manage to evade it and come in with a right-hand fist that catches him on the side of the head when he goes after my legs. He backs up quickly, visibly shaken. A look of surprise is on his face, as he now knows that this is not going to be an easy win, at all.

This is now a serious fight and just what I was hoping for. I will need to be in peak form when I go after Dennis. I focus on the job at hand, looking for openings as we circle each other. There is a group of people around the ring, shouting, as things have just gotten interesting. If I didn't have all the training behind me, I would be in big trouble about now.

I don't bother holding back anymore. I want to win this fight just as bad as he does. He feints a couple times and then tries to connect with a series of foot and hand shots as we bounce around the ring. I manage to block them but they hurt anyway. I catch him coming in with a kick to the inside of his left leg. The force of the kick is heard throughout the gym. He groans slightly as I circle to the left, forcing him to put extra weight on the affected leg. His right-hand drops enough to create an opening. Immediately, I bounce back to the right with a left hook that catches him totally off guard. He staggers a little as his hands drop farther down.

I come back in, moving the other way with a right hand, and finish with a front kick to the abdomen. Down he goes as I swing in behind him with a submission choke hold. He can hardly tap out because of the unexpected turn of events that have left him in a real daze. This guy is really good and, if I'd have met him on the street, I would probably have underestimated his abilities. He got in quite a few really good shots that are going to hurt tomorrow.

A couple of the other guys want to get in the ring with me but the manager shuts them down rather harshly. He follows me to the change room and asks me to join his club. He tells me that with the proper training I could be a contender. I tell him that I will think about it and let him know. Of course, I have no intention of coming back and getting into this type of fighting, despite the fact that I enjoyed being able to let loose for a bit.

Sunday morning, I wake up with a few aches and bruises where I got hit, and some of the spots that I used to block his shots. I feel real good about the way things went. Of course, I'm sure that, if I am in a similar situation with Dice Man, he will have a gun or a knife, so hand to hand will probably not occur.

The weather is warming and I spend a little time getting the garden prepared for planting. Around eleven o'clock, the phone rings, and I hear a voice from work. Jim the inspection guy tells me that he is really sick and won't be in tomorrow. He asks if I can take over for a day or two.

"Yeah, no problem," I say, "What is it that you have?"

"I think it is the flu and, man, do I ever feel like crap."

"Sorry to hear that. I hope you feel better soon," I say and hang up.

Downstairs in the basement, I look over the information Bill gave me and don't learn much that I didn't already know. I still think the guy is going to head to California, and so I try to make plans for the interception. I'm sure he got himself a newer RV, and the last place he hit looks like it didn't yield too much, so he'll have to make another withdrawal in about two weeks.

I'm going to have to take some time off in order to be ready for him but unsure of how much to take. If I don't catch him, I'll have to take more time off later, and I can only get so much. It's probably best if I book a week off. If I miss Jackson, I can always come back early, thus saving the extra time for later. It may look funny coming back sooner than anticipated, but I'll think of some excuse for it.

I take over inspection at work for two days, and then I'm back to my position. I collect some heavy zip ties and work on a little project in my spare time. I build an attachment for my car which may come in handy. It takes a bit of ingenuity to come up with a working model, but, by the beginning of the following week, I am ready to install it. This takes a bit of time too.

What I have installed has to be hidden from view and still work properly. It takes a bit of trial and error to make it operate properly and also to get my angles right, so distance will be fairly crucial. I'll have one shot at it, so everything has to be perfect. The device fits under the car and just inside the front tire. In order to maintain ground clearance, I have to use a three-inch hole saw to make an opening in the plastic air deflector in the lower part of the plastic bumper. I make an insert at work and, in the end, I manage to make everything look fairly normal. I take a few practice runs through to make sure all works the way I need it to and that I have my distances worked out. In the end, I have rigged up a little lineup device near the windshield so I can tell when I'm in position.

February journal entry: *Will this be it? Will I catch up with the man that took away everything from me? I desperately want to make him pay for…*

I'll be leaving Friday after work to head down to Yuba City. Everything is packed, and I even manage to create a small but long storage area under the back seat. Nobody ever sits in the back, anyway, so I should be fairly safe. I get the scanner ready, as well as the GPS, and even pack the tracker that I attached to the car to follow Angelo, just in case I get the opportunity to use it. I plan to keep Jackson in the trunk when I transport him to a cabin in the woods. With this in mind, the storage compartment in the trunk now has two really good heavy duty locks to prevent entry.

It would not do to have him gain access to my things in there and use them against me. I can't very well put all my stuff in the back seat where it would be hard to conceal. So when Friday comes I am on edge all day, waiting to get moving. A few of the guys notice this and ask what's up. I give them an excuse about being really excited and they ask why I'm not smiling.

"Oh, wasn't I?" I ask.

"No," one guy says.

"Oh, just a lot on my mind, I guess."

So I go to the bathroom to avoid any more questions and then watch myself the rest of the day.

The time is at hand, and I'm on my way. There is a knot in my stomach and my nerves are playing havoc with me. Even my hands are shaking a bit. I really need to settle myself down, so I do some deep breathing and bring myself to a place mentally where I can relax somewhat. If I mess this up, Jackson may easily get the upper hand, and all will be for naught. This guy hasn't gotten away from the authorities for this long by being a push over. He also has become more and more violent in his encounters with the victims. It takes me seven hours to get to Chico, California, and it is almost midnight by the time I get a room.

Because I will need to have my things handy, I now have to use my own car to do my surveillance. This is not my first choice, but there are no other options available to me. It's surprising that I actually feel more vulnerable this way but it can't be helped.

He usually hits places before eight in the morning on Saturday, so I need to be up and already monitoring the scanner by this time. I've already picked the most likely places he will target and find a place to hole up and wait. Eight o'clock comes and the tension starts to build. Time drags by slowly as I wait. I scan across all the police bands only hearing routine calls. Nine o'clock comes and goes, with nothing to show for it.

I'm starting to think that he has decided to wait for another week or so. I spend most of the day listening to the scanner without hearing what I am waiting for. Supper comes, and I have to make a decision.

The next morning after nothing happens again, I decide to call it quits, telephone Abe at home, and tell him that my plans on meeting with an acquaintance have been canceled and that I will be into work on Monday. I ask if I can move my time off to the next week. He assures me that it won't be a problem and asks what happened. I tell him my friend has had to change our rendezvous because of an illness in the family.

The guys at work are surprised to see me so I let them in on why I had to postpone things. The week drags by so slowly that it feels like it will never end.

Harry calls. "Would you like to come to dinner on Saturday?"

"I regretfully have to decline as I will be out of town. I'll get back to you when I can." Before I hang up he tells me that things with Gord have gotten much worse. He hardly speaks civilly to them anymore. I feel sorry for them, and say so, but I can't do anything about it right now.

I really have to watch myself at work, because it will be so easy to show my frustration. Finally, Friday comes, the workday is finished, and I am on my way again.

Back in Chico, I am on the scanner again the next morning.

Chapter 53

Dennis

What the hell? I buy a new RV, spend my hard earned money, and the bloody thing breaks down," Dennis says to himself, almost shouting.

He takes the thing to a repair center and finds that it will take most of his money to have it fixed.

"Bloody hell, now I have to get more money."

He wasn't planning anything for about two weeks but now he will take a cruise around to find a good spot that might yield a decent return. He leaves the campsite and drives around town on his motorcycle. There are a couple of places in Chico but this is where he is living, for the time being, so he heads towards Yuba City. There are a lot of places in and around the city, and he is tempted to hit more than one. It really paid off last time he did it. If he does, he will have to make sure there is quite a distance between them so the cops aren't too close when he enters the second place.

He has three days to make his plans and does as much scouting as he can. The RV is fixed, and he drives it back to the site. It took a bit of persuasion to have the owner let him sleep in it while it was in the compound.

                              Leonardus G. Rougoor

He locates a couple of cars he can jack and picks the two easiest B and Bs. He wants to have back roads to use and a fairly direct route from one to the other but still, have quite a distance between them.

"Yeah, it looks like Saturday will be a double header again."

A smile crosses his face in anticipation of the rewards coming his way. Saturday, about five-thirty in the morning, he is about to steal the car he has in mind, but the damn thing isn't there.

"Shit, now I have to get back to the bike, go to another neighborhood, and take the car from there." This pisses him off somewhat. "Not a good start to the day. Nobody better make things worse for me."

Half an hour later and he has his car and heads toward the first B and B. He is early and has to wait for an hour. He doses off for a while and wakes with a start.

"Shit, I almost slept right through the withdrawal time."

His mood is not elevated when he has to wait for some stupid old people to get out of the parking area. He is beginning to wonder if he should change his plans. There are too many things just a little off this morning. The old folks leave, and it looks like a go as far as he can see.

"The hell with it, I need the money now, not later."

He drives into the lot and, after a quick look around, walks briskly into the building and straight to the desk. The smile on the man's face disappears and is replaced by fear. Dennis hands him the bag and tells him to put any and all the cash into it. A quick look tells him where the guests are having breakfast and he tells the desk man what is expected of him. "If there is any trouble from you, I'll bash your brains in. You understand, asshole? Now get moving and be quick when I tell you to do something."

They walk into the room and the announcement is made. There is the usual look of shock and the first sign of resistance, but the pistol and the knife he has just brought out convinces most people to cooperate. The possessions are dropped into the bag by all but one. The old man who seems a little reluctant to part with his wallet needs a bit of convincing. The butt of the gun to the temple draws blood and the man falls to the floor.

"Get the wallet, moron," Dennis tells the desk man.

One of the men near the door makes a run for it and is almost out when he gets a bullet in the back. The rest of the people scream as Dennis makes a run for it himself. He almost drops the bag as he runs to the car. He flies out onto the road, almost running over a pedestrian, and hits as many side roads as he can to get out of the area.

"What is the matter with these damn people? Can't they follow simple directions?" he says out loud to himself.

He pounds the steering wheel a numbers of times, but it fails to change anything. He leaves the car near his bike and heads back to his now fixed RV.

"To hell with the second place. There's no point in getting into more trouble."

This has just become a bad day, and he needs to think about what to do.

Chapter 54

Joseph

I get up nice and early Saturday morning and have a little breakfast, while listening to the scanner in my car. My stomach gets butterflies when I hear the alarm. A robbery at a B and B in Yuba City, shots fired, and an ambulance is needed. *This is it*. I can feel it in my bones that this is it.

I have already located all the RV campsites in Yuba City and Chico. I am not sure which ones to check first. Should I go to Yuba City or check the ones here? If it was me and I was following the route I think he will end up taking, I would have a spot in Chico. I would probably hole up there for a few days at least.

On the scanner, there is a report of a dead body and a severely injured senior. The alarm is spread and road blocks are set up. A description of the getaway car is sent out and it is very similar to the ones Jackson has used in the past. The police will be looking for the car, which I doubt very much he will be driving anymore.

It is probably good for me that the car Jackson used is totally different than mine. This way, I won't be stopped by the police, at least I hope this is the case. There are a lot of secondary roads that will take Jackson from Yuba City through Palermo and Oroville to Chico, so I doubt that I will catch him on the road. I think my best chance will be to spot him in one of the RV sites. I start doing a drive through the closest ones.

I'm looking for an RV with a bike mount or bike trailer on it, because he has to be using a motorcycle to get around after he dumps the car. It's the only thing that makes sense. There are only a couple in the area but they are spaced fairly wide apart so this takes time. I figure he will get back to his place as quick as he can but that it will still take a bit of time. I ask the front office in each place if my friend, who is driving an RV with a motorcycle is here. After going through the second one having done a quick search in both places, I head for the third. All this has taken quite a while, because some RVs are parked so you can't see the back end. This means that I have to do a walk around and, since I don't look like the type you would find in a place like this, I have to be careful, or I will give myself away. I am sure he will know something is up if he sees me nosing around.

So the first two places yield nothing and I am sure that I checked things close enough that I didn't miss anything. That means number three has to be it if he has chosen Chico as his hide out. My adrenalin level is making me jittery.

Chapter 55

Dennis

S hit! How could it have gone so wrong so fast?" Dennis wonders.

It all started with the first car not being where it was supposed to be, and it all went downhill from there. He is almost back to the RV, and he still doesn't know what he should do. He is driving his bike on all the back roads, in order to evade the cops. Finally, he gets back to the site and parks the bike on the small trailer behind the RV. He ties it down, grabs the bag, and gets inside.

All he can think of is getting the hell out of here. He hops into the driver's seat, starts the RV, and rolls out of the site. He has paid in advance and so he doesn't alarm anyone by leaving. He drives out of town on Route 99 and heads north. He goes right through one of the roadblocks without a second look from the cops. He almost panicked but managed to keep hold of his nerves.

He hasn't even looked at the money in the bag. Looking at the gas gauge, he sees he has to gas up soon but only has twenty dollars in his pocket. This means he will have to pull over and grab some of the cash from the robbery before he gets to the gas station.

When he finds an open spot, he pulls over and goes to the cupboard, opening the bag. There is blood on it from the old fart he had to hit. He reaches inside, pulls out some of the loose cash, and stuffs it in his pocket, making sure he has enough for the gas. He continues on until he sees a gas station and pulls in to fill up.

Chapter 56

Joseph

As I enter the third RV site, I scan all the units to see if he is in this one. It takes ten minutes and nothing. Damn! On a hunch, I go to the office here too and ask if a friend of mine is here. I tell the man that my friend drives an RV with a motorcycle on the back. He says that I just missed him. He left about twenty minutes ago. I ask if he knows what direction he went and the employee just points north.

Finally, a stroke of luck has come my way. I have been after this bastard for a long time and finally have his scent. There are two main routes that I can go. He will probably go either west on Highway 32 or north on Route 99. I hit a road block and, after a cursory once over, I am waved through. Once I'm on Route 99, I boot the car as fast as I can, making sure I don't draw too much attention to myself, and listen to the scanner at the same time. I try to keep an eye peeled for any RVs in the distance and down any side roads.

I am well out of town when I see it. There, in a gas station, is an RV gassing up. I have more than half a tank but pull in any way. I park at a pump well away from what I think is Jackson. The RV has a small narrow trailer attached to the back with a motorcycle on it. The bike is an older six fifty Honda meant for off road as well as street riding. His back is to me so I can't be certain yet. I go and pay for twenty bucks worth of gas and start pumping. I keep an eye on him with the adrenalin coursing through my veins. He slowly turns sideways. My heart skips a beat as I see it's him. My hands shake as I look at the man I have been hunting for so long. I have to look down to hide my anger and keep from giving myself away.

If I was an animal, I think I would be frothing at the mouth about now. My hands are shaking, and it is all I can do to keep from running over and beating him to death. He finishes gassing up, doesn't even look in my direction, hops into the RV, and rolls out of the station, heading north.

I wait a minute, set up my GPS unit, and keep the scanner handy. This way, I can see what the roads are like ahead and can hear if the police are on the trail too. When I get on the road myself, I stay back quite a distance so as not to alert him to my presence. I open the box in the console and pull out my semi-automatic pistol and the knife in its sheath.

The man is sticking to the speed limit and taking care not to be pulled over. Route 99, according to a map I have with me, ends at Route 36 and going west will take us into Red Bluff. Northeast goes into the mountains. Just before Route 36, there is a section of road that goes through farm land where we will be at least somewhat isolated. I know this only because of studying the map earlier. If the opportunity arises, this will be where I plan to make my move.

It's coming up quickly so I increase my speed and catch up to the bastard. As we start going through what seems to be a good spot, I have to wait for a car that is between me and Jackson to get out of the way. This driver doesn't appear to be in any hurry so I start to tailgate him. At first, he doesn't even notice me so I get even closer.

Finally, he sees me way closer than he likes so the blinker comes on and he pulls out and passes the RV.

It takes about a mile before the driver is far enough ahead for me to make my move. I have practiced this move on a stationary target but never on a moving one. The distance needs to be fairly close in order for this to work right.

The unit that I have fastened under the car is lined up with his trailer tire and, when the time is right, I push the button that releases a spring loaded stainless steel dart that enters the tire and deflates it really quickly, ripping the tire while it spins.

The trailer swerves back and forth and Jackson has a difficult time maintaining control of the RV. He manages to slow down and pull off the road. Luckily, there is little traffic on the road and, as I pull up behind him, I pick up my walking stick and start to exit the car, leaving the knife and pistol behind.

Chapter 57

Dennis

O kay great! I should be home free now. What a relief to finally have this at least work itself out," Dennis exclaims. "Up ahead the road ends, and I can continue into Red Bluff or north into the mountains. I need more money, so on to Red Bluff, it is."

The decision is based solely on his need to improve his financial situation. He wouldn't be in this position if that idiot running to get out of there hadn't forced him to shoot. Now he's on the run, but it looks like things are working out. There are a couple of cars behind him and this also irritates him.

"If you're in a hurry, pass me you, asshole," he yells, but the driver can't hear him.

Finally, the blinker comes on and the car flies by him. The other car just seems to be hanging in behind him. All of a sudden the rear tire on the driver's side of the trailer goes flat and he has a hell of a time keeping control. He swerves back and forth but eventually manages to slow down enough to pull over. He wipes his forehead with shaking hands.

"How the hell did this happen? I thought the tires were

okay. Son of a bitch.”

He opens the door and sees the other car parked behind the unit. Out comes some guy, hobbling with a metal walking stick.

“What does the guy think he can do, limping the way he does? The stupid jackass can’t change my tire for me, so what the hell?” Dennis mutters.

The guy waddles up with a smile on his face and asks in a weird-sounding voice as if he has a hard time getting the words out. “Are you okay?”

“Yeah, yeah I’m fine, just a flat,” Dennis says.

“Looks like you almost lost it for a minute there. Looking at your tire, there seems to be lots of tread on it so I wonder what caused it to blow.”

This makes Dennis curious, and he kneels to inspect the tire more closely. He doesn’t even see it coming.

Chapter 58

Joseph

In disguise, I get out of the car with my best imitation of a handicapped person, while I make my way to the rear of the RV trailer. The bastard meets me near the flat tire, and it is all I can do to speak rationally. I want desperately to kill him here and now.

It comes to me to get his attention focused on the tire and, as he bends down for a better look, I take a quick glance to see if there is any traffic coming. Fantastic, we're in the clear. I give him a hard rap on the back of the head with the walking stick and down he goes. I could have just punched him out but this just seemed easier.

I drag him quickly along the passenger side of my car and then zip tie his hands behind his back and his feet together. I pop the trunk and throw him in. The compartment is locked and there is nothing lying around for him to use to get loose. I quickly gag him and slam the lid shut.

I walk quickly to the RV, open the door, and go inside. It doesn't take long, and I find what I am looking for. I leave it in the RV, pick up the dart by the tire, and hop into the car, motoring it out of there. My hands tremble on the wheel as my nerves almost take over. I switch the GPS over and locate the coordinates that will take me to the nearest of the semi-deserted cabins in the mountains that I found on previous excursions.

I get to Route 36 and get on the turnoff that takes me toward the mountains. After about fifteen minutes, I hear noise coming from the back of the car and, when the way is clear, I pull off and open the trunk. He blinks his eyes in the bright sunlight and tries to talk but can't because of the gag. I tell him to shut up and explain who I am and why he is in the trunk. His eyes go wide and he shakes his head no.

I ask him if I am wrong about him being the robber who just killed the innocent bystander at the B and B. He nods his head frantically, and I tell him about my finding the loot in his RV. The look changes on his face as he realizes that he is done for. I tell him to be quiet or I will make him be quiet, then, after checking the zip ties, I slam the trunk shut again.

The ride to the cabin I have chosen takes almost an hour and it is around noon when I get there. There has been some noise in the trunk but nothing too much. I have disabled the interior trunk release ahead of time so there is no way that he could have popped it open while I was driving. I check out the cabin and, after I'm sure the way is clear, I get some of the things I will need from under the rear seat.

I have the knife and pistol on my hips and go to the rear of the car to open the trunk. He is laying there and, as I reach down to lift him out, he comes up with the tire iron for my spare tire. He clips me on the side of my face as I start pulling back. I am slightly dazed as I stumble back. He jumps out of the trunk and, seeing that I am almost on my feet reaching for the gun, he decides to make a run for it. As he turns, he throws the tool at me, narrowly missing my head, and he is off.

Damn, how could I have missed removing the tire iron underneath the trunk cover and how did he manage to get it out from under the spare tire? It takes me a minute to grab my bow and, by that time, he has a slight head start but not too much. I am after him and hear the direction he is going by his tramping through the bush. He is in a bit of a panic and not thinking clearly. Once he settles down, he may be more difficult to find, so I put everything I have into catching up with him.

Chapter 59

Dennis

How did I get into this mess?" Dennis asks himself. He knows he has to do something drastic, or it'll be the end of the road. An idea comes to him, as he visualizes the interior of the trunk. When he finally gets his hands in a position to reach far enough under the carpeting and then bending the pressed paper cover over the spare tire, he is fatigued. He has a hell of a time trying to loosen the hold down clamp and get the tire iron out because his hands are held together behind his back.

Bouncing around in the trunk of the moving car makes the job even harder. His shoulders are aching and the things around his wrists are cutting him badly. It seems like forever before he can loosen the clamp enough to twist the tire iron out from under the tire.

When he finally has it in his hands and in position to break the plastic, it is all he can do not to scream out as the zip tie cuts through the flesh on his wrists. Once this is done, he frees his ankles and rests for as long as he dares. The important thing is that he got them off. He straightens the cover and carpet as best he can, putting himself in the same position he was when the bastard threw him in the trunk. He wants to remove the gag but this will alert his captor, so it is left on.

It has been hard waiting long enough for the trunk to open and time the swing properly. He didn't catch the guy the way he thought he would. The son of a bitch is fast, really fast. Anyone else would have been caught totally off guard, but not this guy. If he didn't have the gun already in his hand and was almost on his feet, he might have gotten the better of him. This guy isn't like the types he runs into during the robberies, though.

The son of a bitch said he is the husband of that woman he killed in Napa Valley. It wasn't meant to happen the way it did, but the bastard isn't the type that's going to listen to any excuses. Dennis knows he is in big trouble, but this isn't the first time.

"Is the bugger after me or will I get away? I don't hear him behind me, but then again I have been making too much noise to hear anything. It's time to start going on the offensive," he tells himself.

He starts looking for anything he can use as a weapon. There are plenty of stones but he never was very good at throwing, so the search continues. His cuts are starting to hurt again as the adrenaline leaves his system. Ahead of him, there is a straight branch from a tree lying on the ground. This needs no work and will make a nice spear if he can get close enough. He cocks his ear as there is a sound of someone approaching. He ducks quietly behind a large tree and waits.

Chapter 60

Joseph

The noise has stopped, so Jackson must either be resting or waiting to ambush me. I am sure he will have no hesitation in taking my life if he gets the chance, so I better slow down and be prepared. I put the bow on my shoulder and bring out the pistol. I doubt that there is anyone in the area and, if I have to shoot him, I will try to hit him in the arm or leg. Then I can force him to walk back or drag him.

I look for signs of the ground having been recently disturbed and find some of the leaves on the ground have been moved by someone walking. I have a trail now and follow it. There is still no noise, so I am sure that he is preparing an ambush for me. In his position, I would do the same thing.

I stop and survey the area. There is a spot where he must have stopped and picked up something because the leaves have been disturbed and it looks like there is still the pattern of a long branch that was removed on the ground. So he has himself a club or spear and is waiting for me.

I look around and try to pick out the most likely places that he would be. There is a slight knoll but I don't see any tracks leading to it and it seems too low for him to be hiding behind it. There are several large trees spread out over a small distance. This seems to me to be the most likely place to hide. The problem is they are wide apart and while I am looking behind one it will leave my back exposed if he is behind another nearby.

I look for leaves that have been disturbed and find none. He must have smartened up and taken greater care not to leave a trail anymore. I pick the first tree and start to circle it from as great a distance as possible. I try to listen for sounds that will give away his position but hear nothing. One by one I eliminate the spots he could be hiding. I finally get to the last tree.

"Come on out because you're trapped," I say.

There is a noise and I realize that I have made an error, again.

Chapter 61

Dennis

Dennis hides behind one of the largest trees near a small rise in the ground. It is too low to conceal him, so he dismisses it. Off in the distance, he catches a glimpse of the bastard that is after him. Shit, the guy has a bow and arrows and a pistol too.

"Damn, damn, damn. I should have kept running."

This changes things a bit for him. He knows now that he will have only one chance to turn the tables and decides to very carefully move to the rise and see if he can hide there. He gets there without being seen and without leaving any evidence of the maneuver.

To his surprise, he finds a low spot that is filled with leaves and very carefully partially buries himself. He has also found a shorter branch that he can use as a club or he can throw it with considerable force. If he is lucky, he can stun his enemy and grab the spear to finish him off.

He is almost starting to enjoy this as he sees that the situation may end with him once again being the victor. He takes the occasional peak through twigs and leaves on top of the rise and watches as the guy checks all the big trees and, as he does, this he moves closer and closer.

After each tree is eliminated the guy's back is momentarily to him as he circles it. He is near the last tree and has his back to Jackson. The guy yells out that he is now trapped and just to come out.

Little does the asshole know that his intended target has now turned the tables on him? While the dummy is talking, Dennis rises up and throws the club straight at the back of the guy's head.

Chapter 62

Joseph

As I hear the leaves rustle behind me, I drop to the ground, knowing that I have made another major mistake. I am almost fast enough to miss getting hit, almost! There is a pain on the top of my head, and I am close to passing out, but not quite.

I roll on the ground and almost lose the pistol. Through the haze, I see him coming at me with what looks like a spear. Am I done for? Have I missed my opportunity?

I fire the pistol, in a desperate attempt to stay alive, and am rewarded by a scream of pain. The guy falls on my legs and still makes a grab for me. With my free hand, I try to block his desperate attempt to take control of the situation. He grabs my hand, but I manage to swing the other hand and the butt of the gun down on his head. He stops moving.

I lie back for a moment, just about passing out. I shake my head a bit to stay awake. The pain is excruciating. Pushing him off me, I back up and lean against a tree, trying to recuperate. It takes a few minutes to get my bearings back, and I check to see where I shot the scumbag who almost took me out.

There is a wound in his side. It's bleeding but not profusely. He will survive, at least for a while. Tying his hands behind his back, and then using my knife, I cut a strip of cloth from his shirt and stick it in the wound, in an attempt to slow the bleeding.

I have been after this man for far too long to have him die on me before we have a heart to heart. This man has traveled the country, doing as he pleased. He has killed and hurt countless people. No more!

I sit and wait for him to come to. It takes about fifteen minutes, and he begins to stir. There is a moan as he regains consciousness.

Chapter 63

Dennis

What the hell happened, Dennis wonders. *I had him dead to rights and he still manages to get me?*

Dennis knows, without a doubt, that he is in more trouble than he has ever been in. There will be no escape from this one, unless he catches a major break. But he doubts there will be another one for him. He has never encountered anyone like this guy before. How can anyone react this quickly? *You would think he's a covert ops soldier or something.*

His head hurts like hell, but Dennis opens his eyes and sees his captor sitting against a tree about ten feet away. He is a tough-looking bastard, that's for sure. Quite good looking but you wouldn't want to cross him. However, it's too late for that.

Dennis realizes that he made the biggest mistake of his life when he robbed that B and B in the Napa Valley so long ago.

Bloody hell, his side hurts, and he recalls that the son of a bitch shot him. The guy gets up and roughly grabs him, yanking him to a standing position, causing the wound to hurt even more. With his hands tied behind him, Dennis has a difficult time staying on his feet. A hand pushes him back in the direction of the car. He is not looking forward to what he knows is coming up next, not looking forward to it at all.

Chapter 64

I won't be taking any more chances with this guy that's for sure. I almost got taken out twice by him. I am amazed that this has happened. I thought I was being super careful.

I look at the man I have been after for so long. "We're going to walk back to the car, and if there is even the slightest attempt to try something, I'll break your leg, got it?"

Jackson just nods his head and starts walking, almost stumbling as I roughly push him from behind.

He'd managed to run quite a distance before I caught up with him, so it takes us fifteen minutes to get back to the cabin with Dice Man's wound slowing him down. When we get beside the car, I sit him on the ground so he can't make a run for it. I open the trunk and remove what I want, and we head into the cabin. He hasn't said a word so far because he knows now that it is hopeless. Once inside the old run-down cabin, I tie him to an old chair with each leg bound separately to a rear leg of the chair. This way, it'll be nearly impossible for him to stand up. Because the dust has been stirred up in the long unused cabin, he sneezes a few of times.

I've had a plan for what I would do to this man that destroyed my life for so long. Now that I have him here, I'm not exactly sure anymore. I wanted, at one point, to torture him the way I did to Jake when I finally got him, but now…

I walk around behind him and see the tattoo of the dice on his inside forearm. I take the knife and cut it off. He screams. "Why did you do that?" he asks after he regains control.

"Your luck has just run out."

The rage that has been with me for so long has, over time, been reduced to a simmer and no longer boils over constantly.

"Why did you have to kill my wife and unborn child?" I ask him.

"I swear that it was never my intention to kill her. It was actually just an unfortunate accident. I wasn't used to the pistol, and it had one of those hairpin triggers. It just went off when I was waving it around to scare her," Dennis relays, deliberately leaving out the part about how he would have liked to have spent a little time with her.

"I have a hard time believing you because of all the people you have hurt and the ones that you killed, you stupid shit."

"I'm sorry but in the past year things have gotten out of my control and the anger issues I've got have gotten worse and worse. I really don't know why this is," Dennis cries out.

I go outside and sit on the porch, leaning against one of the posts facing the door for a while and go through things in my head. I have for so long wanted to slowly beat this man to death and make him feel the pain I have felt for all this time. I wanted this more than anything else. Looking forward to this moment is the only thing that has kept me going.

Now that the time is here, I find that, despite everything, I don't have the heart for it. I try to talk myself into it but I just can't. This man will die, but not the way I intended.

Taking the pistol from my belt I walk back into the cabin.

"You have caused far too many problems and pain for way too many people, and it ends now. I could take you and turn you into the police." At this, a glimmer of hope fills his eyes. "But I won't."

"I'll stop, I swear I will," he pleads.

"I know you will."

I look him in the eye, raising the gun, and shoot him in the heart. He dies immediately and, even though I feel justified, I don't really feel any better. Kathleen is still dead, and I don't have my unborn child either.

I go to the car and remove the back seat. Grabbing the shovel from the storage area, I go into the bush and dig a deep hole in where I bury Dennis Jackson. The body is covered with the bag of lime poured over him that I brought to help decompose the body. This should also deter any animals from digging up his remains.

I leave the burial site looking like nothing has been disturbed for years. Hopefully, the tightly packed earth and leaves covering the soil are enough to keep the spot from being discovered for years. I spend another hour or two weeping off and on. My life is nothing like I want it to be. I doubt very much that it ever will be. A normal existence is not in the cards for me.

I have a week off and so I drive to the coast and stay in Carter House Inn located in Eureka, California. It is a beautiful inn, and I take the time to unwind and try to let go of the past. I visit a clinic and have the wound on the top of my head taken care of at the same time. It has been a hard year, and I am not sure where I'm headed, now that this episode is finished.

Lying on the bed with the television on, I watch distractedly a few programs, trying to take my mind elsewhere. My attention is caught when Franklin Graham comes on. Billy is sitting on a chair behind him, looking very old. It is almost sad to see him this way.

Franklin preaches for a while, and I am tempted to turn it off. I don't feel like hearing this right now. As I reach for the remote, he looks at the camera. "You need to hear this. All of you who are watching need to know that, 'The wages of sin is death.' You have an opportunity now to be cleansed of your wrongs. No sin is too great."

I grab the remote and shut it off. I can't listen to this because he has to be wrong. There are things you can't undo and there is no turning back. I realize that I have to stop watching him anymore. I feel guilty enough without being offered things I know I can't be given.

After a couple of days, I decide to head home. This cloud that has been with me for so long is still there.

March journal entry: *I have finally done what has taken so long to complete and yet still, nothing has really changed. There was only a brief satisfaction and even that is fading. I am still alone. Is this what's in store for me the rest of my life? The only real bright spot in my life is Harry, Brenda, and the kids. Thank goodness I have them. I think about Linda and George, the folks I met at the Chain of Lakes Resort. I don't know if I should contact them or not. Almost everyone that has ever really befriended me has paid a high price for it. I don't know what I would do if…*

I make it home late Wednesday and unpack my stuff, putting it all away. There is a message on my machine from Bill, asking me to call when I can. I think that I'll wait till tomorrow. Harry will have to wait too.

The next morning, wearing a hat to hide the wound on my scalp, I go see Ben and go for a long ride on my favorite horse. This has always helped me think things through and relaxed me. I spend several hours with the horse, and we enjoy the countryside and nature.

I wonder if I am at another crossroad in my life because I have no idea where to go from here. The thing that has kept me going for so long is now gone. Do I let things go and try to live a normal life or do I continue the path I believe I have been forced to travel during too much of my life? The choice I need to make evades me. In the end, I decide not to make any decision at all. I'll just play it by ear. I probably should stay off the CDC site and all the others as well for a while. It has a habit of making me want to get involved in eliminating some of the offenders preying on the innocents of society. I wonder if the priests sexually assaulting young boys have been dealt with by the church?

Picking up the phone, I call Bill to find out what he wanted. When I reach him, he tells me that he has the latest information on Jackson and wants to know when to drop it off. It is a shame that I can't let him in on the fact that he has been dealt with and won't be of concern to anyone in the future.

Bill comes over on his way home and hands me the report. He asks me if I am making any progress in finding out how the guy works. I tell him that I am at a loss as to figure the man out, but that I will keep trying. I also let him know that if I have any ideas I will pass them on to him. Bill gives me a look that indicates a little disbelief.

"I know, I know," I say. "But I'm getting weary of this chase and I can't seem to move forward with it constantly in the back of my mind. I'm sure he will get his and the police will sooner or later catch up with him."

I think he still has his doubts but he lets it go. I was planning to get rid of everything, but with Bill in the picture, I think I better hang on to the stuff. If it was gone and he found out about it, he would suspect something was up. I don't need him on my tail again. I wonder if I made an error when I told him I was weary of it all. He will notice that there are no more robberies taking place. When he does, will he put two and two together? Shit!

Oh well, too late now, I need to get on with life. Bill is about to leave when the phone rings.

"Hello." As I listen, my mouth drops open and I hang up.

"Is there something wrong?" Bill asks.

"There's a real problem that I have to take care of immediately. I've got to go. Can you come with me? Your help may be needed. I'll explain on the way."

TILL WE MEET AGAIN!

About the Author

Born in the Netherlands, Leonardus G. Rougoor moved to southern Ontario at the age of four and grew up in the Niagara Peninsula. As an adult, he worked in various fields, until settling down in the tool and die industry. Moving to Kelowna in his mid-forties, he started working in the steel fabrication industry. Quality control, safety rep, machining, and training other employees in various areas of the industry led to a fulfilling career.

One week after retiring, Rougoor started writing his first novel. He has a heart for the underdog and dislikes injustice intensely, so this was the driving force in his first mystery/thriller series. Now, having six novels in several genres contracted with a publisher and more on the way, this is turning out to be a wonderful and satisfying new career.

Rougoor is married with two children and several grandchildren. Living on Vancouver Island in the Maple Bay region allows him and his family to enjoy boating on the sheltered portions of the ocean. His philosophy is: If something isn't going to affect your life much a year from now, why let it overly concern you today?